STRANDED

Stuck in the Recesses of the Real, the Surreal,

and the Supernatural

The Writing Journey

04 January 2020

Other projects of the Writing Journey

Infinite Monkeys (2009), edited by Katherine Lato

The Letter (2012), edited by Claire Somersville

Drops of Midnight (2012), edited by Steven White

The Day Before the End of the World (2012), edited by Roger Lubeck

Stories from Other Worlds (2014), edited by Roger Lubeck and Ana Koulouris

Voices from the Dark (2015), edited by Roger C. Lubeck, Phoenix Autumn, Ana Koulouris, Sara Marschand, and Kevin C. Swier.

Human: An Exploration of What It Means (2016), Edited by Tim Yao, Melinda Borucki and Mary O'Brien Glatz

Near Myths (2017), Edited by Awnna Marie Evans, Eleanor Roth, Todd Hogan and Tim Yao

Reasons for Hope (2017), Edited by Tim Yao, Sarah Vallejo, and Mary O'Brien Glatz

The Love Anthology (2018), Edited by Tim Yao and Diana Jean

See *writingjourney.org/books/* for a complete, up-to-date list.

STRANDED

Edited by Mary O'Brien Glatz, Tim Yao, and Milda Willoughby.

Copy editing by Todd Hogan, Mary O'Brien Glatz, Milda Willoughby, and Tim Yao

This Anthology is a project of the Writing Journey (writingjourney.org), featuring stories and poems by

Barbara Bartilson

Susan Ekins

Elaine Fisher

Leslie Gail

Margie Gustafson

Elizabeth SanFilippo Hall

Todd Hogan

Yolanda Huslig

Debra Kollar

Jessica Kosar

Stéphane Lafrance

Karen Stumm Limbrick

Barbara Lipkin

Edward Martin

Sam McAdams

Mary O'Brien Glatz

K.V. Peck

Savannah Reynard

Julie Rule

Tauna Sonne leMare

Jennifer Stasinopoulos

Gwen Tolios

Susan Wachowski

Milda Willoughby

Greg Wright

Tim Yao

ISBN-13: 978-1654164836

Cover Design by *Chris Jones*

Contents

Run Aground on Reality

Lost in Love

Author Bios

Acknowledgements

The Editors of this anthology would like to thank the hard work by Todd Hogan, Mary O'Brien Glatz, Milda Willoughby, and Tim Yao to copy edit the stories and poems. Savannah Reynard, Elaine Fisher, and Tim Yao contributed to the development of the anthology cover concept.

Many thanks as well to Patti Naisbitt, Program Coordinator of the Woodridge Public Library, and to Amy Franco, Adult Programming Librarian of the Glen Ellyn Public Library, for their generous support as sponsors of the Writing Journey.

Foreword

Perhaps you have never been stranded on a desert island *Robinson Crusoe* style, but hasn't each one of us felt stranded at one time or another? *Stranded* – to be stuck, abandoned, forgotten, left behind, trapped, marooned, held hostage, caught in a mental loop, isolated. Your choices narrow, freedoms disappear, perceptions alter. Held against your will either internally in your mind or externally by forces beyond your control, you begin to think of ways to survive.

The Writing Journey of Naperville invites you to explore the colorful plots, characters, and settings of *Stranded*, an Anthology of fantasy, science fiction, romance, humor, horror, mystery, adventure, realism, dystopian, and steampunk.

The psychological, emotional, and behavioral impacts of relationships gone bad, of arrested adolescence, of unresolved sibling rivalry, can drive us to search for tiny moments of redemption and escape. The characters that come to life in *Beached, Static, Heat, Cold Upon You, Fever, Rewinds, What Lies in the Cracks Between Us, Moonlight Sonata,* and *Quicksand,* open windows to the heart so we can peer into those spaces where we often get lost.

Generational, cultural, or religious identities can trap us into isolation from what we need most – to connect, belong, fit in, relate to one another. *The Immigrant, Benediction, Grandpa, Flotsam and Jetsam, People's Paradise,* and *The Great Divide,* investigate these themes to capture the quandary of the stranger in a strange land. Stuck in our identities, we are often lost to what binds us together.

The supernatural, the afterlife, ghosts and spirits, travels in time – the exciting stuff of the speculative and science fiction that we love to imagine. But would we want to be stranded there, where our dreams become our nightmares? *Be Careful What You Wish For, Date of Death, Stranded in Time, Happy Travels, Tapestry, Waiting for My Family, Haunted, Ghost Diner, At the Other End, Lady Eve and Adam,* and *The Ruin of Alder Lincoln,* maroon us in the quagmires of eerie realms.

Last but not least, harsh reality – horrifying or humorous – can leave us stranded when things go wrong. Reality can hold us hostage and compel us to look for a way to slide back home, set things right, get out, fly away, change things to become unstuck. In poem and story, *Baseball, Stuck in the Muck, Protecting the House, Slight Delay, Ready Or Not, I Stand to Speak, Cold Feet, Schooled, The Elevator Pitch, Neither Here Nor There,* and *Stranded at Valley Forge,* speak to the dangers and the follies we face when we are abandoned, alone, on our own with only our foibles or talents upon which to rely. Sometimes we find a way out and sometimes not.

The 2019 Anthology is a fun read. Join us on these imaginative journeys, but don't get stranded in just one. Read them all to savor the diversity and talent of The Writing Journey.

Mary O'Brien Glatz, Co-Editor with Tim Yao and Milda Willoughby
The Writing Journey

Run Aground on Reality

Ducks

MARGIE GUSTAFSON

The duckling can't get
Reunited with Mother
Cars keep whizzing past

Inspiration

My haiku was inspired by an early morning drive.

Stealing Down the Basepath

Todd Hogan

The Mariners' quick-footed shortstop Emilio still smarted from the play in the eighth inning of this last game of the World Series. The Cubs catcher had an arm like a rocket-propelled grenade and Emilio had dared him to use it. Emilio had stolen second and a long fly ball had advanced him to third. With only one out left, he had taken an aggressive lead, threatening to steal home. Any error in the throw or bobble in catching the ball and the runner would cross home plate. Sure enough, the catcher fired to third. Emilio dove headfirst to regain third base, his fingers brushing the rough fabric of the base just before he felt the third-baseman's glove sweep across his right shoulder.

"Safe!" he thought.

"Out!" the umpire bawled.

The partisan crowd erupted with cheers and boos, provoked by the replay showing on the big screen. However, after huddling for the length of a beer commercial, the replay crew could not find definitive evidence to overturn the umpire's call and so it was upheld. The eighth inning had ended with that pick-off at third. Emilio bristled with anger, knowing he had blown a crucial opportunity for his team to take the late-inning lead.

In the dugout, Emilio's teammates sympathized briefly. They clapped his back, understanding how frustrating it is to be left stranded ninety feet from scoring a run, especially the potential winning run. But the game continued and there was no time for anger or self-pity.

This very last game of the very long season drove each manager's strategic and tactical decisions. They engaged the bullpen early and rotated pitchers quickly. If a reliever looked weak or uncertain, he was pulled and replaced by a more aggressive teammate. The Cubs had a near-monopoly on intimidating relievers and big bats. They counted on that one mighty swing, sending a resounding crack echoing through the park, giving them the lead. Each time a batter connected with a pitch, the sharp clap of horsehide on ash wood sent a shiver racing down Emilio's spine. The crowd screamed with ear-numbing delight and horror until the ball dropped short of the wall or swerved wildly foul, followed by the fans' lung-depleting groan.

After nine innings, the score was tied. The game entered extra innings.

The tension ramped up exponentially with each extra inning. The crowd felt the pressure, the announcers stoked it, and the players' shoulders hunched under its burgeoning weight. By the thirteenth inning, impending disaster dangled over the eventual losing team by a thread stretched as tightly as a steel guitar string. The slightest error would send boyhood dreams, sky-high hopes, and bookmakers' astronomical bets crashing to earth. Blame would fall on anyone who screwed up. At this point the horrifying fear of losing, more than the joy of winning, drove each team.

In the bottom of the thirteenth, the first batter, Emilio, stepped into the batter's box. When the gangly, scraggly-bearded pitcher, all legs and arms, took his stride toward the plate, he seemed to cover half the distance to home before the ball materialized from somewhere behind his head. After three deceptive pitches, Emilio faced two strikes and one ball. He stepped out of the box, seeking reassurance from his manager's flinty face but found a hard-eyed stare and a wink.

Emilio stepped back up to the plate. He bounced from foot to foot.

Perhaps that nervous movement shook the pitcher, because his next pitch took off, veering just before the plate and to the outside. Emilio judged the ball might be a problem for the catcher, who had an octopus-like quality of capturing everything. Emilio swung, his third strike, which distracted the catcher. The ball skidded away from the catcher's mitt, propelled by the baseball's vicious rotation. It scudded to the rear wall while Emilio took advantage of the rule that allows the batter to run to first on a dropped third strike if he can beat the catcher's throw. Emilio, head down and knees high, made it to first before the catcher had corralled the errant throw.

The fans jumped up and crowed their approval of the long-shot move. It was the kind of play that a successful team needed to win. Now, Emilio stood on first base. He needed to travel ninety feet to second, another ninety feet to third, and finally the last ninety feet to home plate.

The pitcher fired to first; the ball slapped loudly in the first baseman's mitt. It was his warning to Emilio. Don't dare take a lead-off. The catcher's eyes glared at Emilio through the steel grid protecting his face. He hungered for an opportunity to pick off Emilio again with his RPG arm. Emilio accepted the challenge with a cold stare and tight smile.

Emilio stretched his lead precariously toward second, watching both the pitcher and the catcher for any movement in his direction. On the third pitch, while the tall pitcher was still completing his stride, Emilio took off. His speed allowed him to slide into second and stand up before the ball reached the second baseman's glove.

The crowd stomped and hooted. The decibel level in the park increased to rock concert levels. Emilio savored the cheers. The crowd knew what he had done for the team. Tactically, his steal meant that a ground ball no longer threatened a double play. Although the current batter had a count of two strikes and two balls, Emilio had reached second with no outs.

With the next pitch, the batter struck out.

Emilio's shoulders sagged a bit, but he tapped his foot at second. He and the Cubs waited for the next batter to approach the plate. There was a substitution. The new batter was Bret MaCough, a thick-armed slugger whose name sounded like a well-hit line drive. He had the second-highest home run total on the team and would have played earlier but for a healing muscle tear near his groin. Late in the game, his potential firepower made his weakness in the field worth the risk, especially if he could end this game with one long ball.

Emilio's third base coach signaled frantically. He ordered Emilio to steal third before Bret finished his at-bat. That way, a long ball afforded Emilio a better-than-average chance to score, even if the ball were caught on the warning track. Emilio could tag up and take off toward home. The third base umpire's face was fixed in a permanent scowl, especially when he looked at Emilio. The crowd chanted the batter's name, "MaCough! MaCough! MaCough!" It sounded like a jungle full of screaming parrots.

Bret's first swing would have crushed the ball if he had connected; he did not. He corkscrewed into the batter's box, his knee scraping the dirt, like Atlas posed to support the world.

"Stee-rike one!" the home plate umpire roared.

Chanting resumed, louder this time. The pitcher's eyes, nearly hidden by his cap, studied the target—which edge of the plate would he hit? Emilio darted towards third, but held up after about fifteen feet when the pitcher whirled toward him. Emilio made it back to second, his arms jittery like he'd dodged a bullet.

Another pitch. "Stee-rike two!"

Two pitches, two strikes. The crowd fell silent. From beyond the fence, the brisk autumn wind whipped the pennants and snapped the flags in toward the park. Bret would need every bit of his power to push the ball out of the park. The third base coach renewed his frantic signs. Emilio nodded; he knew he had to get to third.

The pitch flashed inches from Brett's knees. Ball one.

The next throw swerved wide before dipping toward the outside corner of the plate. It just missed. Ball two.

The catcher fired a warning to third. Emilio understood his message. "See how quickly I can get the ball into his hands? It's not like stealing second. It's one-hundred-twenty-seven feet and three and three-eighths inches from home to second. The distance from home to third is only ninety feet. My throw can cover that before you can blink."

Emilio hunkered down into a sprinter's stance, waiting for his opportunity.

Bret stepped out of the box and stretched his legs and his torso. He shook his shoulders like some great bison. His fingers flexed around the bat handle and squeezed. He stepped into the batter's box with a hunter's stare in his eye.

Batters have to guess what the pitcher will throw next. Will it be his fastest pitch requiring that the batter start swinging almost as the ball leaves the hand, or a slower pitch, catching the batter swinging too early and awkwardly trying to make contact. Occasionally, the batter guesses correctly and his swing is precisely timed with the pitch.

Bret must have expected an off-speed slider. He held up his swing a bit and when his bat met the ball, it sounded a solid smack, "Bret MaCough!" The crowd exploded in cheers as the ball sailed high toward the right field fence.

But Emilio appreciated what the crowd didn't. First, the extra movement on the slider meant that Bret's connection with the ball had not been as solid as it sounded. Second, the October wind blowing into the park would form a wall of resistance to prevent the ball leaving the park.

Emilio waited on second as the ball threatened to cross the right field wall, then didn't. The ball fell into the right fielder's glove in the farthest fair corner of Tropicana Field. It was Emilio's best chance to advance to third. The fielder had to come out a few steps from the wall to throw all the way across the field to third base. By that time, Emilio's spikes dug hard into the ocher base path.

He slid into third arms first and felt the base's rough fabric against his fingertips and palms. The third baseman was poised to catch the long throw and sweep it against Emilio, blocking him from the base if he could do it without the umpire calling him. Emilio slid underneath and heard the ball connect with the glove.

Swop!

He felt a bruising tag on his right shoulder. But it was too late. He was safe.

"Out!" the third base umpire bawled.

His scowling face wore a snarl when he stared at Emilio. The crowd went nuts, cheering, booing, cursing, laughing. The catcher took off his mask and headed for the dugout. The pitcher shrugged and stepped off the mound. It was all part of baseball theater.

A replay review was called for while various television angles played on the gigantic on-field screen, encouraging more strenuous calls from the fans. The umpires huddled like MacBeth's witches while Emilio squatted on third base awaiting the final decision, wondering if he had offended this umpire somehow. But that kind of thinking was nonproductive. The review seemed to drag on a good fifteen minutes when it was more likely only fifteen seconds.

The umpires broke their confab. The head umpire gave a signal that sent the crowd screaming their divided opinions. The call was reversed. Emilio was safe.

The catcher returned with the pitcher to the mound. The jeers of the crowd might rattle a less experienced battery, but this pitcher and catcher combo had been through the wars. While they talked, the third base coach machine-gunned instructions to Emilio who waggled his head. Emilio imagined all the ways the ball could go for the next batter and which opportunities might arise for him to score. It could not be planned with any degree of certainty. The movement of the ball could only trigger aggressive reaction.

Another power hitter was the next batter scheduled, but the Mariners' manager swapped him for a meteoric runner. Frequently, the substitution was done after the batter had safely reached base. But the stakes of this final decisive game pressured the manager to use this runner's speed now.

Both defensive corners were pulled in. The first baseman was nearly halfway down the line. The third baseman also cheated toward home but Emilio on third made it impossible for him to stray too far.

Emilio knew the Cubs manager had a decision to make. He could load the bases so that an out could be forced at any base. That was risky though, given Emilio's propensity to try stealing home. He had no choice but to pitch to the substituted speedster and try to hold Emilio at third.

Even before the pitch was thrown, the batter showed bunt. The corners were ready. Second base would cover first if a play were made there.

"Stee-rike one!"

Emilio shook his arms and legs to loosen them. He overheard the third base coach mutter, "How hard is it to lay down a frigging bunt?" together with other salty questions.

Emilio played out the bunt scenarios. The Mariners' best chance was to execute a squeeze bunt, a bunt down the third base line. If it rolled too slowly, the catcher would gather up the ball and wait for Emilio to attempt to score. If he couldn't score, the catcher would make a quick throw to first. Out! If the ball rolled too quickly, it made it to the third baseman who could run Emilio down or toss the ball to the catcher at home. Out! And then the Mariners would be required to play with its substituted players, MaCough with a groin pull and the speedy batter. It required a remarkable bit of skill and extraordinary luck to lay the bunt down exactly between home and third at just the right speed. Otherwise, Emilio would be stranded at third, a situation every player hated, especially in the final innings of a big game.

"Stee-rike two!"

Reset. Reset. Everyone on the field and in the dugouts repositioned themselves for the next pitch. The fans in the stands hugged each other or hid their faces awaiting the next pitch. What had gone before could not be considered. Only the next pitch counted.

The batter squared up to bunt. Very risky, with two strikes. If the ball drifted foul, the batter would be called out. But this time, the batter made solid contact. The ball spun and rolled toward the third base line. Emilio had no choice but to sprint toward home. He raced the third baseman who stretched forward toward the ball. But Emilio was quicker. He passed the ball before it reached the third baseman by a fraction of a second. The third baseman did not use his glove but swooped in with his throwing hand. His fingers curled around the white sphere the way they had thousands of times.

Ninety feet never seemed so long.

But the catcher made a fatal error. He had charged the ball to reach it before Emilio did, then tag him. In charging the ball, he left home plate open. It would be covered by the Cubs giraffe of a pitcher. The catcher could not retreat even when the third baseman reached the ball. The pitcher must cover home.

Emilio passed the catcher. He expected to be jostled, but it didn't happen. The pitcher, an oil derrick of a defender at home plate, awaited the throw from the third baseman. Emilio not only heard, but felt, the ball whiz past his ear, thrown furiously by the third baseman. The blood pounded in his ears as he ran. If the crowd were roaring, Emilio didn't notice. He focused on finding the point where home plate was vulnerable.

There it was. The pitcher was so tall that he needed to kneel to completely block the plate. That was a position the pitcher was reluctant to assume. A catcher was heavily padded against collision. A pitcher had no such protection. Emilio saw he was eager to apply the tag. Emilio ran upright toward him. The pitcher stretched his arms out straight to tag him in the chest but Emilio fell backwards and poked his legs underneath the pitcher's glove. The pitcher hadn't kept his glove low but tried to catch Emilio chest or belt high. Emilio slid under the tag through the plate and nearly into the home plate umpire.

"Safe!" Emilio thought.

He heard no call for a moment while the blood pulsed in his head. He saw stars from the jolt of landing on his back. He rolled to his left. Was the game over? Where was the call? He listened intently.

"Safe!" the umpire cried.

His teammates surrounded Emilio who was still lying outstretched past home plate. They carried him and the speedy batter around the field for the fans' hoarse acclamations. The cheering filled the park and he hoped it would never end. But the season was over now. He would forever remember and savor the victory they had won. For now, he was grateful that he had not been left stranded.

Inspiration

Chicago Cubs radio announcer Pat Hughes has 36 years experience describing baseball games. He generates tremendous listener involvement while communicating all the colorful details of the three hour game. I thought I'd try to imitate the excitement his masterful reporting delivers daily, giving myself the unfair advantage of placing the story in the last game of the World Series. The selection of the Mariners was made because they have never appeared in a World Series game, until now. My wife is a lifelong Cubs fan, but forgives me.

Protecting the House

GWEN TOLIOS

I stare at the six-dot grid of my phone's lock screen and go over my options. I could call a Lyft. It would be pricey, maybe $25, $30 plus tip, but it would be the most discreet option.

Or I could call Claudia. We're not exactly friends, but she's the only one I talk to who has a car. Except Claudia has a date tonight. She might not pick up her phone. And if she did, she might not be willing to drive almost an hour to pick me up. She would also know instantly what had happened.

Lastly, I could call Mom, who would no doubt ask questions and make demands, making me feel worse than I already do.

My screen goes black. I press the home button, swipe in, ignore the text from my teammate Joshua (*Sorry*), and call Mom. I don't want to spend the cash on a ride, and she is the only one guaranteed to pick me up before dinner.

She answers on the second ring. "Hey, Nicki. How'd the game go?"

I stare at my bag of gear on the sidewalk. "Good. We won. It was a shutout."

"That's because you're an incredible goalie, sweetie."

"The best," I agree. I have to be, with how little my team helps out. Even when we have an advantage, I feel like we play short-handed with how badly my team passes in the defensive area and fails to clear the puck. "Not that I'll get MVP," I mutter.

"What was that?" Mom asks.

"I-, Mom." I'm not sure how to say it, so I force the words out quickly. "The team left me behind."

"What."

"I mean, the bus left without me. I, I spent too much time in the locker room."

"Where was this again? I'm on my way."

I can hear the sound of keys jangling through the phone. "Um…Stentson."

I imagine her freezing as she realizes how far away that is.

"The school left you behind after a hockey game in a town an hour away?"

Her tone is cool and I regret calling her. I should have spammed Claudia's phone. Mom will call the school about this. Coach will get a mouthful from someone, I'll get a mouthful from Coach, and my life on the team might get worse.

"I… yes," I whisper. The doors say they close in thirty minutes. I'm sweaty, starting to get hungry, and a cold early December breeze makes me shiver. It's dark. I want to be home.

Mom doesn't press and I love her for it. "Where are you exactly?"

"Stentson Center Ice Rink."

"I'm hanging up, so I can bring up Waze and start driving. Do you want me to call you from the car?"

"No!" No one would know, but it's still embarrassing. Fifteen, almost sixteen, and talking to your mom to stave off the encroaching dark and cold. I didn't need a security blanket. "I'll wait inside the building. There's a snack stand. I'll grab a smoothie. Do some homework."

"I'll be there as fast as I can."

"See you soon." I hang up, pick up my bag, and head back inside.

There are a few stragglers. Free skate in one of the rinks just ended, so people are turning in their skates and getting ready to leave. The snack stand I saw earlier is closed, and even then it didn't have anything like smoothies. I dig into my duffle for a snack, any snack, and come up with a package of peanut butter crackers.

It'll do.

I sit on a bench and watch the people around me pack up and leave. I don't want to play with my phone. It hasn't charged it since this morning, and while 40% will last a while it wouldn't if I pulled up a game or YouTube. I wish I had my school backpack with me, but I left it on the bus. The entire team did.

I text Joshua. *Grab my backpack.*

My backup goalie would never encourage the team to leave without me, insist to Coach's face that *yes, Nicki is on board. She's sleeping on a bench in the back.* But he wouldn't call the team out on their lie either. He already got flack for being my backup and the first few times he supported me led to a flurry of teasing about us in a relationship. Which in turn resulted in Coach establishing firm rules that further separated me from the team. All for my protection, of course.

Not that I need it. I'd skated with a few of these boys in younger co-ed leagues and checked them. *Hard.*

But without my fellow girl skaters, and the teasing other schools gave them for having a girl player, and me being singled out by Coach, the school, *and* the district, was it any wonder the majority of my team made things hard for me?

I just wish they kept it to the ice.

Why did this have to be the farthest game this season *and* a night Claudia had a date?

I slump, shoulders curling in. The first time Claudia picked me up, fully aware I had called because of her car and not because I thought she was a friend who'd do me a solid, she'd raised an eyebrow but didn't say anything as I slunk into the seat. I offered a mumbled reason, "missed the bus". The second time, she called me out.

"You didn't miss the bus. They left you. Twice."

Beet red, all I had done was nod.

Claudia hadn't told anyone. Hadn't asked me questions. Hadn't given me advice on what to do. We didn't have a relationship deeper than ex-lab partners who shared a taste in music and once in a blue moon swapped links to new songs. I appreciated it.

"Boys suck," was all she said. My own thoughts about my teammates are a bit more colorful.

As I stare out the window, I huff and lament, not for the first time, that some of my girl hockey friends hadn't made their own teams. I'm not the only girl who had been playing co-ed since five, the only girl who complained about a lack of a high school girl's team, or the only girl who had tried out for the boy's team.

I am simply the only girl who made the roster.

I skated as fast as I could, as clean as I could, as steady as I could. And made the team as goalie.

Covering goal is my second-favorite position, I love the sweeping speed of forward. But Coach, concerned I'd get hurt despite the ridiculous amount of padding hockey players wear, my skate test, and my shot tests, refused to consider me for anything other than protecting the goal. And the only reason I got that position was because my save percentage is double Joshua's, despite the team sending harder pucks my way than his.

It's hard being the only girl on the team. Coach only stops the really bad locker room talk, and he can't hear what's said on the ice. I constantly have to prove I'm amazing at the sport, all-state level, just to keep my jersey. Most of the guys get pissed I make more shots during shooting drills and take out their aggression on me in a few ways. They ignore me in the hallways and in class. Slam me extra hard against the rink walls, accidentally get their sticks caught in my skates. I work my ass off to keep my spot, but the better I am, the more bruises I gather.

They're not always the black and blue kind either. Some of my old hockey friends don't talk to me anymore. As Joshua learned, being friends with your girl teammate puts you in the line of fire too. Being seen as friendly to the girl player is an automatic penalty.

I don't change with the team. I go to the women's locker room. Usually, I put everything away fast to finish before the rest of the team and claim a seat on the bus.

Occasionally, circumstances mean I take longer to change. Under all my goalie pads my small breasts make it hard to identify me as female, and why would a girl be playing on a high school team? Not everyone lets me into the locker room right away. Sometimes I get bombarded by questions from other girls I feel compelled to answer. Today, not expecting a female player, the locker room had been locked and it took staff almost ten minutes to locate the keys.

Most days, I make it to the bus before it leaves. Today was a rare opportunity for my teammates.

I know in a crowded bus it's easy to count someone twice, easy to believe a chorus of guys when they chant "yes, we're all here". From what Joshua has told me, Coach doesn't mean to leave me behind. The first time, the team just didn't point out my absence. And the second, my teammates told Coach I left with my dad. Who knows what they said today.

They'd lose without me. I'm loads better than Joshua. But apparently getting rid of the girl is more important than winning the district championship, and they escalated their efforts when all the slams on the ice hadn't driven me to quit.

I stick through it, silently to not draw official attention to everything, mainly from spite. But also because a lot of my old hockey gal buddies look at me and see a future for them next year on their own high school teams. They miss playing, the *swish swish* of skates on smooth ice, the cold air in your heated lungs, and the thump of bodies against the wall. I would too.

"We're closing."

I turn to look at the guy who spoke. He's wearing the rink's uniform, a red shirt with the building's name on it and has a temporary tattoo of Stentson High's mascot - a bear - on his left cheek.

"Okay." I stand up and shoulder my hockey bag.

His eyes catch on my duffle, specifically the blocky GHS on a manta ray's back on the side. Then he looks at me, in my under uniform gear and long braid. "Didn't Gabriel High leave already?"

I shrug. "I missed the bus."

He purses his lips and gives me a quick full body glance. "You're the girl goalie."

I glare at him, not gifting that with a response. It's pretty obvious, based on my boobs, long hair, and school provided gear. "My mom's on the way, but she won't be here for a bit. Can I just... sit here while you clean and close or whatever?"

He looks out the windows to the near-empty parking lot lit by five overhead lights.

"Yeah, you can stay. But when the staff leaves you'll have to too."

"Thanks," I say, collapsing back into my seat.

He walks away and I pull out my phone. Joshua texted to say he'd grab my backpack and take it to my house. Mom had sent an ETA text. If she held her pace, she'd arrive in twenty minutes. I hope it takes longer than that to close an ice rink.

I spend the next fifteen minutes scanning the darkness outside for Mom's white Prius, phone between my hands so I can feel it vibrate with a text. Nothing.

"Your mom here yet?"

I jump, turning to see the guy from before. He's standing a few steps away, temporary tattoo gone. The black hair on that side of his face is wet. Behind him are two other teens, also employees of the ice rink. They look at me curiously but don't say anything.

I wave my hand to the empty parking lot, making the gesture sarcastic with an eye roll. The action takes my mind off how alone and small I feel.

"You have to wait outside," the guy says.

"Yeah." I gather my stuff, zip up my coat, and step outside with the three of them. When the door locks behind me, I shiver.

The two new teens wave to their coworker and he calls out goodbye. They head to a beat up sedan. Instead of heading towards his own car, the guy turns to look at me. "You didn't miss the bus, did you?"

I turn my face away. I don't want him to see the shameful blush on my face.

He takes my silence as confirmation. "That's shitty."

"You're telling me."

"Is your mom really on her way?"

"Yeah." I re-hoist my duffle over my shoulder, turning back to face the parking lot. I still can't bring myself to look at him. "It's just a long drive."

He stuffs his hands in his pockets and makes no indication of moving.

"You can go home," I tell him.

"I know." He rocks back on his heels.

I keep my eyes on the entry to the parking lot, very aware of his presence two feet to my left. We stand there, side-by-side and silent for another ten minutes. I want to tell him to go or ask his name. I don't because I worry that if I open my mouth I'll babble insecurely or my voice will warble.

My teammates have trained me well; anything that can be taken as emotionally weak, as "girlish", is teased and made fun of. I can't handle that tonight. I can't risk the tears I want to shed in private will push through.

Especially in front of a stranger.

When Mom's car pulls up, I breathe out a sigh of relief.

I stand up straight, making sure my voice is steady, and turn toward the guy next to me. "Thanks, for, you know, waiting."

He nods. "I'm sorry those guys were dicks to you."

"Yeah, well. Not the first time."

Out of the corner of my eye, I see him turn to me with wide eyes, but I ignore it. I sprint down the stairs and into the car.

"You didn't tell me the place was closed!" Mom yells.

"Wouldn't have made you drive faster. Speed limits are laws."

"What happened? I can't believe the bus just-"

"Mom," I hug my duffle to my chest. "Can we, can we just go? I don't wanna talk about it."

Here, in the car, safe, my eyes start to water. My voice is thick. Tonight has been awful. I don't want to think about it. I want to curl up in bed and cry. I want to know why my teammates hate me so much. I want to tie on my skates and practice for a hundred hours to show them this won't stop me.

I want to play hockey. I want to win district, then county, then state. And I'm not going to let something as stupid as being a girl, as stupid as people who hate girls, stop me.

"Okay, Nicki," Mom whispers.

As she puts the car into drive, I look out the window. The guy from before is unlocking his car. For a moment, our eyes lock, and I hope I don't appear too weepy. He gives a small wave; I give a small smile. It makes me feel a little better, that it's not just me and Claudia who think the hockey team is full of jerks.

We have another game scheduled in Stentson this season. Maybe he'll be working.

I'll think about it all later: Mom's call to the school tomorrow, Coach most likely pulling me aside, the potential fallout with the team. I close my eyes and drift off as Mom drives home.

Inspiration

There are certain moments in childhood that stick with you. One of mine is a very delayed pick up from my mom. Another are conversations I overheard in high school from yes, the sole girl hockey player on our team.

I wish that when I waited all those years ago, the person waiting with me had been kind instead of indifferent. And I wish my bandmate could have had at least one supporter on the hockey team. In fiction, those wishes can come true.

Stuck In the Muck Of Corrupt

MARY O'BRIEN GLATZ

Bright white frozen glares, crossed arms
pouty lips, glowing skin, yellow hair growing thin
mouth open screaming, screeching
all our decency from troll farms leaching
out onto three long winters of discontent.

No compromise from him brings harm,
he makes US forget what we meant
In the first place when we knew
who we were supposed to be through
all the springs, summers, falls of our nation rising.

We the People are a nation of integrity,
dignity, diversity, truth, a democracy
risen from a Constitution and precedents
from laws and sea to sea examples shining
overriding lawless presidents.

He distracts us with lies, little things he makes big
so we don't remember who we are
lies grow like fungi that don't show
their ill effects until it's too late
let's not wait for planks to rot, keel to bow.

Let's be candid, we are stranded
in his muck of corruption, destruction
until a blue wave rises to lift us up
to forge a new vision, heal the division
as united we stand on an old proposition.

We are one, you and them, me and thee
yet here we are shipwrecked in a swelling sea
so close to shore drowning in our own despising.
Sail on Oh Ship of State
clear these shoals of grifting greed and hate.

Inspiration

Inspiration for this poem is the President of the United States who was elected in 2016 with social media help propagated by the Russian GRU, the successor agency to the KGB, as verified by the United States Intelligence agencies. This poem is also a plea for a democratic exit from the dangerous path of division, dishonesty, and destruction of our democratic norms, institutions, and laws as he purposefully polarizes our country for political and personal gain.

There Will Be a Slight Delay

Greg Wright

The first day.

Eric and Cheryl glanced at the airport departure board. The times slowly faded from accurate times to a single word: *DELAYED.* They stared at the 5:30 pm flight to Miami; it was holding. The light snow falling outside the window was ramping up to a full-blown white out.

The Chicago to Miami shuttle was the last leg of their journey. Flying from Minnesota, they were excited about spending a week together, but there was some trepidation. They had never been on a long trip together before and with their new relationship, it was a gamble. In February a warmer climate is a requirement and South Beach is a place where two twenty-somethings can play, so it was an easy decision to book it.

But now things were slowly unraveling as the winter they sought to run away from had them in its grasp. They sat in the black padded leather chairs, staring at the board, watching the flights slip into purgatory. Their flight held its time, still ready to board in twenty minutes as promised, like a secret portal that would slip them into an invisible jet stream and land them in a world of palm trees and margaritas.

Cheryl grabbed Eric's hand, laced their fingers together, and curled hers tightly over his knuckles. He looked at her and tightened his grip. She looked back at him with large doe-eyes, the skin on her cheeks taut with anticipation and fear. They looked like two sacrificial virgins on the edge of the volcano who suddenly realized that maybe this wouldn't end like they thought.

The storm edge tipped and the snow hit critical mass. The status board flickered. Like a broken dam, the word *CANCELLED* started at the top line and fluttered down to the bottom where their flight was listed. As the 'word' came crashing down the column, they had hopes, aspirations that somehow miraculously they would be skipped. They held their breath and tightened their fingers with anticipation that the verb would blast into their flight's slot to obliterate their departure time and crush any hope of hitting South Beach before midnight. Cheryl blurted out the word 'F***!!' as the demolition continued down the board.

It was quite the shock. Eric had never heard her express herself in the same way a plumber would when his pipe wrench slipped off of the nut. He had known her for almost a year and in all the situations where he thought he would hear it - the Vikings making a miracle throw to knock her beloved Saints out the playoffs, the time at the grocery store where someone had pulled a car so close to her driver's door that even if she were Gumby she didn't stand a chance of getting in it, or the time at her favorite sidewalk restaurant when they just missed the last seating and had to watch the couple in front of them get seated at 'their' space on the patio.

Cheryl threw his hand away like a wet dishtowel, crossed her arms, and scowled. She stared out the window at the sheets of white filling the glass, then at the scheduling board, then at him. She was trying to place blame and the fact that the final stare was on him made him a little uneasy.

"I'm sure we will get out in a few hours," he said with a deep sense of self-preservation.

She exhaled and leaned her head back. "I don't want to be here."

He scanned the people and noticed that everyone was settled in for what may be a long stay. An old man placed his soft duffel behind his wife's back so she was more comfortable. A group of seven teenaged kids abandoned their seats and stretched out in a corner of the waiting area. Another couple, apparently experienced travelers, built footrests out of luggage, pulled out blankets and pillows, and settled in to sleep. It was the little girl with her parents that made him edgy when she reached into her carryon and pulled out a recorder.

"I can practice!" She proudly told her mom.

Soon the strains of a screaming cat, its register oddly similar to the Minuet in G, interrupted the calming overhead music. At some point, this could not would not stand.

Day two.

Eric awoke, alert and aware of everything around him. He stretched his legs, twisted his back to loosen it and sat up. He remembered that he had transitioned from the chair to a place alongside the window heater. It was warm but that made him thirsty from the dry heat. He glanced at his phone. 6:00 am. It was about midnight the last time he looked and Cheryl had already fallen asleep next to him. She was still there, curled up, using her thick overcoat as a blanket.

He glanced outside. The storm hadn't subsided. However, the intensity had slackened and through the steady fall of snow he could see the shapes of planes and snow machinery moving between the drifts in the background. The airport had completely shut down and people were sleeping in heaps like odd collections of clothing gathered for laundry. Those that couldn't sleep were on their devices, the light blue glow of the screens reflected on their faces.

Standing slowly so as not to fall into Cheryl, he kept his balance and stepped over her to walk out of the gate area into the concourse. He felt a chill, and it got colder as he walked down the wide, barren aisle looking for something to drink. He was now in hunter-gatherer mode walking past kiosks and storefronts to see what was open and had food. He found a fruit juice stand and looked at the options. Behind the counter was a blurry-eyed woman. A much larger man was lying on the floor asleep.

"Can I have an orange juice please?" He asked, reaching in his back pocket for his wallet.

"Juice is gone," she said in a halting accent as she rubbed her eyes.

"Ok, apple, then."

She shook her head no.

"How about lemonade."

Same response.

He tried to pick something from an already limited selection.

Finally, he just asked. "What do you have?"

"Pomegranate and lime."

"That's it?"

"Pomegranate and lime," was the answer again. "The truck is stuck in the snow. No new drinks."

"Don't you carry supplies in case of an emergency?"

"This is an emergency. You think you're the first person to come here?"

"Alright – I'll take two." He relented.

She pulled two bottles from a cooler, empty except for lots of bottles of pomegranate and lime juice, and handed them to him.

"Is there anything to eat around here?" he asked but it was a pointless question. She shrugged and leaned on her hand after a heavy sigh.

Returning to hunter-gatherer mode, he continued down the con-course. After almost an hour of walking down different hallways, crisscrossing concourses, and discussing the unavailability of food with vendors, he started his return to Cheryl and Gate 43, holding one twisty pretzel with cheese and horseradish, a large box of cold French fries, a small packet of chocolate donuts, and a slice of pizza with one pepperoni in the center. He convinced himself that his expedition to gather sustenance had been a success. But now he was confused. Where was the gate? Despite the numbering system, he wasn't sure which hall to enter.

He struggled to guess the way back, but then the sound of the recorder, the siren's call, reverberated through the gates and echoed down the halls. The scratchy, reedy voice of the recorder butchering the Minuet in G, and yet in its odd way, calling the sailor home. He followed the sound until, at last, Gate 43 appeared. Cheryl was up as expected, sitting with her knees bent, eyes black and puffy from a rough night of sleep, staring with murderous intent at the little girl with the recorder.

"Breakfast!" he said, using the word loosely and trying to show some glee in the items he held.

She looked at him, scanned over the choices, and turned away. She pulled a small toilet kit out of her backpack.

"I'm going to the bathroom," she mumbled, stood up and walked to the restrooms.

He laid the food on the heater, hoping the warmth would make it more appealing, but the faces on the people near him showed repulsion at the smell of twice warmed food, so he removed it.

Eric looked at Cheryl as she returned. She had removed all of her makeup, pulled her hair back into a ponytail, and had a dark look in her eye. She walked differently too. Her shoulders were slouched slightly, her movements dull and almost threatening, and her face had the look of disappointment, like a softball player walking away from third after being thrown out. She sat down next to him in silence.

With the gate attendants having long abandoned them, they were left to gather whatever news they could from the cable networks in the corner of the seating area. After constantly hearing about the paralyzing snow-storm, and with the kids getting restless, one of the fathers climbed up and switched the channel on the TV from the weather to a kid-friendly station. This distracted the children enough so that they didn't annoy people.

Families moved closer to the monitor. Singles and older people began to move away. Like-minded people started to move closer together, those that were different moved away. Everyone was assembling into tribes; and although there was no hostility, there were definite boundaries.

Parents encouraged wandering children to stay with their group. One child wandered close to the collection of teenagers. Their conversation stopped as the five-year-old stood in front of their group and stared at them. One of the teenage girls pointed to the child and shouted "Hey!" at the group of parents that had foolishly allowed the child to escape. The mother quickly ran over and grabbed the child with the urgency of a mother saving a child from being eaten, scolding the little boy for wandering.

Older people talked pleasantly while the younger passengers worked their devices. The only exception from the collections of people were the two travelers that had been prepared all along. Hungry, they pulled out food. Thirsty, they had their own canisters so there was an ample supply. They never left to forage, they drew from the reserves they had. Grasshoppers vs ants. Above all this divisiveness was the crackling sound of the recorder, grating and carving a cranial tattoo on their memories.

Day three.

It was now almost noon, but nothing had changed. It was still snowing. The groups still kept their distance and a collective mood of misery had descended on everyone.

"Do you think we will ever get out of here?" Cheryl asked softly in a desperate voice.

This was a treacherous question. Yes was too optimistic. No was too depressing. Should he even answer at all? Was it just an open-ended question to ascertain the level of one's madness? He chose the first.

"Yes. We will," he said, not in the weak voice of someone waiting for retribution, but in the strong voice of someone willing to lead everyone out of the wilderness.

She turned to him. "I really wasn't looking for an answer." Then she breathed deeply and turned to watch the snowfall. On his part, a lesson learned.

Since the food options were minimal, they subsisted on water for a time. In the distance, he heard a man yelling. "Out of vodka!! How is that even possible!!"

Eric and Cheryl went to the bathroom in shifts, each watching the other's stuff. Every time she came back, she appeared more and more dismal. The laughter and good times he was hoping to create and share were slowly sinking into a morass of despair, but she was doing nothing to pull herself out of it. She constantly mulled on her own hopeless situation with little concern about those around her. Crying babies were causing her to withdraw into her sweatshirt. People trying to entertain themselves were laughing and she appeared unable to appreciate it. She didn't seem to have the ability to see beyond herself and to see that in this situation everyone was affected, not just her.

Around 4:00, Cheryl returned from the bathroom, and on the path towards their little camp she looked up from staring at the floor and saw an opportunity. Eric watched her as she hesitated slightly when she saw the recorder, alone and unattended, laying on the floor. The little girl was distracted by a circle of children. Eric watched Cheryl gauge the distance, adjust her stride, and set a course for the object. Focused, she took four steps, and on the fifth, with the force of Voldemort on Harry Potter's wand, brought her heel down on the thin piece of plastic.

With a snap that everyone heard, she walked on top of the recorder. Its spine was broken, it lay there in two parts, helpless.

"Oh God, I'm so sorry!" She exclaimed. "Let me know how much it is and I'll pay for it!"

The mother said it wasn't a problem, the instrument shouldn't have been there in the first place, and they parted with no harm done.

The smile on Cheryl's face showed her satisfaction. Behind her the little girl held the two pieces apart and watched Cheryl walk away with a steely stare and tight smile. The little girl didn't cry or complain, but watched Cheryl. Revenge as a method had been learned and successfully passed from adult to child.

Around 10:00 pm the snow let up appreciably and soon ended. The crews started to de-ice the plane and the lights on the runways became clearer as the snow was cleared. People stirred in anticipation, and when attendants showed up at the gate, the passengers began to organize and collect their things. Like the early pioneers waiting along the trail for the guide to return, movement was stirring. When the intercom opened up and the scheduling board rebooted to display times and gates, everyone knew salvation was at hand.

Eric grabbed his bags and helped Cheryl with hers.

"Finally!" She said in a cheery voice, one that he thought had been abandoned and long forgotten. "We are on our way!"

She looked at Eric, her bloodshot eyes welcoming.

"Hope we don't have any problems at the hotel. Wouldn't it be great if there is a Cuban band at the airport?"

"Wouldn't that be wonderful?" Eric replied slowly. He prayed silently that the band would be on key.

Inspiration

This story is a mixed bag of scenes that I had actually witnessed at an airport or had been informed of by friends, and by my own bad relationship reveal on a ski trip. As any battle-hardened traveler will tell you, there are challenges.

Stranded at Valley Forge

Sam McAdams

"I hate that painting." Albert looked away from the bar's TV which displayed the iconic painting of Washington Crossing the Delaware.

"Are you British and still hold a grudge?" asked a stranger entering the bar. He grabbed a free stool a couple away from Albert and glanced at a flickering dust-covered neon Falstaff sign.

"The owner calls it classic tavern décor," said the bartender, handing the stranger the beer list. "I say the place resembles a bus depot bathroom."

"Every Christmas they show that damn painting and repeat the story of lies," said Albert staring at the smoke-stained ceiling tiles.

"You must be British," said the stranger studying the beer list.

Albert spun to face the stranger in pressed slacks. "Do I sound British?"

"Sorry, I didn't mean to offend," said the stranger.

"My great ancestors drove the British out of this country, so don't go accusing me of being British. I'm a patriot." Albert pushed his empty can of Hamm's and drained shot glass to the edge of the bar.

The bartender grabbed a fresh beer from the bar fridge and a bottle of Goldschläger on his way over to Albert's spot.

"My great-great-great-grandfather, Corporal Albert Hampton was at Valley Forge. I was named after him."

The stranger motioned to the bartender. "Let me get that round for Albert, the patriot, and I'll have a Bourbon County Stout."

"You're only encouraging him," said the bartender as he placed new drinks in front of Albert.

"So," said the stranger slapping a couple of twenties on the bar, "I get your disgust with the painting. I don't think anyone believes George Washington stood up on the boat like that as they crossed. What else about the crossing is not true?"

"Like, he wasn't in the boat at all."

"What do you mean?"

"He stayed behind at Valley Forge while his troops made the historic raid." Albert downed his shot.

"You don't know what you're talking about."

"Buy me another shot and I'll tell you all about it."

The stranger nodded to the bartender who shook his head.

"I tried to warn you. You really don't want to get Albert started about Valley Forge," he said as he grabbed the bottle of Goldschläger.

"All right Albert, tell me about George Washington not being a part of the Christmas night crossing of the Delaware."

Albert moved himself and his drinks to the open stool next to the stranger.

"Because it was my great ancestor Corporal Albert Hampton's job to make sure everybody got on the boats. He had a list of which boat everyone was to be on and he checked off every soldier as they boarded their boat."

"Let me guess, there was one name he didn't check off," said the stranger as he motioned for another IPA.

"Precisely. You want to see the list?"

Albert didn't wait for a response. He scurried back to his stool and fumbled through the pockets of his winter coat before pulling out a folded set of documents. He plopped the stack on the bar in front of the stranger.

"You carry these with you?" asked the stranger.

"They're not the originals. I'm not going to carry around 240-year-old historical documents. I'm not crazy."

"Ok?" said the stranger, as he began paging through the sheets.

"There's a page for every boat with the list of the soldiers assigned to it."

"I see that. Every name has a checkmark in front of it."

"Precisely."

"I don't get it. That means everybody got on their boat."

"Ah, but do you see the name George Washington?"

The stranger scanned through the stack again. "No."

"Bam!!" He downed his shot and slammed the empty shot glass upside down on the bar.

"That proves nothing. Without a check or a missing check by his name, we have no idea whether he was on a boat or not. All we know is he wasn't on the list."

"Well, I know for a fact he wasn't on any boat. He was stranded in Valley Forge." He snatched up the checklists and stuffed them back in his coat pocket.

"I honestly don't know why you carry those documents around with you," said the bartender clearing away the empty shot glass.

"It's history. You wouldn't understand."

"Oh, I understand," said the bartender. "I understand that you come from a long line of idiots and you're proud of it. You can't wait to tell everyone you meet that your great ancestor was a moron and left George Washington stranded in Valley Forge during the raid on Trenton."

"It wasn't his fault. He didn't make the list. He checked off everybody's name and figured they were all aboard."

"So, why wasn't George there when they were boarding the boats?" asked the stranger after taking a long sip of his beer.

"Maybe he had to go to the bathroom or went to brush his wooden teeth. How am I supposed to know?" Albert scanned the bar looking for his shot glass.

The bartender rolled his eyes as he grabbed the Goldschlager bottle.

"So, you know anyone at the Smithsonian?" asked Albert as he closed his eyes and let out a quiet belch. The bartender and stranger flinched, expecting more than a burp to come out.

"Sorry, I can't help you with that," said the stranger.

"Albert," said the bartender pouring the new shot, "why do you want your ancestor's great blunder on public display?"

"These are historic (belch), historically significant documents. They belong in the Smithsonian." Albert grabbed his drinks and returned to his seat.

"So that's it. That's the story?" asked the stranger.

"Yep. Pretty frickin' earth-shattering, aye."

"OK, but what happened when everybody got back? How did George Washington react?" asked the stranger.

"We don't talk about that. Let's just say, from that point forward, grand-pappy Albert made sure to put George's name on the list first."

Inspiration

The announcement of the Stranded *theme reminded me of the time my daughter's middle school band director got left at the school as the two buses headed off to a band competition. My wife had the responsibility of checking off names for her bus. With all the names checked off for both buses, they took off, leaving the band director at the school. She was not happy when she caught up to the bus or when my wife explained that her name was on the list and they assumed she was on the other bus. I didn't want to retell that exact story and figured I would skip submitting to the anthology. But then we watched an episode of* Drunk History *on the Washington crossing the Delaware and I thought, "Wouldn't it be funny if they left George back at Valley Forge because his name wasn't on the checklist."*

I Stand to Speak

Edward Martin

"Breath in, breath out."
Before them, I stand
Hands without pencils
And heart in hands.
My words, they say, are short, bitter-sweet,
Of life and death, and beauty with heat.
Before them, I stand
Hands without pockets
And heart in hands.
My shirt, less torn, my jeans, less worn,
My face and self, for once, unadorned
With trinkets, bits, or bobs,
Despite my comfort with them all,
Because *"Professionalism is all,"*
Alone I stand.
Above them, I stand.
Aware again again of my faults,
Judging eyes, a liar's tongue, hands that long only to assault,
A heart that's torn twain by twain,

For right and wrong and love and hate,

And my brain, oh my brain, the conceiver of imagined pain,

Lust, greed, pride, my mistakes, none of which I want as mundane.

Alone I stand, and my self-loathing tells the truth, I know

Brought low, I stand.

Hands without right,

And heart in hands.

My voice speaks woes

With passions low.

So I murmur in hope of setting the tone,

But that whisper dies in the dark, alone,

And my treacherous voice betrays me now

As a childish squeak is all I sound.

My speech leaves for heaven, my heart leaves for hell,

And I stand truly alone, until I cease to stand.

Cold Feet

Leslie Gail

Left
tuxedoed
at the altar
down the aisle
of a church.

Left
abandoned
right at crunch time
while the best man
sprints to search.

Left
forsaking
motivation
to veil jitters
or escape.

Left
concluding

to do nothing
snapping tersely,
"She's just late."

I hold
quiet
time suspended
facing facts here
on my heels.

Left
out cold since
the proposal
when she griped I
should have kneeled.

Left
high and dry
left cast ashore
the knot not tied
no solemn vow.

Left
undone from
this day forward,
"What the hell do
I do now?"

Hand
still ringless
guests a twitter

promise premise
most betrayed.

Left
less certain
boldly bachelored
disconcerted
and dismayed.

To my right a
door swings open
the best man
leans in
towards my head.

Left
me stranded
at the altar
for, "She never
left her bed."

Inspiration

My inspiration was the Stranded Anthology *theme. I considered different places someone could become "stranded" and stumbled upon "stranded at the altar." In addition, poking around a thesaurus brought up "left" as a synonym. I am left-handed and have an unhealthy attachment to the word.*

The Elevator Pitch

Debra Kollar

At the exact time I was supposed to be upstairs in a pitch session on the eighth floor of the Montgomery building for the job interview of my life, I stepped into a crowded elevator. I had been up all night figuring out the perfect pitch that would be so funny, so amazing, they would have no choice but to hire me as a writer for the Sunday evening comedy showcase, *Just Laugh!*

"Maybe a comedy skit about a hairstylist in training who dyes her client's hair fire engine red?" I said as the elevator went up. I had to figure out a comedy bit by hearing it out loud. I let out a sigh in frustration. "Too obvious..."

I only noticed the elevator had stopped between floors because someone broke the background music of Kenny G's "Songbird" by yelling, "Oh hell, not again."

I threw up my hands. "It figures. I'm an anxiety-ridden comedy writer stuck in an elevator the size of a walk-in closet. Oh, and I'm late for an interview."

"Hey, crazy girl up front." A man yelled from behind. "When you're done having a full-blown conversation with yourself, maybe you would be so kind as to push the emergency button for the real people behind you."

"Of course," I sneered. After pressing it, I shimmied to the right, away from the panel and by default, the leadership position.

The tall man standing to my right, in front of the doors, turned and looked at me. "I ain't budging, sweetie." He was probably used to getting his way since he looked like a Ken Doll with his thick bolt of blond hair, high cheekbones, tall stature, and pressed suit. He surveyed the group, shook his head disapprovingly, and stood firmly planted in his position, preferring to eye the gloss of the steel elevator doors instead.

"Fine," I uttered.

The man behind shouted again. "You didn't press the emergency button correctly!"

"Are you the button police? I pressed the damn emergency button, see…" I pressed it a second, third and fourth time. "It's not working!"

"We're packed in here like sardines. We're going to die!" A woman yelled from the right back corner.

"Great. Another crazy person." I heard Mr. Button Police announce.

A tall, thin woman standing in the middle with caramel-colored skin in a floral pantsuit raised her arm to gain attention. "Excuse me! What are your names?"

I immediately recognized the royal blue chin length pageboy bob and matching heels. I had caught her drag queen comedy show in Brooklyn last month.

Ken Doll smirked. "Why do we have to give you our names?"

"Because of manners. Clearly, you're all eye candy and no substance, Mr. Dolph Lundgren from Rocky IV." She turned her back to him. "My name is Miss Deedee Divalicious," she said to the rest of us. "And I have no problem giving anyone my name. Cause everyone will know it one day."

Ken Doll rolled his eyes. "Dolph Lundgren? I'm from the Netherlands, not Sweden."

Deedee sighed. "What's the difference? You're all tall and up north."

"Alright then, Apollo Creed," he told her.

Deedee shifted toward him for another attack.

I tried to deescalate the situation. "By the way, big fan of yours, Deedee. My name is Louisa Grayson. I am a comedy writer and if you're ever in need of some material for a show of yours, I have a business card right here in my purse somewhere..."

Mr. Button Police chimed in from the back corner. "We're not here for a meet and greet. We're freaking stuck on an elevator."

I placed the cards back in my purse.

"Fine," Ken Doll turned around. "My name is Hans."

Mr. Button Police propelled toward Hans. I now knew who smelled so strongly of cigarettes and alcohol. "Say, Hans, I have a slick Mercedes Benz you'd look great in." He opened his wallet and held out a business card. "Last name is Sanders. I sell used luxury cars."

"So, you get to pitch your business on the elevator, but I can't?" I snatched his card and threw it on the ground. Nothing made me angrier than an unfair world. A lesson I learned in high school.

"Like I said. Crazy girl." Sanders said to me before bending down to retrieve his card.

The woman in the back in a rainbow knitted dress and a beret to match—who was adamant we were all going to die—introduced herself by the nickname she received as a younger woman, Sissy from the '60s. Based on her paranoia, I had a feeling she may still be using those recreational drugs from the '60s.

Sissy tugged at the collar of her knitted dress. "It's hot in here. Why is it so hot in here? We can't be stuck for long? What about air? There's air in here, right?"

"You're all in need of a psychiatrist," Hans decreed.

"Did anyone try their cell phone?" Sanders brought it out from his side pocket. "Nope, no bars. Can't get a signal in here."

We tried our phones except for our resident fatalist Sissy who prophesied we would all be dead in five years from cell phone induced brain cancer.

These people were getting the best of me. We had been here for twenty minutes, succumbed to passing around plastic baggies of homemade holistic snacks from Sissy's purse: kale chips, date bars, and dehydrated fruit strips. She said that one must always carry a food stash in preparation for doomsday.

I hoped *Just Laugh!* would somehow be able to fit me in for an interview with John Erickson, the producer. I had to be ready. "Okay. It's the apocalypse. The last man on Earth is surrounded by, what else would be left? Cockroaches and Twinkies. He has a Twinkie on his dinner plate, and he says to his dinner guest, the cockroach: 'So, Floyd. What did you do today?'"

Hans grimaced at me.

"Lord Jesus, it's hot in here." Deedee started fanning herself with her hand. "I mean, I could see an elevator break down in Brooklyn or Queens, but this here is Midtown Manhattan."

"It does this," an elderly woman interjected from the back corner. No one noticed she had been there tucked behind Sissy and statuesque Deedee Divalicious, because either we were preoccupied with our own problems or because she was not more than four feet tall. She appeared like an uninvited child who snuck into an adults-only party wearing her mother's knee-length mink two sizes too big.

"Where did you come from?" Sanders eyed her. "Is there a trap door in this elevator?"

"Morty will save us," the elderly woman in the oversized mink spoke up.

"Who's Morty?" Sanders asked.

"Morty is my husband."

"Where's Morty?" Sanders pressed.

She looked at the ceiling and pointed.

"You've got to be kidding." Sanders threw up his hands. "We're stuck on an elevator with a madwoman wearing a fur in July."

"She probably has dementia," Hans added flatly.

"Quiet," I told the two. "What's your name, ma'am?"

"Rosa Gerstein and I see dead people."

"Oh, for crying out loud." Sanders slapped the metal wall of the elevator.

"Girl, shush now, you don't see dead people," Deedee laughed nervously.

Rosa turned to Deedee, "Your grandmother Ernestine says, 'Sweet Jesus, Dwayne. I can see that whorish blush of yours clear up in Heaven. Take that rouge off before people get the wrong idea.'"

Deedee screamed. "Ah, hell no! There's a ghost in this elevator!" Charging like a football player rushing an opponent, she slammed her body against the doors and fell back with a thud.

"I could have told you that wouldn't work." Hans looked down at Deedee on the floor.

Rosa inspired an idea for my interview. "A medium is sitting in front of a crystal ball inside a tent. A girl enters to see who she'll marry. She is outraged. It's her cousin Billy Bob. The medium says, 'You aren't from Kentucky by chance?'"

Rosa touched me on the shoulder. "Don't try so hard, dear. Real life gives you all the material you need."

After another fifteen minutes, we sat on the floor, leaning against the walls, tired and thirsty. I almost asked Sanders for his flask peeking out from his breast pocket which would not quench my thirst, but it sure would make me feel better. The air smelled stale with our desperation sweat added to Sanders' smelly suit of cigarettes and alcohol. I took off my shoes and suit jacket. I rolled my hair into a bun and stuck a pen through to hold it in place. We didn't have much ventilation and it was hot as hell.

"We're goners," Sissy cried. "I know it. We're out of air. It's the final countdown. Mama, I'm coming home."

"I wonder who'll play me in a Lifetime movie when I die?" Deedee took a cosmetic bag from her purse to apply makeup. "At least I'll look good when they find me." She pointed to the ceiling. "And Granny, I do not look like a whore!"

Sanders stood up. "I'm not staying here any longer. Hoist me up to that panel in the ceiling guys."

"You do know this only works in the movies?" Deedee told him. "Hell, you drink, smoke and you have to be at least fifty."

"And you yap your mouth too much," he snapped.

"And you need the triple threat of Alcoholics Anonymous, NicoDerm CQ, and Weight Watchers," she rebutted.

Hans shook his head in disbelief. "Hello! How old are you two?"

"Just stop being a pain in my ass and help me, Deedee Delicious," Sanders begged.

"Delicious is not my name, but I'll take it."

If I ever saw a comedy routine this was surely it. A metrosexual Ken Doll, a dramatic drag queen, a mini elderly woman and me hoisting up a fifty-year-old man with no athletic ability whatsoever. Thank goodness, it was Sissy who suddenly came over and saved us. Clearly, something she took in the 60s had given her uncanny strength.

"Can't get my gut through. I'm stuck."

We pulled and rotated Sanders until he fell back down to the floor.

Sanders brushed himself off. "What about one of you ladies climbing up the shaft?"

I raised my hand. "Fear of heights. No way."

Sanders looked at Rosa in the mink and bypassed her. He then looked at Sissy and after thinking for a moment, bypassed her too. "We need someone that won't go mental up there. How about you?" He stared at Deedee.

"Hell no. This here's a designer suit. Don't remember the name of the gal who sold it to me on 5th Avenue. My friend Gigi swears it's Versace."

"That isn't Versace," Hans laughed. "More like dumpster diving couture."

Deedee ignored Hans and turned to Sanders. "The point is, I'm no Tom Cruise and this sure the hell ain't Mission Impossible."

"My Morty bought me this mink."

We had forgotten the elderly woman.

Sanders motioned at Rosa. "You sure we can't push this little thing up in the elevator shaft."

"Of course not." Spirits or no, the woman had to be over 80.

"They have to get us out of here, right? We're American citizens." Sissy was losing it again. She had taken off her knitted beret and was kneading it like it was a stress ball.

Deedee shook her head. "You would think that, wouldn't you honey? When I was beaten leaving a drag club a few years back, nobody did jack. I look fierce, but it ain't always easy keeping up a brave face for everyone."

"No, it's not." Sanders retrieved the flask from his breast pocket. "Lost my family over this. My old man drank. Promised I would never do it. So hard to change."

"I live with thirteen cats," Sissy spoke up.

"Good grief," Hans rolled his eyes. "Why am I not surprised?"

"That would make anyone depressed," Sanders added.

"No," Sissy explained. "They make me happy. It's my sister that depresses me. Lived with her for fifty years. She says I can't take care of myself. I can though, if she would let me try."

Hans huffed, "Don't expect me to do this heart show-and-tell thing. My life is perfect."

Deedee shook her head. "You're lying. Nobody's life is perfect."

"Fine," Hans mumbled. "My parents died in an accident when I was six. My uncle shipped me off to boarding schools. My life is my work. I'm 40 and I'll probably never have kids. All I know is how to be alone."

"Man, you're well preserved," Deedee assessed. "I thought you were thirty, tops."

Hans shrugs his shoulders. "I'm Dutch, what can I say?"

"I know what it's like to be alone," I spoke up. "My twin sister died when we were in high school. Drunk driver. The one thing I could do to make my parents forget was to make them laugh. So, surprise. I'm a comedy writer." I bit my lip to keep the tears from coming. The last thing I wanted to do was break down in a stuck elevator with five people hovering around me.

Rosa came over and patted my hand. "Your sister's okay, honey."

Before I could ask Rosa about her comment, the elevator began to shake. We all stood up with smiles on our faces.

"Yippee. We're going to be saved." Sissy began clapping.

The elevator shook again and then plummeted toward the first floor. Everyone screamed except for Rosa and me. I watched her as she watched me. We both had someone in the afterlife we were ready to see: my sister and her husband, Morty. I took a deep breath. For once, the anxiety left me.

Then Rosa gave me the most peculiar smile. The elevator stopped at the second floor with a sudden jolt and coasted down to the first floor—as if this was all part of the ride.

I looked around in disbelief. How petty we had been, judging one another. Complaining about our lives. For a brief moment, we were no longer defined by our labels or issues—we were all happy to be alive. We shouted with excitement.

Someone yelled from behind the elevator doors. "Stand back." After a lot of commotion and maneuvering on the other end, the doors opened to the lobby. A firefighter was there to greet us. "Are you ladies and gentlemen okay?"

We had been faced with who we were and most of us didn't like what we had seen. Maybe, a few of us would see things differently and change.

Hans took off to the stairway door to climb the stairs back to his office, to make up for lost time and missed work obligations.

Sanders went over to the trash can, dropped his flask inside and yelled, "I'm a free man baby!"

Sissy looked back at the elevator as if she was leaving a nest, going back out into the big scary world again. She went through the front revolving door.

Deedee walked past us in her electric blue heels, already on her phone sharing her near-death experience with someone.

Rosa walked out of the elevator. "I promised you Morty would save us." She kissed her fingertips and raised them to the ceiling. She grabbed my hand and held it there for a moment. "And Lucy is with you, dear. Always."

I watched her hobble across the lobby and back out into the sunlight, realizing I never mentioned my sister's name.

Two hours after my initial interview time and eight flights of stairs later, I finally made it to the eighth-floor offices of *Just Laugh!*

I had called hoping to reschedule, but they stated that Mr. Erikson was leaving tonight for Los Angeles, so it had to be today.

The secretary looked me over. "Here's a wet wipe."

"That bad, huh?" I took the wipe and went to look in the bathroom mirror. My natural curls had morphed into a frizzy Chia Pet and my makeup had sweated off. My suit was wrinkled. The worse part: I smelled like Sanders' rock bottom cologne of cigarettes and alcohol. No, a wet wipe would not do.

A menagerie of sprays and perfumes lined a metal tray. I tried one. I smelled like Sanders and—looked at the bottle—orchids.

The secretary looked up as I walked out of the bathroom. "They're ready for you, Miss Grayson."

I walked through a door and was caught by surprise. I was interviewing in a theater, center stage. No pressure, right? I looked at the filled seats. The secretary mentioned a lot of the team would be in the interview since everything is collaborative, but I didn't expect this many.

After being asked extensively about my writing skills and experience, it ended with the one thing I wasn't able to figure out in the elevator—a finished pitch for a short comedy sketch.

I stood frozen for a moment. Which idea should I use? I remembered what Rosa had told me: real life gives you all the material you need.

I took a deep breath. "Okay, picture this. Five types of people are stuck in an elevator. A drag queen, druggy, car salesman, Ken Doll look-alike, medium and… one with anxiety. They all first appear normal, right? The elevator gets stuck and they try to be civil and work together; but all of these quirks start coming out. They argue and bicker. Then try to save themselves by escaping out of the elevator panel. It doesn't work. Defeated, they open up about their vulnerabilities, issues and what they want to change about themselves. The elevator suddenly plummets to the ground and they scream, fearing death. It stops at the lobby. The doors open and they walk out—ready to tackle life. The camera shows a therapist in uniform standing by the doors with a clipboard and a long line of people waiting to get on. It zooms in on the sign above the doors: *Elevator Therapy*."

"It sounds unbelievable," someone called out. "Our audience will never buy it."

A figure walked down the aisle of the theater. "Oh, believe me, gentlemen. It's crazy enough to be true."

I recognized the bolt of blond hair immediately. "Hans?"

He stepped onto the stage and whispered. "You can imagine my surprise when I saw you on the stage. I suppose I'm the Ken Doll look-alike in your story?"

I was speechless.

"We could use a little more feminine perspective. Besides, anyone crazy enough to go around talking to herself in comedy sketches has to be made for this job."

"What are you doing here?" I whispered.

"I'm the producer. I never mention I'm in the comedy business because I get all kinds of weird pitches, like a man who followed me around dressed like Wanda from *In Living Color*. His bit wasn't funny and he looked more like Al Sharpton than Jamie Foxx. I think I still have a restraining order on him?"

"No, John Erickson is the producer," I insisted.

"Hans is short for Johannes which is John Americanized. Now, we can debate the complexities of my various names the rest of the day or you can stop, realize you have the job, and get out of here before I change my mind. Go home and take a shower, Grayson. You smell funny." He winked, walked through the side door and disappeared.

"Congratulations, Miss Grayson," the secretary greeted me outside of the room. "Oh, yes. A woman handed me a card as I was coming up on the elevator for work this morning. She asked me to give it to you after your interview."

"Why would someone give you a card?" I didn't have any family left. Nobody knew I was here. I opened the card and stood there in disbelief.

Congratulations on your new job, Louisa. Now go and spread laughter to the world.

Love Lucy & Morty and Rosa Gerstein

Inspiration

I think it's bizarre and comical when people get into an elevator. It's as if time stands still, while the people navigate the few minutes from one floor to the next. People stare up, down and ahead. They stay silent as if they need to be completely nondescript. Now add an issue and their true personalities come out. This is the inspiration for "The Elevator Pitch."

Neither Here Nor There

GREG WRIGHT

He sat on the edge of the bed wearing only sweats and a thin t-shirt in the motel room by the airport. In his right hand he held the TV remote and deliberately, daringly, pointed it at the screen as if casting his first spell. The screen lit up quickly upon his direction, then he shuffled through the channels, pausing for only a moment at each one.

"Phil…Ellen…Jerry…Rachel…Maury. My new friends, " he reflects.

Every minute or so he would shuffle through them again, pausing, oddly enough, at women who were crying. Perhaps it was carved in the DNA - a primal response to a threatened cave mate.

Finally, he ended the tv watching when the news came on. It was late in the morning and a lot of the early travelers at the hotel had gone. New ones wouldn't be in until late this afternoon, so the hotel was empty.

"I should go out and get something to eat," he thought to himself, but he really wasn't hungry and didn't feel like getting fully dressed. Refusing to leave without changing out of his sweats was a dignity he held onto.

He went over to the nightstand and checked his phone. No messages, emails or texts. Back to looking at the parking lot as the gulls were now beginning to feel safe. They began to sift through the Styrofoam meals the tenants had left.

"Jesus, I wish she would call. I really need to talk to her," continuing the confession he was making. It provided some validation hearing it.

"I made a mistake. Can't you just talk to me," pleading the case for the confession he was prepared to make.

Frustrated, he returned to the edge of the bed and continued his muted surfing.

"*Phil...Ellen...Jerry...Rachel...Maury. Wait a second.*" He flipped back to Jerry. Along the bottom of the screen was the caption: *Husband slept with my best friend.*

"Huh." He turned the volume up.

The screaming had yet to begin, so he could get a full picture of the issue. The deceit, the lying, the excuses. The pleading by the husband that it was a one time thing, he didn't mean it, and it was the friend's fault that this happened. The husband really loved her. He could relate. The husband really needed her – again relatable - and that this wouldn't happen again.

"Bingo! That could be me on that stage," he thought.

But the ending wasn't what he hoped for. Within a few minutes the two women were thrown into the gladiator pit with the Roman crowd giving the temptress a solid thumbs down.

*"*Yet, is there a path here to get her back?"

After all, his wife told him to pack his crap and get out of the house, which he did, hence ending up here at the hotel. That was two days ago and she had yet to respond to his calls, texts, or any other communications.

Turning the TV on mute, he texted, "What do I need to do to come back?"

Surely she'll send a reply. In the meantime, all he could do was wait.

Returning to the TV, he began the check down again.

"*Phil...Ellen...Jerry...Rachel...Maury.*"

When he reached Maury, he hesitated. Then he turned back to Phil. Then back to Maury, then back again. The woman sitting in the tall chair, Kleenex in her hand with Dr. Phil consoling her on her situation, was the same one pulling the orange dreadlocks out of the woman's hair on Maury. The exact same.

"This is not helpful."

He strode out of the motel and onto the patio. He glanced over the parking lot from the railing and watched as a late model Ford sedan pulled into the lot. The car settled into a parking space by the front entrance. It had seen its share of road time - tires were mismatched, paint thin on the hood.

A woman that looked as if she had a similar amount of road time exited out of the driver's door in an oversized yellow tee shirt and woefully undersized black yoga pants. She walked over the chipped red mulch in the center island, made an attempt to throw a coffee cup in the garbage can, then didn't return to pick it up when she missed.

She disappeared into the lobby and when she did, someone more intriguing appeared out of the passenger side. A thin young woman with shoulder length blonde hair, dressed in cutoff jeans, a loose white blouse and a figure any man would want to hold close. She walked to the back of the car, leaned against the trunk, then casually pulled out a pack of cigarettes from her front pocket. Lighting one, she slipped the pack back in, then pulled out her phone from her rear pocket, glanced at it, then returned it to her pocket.

Since she was the only thing of interest in an empty lot, he watched her smoke the cigarette, look at her watch, and scan the scenery. Possibly feeling his gaze, she looked up and noticed him standing at the railing. For a while she just looked, then nodded an acknowledgement. He nodded back.

"Where you from?" he yelled.

"Cincinnati," she yelled back.

"That's a long way from Jacksonville."

She smiled and nodded, "Just looking to get some sun, have a few drinks."

"Get some rest," he finished her sentence.

Still smiling, she added, "I doubt that."

Her friend came out holding some papers and a key card. The friend moved her aside and opened the trunk. The two of them sorted out a few backpacks and pulled them out of the trunk. Setting them on the ground, the blonde said something to her friend as she turned and looked at him, offering a mild wave.

They slung the backpacks on their shoulders and started to walk toward his building, the driver in the lead. As the blonde fell in behind, she looked up at him, reached into the side of her backpack and pulled out a bottle of Jameson.

"201," she said, adding, "in thirty minutes if you're interested."

"Wow," was all he could say.

They disappeared into the building and he walked, almost stumbled into his room. Sitting on the edge of the bed, he thought about his options. They looked good on paper, but the downsides were bad. Really bad. If his wife called, he could be out of here. Yet if she didn't, here was an option to really be out of here. If he partied, it wasn't really his fault; the wife sent him here. If he left the two 'opportunities' alone in the room, he could be missing a lot of legendary fun.

Picking up the remote, he turned on the TV and muttered, "What would Jerry do?"

Inspiration

Easy. Someone I know has a husband that occasionally cheats on her. He leaves for awhile, then comes back in a few days when she forgives him. Rinse, spin, repeat. They have been married for fifteen years. I just tried to imagine where he would go and what he would do, because he never tells anyone.

Schooled

Leslie Gail

I am certified
yet unpracticed.
A substitute aide
assigned to a
Behavior Disorder
middle school classroom.
Instructed to,
"work upstairs with Nick."

Nick leads me up a
    back
  stair
case
to an unoccupied
third floor classroom
scattered with empty desks.

Unschooled,
I take it in.

Nick begins to
side
step
long division with conversation.

I learn Nick is from Florida.
They sent him up north
to live with his aunt and
attend a better school.

Responsive,
I take it in.

Nick recalls his
Portable Classroom, a
crammedclaustrophobicsolution
to elementary overcrowding.

Inside,
a classmate
bad-mouthed his mother.
Impulsive retaliation
all at once
a desk rammed up AGAINSTHISTHROAT
ca
n't
breathe as it was released
a PUNCH
to the stomach

a PUNCH
to the nose
blood pulsed
out through
airways.

The Principal
sent him home
but
Nick's Stepfather
RAGED
and returned him to school.
End of discussion.
Off the hook!
Lesson not learned.

Within weeks another insult
BLOW FOR BLOW
yet again.

And again.

At 13, Nick is up north
in *Behavior Disorder.*
Labeled.
Unstable.

Disconnected
from his peers
and not-so peers.

Long division and Rutherford B.
fill the gaps
between the days
of talking back
and mischief.

Sent to the third floor
to
do
long division
when he flouts the rules
choosing to
skip lunch
rather than MAKE GOOD CHOICES.

separated from
his perceived rivals
and his somewhat peers

stranded
on the third floor

not
accomplishing
long division

$$86 \overline{)350303}$$

I prompt.
What is 86 x 3?

too low

Try, 86 x 4?

> *I'm on probation right now.*
> *If I'm in the car when my cousin gets pulled over?*
> *That's. It.*

Put down the 4.

8 times 4 is…

> *32*

plus 2

> *34*

344. Will that work? 350-344 =

The smell of

microwave popcorn

radiates from a break room.

My stomach rumbles.

I substitute there three days.

Listening beneath

Nick's bravado.

Taking a

stab

at

long

division.

Taking it in.

Inspiration

I spent one full year working as a substitute teacher and aide after earning a Type 3 teaching certificate. My assignments were varied and challenging. This experience in particular stuck with me and I wrote about it in my journal at the time.

Beached on the Jersey Shore

Barbara Bartilson

Laurie turns south onto the Garden State Parkway heading away from Red Bank. Another Friday night. She and her co-workers scatter for home as early as possible, seeking relief from the pressure of tending to people with mental illness in Monmouth County.

"How did I ever get here?" Laurie reflects on the clients she encountered this week and puzzles over her decision to move to this decaying corner of the country.

"What was I thinking to have studied this line of work?"

Mid-twenties and single, Laurie wants more from life than trying to find humor between counseling sessions with the parade of abnormal psych types, schizophrenics, psychotics, sadists, flashers, the manic-depressed, the mentally and physically-challenged.

Laurie slams coins into another toll basket at 20 mph and wonders what she might do this weekend to relax and think brighter thoughts. Doug, her only unmarried friend at work, is busy this weekend visiting his girlfriend in Philadelphia.

"I don't make enough money to travel and forget the sadness of seeing the outcomes from the cruelty people (especially relatives) are capable of inflicting on each other.

"Maybe I should go see the new movie, *All the President's Men*," she says out loud and shifts into fourth gear, "although I'm not sure even Dustin Hoffman and Robert Redford can cheer me up. Besides, living through Watergate was depressing, why watch the movie so soon afterward."

Twenty miles down the Parkway, Laurie takes the Bradley Beach exit toward the shore. At the east end of LaReine Ave, one block from the T-intersection with the Atlantic Ocean, she pulls up to her apartment building. Changing clothes quickly, she walks north up the boardwalk to the rock jetty before meandering back on the beach. The waves lick her bare feet, reminding her to avoid the jellyfish left by the retreating tide.

Seeing a crowd further ahead, Laurie sits down in the sand and laments being stuck at the edge of the continent, too proud to quit her first professional job, but distraught about staying. *What to do?*

"Excuse me, Miss, do you have any matches or could I use your cigarette to light mine?" a man's voice behind her interrupts and approaches.

"Here you go, you can keep them," she turns and hands him her extra matches.

"Did you see the beached whale here this afternoon?"

"Very funny! Or are you just name-calling?" she jokes with her best wry expression.

"No, really, a whale! The shore patrol, fire department, volunteers, lots of people were pushing it back into the water to save it!" He recovers, she observes. Dark hair. A talker. Funny. Not her usual type, but attractive and she decides to play the hand. Not too many shy, blond men here.

"I wondered why there are so many people down there. Did it survive?" He nods yes and cups a match in his hands.

"Why did it strand itself? Was it sick?" she quizzes.

"Maybe chasing a girl! " he smiles. "Just kidding. Mind if I sit, I'm Evan."

Laurie gestures and Evan charms her with his story, "Apparently whales lose their sense of direction when the iron content of the water is high because it interferes with their sonar. Interesting, huh?"

"Yes, maybe it affects people that way, too. I'm feeling a bit stuck here at the beach! Do you ever feel that way?"

"Not me, I love the beach! Born and bred here, my oasis! Where are you from?"

"I grew up on the other Coast. I've only been in New Jersey seven months. Graduated from a college in the Midwest and found work in Red Bank. What do you do?"

"I own a Driving School in Belmar, teach kids to drive."

"Ah, all the crazy drivers here are your fault then?! Just teasing, although I still haven't figured out roundabouts!"

"No one has figured out roundabouts! Have you figured out New Jersey turns yet? The first car in line at the light gets to turn left before oncoming traffic can enter the intersection."

"Look, the whale watching crowd is finally starting to disperse."

"Yep, here comes my gang." Evan's friends return, clamoring to get something to drink and eat. Evan insists Laurie join them and seems genuinely happy she agrees to come along. Relieved to be included, Laurie is glad there are both men and women in the group. Makes getting to know each other easier.

"Hey, everybody, this is Laurie. Introduce yourself to her. She just moved here."

She tries to remember names as they all collect their bags and head toward the bar on the pier. She checks her tendency to lean into an adventure too quickly and too naively by listening to his friends interact with him.

"Evan, weren't you going to Fredonia this weekend, what happened?" one of them asks.

"Yes, but I had a flare-up of the old sports injuries. Eight hour drive is too much today! I called Katie and told her I would have to visit later in the summer." Turning to Laurie, Evan clarifies, "Katie is my god-daughter. She is having her first communion this weekend up in Fredonia and I wanted to be there."

"Sorry to hear, that's too bad. Do you mean Fredonia, NY?" He nods, she adds, "I have a couple friends from Fredonia, Sid and Lou. Went to school with them in Wisconsin."

"What? Seriously? Sid and Lou? Lou Cavallo?" he chokes, spitting his water. "She is my god-daughter's older sister. I am supposed to be staying with Sid and Lou this weekend. You know them?"

"Yes! We went to college together the last couple years."

"No way, Laurie, this can't be!! You are making this up."

"Small world, Evan!! We really are stranded here by the iron-laden water, on the edge of the continent, beached just like the whale!"

"Too funny!! But true!! Maybe that's why we were drawn together? Our sonar navigation!!"

"I guess we will find out," she smiles fully for the first time all week.

Inspiration

Been there, done that. Giving voice to a memory that cheers me when I am low; there is usually something good right around the corner. Composite conversation made dramatic with passing similarity to reality experience.

CAUGHT IN CULTURAL DIVIDES

The Immigrant

Milda Willoughby

Greta sat in the dingy office, watching George in front of her shuffle papers; they appeared to glow in the rays of sunshine that found their way through the gaps of the mangled window blinds. The smell of stale old smoke and hints of alcohol permeated the air.

"Sign here, here, and here," George scribbled a few exes on the papers. Greta's mom, Ilena, reached over, pulled the documents to herself and started scanning the small print. Greta watched George take a swig of water out of a crumpled plastic bottle, noticing the all-but-gone label. At least George opted to save the planet by reusing his water bottles. His hair was shaggy around the ears and too long on the forehead, yet a growing bald spot betrayed the top of his crown. George wasn't even his real name; he just went by it to appeal to a broader clientele. His real name, Yuri, was infamously associated with poor law practices, so George decided to Americanize it in hopes of salvaging—or at least prolonging—his career.

Greta watched her mom sign the documents and slide them back to George. Those papers were the ticket out of the limbo the family was stuck in. Like many, Greta and her folks came to the States searching for a better life. Everything had been arranged: her parents had jobs lined up with employers ready to sponsor them for workers' visas, Greta and her brother were supposed to finish out their education in America, and a much brighter future would await the family than the prospects offered by their Baltic homeland. But then, 9-11 happened and everything came to a screeching halt.

"You must get a physical next. I know a doctor—easy going. No trouble at all. Just give him a small thanks, and you'll be in and out," George explained, digging out a stained business card from his drawer. "You can probably call him today, and he'll get you in. Tell him Yuri sent you." The man used his original name, implying an established under-the-table partnership.

Ilena took the card from George, gratitude in her tired eyes. She tucked an unruly strand of pale blonde hair tinged with silver behind her ear and forced a smile at the man.

"What about Greta? Can you do something for her? She's such a bright girl!" Ilena asked, wrapping one arm around her daughter's shoulders, a glimmer of hope infusing her words. Greta was hardly a "girl" anymore, as she had just left her teenage years, but her mother seemed to have missed this. George leveled his gaze at Greta, making the young woman recoil in her seat.

"Easiest way for you to get citizenship is to get married," he spoke directly to Greta and barked a laugh, as if his suggestion was a brilliant idea. "That shouldn't be too hard."

Greta's eyes filled with angry tears—tears came so easily these days. She bit her lower lip trying to pull herself together and tasted blood. It was time to leave. Any small hope she had held onto was dispersed. Other lawyers had hinted at marriage as the easiest way out before, but never this bluntly and never without first looking for other loopholes. George didn't care. George only cared about making a buck by completing an easy case. Greta stood up, forced a smile that was more of a grimace at the man and left the office. She heard her mother thank George for his help and leave him with an added monetary bonus "for his troubles" before scurrying out after Greta.

"It will be ok, Birdie. We'll figure something out," she whispered as they both slid into a white Subaru. Gretta watched the trees lining the sides of the road and the people scurrying down the streets, purpose in their steps. She wished she could be one of them. For the hundredth time, she wondered, why this country didn't want her so much.

"This can't be happening! How can it be exam day?! I'm not prepared...and I always prepare! I'm going to fail. I just need to write something, anything!"

Greta's eyes sprang open in the still dark room. It wasn't the first time dreams of going to school visited her at night. It's been five long years since the move to the States and not much had improved. She stared at the swirling patterns plaster and paint made in the shadowed ceiling and allowed the last fragments of her dream to fade from memory.

Greta sat up in her bed and listened. The only sounds came from the birds greeting another day outside the window, which meant that the old lady must be still sleeping. For the last couple of years, Greta had been working as a personal caregiver for an elderly Italian woman, Josephine, with late-stage Alzheimer's. It was a lonely job, as the woman couldn't recognize her own children, let alone carry a conversation with a relative stranger.

Greta got up and made her way to the small bathroom. She stood at the sink, letting the cold water run over her fingertips and looked at the face in the mirror. Sad, haunted eyes stared back at her. She had once been promised a bright future.

She was supposed to go to a university, get a degree, make something of herself. She was supposed to have a husband and beautiful children who sported their mother's copper hair and blue eyes. She wasn't supposed to be stuck between four walls, living to keep someone else alive. Deep in her heart, Greta understood that she was being unreasonably bitter. The care she provided made the patient's last years easier, but Greta longed for a typical life of a 20-something-year-old. Her friends from back home – "friends" is a loose term, as Greta didn't believe in online friendships lasting—did all the things Greta longed to do: they travelled, they completed their education, they built families. The cold fingers of jealousy coiled tighter around the young woman's heart each time she looked at the faces of her former friends, smiling from pictures with pyramids or palm trees or sparkling oceans behind them. Sometimes, Greta wished she were a bird, so she could just spread her wings and fly freely wherever she wished. Instead, she felt caged living in a land that didn't want her.

Greta splashed cool water onto her face. It was early spring, and the sun was beckoning the smattering of freckles across her nose to reemerge. She brushed her teeth and her hair, dressed, made the bed, pulled back the curtains on her window to let the rays of the rising sun spill into the small room, and headed to the kitchen to make breakfast. It was the same routine every day. Some days the simplicity drove Greta mad but other times, she switched to auto-pilot and allowed her mind to venture elsewhere. The coffee maker coughed and sputtered a few times and the steady flow of dark liquid began filling the glass carafe. Greta tiptoed down the hallway to a door cracked open and listened. She heard quiet mumbling, accompanied by an ever-present groaning. Josephine was finally awake.

"Good morning, Jo." Greta entered the room, a broad smile that had nothing to do with how she felt on her lips. "Are you ready to get up?"

The small woman lay in bed, watching Greta as if she were seeing her for the first time—which, her brain likely perceived exactly as such. At the age of ninety-three, she was still a handsome woman–silky soft skin, albeit wrinkled, and high cheekbones that she loved to have blush on. She was small–not even five feet when standing—and frail, yet her children swore that they had to hide her high-heeled shoes two years ago, because she insisted on wearing them around the house.

"Are you my husband?" Jo croaked. For a tiny woman, she had a surprisingly low voice. Without having seen her, one would easily assume the baritone belonged to a man.

"No, Jo. I'm not your husband. I'm just here to help you." Greta pulled a pair of slacks and a pink cashmere cardigan out of the closet. "Now come on, let's get you up." She gently pulled the woman to a sitting position on the edge of the bed. "Did you sleep well?"

Jo didn't answer, she just groaned. It's what she did. The doctors assured the family that the woman wasn't in any pain, Jo just made an omnipresent sound. Maybe, much like cats purr to comfort themselves, Jo was trying to reassure herself that she was still alive.

Gretta worked methodically to wipe Jo's face with a damp cloth, to tug socks over her arthritic toes, to pull on the slacks, and to put the soft sweater over the silk shirt the Italian woman slept in. She then fixed up the grey curls that got squashed onto one side of Jo's head and dabbed some rouge onto the pale cheeks.

"There. Look at how nice you look!" Jo stared at Greta vacantly, failing to piece together the words she was hearing. "Let's get you some breakfast."

Greta sat at the small, round kitchen table nursing a cup of coffee while Jo tackled scrambled eggs with a spoon. The woman mumbled about chores of years gone, her children, and whatever else flitted across her mind. Occasionally, she would stop eating and polish the spoon with a paper napkin, and after inspecting her own work, would dig it back into her food. Greta watched her client, so lost in a world of a fragmented mind, wondering what it was like for Jo.

"A mind is a terrible thing to waste," whispered Greta.

She frequently thought about Arthur Fletcher's famous words because she felt like her mind was being wasted. When she was growing up, Greta was an overachiever at school. She thrived on education and took pride in her grades. Having to live the life of an undocumented resident in the States felt like a prison sentence. She often hoped for change, for some miraculous encounter that would turn her mundane reality upside-down, but the monotony was ever-present. Her options for change were limited–either get married to an American or leave. Neither of those was a viable solution.

Greta was happy that at least her mother and her younger brother were now fine. After signing the paperwork with George a few years ago, her mother was granted permanent residency and she and Greta's younger brother now lived with mom's new husband in a small town in southern Illinois. How would they have coped if all three of them had remained undocumented?

Greta often heard about "illegals" and all the "free stuff" they got. It baffled her. She couldn't even get a library card because she didn't have a valid ID, let alone a driver's license or some undeserved benefits. Her health insurance was prayer, her means of transportation—Pace, a suburban bus service that was aptly named for pacing itself.

Greta was over eighteen when her mother married Frank, a jovial carpenter who upon hearing that the family were "aliens" was more concerned with where they hid the spaceship than the legal implications. It felt like Frank was the saving grace to the rest of the family but Greta was left behind. Her mother could no longer fix all that was wrong and Greta was left on her own. If there was going to be a solution to her problems, Greta would have to figure it out herself. It felt unfair that the country Greta had longed to live in was so unwelcoming to her. She yearned to be a contributing member of society but was only able to work under-the-table jobs that helped her survive.

Fear was also an omnipresent companion. Legally, Greta had no business working any kind of job, even jobs nobody else wanted, but she had to take the risk and apply. Almost all applications required a social security number, nine digits that separated Greta's reality from where she yearned to be. Whenever questioned about leaving the field blank, Ilena's words echoed in her mind: "do not tell anyone you don't have documents. They'll send you back and you will never be able to return." Life felt like a dark tunnel pulsing with despair and lacking the light at the end of it.

The clang of Jo's spoon on the floor brought the young woman back from her reverie. Jo was done with her breakfast. Greta picked it up, washed it, and tossed it in the cup of the dishrack.

"Alright Jo. Let's go to the living room. You can watch some TV." She helped the old woman up and they both shuffled the few steps to Jo's armchair. Greta brought her a small glass of Sprite—the only "water" Jo would drink—and as she was retreating to clean up the dishes off the table, heard Jo murmur an angry *puttana*, a "colorful" name for someone in Italian.

"You're welcome, Jo," Greta murmured, more to herself than the old woman. The rest of the day was filled with daily chores of laundry, cleaning, mindless day-time shows, reading, and general care for Jo. Jo seemed oblivious to the world and lived in a time where her babies needed her and her husband didn't. Her moods swung from happy to sad, either one lasting only a few minutes before flitting away.

At eight in the evening, Greta cleaned Jo up one final time and helped her into bed. Once everything was put away, she stepped out onto the balcony and collapsed into the plastic chair. The weather was starting to warm and her light sweater kept her comfortable. Greta stuck an earbud in each ear and tapped a button on her mp3 player. Jem's voice, questioning an unnamed "they" filled the silence and overtook Greta's thoughts.

Bzz-bzzzt, bzz-bzzzzt.

Greta glanced at her phone and yanked the headphones out. She flipped the pink Motorola open and answered.

"Hey, cutie. Whacha up to?" A velvety male voice greeted her.

"Hi, stranger. Just listening to music. What are you doing?" Greta smiled. She loved these evening calls. They were a welcome distraction, a drop of normalcy to her life of relative isolation.

"Packing. I've decided to go back." Julian paused. "There's a program...if you go back for a while, they help you get your papers and then you can come back legally."

Greta had met Julian while indulging in one of her few pleasures—video games. They had hit it off immediately, engaging in friendly banter and online flirting. Although the relationship started with romantic undertones, the friendship grew beyond it. Even though they had never met in person, they learned about each other during their phone conversations that often spanned several hours or until one of their phones died. Eventually, romance was replaced with mutual understanding and support. Part of the reason the friendship was so easy was because much like Greta, Julian was undocumented. His situation was slightly different but he understood her pain, hopelessness, and frustration better than anyone else.

"You're going back to Haiti?" Greta felt her heart ache. "For how long? What if they don't let you come back? What if something happens to you? What about your family?"

"Woah, woah. Slow down," Julian interrupted her barrage of questions. "The family is coming with. We're all going. We will come back. It's only for six months. And then we'll be ok. We'll have papers."

Papers. Over the years, the word had become synonymous with "joy" or "freedom." Some days, In Greta's mind, nine digits stood between her and her future. The same nine digits that made everyone around her belong in the States and excluded her. And Julian may have discovered a way to get them.

"How does this work? Are you sure it's not a trick for the government to find you and just get rid of you?" Greta challenged, letting her fear rise.

"Hey now, I'm the paranoid one here, remember?" Julian chuckled. "I guess that's a possibility. But I think it's worth a shot. We can't continue like this…it's not really living. I'll take a chance for it to change."

"I see."

"I won't be able to call while I'm there, but I'll call you when I come back, ok?"

"Yeah," Greta sniffed. "I hope it works out."

"Me too. When I get my papers, I'll marry you. And we'll make you legal."

A sob mingled with laughter escaped Greta's mouth. "Funny. We should probably meet prior to you proposing."

"I'm serious," he paused. "Well, unless you meet someone in the meantime."

Greta didn't answer. Hot tears were making their way down her cheeks. What if like her mom and brother, Julian would get his papers and she would be left behind again? Maybe she should go back, too, take a chance on the unknown. Anything would be better than this.

"I'll marry you," Julian repeated. "Hey…I have another call coming, can I call you back in a few and we can talk more?"

"Yeah," Greta wasn't sure if Julian heard her. She sat alone in the dark, gazing at the twinkling stars in the sky, wondering why life had brought her here. Briefly, she wondered, if she died today, who would come to her funeral, what would she be leaving behind as her legacy. She stuck the headphones back in her ears, turned the music a couple of notches up and closed her eyes. Maybe, he would marry her… Hope was dangerous.

Inspiration

I had multiple reasons for writing the story. Immigration is a hot topic these days, especially with the troubles at the Mexican border. I often hear those anti-immigration speak about "illegals" taking our jobs or getting free healthcare, education, etc. The truth is that I'm certain that there are people who find loopholes to take advantage of the system, but that is not the reality of a typical undocumented person. I was the "The Immigrant" at one point in my life, and it was not an easy life. In writing this short story, I hoped to bring to attention the fact that living undocumented is living in a constant state of fear and frustration over not being able to change anything. The statement, "well, they should enter the States legally" also doesn't account for situations where people do, but just end up staying beyond their allotted time because they have nothing to return to. I hope this story gives readers an alternate point of view when it comes to undocumented immigrants.

The Great Divide

Tim Yao

We played together from before you could stand.
I helped you learn to walk.
"There they go," our mother would say.
"Saari and Noori, filled with love for each other."
Two sisters like the two moons *Soren* and *Naarun* that
circle our world together.
Even now we hold hands more often than not.
Dry your tears and do not fear, dear Noori.
I will not forget you.

What have you brought me today?
A beautiful bead you carved from the *janko* tree.
How wonderfully you polished it,
making it shine almost as brightly as the *nedu* beads
that our aunts and cousins will braid into my hair
in my stranding ceremony next week.

Yes, you can add your bead into my hair.
Your hands are always gentle, your fingers clever.

Haven't we played with each other's hair often?
Still, you must realize that all those things from our childhood
will be stripped away from me in the stranding ceremony
as I become a woman.

No, don't cry, Noori. Even though I cannot
wear *janko* beads after I have been stranded,
still I will keep and treasure your *janko* bead
Wait! Don't go!
Don't run away!
But her lithe form vanishes into the jungle.

I know how she feels.
My pain when our cousin Esra was stranded
leaving Noori and me to play by ourselves
still stings.
Esra became a woman,
spending most of her days in the caves,
helping the others to sustain our village.
She was still loving and caring but never quite the same.
The tales she told us were not the daring, imaginative
tales of glory we had dreamed together.
Something essential died within her.

Will that happen to me?
Boring and bored, never to have fun with my beautiful Noori again?
Tears come to my eyes at the thought.
My fingers play with the smooth, glossy *janko* wood bead in my
hair,
imagining the cold metal *nedu* beads that will weigh

my head down to remind me of new responsibilities.

Our mother and our aunts labor in the secret *nedu* caves,
digging out the precious *nedu* metal and *boresi* crystals,
transforming them into the wonders
treasured by so many in the world.
No woman may go there before she is stranded.
Mother has warned us of this since we were old enough to walk.
It is a mystique and an honor to be thus called
to provide for family.

A fearful thought creeps into my head.
I told Noori of my deep regret that I would have
to put aside the *janko* bead
so carefully crafted
to make room in my hair for the *nedu* beads to come.
Her face fell.
But Noori is clever and fearless.
She doesn't shy away from taking frightening risks.
Would she dare to venture into the *nedu* caves?
She hasn't been prepared yet for stranding as I have.
She hasn't been taught the secrets of *nedu*.

Once, curious to the point of bursting,
we carefully tracked our mother to the *nedu* cave,
hiding in the tall branches of the *janko* tree
when she and our aunts passed beneath.
They never realized our discovery.

Now, faster and faster I run, hoping that Noori

has better sense than to go into the *nedu* caves.
Heartsick, I go to find her,
to stop her from harvesting and crafting
a *nedu* bead for me.
My fear turns to anger at Noori.
How dare she do such an immature thing
that might jeopardize my stranding?

What a child…!

But that anger shifts to guilt
and then fear again.

I reach the *nedu* caves and hesitate.
If any women find me here, the punishment will be fierce.
I imagined my stranding cancelled,
trapped forever in a permanent childhood.
Or ostracized and outcast.
If Noori is here, the risk is worth it
if I can save her,
my sister and dearest friend.

The *nedu* caves are dark
compared with the bright sunlight of our jungle world.
There are no signs of our mother
or aunts or older cousins.
They must be much farther within.
Only twenty paces in, I feel it -
a burning sensation in my head
pulsing with the faint, dark light that emerges

in rhythm from the *nedu* strands
and *boresi* crystals that sparkle from the cavern walls.

Then I see her. My heart races.
Noori, sprawled upon the floor
as if she had grown too weary
and took a nap,
though we outgrew naps long ago.

In spite of the pain the rictus of her face betrays,
her right hand is gnarled around a large chunk of rock
gleaming and heavy with raw *nedu*,
the reason we are forbidden from these caves.
We are not yet stranded,
not yet protected by the processed *nedu*
beads to be woven in our hair.

My hands tremble, tears blurring Noori's still form.
I shake her arm to dislodge her grip,
trying not to touch the deadly *nedu*.
I ignore the pain burning in my head
and drag both of us out of the caves.

Into the sunlight
that blinds me before
all turns
to black oblivion.

The next several days are a blur.
My weeping mother cradles me,

my head burns with a strange fever
that brings wildness.

They have to
   tie
     me
       down

"Noori!" I scream over and over as her name echoes.

My hair falls out in bloody chunks.
I vomit out my guilt and grief.
Has my foolish pride in my upcoming stranding
led to my sister's death?

At last the madness ends.
I awaken, weaker than I have ever known.
Noori lies beside me, one small hand in mine,
her other wrapped in healing *khthalu* leaves,
a poultice they change daily.
Like me, her head is wrapped in a cool, wet cloth of white.
Mother says that we will both recover,
though it will take a long time for our hair to grow
long enough to be stranded.
We may even go through our *stranding* together.

We whisper stories to each other,
happy to be alive
and together again,
hands clasped,
sisters forever.

Inspiration

My first thought in coming up with this story was to be clever in the meaning of the word stranded. It could, for instance, mean how a cord or hair is braided. Somehow, this made me wonder under what circumstances the act of having ones hair braided would be noteworthy. I imagined a culture where there would be a stranding ceremony, involving weaving elaborate beads into the hair. Why would this be done? Perhaps the beads conveyed some kind of protection for the wearer; and the life of the wearer would be undergoing a significant change–a coming of age and a taking up of a significant responsibility.

When this story began taking the shape of a poem, then the whole world began coming to life for me. I hope it came to life for you as well.

Benediction

TODD HOGAN

Anthony, dressed in his server's red cassock and white surplice, genuflected before the marble altar. He saw two fluttering candles and a single bright light trained on the golden starburst monstrance. Quiet prayer before the Blessed Sacrament, a one-hour act of adoration and humility, was not easily accomplished by an eighth-grader. This Eucharistic practice had its roots in the Middle Ages, well before the development of basketball hoops and baseball diamonds. In the silence of the church, Anthony heard the boisterous call of the outside world and his unruly classmates as clearly as if he had been racing among them. But he was not outside; he was alone in St. Jude's. Anthony hiked up his cassock a little before settling onto the thinly cushioned kneeler with a huge sigh.

The heavy air carried the slight aroma of incense which nested near the church's apex. Built in the 1950s, St. Jude's roofs pitched steeply and all the pews faced forward in two sections of thirty rows. Votive candles, prayerfully lit by silent parishioners, flickered in red glass. Vatican II had turned the altar so the priest faced the congregation during the celebration of the Mass in English. Anthony had never heard a Mass in Latin, although his father had told him how awe-inspiring, solemn, and spiritual the old Masses were. He listened to his father but couldn't imagine it. The church seemed less sacred these days.

His blacktop-scraped knees felt the pressure of kneeling despite the padding. Anthony shifted from side to side, groaned, and refolded his hands. From his position, he couldn't see the clock, so he didn't know how much time had passed. Perhaps it had been an hour already, but more likely only a few minutes. He sighed again.

The priest put forth the argument to all the servers that an hour wasn't that long a sacrifice. He gave examples of the sacrifices endured by those who served the Lord our God—three hours on the cross, a night in the Garden of Gethsemane praying, three days in the belly of a great fish, forty days and nights in the wilderness, forty years wandering in the desert. Not counting the hundred years the Cubs spent chasing a World Series. In comparison, an hour was nothing.

Anthony's breathing slowed. His eyelids felt heavy. His shoulders sagged. Even his lower lip relaxed. He felt as though he were slipping into a daydream. "I'm here, Lord," he prayed to reassure himself as well as the Almighty. "I'm here."

The minutes slid by unmarked by any clock's tick. Slowly or quickly, impossible to tell. He lifted his eyes to the white Host, struggling to recall the kind of prayers he should say or the kind of thoughts that should occupy his mind. The church was entirely quiet. He no longer heard the sounds of his classmates' excited play outside. He did notice his pulse, the blood coursing through his body and eardrums and brain.

Anthony reasoned that if he prayed for specific people, his allotted hour might be better used. He prayed for his mother, his father, his sisters and brothers. He prayed for his grandparents, both living and dead. The objects of his prayers flashed through his mind, like face cards sliding past each other. Then the cards began to swirl wildly as if he weren't doing the shuffling.

He glimpsed his father and mother when they were younger. He'd seen their photographs. Then he saw them grow older, much older. His mother not yet sixty—was that old?—weak, emaciated, breathing with difficulty. A shiver of dread slithered beneath his collar. His brothers and sisters and his father, all older, with spouses and children, gathered at a funeral. His feeling of profound grief elided into compassion and mutual support. An exuberant wedding celebration, then more weddings and parties, joyful. College, pressure, achievement. Charming girls with his brothers, shy friends of his sisters. He saw with horror a hospital room where his oldest sister lay in perfect stillness, a pain-numbing drip in her arm.

He recognized himself, in high school, in college—which college?—and after. Lovely girls smiled and drank icy, neon-colored beverages with him. One became angry or sad, tears coursing down her cheeks. The same woman wore a bridal gown. Then a slide of that woman handing him a toddler. His heart nearly burst.

Throughout all these images and emotions, he recognized a Presence, One whose Image he could not see.

There were vistas of mountains and lakes and river waterfalls. There were tents, apartments, and homes. He wandered through them, hoping to capture some emotion, but satisfied with a glimpse of faces. Sadly, he saw his aged father in a hospital bed, unable to speak. Even then, comforting his mute father, they were not alone. He understood that he was never completely alone.

He felt…

A hand touched his shoulder. Elspeth, dressed in her cassock and surplice, smiled her timid teen-ager hello, her bright eyes lowered so as not to meet his. Anthony shook himself out of his reverie, his face flushed. He felt drained yet refreshed. She took his place before the Host, and he bowed deeply toward the altar and crept to the sacristy.

Anthony never spoke of his experience that afternoon, not even to

Elspeth. After all, it had only been his crazy imagination. After graduation from this grade school, he would never be forced to spend an hour kneeling in prayer again.

Inspiration

Praying, like meditation and deep thought, can feel isolating, as though one were stranded. However, the images that the mind encounters in moments of intense contemplation can be striking. Are they pieces of the future, paths that are possible, or grace from an All-Knowing and Loving Deity? It happens frequently to those who engage in prayer, meditation, or contemplation, and I thought I would describe the time it first happens to an unexpecting young boy.

Flotsam and Jetsam

MARY O'BRIEN GLATZ

How does one create a life from broken pieces that wash up upon the shoreline? How did we do it? Antonia sucked on the rim of her wine glass and gazed out from the white stone patio of her hotel room to the translucent blue green Adriatic Sea lapping the beach below in gentle rhythms. *I don't know,* she mused, *but we did it and here we are.* She felt happy, content, peaceful in her contemplation.

"Antonia!"

She turned to see Margaret in a gossamer yellow floral dress and wide brimmed sea-blue hat standing at the open patio door.

"Come on, let's go, the ship is sailing in a few hours. They already picked up the luggage. Let's get a little more shopping in before we have to leave."

"OK, I'm coming." Antonia rose, raised her arms up over her head in a lazy stretch, and walked toward her lover. Margaret's flash of long red hair, now hanging loose instead of tied back into its usual tight bun, her pale freckled skin, and her sleek bony frame, always caught Antonia by surprise, as flashes of beauty often do. She inhaled a quick breath and softened her eyes as she looked at Margaret, comparing her own cap of close-cropped, nappy black, white fringed hair, her brown skin, and her slightly plump body ripe with age.

She stepped into the room, planted a quick kiss on Margaret's cheek.

"Margaret, remember when we met in Kathmandu? Life was so unsettled and harsh back then. Don't you think we've come a long way, baby?"

"No, honey, just a different set of prejudices and power struggles to let go of today, that's all. Let's get out of here before the boat leaves without us!"

Antonia chuckled, slung her backpack over the shoulder straps of her white sundress, and slipped on her red Calvin Klein ghita flats to head out the door with her friend and compatriot. Margaret was Antonia's balm of Gilead that kept her glued together and at the same time lit her up like a spark flung on dry straw in a hayloft on a hot summer day.

Thirty years ago, at the end of a silent summer Buddhist retreat, they spoke to each other for the first time and learned of their common interests in medicine, women's rights, and women's health. They became fast friends and opened the Cleveland Women's Clinic together after both completed medical school.

Margaret helped Antonia put the pieces of her life back together after an abusive husband and a stillborn child at the tender age of eighteen - the trauma that had led Antonia to Kathmandu so long ago. And again years later, after the attack on the clinic when Antonia was shot by a fanatical right wing pro-lifer. Yes, Margaret had saved Antonia's life many times, in more ways than one, and never judged her.

Antonia always felt that she didn't deserve such good fortune. But she also knew that Margaret loved her dearly, and not simply for her motherly persona or her fierce warrior skills. They had been fighting together for many years to ensure women's rights to own their own bodies, souls and minds. Margaret knew all her flaws too, Antonia thought, knew about her not quite pristine past, and knew that she had done some unsavory deeds just to survive. Antonia kissed Margaret again, feeling gratitude for their life together.

They walked outside down the white washed steps of the hotel and entered the side alley with the tourist shops. Spicy sweet aromas of red peppered *kulen*, garlic, roasted lamb shashlik, and salty sea filled the air around them as they sauntered over the cobblestones like two school girls.

"Hey, *zena*, lady, look at this beautiful scarf. It will be *lijepo, beautiful*, on you. I can give you a bargain. Lady, lady, you need this to make you even more beautiful than you are. *Stara koka, dobra juha.*"

"Margaret," Antonia whispered, "Can you believe it? That guy is hitting on me. Did you hear him? He said, 'Old hen, good soup.' That means an older woman has more appeal. Gross! Honestly, haven't they heard about #metoo over here?"

Antonia waved the shopkeeper away with a disdainful hand and a grouchy sneer. Margaret laughed and snatched the scarf from the man.

"Oh, come on, Tony, let me buy this scarf for you." She draped it across Antonia's shoulders. "It is beautiful and the pale blue will be a lovely contrast with your dark hair and eyes. It'll remind you of this glorious sky! Although, it looks like a storm is moving in. Look at those thunderheads over there. We better get to the ship."

Antonia loved that Margaret called her Tony. She watched Margaret pay the man, stood still while Margaret gently wrapped the scarf around her shoulders, then grabbed Margaret by the hand and ran with her, laughing, the few blocks to the ship's plank. Breathless, she squeezed Margaret in a hug and inhaled her lavender scent as the ship left the dock. In a few days, they would be in Greece to catch their flight home and back to work at the clinic in Cleveland.

The sea turned rough that day soon after they departed. A storm on the horizon pushed in a thick fog. By the time they got out of port, huge waves crashed and collided with each other and with the ship that felt like it might buckle in the forty foot swells. Wind howled and whistled outside of the rooms below deck. Antonia and Margaret, like the few other passengers on the small schooner, hunkered down in their cabin to wait it out.

Antonia got up to pour a glass of water, lost her balance and fell on top of Margaret like a woman without bones. The ship heaved. Margaret retched and covered her mouth. They both lay there trying to be still and not roll off of the bed. Antonia reflexively reached over to the night stand to clutch her backpack against her chest with her arms through the straps. It had her passport, her wallet, her glasses, her hearing aid charger, her phone, all her important traveling stuff, just in case they got shipwrecked. Antonia liked to be prepared for every eventuality, like a wizened survivor of many lifetimes.

They heard a loud explosion coming from the back of the boat. It lasted for quite a few minutes, then everything went black and silent. Smoke crept through the cabin door.

Right after the explosion, Antonia felt Margaret pull her by the arm. They struggled to climb, swim, out of the cabin, but her arm slipped away when the water came rushing in on them with the full force of the raging sea. Margaret moved forward while Antonia flipped backward. She watched helplessly as Margaret struggled to swim up the narrow stairway to the top deck.

She barely heard Margaret scream, "My friend is still down there. Please! Someone get her!," as the captain lifted Margaret into the last lifeboat leaving the sinking ship before it submerged into the deep.

Antonia opened her eyes. Where was she? Had the ship sunk? Was she under water? She couldn't tell from her surroundings. She tried not to panic and remember her Buddhist teachings to dispel any terrifying thoughts. She had been through one near death experience already and this felt familiar. But fear took hold. Was she alone? Where was Margaret? Was she dead?

Everything uncoupled from its moorings from the force of the water and floated around her – the cabin furniture, the luggage, a water glass, her backpack. She peered into the opaqueness trying to make sense of it, but it was like looking through eyes with macular degeneration, blurry objects in a nameless, dark, impenetrable blackness. A pale, ashen, gun-metal light shone in the murky distance.

Ok, thought Antonia. *Let's try to move. One leg, then two. Move the arms.* It was like swimming in a dense soup of an unknown substance. But she knew she had to keep moving. Her mouth filled with the taste of acrid water and cold aluminum. The smell of charred flesh and raw ozone flared around her. She tried to feel for her body, imagined that she was touching her head, face, shoulders, ribs, arms, legs. But she could no longer identify her own outlines. *Just keep moving,* she told herself.

Antonia floated, looking down at a kaleidoscope of scenes that appeared as faint shadows beneath her. She only half realized that, yes, she must have died and that she was now in the Bardo, where consciousness has seven days to find a new incarnation. She tried to focus her intentions on moving toward that light, but it kept getting farther away the more she thought about it.

She remembered the teachings. They say that once a body has died, a bright red ball of pulsating light moves up to the solar plexus and a radiant white light moves down from the crown of the head to meet the red. They merge into one glowing luminescence - the life force that shoots out the crown of the head and enters the Bardo.

One's rebirth is not an accident, they say, but the result of all the flotsam and jetsam of one's life coming together again in a new form. Everything good and bad – flotsam remains of life's explosions and jetsam that one threw overboard to lighten one's load in each lifetime – it all comes back together in the Bardo. The karma of past deeds shapes the present and the future. Each lifetime offers new opportunities to learn and become more compassionate.

All this was imprinted onto Antonia's consciousness during her months of study with the Buddhist monks of Kathmandu, and she reflected on it now as she floated along in the fuzzy stream. The light she had seen in the ship kept appearing just out of reach ahead of her.

Using her mantra, Antonia chanted out loud, or so she thought, to focus her energy on a good journey to her next life. But it came out as a muted mumble of indistinct sounds.

Below her and around her, forms appeared as if in bas relief - a mother and a child passed by, an old woman wearing a long dress and a scarf, a mangy dog, a sleeping lion, a young boy, a bedraggled beggar. Were these her potential new forms, she wondered. How would she know which one? A pregnant woman stopped in front of Antonia and smiled at her with what felt like a deep love, then moved on into the blackness.

Exhausted, she needed to rest. She paused her mantra and stopped moving, closed her eyes and fell into a deep sleep.

⌀ ☆ ⌁

"Mother, I know it's gonna be a boy. Maybe he'll be our next president who will outlaw them evil women's clinics that kill babies before they are born. I can feel it, or a famous preacher who will convert all them heathens, harlots, and them #metoo women." The old man drawled with the long, lazy vowels of the south.

The woman flinched and held her breath when the man raised his arm toward her, but exhaled when he placed it on her belly. His gnarled, grimy hand patted the woman's large watermelon-like protrusion with pride, grinning through almost toothless gums.

"Let's pray, mother. Praise the Lord." He pushed her down onto her knees.

The man and woman knelt next to the small bed they shared in a crumbling shack hidden deep in the woods of Appalachia, clasped their hands together, closed their eyes and intoned, "Heavenly Father by who we are saved, praise be …"

Waking from her sleep, Antonia heard voices, heard those words coming from somewhere outside of her and wondered where she was. It felt like she had been floating for some time now, several days at least. It was still dark. A syrupy, viscous fluid held her attached to some type of cord. She felt safe, anchored, no longer panicky, and stretched her legs and hands to get her body moving again. She could feel her limbs now.

"Father, did you feel that? The baby just kicked. Praise the Lord." The mother beamed, struck a match with nicotine stained fingers to light her hand-rolled cigarette, inhaled and blew out little smoke rings.

"Mother, let's call him Anthony, after Saint Anthony, the saint of lost souls." He took a celebratory swig from the unnamed bottle of amber colored whiskey in his hand and passed it to his wife. She chortled it down and wiped her mouth with the back of her hand.

Antonia heard their words clearly. *What? Where was she?* Anxiety rippled across her body like a fast moving dark cloud eclipsing the sun. She pounded her fists and kicked her legs as hard as she could.

The woman yelled, "Ouch, cut that out you little devil or your daddy's gonna whip ya' when you come outta there."

Father rubbed the woman's belly, "How ya' doing in there, Tony? Behave yourself now, boy. We're waiting on ya', son. It won't be long now. Praise be."

"Oh my God!" Antonia tried to scream out, kept kicking and screaming until her voice was lost to even herself. "No, No, No! This can't be! HELP ME! HELP ME!"

Inspiration

The state of perpetual conflict in our contemporary American political culture. Identity issues - gender, women's right of autonomy over their own bodies, ethnicity, citizen status, LGBT rights, racism, sexism, extremist religious lobby groups influencing policy, the breakdown of separation of church and state - have dominated our discourse. These issues are all complex, yet modern media and politicians exploit them in simplistic, manipulative ways. As a student of psychology, theology, world religions, and Buddhism in particular, I want to express my own wonderings about what kind of karma might befall a character who personified several of those identity issues. The karmic outcome of the main character will be evaluated differently depending on the reader's perspective on any given issue. Also, it occurred to me that, in the context of the extreme polarization in contemporary culture, the most horrific type of stranding might be to be reborn into a form that is the polar opposite of one's self-defined identity in a prior lifetime. Punishment or Redemption? Must we be stuck first before we can become unstuck from our illusions of fixed identities? That is for the reader to decide.

Generations

TODD HOGAN

Fourteen-year-old Nicholas arrived at his grandfather's remote cabin a little after nine on Sunday morning. The quiet lake looked silver, with tendrils of fog hanging near its surface. Nicholas wrinkled his nose at the smell of damp vegetation surrounding the shoreline. In the middle of the lake bobbed a small gray fishing boat with his grandfather.

The boat glided through the fog toward him. It had been years since Nicholas had last seen his grandfather. As Nicholas reached the pier, the water now reflected dark greens and blues.

His grandfather secured the boat with an expert mooring hitch. He stepped onto the dock, brown boots covering his legs to the knee. Long silver hair obscured his face until he lifted his wide hat and scraped it back with his hand. He handed a stringer of freshly-caught small fish to the boy.

"Nicholas, right? Your mother wouldn't stay for coffee?"

The boy shrugged.

"Have you eaten? I can fry up some fish."

"For breakfast?" Nicholas shook his head. "We stopped for donuts and coffee two hours ago. I'm good."

The old man took back his string of fish and started up the hillside with large, powerful strides. When they reached the cabin at the crest, he placed his fishing pole handle-first in an old wooden box that used to keep milk bottles upright. Nicholas followed his grandfather inside.

"What's your WiFi password?"

"What's that?"

"You know. To make a connection with the Internet. You have Internet?"

"Sorry. I don't even have a TV. Can't get the replacement tubes I need." He started cleaning the fish with a sharp knife.

"What are you doing? Gross!"

"Need to clean the fish before we eat them. Come here, I'll teach you."

Nicholas shook his head.

"Can I use your phone, Grandpa? My phone has no bars. You have a phone, right?"

The old man nodded. He lit a fire under a black iron skillet.

"Sure. It's in the hallway. Right there on the telephone stand, that small table."

Nicholas checked the table but only saw a black pyramid with curled wires attaching a curved barbell on top. A ring of numbers in smaller circles leaned against its front.

"Where's the buttons? Where's the screen?"

The cleaned fish hissed and crackled in the hot pan. Nicholas frowned at the odor of fresh fish frying. He lifted the black dumbbell, which buzzed annoyingly.

"What is this thing?"

"I'll show you later. Come on, sit down. Eat something."

"I'm not hungry."

Nicholas hefted the receiver from hand to hand. The buzzing stopped when he replaced the receiver.

The old man forked two fish fillets onto Nicholas's plate. He grabbed two oranges from the refrigerator. He broke a piece of bread, passed it and the butter, poured himself a large mug of coffee and offered the pot.

Nicholas shook his head and sat with his arms crossed.

"Just try a bite."

Nicholas broke off a minuscule flake of fish. He balanced it on his fork while watching his grandfather dig in.

"Your dad never liked fish either."

Doc finished three fish fillets before Nicholas had the nerve to taste the tiny flake on his fork.

"No school this week?"

"Three-day week. A short break starts Wednesday at noon."

His grandfather stared at him, silently demanding an explanation for missing school.

"My dad said you couldn't get me to school on time anyway, so why bother."

Doc pursed his lips but said nothing. He finished his coffee with a long swallow and cleared the dishes.

"Where are your parents going this time?"

"Some convention. My dad is always going to conventions. They said this one was at Disney World. Like I care."

Nicholas tasted a bit of fish and chewed it slowly.

"Did you want to go?"

Nicholas shrugged and took a second bite. He quit after that bite and brought his plate and silverware to the sink.

"I need an Internet connection, Grandpa. I've got friends there."

"You mean your friends who are at school?"

"It's Sunday. Nobody's at school."

Doc finished washing the dishes while Nicholas waited.

"I said I need the Internet, Grandpa."

"Sorry. I don't have any of that Internet stuff. What else would you like to do?"

"You don't have any Internet, you don't have a TV, you don't have a phone that was made in this century, and you expect me to stay here a week?"

Nicholas stood with arms crossed staring at the old man. The pose often worked to aggravate his parents. But his grandfather only smiled back.

"Let's be clear. Your parents sent you here. It had nothing to do with me. Honestly, I forgot you were coming. You're always welcome. I just hadn't planned anything to do, is all."

Nicholas rolled his eyes and slouched in a chair near the fireplace.

"It's only one week. Come on. What would you like to do? Fish, hike, explore, play games?"

"How far is the nearest Best Buy? Apple Store? Civilization?"

Doc laughed. "Calm down. You might find you like it here."

Nicholas could feel the walls pressing in on him. His breath caught. He raked the cabin walls with his eyes for something to do and found nothing.

"We could play chess or Uno or read. Do you like to read? I've got some really great stories. What do you and your dad like to do?"

"I read graphic novels or Manga, unless it's schoolwork. Don't ask what my dad and I do. That's easy. We don't do anything. He's always working."

"Well, your dad is an important executive. He has the responsibility for a billion dollar company and thousands of jobs that help it run."

"So my mom likes to brag."

Nicholas got up from the table and walked to the bookshelf, running his finger over the colorful, wrinkled spines. "How old are these dinosaurs?"

"Since your dad was young. A lot of these he no longer wanted." The old man pulled a few out, checked their titles, and chuckled. "Jules Verne!–wrote about going to the center of the earth, and riding in the first submarine. If you like knights and castles, here's *Ivanhoe*."

Nicholas pulled out his own thick, heavy book. "Who reads this stuff?"

"Not too many people nowadays."

"*The Hunchback of Notre Dame.*"

Doc frowned. "Hmmm. I think that may be too mature for younger readers."

Nicholas huffed and opened it.

"My dad went to Notre Dame."

"I remember."

"If I have to, I'll start with this one. It's not like there's anything else to do."

"Well, there's nothing else to do if you don't like to fish, hunt, explore, or play games. Let's do this: I'll read with you. We can take turns. Some of the parts are pretty intense and others are just plain boring. I'll help you get through both of them."

They found a comfortable spot with plenty of light. Doc pushed his hair back and Nicholas began reading aloud. The scene involved a play performed for a celebration that was part religious, part secular. Doc stopped Nicholas every few lines to explain what was going on, what Fifteenth-Century France was like, and who the characters were. They took it slowly, carefully.

After a half an hour, Nicholas said, "I think there's a Disney movie of this. It would be easier to just watch that."

Doc smiled. "You're right. That would be the easy way. But since I don't have a TV, you'll have to wait until you get back home to watch the movie."

"This is boring. I'm going for a walk."

"Take those green boots near the back door. They will protect your tennis shoes."

Nicholas smirked. " 'Tennis shoes'? What are 'tennis shoes'?" He went out the door without taking the boots. Glancing back, he caught his grandfather watching through the window.

Nicholas walked to the lake, then along the shore. He heard tree leaves rustling, small amphibian plops in the water, and the sluggish roll of a possum into the brush. He was sure if he delved into the shrubbery more deeply he would find bird nests, rabbit warrens, snakes coiled on flat rocks, and who knew what else? He picked up a three-foot branch to defend himself.

His grandfather was pathetic, a long-haired hermit in a lake cabin. His own father owned a much nicer home with a four-car garage, five bedrooms, a gourmet kitchen, wrap-around deck, an office, a gym, and a hot tub. His mother planned a pool installation this summer, which would make the place just about perfect. His classmates would chew their nails in envy when they saw it. If they ever came over. "Soon," his mother had promised, but some pressing obligation always took precedence.

As he walked, his shoes squishing, he mulled over the strange story that they had begun reading. Set in a different time and a different country, its characters were so bizarre. Were they good people or evil? There was no easy answer. He felt sorry for the deformed little hunchback child that no one else in the story pitied; in fact, the child antagonized most of the people he met. A priest who cared for his own younger brother, now adopted the hunchback too. But the priest seemed dark and secretive. He reminded Nicholas of his own unfathomable father. Despite himself, Nicholas wanted to hear more.

When he returned, the morning was spent. But that still left the rest of the day and the rest of the week to endure. His shoulders sagged. His grandfather rocked on the front porch, a small table in front of him with two opposing lines of chess pieces.

Nicholas removed his soggy shoes. "Ok, next time I'll use the boots."

"They used to be your father's."

Nicholas sat down across the table from his grandfather. "I don't know how to play chess."

"I taught your dad. I think I can teach you."

"I've never seen him play."

"He gave it up a while ago. I still can teach you, if you want."

"Maybe later. How 'bout we read more Hunchback?"

Doc put both hands on his knees and pushed up. "Sure, Nicholas. We can read a bit more. Then after lunch, we can begin with the chess lesson."

Nicholas nodded, his lips tight between a smirk and a grin.

The novel continued. Nicholas struggled over some words but his grandfather added context and explanation. Esmeralda and her trained goat amused him. He didn't know an animal could be trained to count on command. He laughed at the playwright Pierre, whose first production was undermined by the crowd's distraction with the gypsy girl.

They stopped for lunch, a peanut butter sandwich and apple for Nicholas and a bowl of chicken soup for Doc. While they ate, Doc asked about his school, his classmates, and teachers. Nicholas couldn't remember the last time he talked about his school with anyone. It felt awkward at first but his grandfather seemed really interested in what they were discussing.

"You should visit more, Grandpa."

"I'd like to, though your father may object. Your grandmother would have loved to see the young man you've grown to be."

"I don't remember Grandma. I barely remember you."

"She passed before you were born. I have some pictures if you're interested."

Nicholas was tempted to say, "No, don't bother," but his curiosity won out. The photos were taken in the '60s, and the young woman in them had straight, fawn-colored hair reaching to the small of her back. She wore funny heart-shaped sunglasses, colorful shirts, and pants wider at the bottom than at her knees.

"Bell-bottoms. Very popular for a time, Nicholas."

"So Grandma was pretty hot, wasn't she?"

"She was a stone fox."

Nicholas laughed. "So, like Esmeralda?"

"I suppose. She relished her life. She would not approve of your missing school this week."

"What's your plan, then?"

Doc pondered a while before answering. "Let's return to your house. We'll stay there and I'll drive you to school."

Nicholas looked skeptically at his grandfather. "Sure, I guess. At least, I'll have WiFi."

"No plan is perfect, Nicholas. But I want you to go to school, okay?"

"No plan is perfect," he echoed, smiling.

Doc packed and brought the book they were reading, together with the chessboard. His fifteen-year-old Toyota Echo started right up.

It took more than three hours to get to the house following Nicholas's confused directions. At the gated community's entrance, the guard recognized Nicholas but not the aging hippie in the wide hat driving.

"I'm staying with Nicholas this week while his parents are away. I'll pick him up from school, so what do you need from me?"

The guard noted Doc's license plate. "I'll need your home address and cell phone."

Doc gave him the cabin's rural route address. "No cell phone. Landline."

The guard let them pass with a wave.

Nicholas's parents built their home on a ridge away from neighbors. Nicholas punched in the garage code but the four bays were all occupied. Doc left his black Echo looking incongruous on the driveway.

"Well, you're home. You've got your computer, your WiFi, your friends."

Nicholas nodded. He fingered some headphones, then put them aside.

"Can we do a little more Hunchback? And you promised some chess."

Doc nodded and patted his grandson's back. "Sure. Do you remember where we were?"

"The priest asked Quasimodo to kidnap Esmeralda but he got caught."

"Right. Now comes the hunchback's trial. The judge is just as deaf as

Quasimodo. Poor communication often leads to misunderstanding."

They read, alternating pages until Nicholas insisted on reading all of it. They finished the trial, the hunchback's public flogging and pillory, and Esmeralda braving the jeering spectators to offer him some water.

"She's a rebel, isn't she?" Nicholas said.

"She's remarkable, certainly."

For supper, Nicholas showed Doc how to order from Grub Hub and used his mother's standing account. Nicholas ordered tacos, Doc ordered a burrito.

"It's okay if you want some friends over this week. I'll stay hidden." Doc raked his fingers through his silver hair before replacing his hat.

Nicholas finished one taco. "Probably not. Most of my friends are on-line gamers."

"You'll have to show me sometime."

"Sure. So, you don't work. Did you have a job?"

Doc touched a paper napkin to his lips. "College professor."

"Hah! No wonder you're so crazed over school. What did you teach, French History or famous books?"

"Philosophy."

"Doesn't pay as well as a corporate executive, I bet."

"Your dad figured that out early. More taco sauce?"

"Thanks." Nicholas squirted out a dollop and took a large bite. "Better than fish, right?"

It was still light outside when they finished eating so they went out to the deck. It was quieter here than at the lake. No plops into the water, no furtive rustling in the undergrowth. It was peaceful, like a cemetery.

"Teach me to play chess."

The chess lesson went slowly but by bedtime, Nicholas understood all the pieces' distinctive moves.

"The fun comes when you learn to combine the moves and create strategy. Now, what do you need for school tomorrow?"

"I've got everything. But there is something. Don't be mad."

Doc waited.

"I know where the keys are to our Jaguar, the Navigator, and the other cars. You should drive one of them. Save your clown car for the lake."

"You've never been dropped off in a car like mine?"

Nicholas shook his head. "Don't want to start, either."

His grandfather squinted. He stood slowly and clapped Nicholas on the shoulder.

Nicholas blurted, "If that's a problem, we can forget it."

"Not a problem."

Nicholas felt embarrassed for the poor old guy. "Let's read more, ok? It's getting good now."

"Sure." Doc grabbed the book and handed it to his grandson.

They read about Pierre following Esmeralda into the Court of Miracles. They both laughed when Pierre was nearly hanged because he wasn't a thief like everyone else. Esmeralda saves him by marrying him, sort of.

"We'll skip the next few chapters which are just descriptions of architecture and the city of Paris. Goodnight, Nicholas."

"Nite. Esmeralda is outrageous. Oh, and here's a card I found, too. If you want it."

The business card read, "George, One Salon, Hair Stylist." Doc tucked it in his shirt pocket, turned out the light, and closed the bedroom door.

The next morning, Doc drove the Navigator. Nicholas jumped out and walked coolly towards the school, turning around once to tilt his head toward Doc, his thanks for the ride. He walked into the school alone, his backpack weighing on his shoulders. After school, he walked coolly toward the SUV, still alone.

"No homework. So, we have time to play chess or read. Or I can teach you how to use the Internet."

"There's really not much use for it where I live. But you can show me. Where to now?"

Nicholas directed him to an Apple store where they checked out the different ways to connect with the world. Doc took notes.

"I'm a bit overwhelmed."

Back home, Nicholas spent time alone on the computer. Before dinner, he asked to play chess. They played slowly. Doc won but Nicholas experienced the fire of competition. "Again."

They played a second time. "You're really coming along, Nicholas. Now work on controlling those four center squares."

When it was time to read, they began at Book IV and continued until bedtime.

When they stopped, Nicholas asked, "What's with the priest? Why don't he and the hunchback get along?"

"Every reader answers that for himself, which is what makes great books intriguing."

"But what do you think, Grandpa?"

Doc took a deep breath. "Maybe their problems arise from the hunchback's deafness. Plus he can't talk. So, the two can't discuss their problems, or feelings, or reasons. Poor communication often leads to misunderstanding. It had to be frustrating."

Nicholas nodded. "Communication." Doc's words troubled him. He needed time to think.

"We can talk more in the morning, Nicholas."

"Goodnight, Grandpa."

The next morning before school, Nicholas stayed quiet. He smiled his goodbye and walked alone into the building. The day dragged. After school, Doc arrived late to pick him up.

"I'm sorry, Nicholas. I was caught up in something."

Doc took off his hat and scratched the remaining bristles on his head.

"Hey! You got a haircut. I can't say I have a hippie for a grandpa anymore."

"It was nothing to brag about. And I talked to a company about a satellite connection at the cabin. It's possible but expensive."

"Maybe my dad could help."

Doc shrugged and shook his head. "I won't count on that."

They read until supper, a delivered ham-and-pineapple pizza. Nicholas held a slice in his hands until Doc noticed he wasn't eating.

"Don't you like it?"

"I guess. It's not tacos." Nicholas changed the subject abruptly. "Why do you like this book, Grandpa?"

"Well, I'm impressed by how Victor Hugo explores ideas about love—selfless love, selfish love, brotherly love, paternal love, marital love. People in love are just so complex."

"Huh."

"So, do you like the book, Nicholas?"

He didn't answer immediately, then burst out, "I called my dad today."

Doc put down his pizza slice. "Oh?"

"He said I should come to Disney World. He can fly me down tomorrow after school."

Doc sighed. "That might be fun."

"Even if he's busy, he has assistants who can show me the park."

Nicholas waited for Doc's reaction but he didn't speak. The kitchen, the house, the entire neighborhood, seemed oppressively quiet. He wished there was a freeway running outside or a waterfall, just to create some turbulence.

Doc put his hands on his knees and rose. "I can take you to the airport tomorrow, no problem."

"Remember, tomorrow I get out at noon."

"I remember." Doc cleared his plate. Nicholas wasn't hungry any longer.

He felt coiled inside, ready to burst unless he said what he was feeling.

"You should visit more often. I don't care what Dad says."

"Your father doesn't agree."

"Why? What's he got against you?"

"He's had a hard time forgiving me for not saving your grandma."

Doc's face sagged, looking every bit of his seventy years. "She had to live her life, and sometimes took risks. She dabbled with drugs, for fun. But she became addicted. I got her into rehab programs, but she wouldn't stay. Things got worse until she passed away."

Doc paused, then released a deep sigh. "Your dad was devastated. He was about your age, maybe a bit older."

"But she was so perfect and beautiful."

Doc nodded. "I still miss her. Your dad misses her. But I'm the one he won't forgive."

Nicholas smacked their book off the table onto the floor. He shuddered and shook his head.

Doc put his arms on Nicholas's shoulders.

"Nicholas, don't. Things can change. Your dad's changing. Look, he trusted me to watch you this week."

"He had no other choice."

"Everyone has choices. I'm just so glad you came to visit, Nicholas."

Nicholas looked up and saw that his sad, ex-hippie grandfather meant it. He gathered up their book and held it to his chest.

"Grandpa?"

Doc raised his eyebrows.

"Grandpa, I don't blame you. I love you."

Doc swallowed hard. "I love you, too."

Nicholas felt strong arms pulling him close.

"Well, you better pack and get to bed early."

"Sure. But, I was thinking. Can we go back to the cabin tomorrow instead?"

Doc rocked back on his heels. "What's going on?"

Nicholas shrugged. "I'm just getting good at chess. We haven't finished our book. And I miss that silver lake, okay? Let's go back."

"What will your dad say?"

"He can't stop us We'll talk when he gets back."

"Won't you miss the Internet, WiFi, your friends?"

Nicholas smiled. "No plan is perfect."

Inspiration:

I've always suspected that children and grandparents get along better than parents get along with either. There's something about the intervening years that makes children and grandparents more tolerant of the challenges each face. Sometimes, history repeats itself and grandparents can interpret for children better than parents. This story develops the burgeoning relationship between two generations, despite the intervening generation.

The People's Paradise

Mary O'Brien Glatz

Masha exits from customs into the great hall of Moscow's Domodedovo Airport. To her surprise, huge Kentucky Fried Chicken Banners hang everywhere. A familiar voice calls her name across the crowded corridor.

"Masha!" Natalya waves at her.

"Natalya!" Masha shouts, "I'm here. I made it. Finally!" She raises both arms in a double-fisted victory sign across the throng of travelers.

They reach each other with an embrace and three light kisses to the cheeks.

"I told you I could have taken a cab. You didn't have to get me," chimes Masha.

Natalya snorts, "And I told you that you can't travel alone in Moscow. I wouldn't think of letting you go on your own here. You don't know your way around. It's not safe."

Masha rolls her eyes and laughs, "I'm so excited to be here, Natalya! I've traveled the world, but never to Russia. Thank you so much for inviting me. *Bolshaya spaceeba, maya podrooga.*"

She remembers how on one early morning in the states last winter, Natalya had invited her to visit. During their daily walks, the two women talked about checking off Masha's bucket list to see Russia almost as often as they laughed about being stranded in their old age, and how the best remedy was daily walking. No escape, no turning back from the aches and pains of aging. *Carpe diem* was their mutual motto.

Masha follows Natalya outside to the parking lot. A sticky summer heat is in full bloom. Natalya throws the suitcase in the trunk of her car and gestures to get in. They speed off in her Peugeot around the traffic circles and down the busy avenues of Moscow to Leninsky Prospekt in the University District.

One good night's sleep in Natalya's apartment, a breakfast of farmer's cheese, yogurt and cucumber, and they are off to see the sights. Natalya swipes a red card with an electronic strip on it in the Metro turnstile, then hands it to Masha.

"This should cover all your metro trips while you're here. Don't lose it. And do not ever ask police for help here. Police are no help. If you call them, they expect a bribe or they arrest you." Natalya whispers in a dark tone.

"Okay," Masha tells her but wonders about this warning. She shakes it off and thinks, *It can't be that bad; she's just overly cautious since I'm her guest.*

Looking down the long, steep escalator of the Metro Station, Masha can't see the bottom. Her feet feel like they're floating, vertigo strikes. She steps on behind Natalya and they descend into the underground station to squeeze into a crowded subway car.

At Red Square they exit, ascend to street level to walk around the famous cobblestoned courtyard that surrounds the high red brick walls of the Kremlin. Throngs of tourists hustle past and around them. They stop to look at the zero-point medallion, a circular brass marker with an engraving that pronounces this as the exact spot from which Russians measure all distances in Moscow.

Natalya points out the many churches with their multicolored striped, gilded domes and byzantine architecture. They press back into the jam-packed Metro, ride to Park Kultury Station and exit into Gorky Park, a ribbon of green along the Muscovy River that runs through the center of Moscow. A leisurely stroll takes them down tree lined lanes filled with skateboarders, cyclists, and kiosks sending out smoky sweet aromas of *shashlik*, *pirozhki*, and *blini*. Their walk ends with lunch at a bustling riverside café.

Masha kids with Natalya, "So, Natalya, I don't see any intrigue here like in the movie, *Gorky Park*. Where are all the spies?"

Natalya ignores the joke as usual and answers, "Tomorrow we'll visit the other metro stations. They're famous, and we'll go to the Bolshoi Theater."

"Lead the way, my friend. Without you, I do not have a clue. But tell me why Russians never smile. When I smile at anyone, they flinch, frown, avert their eyes and look scared."

Natalya laughs, finally, "That's just the way we are. If you lived here your whole life, you wouldn't trust anyone either. Maybe it's our history that makes us serious and cautious, not our genetics."

The next morning, they set out again, pushing through the crowds to exit the Metro into Teatralnaya Station. They pass through a cavernous central hall that looks more like a ballroom than a metro station. Intricate crystal chandeliers hang from a marble cathedral domed ceiling to illuminate porcelain bas-reliefs depicting the theater arts. Music from various Russian composers, ballets and operas float out from speakers in the walls. Masha slides her hand along the fluted marble pylons lining the walls, immersed and disoriented in the urban cacophony of people, sounds, sights, and languages not her own.

Natalya sees Masha gaping at the beauty of the underground Metro and explains, "Each metro station is a tribute to some significant part of Russian life, culture, and history. Some call the underground the 'Paradise of the People.'"

An escalator carries them up to street level to walk toward the Bolshoi.

It's closed for summer so they stop instead for a lunch of salmon and a crisp Pinot Grigio on the outdoor patio of The Bolshoi Café.

"See that building down there at the end of the block and across the street?" Natalya points to a nondescript apartment building.

"Yes, what about it?"

"That's where I lived as a child in the Soviet Union under Stalin and Krushchev. Four other families lived together with us in that one apartment. Dividers separated the space. We had one kitchen and one bathroom for all the families. My parents were the only ones with a child, that was me. The others were artists, musicians, intelligentsia. I went to the Bolshoi many times when I was young. Since I was the one child in our apartment, my mother made me stand in the lines for the others who were all elderly to get their bread, milk, and meat rations. We all got along very well with cooperative living. No one in our apartment sold out anyone else to the KGB, just to get ahead or to get special privileges."

"Wow! You've come a long way, baby," Masha says in her best American slang and laughs, "There's so much I don't know."

Natalya raises her glass, "A toast to friendship and long life. *Drooshba! Na Zdarovya!*"

"What an amazing living history you are, Natalya, having lived in the Soviet Union under all the dictators from Stalin to Putin, and now you are a dual citizen of both Russia and America? You've lived all the history that I studied. My dual citizenship in the US and Ireland isn't nearly as interesting."

Natalya waves her away in classic Russian style, "Stop it. I'm not interesting at all, but some might say there is a movement by certain people in power here to return to those days. We still have to be careful today. The young people are planning a new revolution."

"That's interesting in a terrifying kind of way. But enough of that. Let's walk, my friend." They head out to continue their walking tour of Moscow.

After a week of sightseeing in busy Moscow, Natalya gives in and agrees to let Masha go on her own. She gives her the apartment keys and tells her, "This afternoon I need to drive to my dacha in Pushkino Village to take care of a few things, so I may not be here when you return. Be careful out there."

"Don't worry, Natalya, I'll take the same metro we took last week to go back to Red Square and do some shopping in the state store, Gum. I have to see the largest department store in Russia before I leave."

It's mid-morning and the air is still fresh. Masha walks the few blocks through the park to University Station, enters, swipes the Metro card, and heads down the long escalator. It's so quiet and empty, not even the guards standing at the entryway. Unusual. But she gives it no more thought. It's past morning rush hour and it's a weekday, so maybe this is the downtime.

She gets on the train. At each stop the subway door opens and closes, no one gets in. Masha realizes that she's the only one in the car. The only sound besides the rattling of the car on the tracks as it speeds along is the mechanical voice announcing, *doors opening, doors closing, please stand back.* All the stations look empty as the car speeds by, no bustling people, no violinists playing classical music to echoing walls for a few rubles, no Lenin or Stalin impersonators in full costume spouting wild, hilarious, gesticulating speeches.

Why is the Metro so empty today? Yesterday it was crowded full, she thinks.

The car flies past the signs in a blur. *Park Gorky, Park Kultury, Oktyabrskaya, Mayakovskaya, Teatralnaya* Stations, and finally it stops at her destination, *Revolution Square.* She exits into the station and walks through corridors of marble tiled floors lined with life-sized bronze statues of the heroes of the 1917 Revolution. It feels like a museum, not a subway station. Still no people. The steep escalator takes her up and out into the daylight of Red Square.

A heavy silence and a rush of hot, humid air wash over her. She walks a little further to stand near the zero-point medallion, looks around, sees no one. The smell of smoke fills the air. She looks up to see a small grayish cloud cover, ashen, sooty, hovering above the high red brick walls of the Kremlin fortress.

A figure appears on the far side of Red Square, seeming small at a distance and black in what might be a long overcoat. A tank that wasn't there last week when they were here sits at the opposite corner of the square. On approach, the dark shape grows larger. Masha sees that it's a man wearing a hat pulled down to hide part of his face. He comes up to her and grabs her arm. She recoils.

"Ma'am, you must go back into the Metro." He gestures to the subway entrance. "It's not safe out here."

He is speaking English with a Russian accent. He touches her arm again, lightly this time, and pauses to look into her eyes. His eyes are lapis blue with wrinkles fanning out from the skin on the corners. He looks intense, perhaps afraid.

"What is going on? Who are you?" She demands. "Why is the Metro empty today?"

He doesn't answer, walks toward the Metro, gestures for her to follow him. She reaches into her pocket and pulls out her phone. No service. She thinks, *I'll go back to the apartment if there is some kind of crisis happening.*

The man looks back at her and says, "I'll take you to safety. You can't be on the streets today in Moscow. Everyone is being detained and questioned. Where are you from? Are you American?"

"Yes."

"You're lucky today, I speak English. But even more dangerous for you to be here. They think an American did this."

"Did what?"

"There's been a terrorist attack. Someone tried to poison the President and smuggle a bomb into the Kremlin. No one is allowed on the streets, you'll be arrested. Hurry, follow me."

Masha gasps. *Oh God, I need to tell Natalya.*

She talks to his back and follows him into the station, down the steep escalator.

"I need to go back to University Station. I'm staying in a friend's apartment in the University District. I need to see if my friend is there."

She remembers Natalya said she wasn't leaving until after lunch.

"I'll go with you," he offers. "I can't leave you alone. I'm collecting people."

They enter the car and it speeds off. *Doors opening, doors closing, please stand back.* He goes silent. She doesn't ask any more questions or offer any conversation. In her head, she rehearses her emergency Russian phrases. Her chest tightens, heart flutters, and her brain kicks into high gear, matching the velocity of the train. *Do I have my passports, money, what else?* She touches her pockets to double check. Yes, they're in the safe places, strategically clipped inside her clothes or inside inner pockets.

Still no people appear in the Metro, empty stations, empty cars all the way back to University. The train stops and she rushes out first. This time the stranger follows her through the lush green park from the station to Natalya's apartment building. She rings the buzzer. No answer. The little grocery store across the lane looks closed. Leninsky Prospekt, the busy avenue on the other side of the building, has no traffic rushing by, no buses, no taxis, no cars, no pedestrians. She sees Natalya's car parked in the enclave and makes a mental note, *Natalya didn't drive to the countryside after all.*

She rings the buzzer again, then remembers she has the entry code to the building, pulls a piece of paper out of her pocket to confirm the number, punches it in. The outside door swings open. The building is quiet. They go in, up three steps to squeeze into the tiny two-person lift and take it to the second floor. The stranger has to lean in to her, it's such a tight space, but they don't make eye contact. He looks away.

They get off the lift and turn left to the apartment door. She presses the buzzer. They wait for what seems like a long time, a few minutes. No answer. Natalya gave her a keyring with the three oddly shaped keys that every steel reinforced door in Moscow has these days, one key to fit each of three different locks. She rings the bell again. Silence. She puts the keys in, remembering what Natalya told her.

If Natalya is home, she would have locked the middle lock from the inside and there is no way to unlock it from the outside, even with the correct key, ensuring her bodily safety. If thieves ever steal the keys, they could get in only if she unlocks the middle lock from the inside. Otherwise, they would have to break down the steel door–impossible– a low tech but complicated home security system set up in almost all Russian homes in the 1990s. After the dissolution of the Soviet Union and the opening to capitalism–the *Glasnost* of Gorbachev– break-ins were rampant, thieves and gangsters looking for anything to sell on black markets for profit. If Natalya is not home, the middle lock will be unlocked, and the top and bottom keys will open the door.

It takes a few minutes with her shaking hands, but the keys turn in the locks. She pushes the heavy door open and enters the apartment, tripping over the raised lip of the new steel door frame installed on top of the existing floor. The stranger doesn't enter. He waits just outside the entrance to the apartment.

Masha walks through the rooms, the front guest room where she picks up her backpack, the living room with its books lining the walls from floor to ceiling, the back bedroom, bathroom, and the small kitchen. A glass half full of kvass and a bowl of creamed herring sit on the table. A breeze wafts in from the open window, rustling the delicate white lace curtains. *Natalya always closes all the windows when she leaves, especially with the daily thundershowers of summer,* Masha thinks as she closes the window.

She walks out to the hallway and with her mind deep in thought almost bumps into him. He is standing just outside the doorway. They are face to face. She thinks about slamming the door shut and locking him out, but decides that she needs to find Natalya. She steps out into the hall and locks the door with the top and bottom keys.

"Now what? My friend isn't here, obviously. I don't know where she is and I can't contact her. I don't know what I'm supposed to do, but I need to find her."

The stranger insists, "You can't stay here. We need to go, now. Back into the Metro, underground. That's where people are going for safety. She might be there."

He starts toward the lift. "Come on. Let's go."

She follows him. They retrace their steps to University Station, descend into the eerie silence. The train arrives, stops. They step in. The car is empty, again. *Doors opening, doors closing, please stand back.*

"Where are you taking me?" Masha half whispers, not looking at the stranger who is sitting very close to her, their shoulders almost touching. She smells his musky cologne.

"I demand to go to the American Embassy." Her voice grows bolder.

"No, that's the most dangerous place to be right now. Stay with me and I will get you to a safe place."

He sounds authoritative but his voice is soft. She goes quiet and thinks back to when she arrived here, trying to remember if anything seemed off before today. *What else can I do? I'm lost and at his mercy. No police, no Natalya, no other people around. There were no signs, except Natalya's ominous warnings. I thought she was being paranoid. This must be a surprise to everyone, unexpected, and they don't know what to do either.*

The stranger nudges her back to the present with his elbow as the train comes to a halt. "This is our stop. Let's go."

She follows him out. They exit into Mayakovskaya Station, walk off the platform down one of the corridors into the Great Hall with its pink rhodonite and stainless-steel columns, white marble walls over white and pink marble floors. And there they are, people, lots of them, some sitting huddled against the wall talking in hushed tones, some standing in small groups under the ceiling mosaic of the Moscow sky lit up by hundreds of hanging filament lights. The hall is full. Everyone looks miserable, terrified.

The stranger removes his hat and overcoat. His white hair falls gently over his chiseled high cheekbones. He pushes it back and smiles at her with kind eyes. He looks about the same age as Masha, old but in good shape and not too weathered. Her brain starts working overtime again. *Who is this guy?*

"Welcome to the Underground People's Paradise. Everyone must stay here until things return to normal. Who knows when that will happen?"

He asks, "Do you have identification?"

She pulls out her two passports from her inside pocket, one American, one Irish, and holds them out for him to look. She always travels with both, just in case. Americans are not too popular around the world these days since they elected a new President in 2016.

He smiles at her again with those blue eyes. "I always wanted to meet an Irish girl. Alexander Mishkin[1] at your service. Hide that other passport for now or better yet, let me hold it for you."

She starts to protest while her brain thinks, *hmmm a Russian made a joke.* A voice calls her name and Masha sees someone pushing through the crowd. Natalya. In her distraction, he snatches her American passport from her hand.

"Masha, you made it! *Slava Bogu!* Thank God! I went out to find you, but the neighborhood district patrol made me come down here too! They

---

[1] *Although entirely fictional in this story, Alexander Mishkin is the name of the Russian agent who poisoned double agent Sergei Skripal and his daughter Yulia Skripal in Salisbury, England, 2018.*

collected all the people from my apartment building right after you left this morning. It's like martial law out there."

Masha hugs Natalya, turns back to Mishkin with a stern face, her eyes glaring at him and her lips pursed downward in a scowl.

"Hey, give it back! Why did you take my passport? I need that."

"Sorry, I'll hold on to your American passport for you. You are now stranded in the Paradise of the People, but it is one of the most beautiful places to be and the safest, deepest underground in the world. Did you know that Stalin used this station as his underground headquarters during the German bombing of Moscow in World War Two? We may well be at the start of another war."

"No, not a fact that I would know. Natalya, I'm so glad you're here too. How long do we have to stay here?" Masha turns to her friend.

Mishkin answers, "We are sealing the entrances to the Metro after all the people are here, then we don't yet know what happens next. All trains and planes have been canceled. The Metro will stop running at five o'clock today. There is nothing you can do. At least you're not Ukrainian. But Americans are also suspect these days because of the anti-Putin movement in your country for his relationship with your own crazy president. Or perhaps an attempt to poison Putin might be just what Putin was waiting for to start the next war. For all we know, he did it himself to give him an excuse."

Natalya scowls at him, "Stop it! Don't say that."

Masha puts a trembling hand up to her mouth, "Oh my God, when can I go home?"

He looks at Masha and winks, "Settle in, Masha. Who will you be now? How about Meg, the Irish tourist? I'll be back before five, I hope."

She watches him disappear down a marble hallway.

Inspiration

I spent a month in Russia in 2018 and traveled on the Moscow Metro, sometimes alone. One day, I was alone when the subway car door opened and closed, with no people getting on or off. I assuaged my anxiety by daydreaming about being stranded in Moscow after a fictional apocalyptic event. At that moment, a story was born. I also wanted a vehicle to show readers the Moscow Metro, perhaps the most famous, safe, beautiful, and interesting underground system of transportation in the world.

STUCK IN THE SURREAL

Be Careful What You Wish For

TIM YAO

Cool hands covered John's eyes. Slender fingers. He breathed in the familiar honey scent of her hair and smiled. "Muriel."

"Guilty as charged, sir," she said, shifting her hands as she stepped around to gently pull him into her warm kiss. "Good book?"

"As good as Psych 101 can be." He smiled.

"Sorry to be a little late, John. I had an errand to run." Muriel sat down cross-legged on the grass in front of him, brushing back her dark red hair. Her green eyes sparkled in the October sunlight.

"Picking up your lunch?"

"Yes," she said, lifting up a plain brown paper sack. "Ye Olde Sandwich Shoppe." She put it down beside her. Her cheeks were flushed.

John's curiosity was piqued. "You look like the cat that swallowed the canary."

"Well, I happen to have a little present for you. But you have to close your eyes first."

John closed his eyes, feeling his lips twitch into a tolerant smile. "Okay." She took his hand into her own and placed a small, cold, hard object on the palm of his hand.

"I was too excited to bother wrapping this up," she said. "Open your eyes."

John opened his eyes. He held a ring of dark metal, black enough that it seemed to swallow the light. The band was wide, its surface worn and pitted to the touch of his curious fingertips.

"Try it on!" Muriel's eyes glowed.

"This is a handsome ring!" John was never one to wear jewelry, but something about this ring appealed to him. He slipped the band onto the ring finger of his right hand. The band was large enough to easily slip on but not so large that it might fall off.

"Thank you, Muriel." He leaned forward and gave her a long kiss.

"I was drawn into the curious little antique shop next to Ye Olde Sandwich Shoppe. The ring was there, sitting on an old, wooden desk by the front. It didn't even have a price on it, but the shopkeeper still haggled with me. Of course, he had no chance against my negotiating skills." She grinned.

"I'm really tickled by this!"

"Think of it as a late birthday gift," she told him with a smile. She kissed him again.

They sat there on the university quad watching students walk by, eating their lunches.

"Oh, hey," Muriel said. "There's Tom."

John looked up to see his roommate Tom Sutton hurrying across the quad. He and Tom had become fast friends when they met as roommates freshman year, though they weren't able to spend much time together due to Tom's busy schedule.

When they met Muriel, their neighbor across the hall, John had felt an immediate attraction to her but was too shy to act. It took a couple of weeks of late night talks before Tom convinced John to ask Muriel out on a date.

John glanced at his watch. "He's headed for his job at the cafeteria."

"I'm still amazed that he has three work-study jobs this semester. It must be tough for him to have to spend so much of his week working."

John spun his new ring around his finger. "Yeah, poor guy. He has an incredible work ethic, but I wish he wasn't so poor."

A dark light flashed by his hand, like the inverse of sunlight glinting off of something shiny. John frowned.

"Oh my god! What is that thing?" Muriel pointed to a small Barbie-sized, blue-skinned figure jumping up and down and jibbering excitedly in a foreign tongue. Its skin was inscribed with intricate white patterns.

John stared at it in wonder. "What on earth is he saying? I wish we could understand him."

The small figure bowed, smiled, and nodded. "Your second wish is granted. I will now work upon your first wish. I apologize for making it happen after your second wish, but it is much more difficult to make happen and I am not as powerful as my brethren."

"What?" John stared at the small being, whose voice was tiny and barely audible above the other sounds coming from the quad around them.

"It must be the genie of the ring," Muriel said, eyes shining.

"What?"

"You haven't read 1001 Arabian Nights?"

"Isn't that the story about the genie of the lamp?" John noticed the small genie follow their conversation with apparent interest.

"There were two genies in that particular story in the book. A genie of the lamp and a second genie that belonged to a magic ring." Muriel bent down to the small genie. "I can't believe we're witness to real magic!"

John smiled and brushed back Muriel's long, red hair. "I love you, sweetie," he said.

She leaned over and kissed him.

John blinked. "Wait," he said, looking at the small genie. "Did you say second wish?"

The genie's smile widened and he vanished. The world blurred around John.

Something hit the back of John's head, knocking him sprawling onto the grass.

"Sorry about that!" a guy called out from behind him.

John pushed himself back up to a sitting position, rubbing his head. A guy in a red sweater ran over and picked up the football that had hit John.

"Tom," John said, surprised. "Where'd you get the red sweater?"

Tom looked at him. "Hey, I think that football hit you harder than you thought. My name's Blaine. Blaine Lazenby. I don't believe we've met."

It wasn't just the cashmere sweater. Tom wore stylish leather shoes. John frowned. His roommate only owned one pair of old sneakers.

John turned to make a comment to Muriel, but she was nowhere in sight.

Tom tossed the football back to his friends, one of whom wore a Delta Kappa Epsilon sweatshirt.

The genie was gone.

John held out his hands–the ring was gone too.

Rattled more by Muriel's inexplicable disappearance than by being hit by a football or Tom's poor practical joke, John found it difficult to pay attention to Professor Lipp's Psych 101 lecture. It was a large class but not so large that he didn't recognize most of his classmates by sight.

Weirdly, though, over half of the students in his class were unfamiliar to him.

John stood up.

Professor Lipp stopped mid-sentence to stare at him.

"Sorry, Professor Lipp," John said. "I'm not feeling well."

The professor nodded absently, continuing his lecture. John slipped out of the room. He reached into his pocket for his phone, but it wasn't there.

"Must have fallen out when that football hit me," John muttered.

He ran back to the quad, but there was nothing there within the space on the grass where he and Muriel had been sitting.

Cursing, John ran all the way back to his dorm.

He knocked on Muriel's door, but there was no answer. Head lowered, he entered his own room and sat down on his bed, frustrated.

"Hey, John," said the guy on the other bed. "Whatcha doin' home this afternoon. Don't you work at the cafeteria on Friday afternoons?"

John looked at the big, beefy guy with curly dark hair. "Who are you? And how did you get into my room."

"You're kidding me, right?" The guy leaned forward, frowning. "It's our room, John, thank you very much." Then, in reaction to John's frown, he continued. "John, it's me, Sam, your roommate." He chuckled nervously.

"Where's Tom?"

"Tom who? Come on, John, stop scarin' me. You feel okay?"

Sam's side of the room featured big heavy metal posters plastered on the wall and a complicated looking stereo with enormous speakers by the bed. "I don't feel so well," John said. Then he looked at Sam again. "What do you mean by 'work at the cafeteria'?"

"You're work-study, bro," Sam said. "Great program. I could have sworn your work schedule has you working shifts Monday, Wednesday, Friday and Saturday afternoons."

"I'm not a work-study student. You must have me mixed up with Tom."

"Tom who? I don't know anyone named Tom."

John buried his head in his hands. "I wish Muriel was here."

"Muriel?"

John raised his head.

"Wait, you don't mean Muriel Johnson, the girl who lives across the hall from us?"

"Yes, my girlfriend."

"Your what?" Sam gave John a funny look. "Dude, I've noticed you noticing her, but you know she has a boyfriend. One of those frat guys."

"What?"

"Some fancy dude. Lame. Brad. Something like that. He's always coming over to the dorm to pick her up in his Corvette."

"Blaine?"

"Yes, that's the one."

John reflexively reached into his pocket for his phone, but it still wasn't there.

"Sam, have you seen my iPhone?"

Sam gave him another funny look. "You, ah, don't have an iPhone, bro."

John rose slowly to his feet. He checked his pockets but found no ring. The backpack he carried wasn't the black nylon Targus, but a rather ratty canvas pack from army surplus. He searched through it but found no ring, no phone, nothing but some very beat-up textbooks.

He didn't even realize he was headed out of his room until he heard Sam ask him where he was going.

"I just gotta get out. Walk around. Clear my head."

"Okay," Sam said. "You're sure you're okay?"

John nodded. "I'll be okay."

On the way to the quad, he passed by three of the Greek houses, including Kappa Delta Epsilon. Out front, just getting out of a shiny white Corvette was Muriel. John's heart leapt. "Muriel!" he called, running to her.

Something in her blank expression stopped him from throwing his arms around her. "Sorry," she said. "Do I know you?"

"It's me, Muriel. John," he said.

Her eyes narrowed and her lips pursed together. "Wait, you do look a little familiar." She brightened. "Yes, I think I've seen you before. You work in the cafeteria in Humley Hall, right?"

"Actually, I live in the room just across the hall from yours in Lazenby Hall."

Her smile went away.

"This dude bothering you?" It was Tom, still wearing his red sweater.

"Tom! It's me–John."

"Stop calling me Tom. I told you, my name's Blaine Lazenby." Tom frowned. "You're the guy from the quad today."

Muriel leaned into Tom. "How did he know your middle name, Blaine?" she whispered to him.

A thought occurred to John. "Tom, is your mother's maiden name Sutton?"

A look of extreme distaste came over Tom's face. "What are you, some kind of weird stalker?" He shook his head, took Muriel by her arm and led her away with him into the fraternity.

Crushed, John stood there outside the Kappa Delta Epsilon house. The frat boys on the porch began making rude comments. With one last look of regret at the big building, John walked back up to the quad and sat down on the grass.

I am in some weird alternate universe, he thought. *If only I still had Muriel's ring. Wishes usually come in threes. I could undo this situation.*

John replayed the events leading up to his sorry present. The little genie had said he was working on John's first wish. Something that John had wished for before wishing that the genie spoke English.

John closed his eyes. Muriel had arrived, surprised him, given him the ring. Then … Tom. They had seen Tom. Poor Tom.

John opened his eyes. He had said he wished Tom wasn't poor.

Somehow the genie had interpreted this as a literal wish, one that he had made come true, in spite of his protestations that he had little real power.

But why had the ring disappeared?

The world had been changed. In this new reality, Muriel had fallen in love with a wealthy Tom. Without Tom's encouragement and possibly burdened by his work study schedule, John had apparently never asked her out. So she had never given him the magic ring.

John was baffled. If she had never given him the ring, then how had the wish happened? He headed back to his room. Sam looked relieved to see him.

"Hey, bro," Sam said. "A student came by and dropped off this note from the work study program. You, ah, apparently missed your shift this afternoon. I told the student that you hadn't been feeling well."

"Sam, what's your major?"

"Physics," Sam said.

"Do you ever read science fiction? You know, stories about time travel and the like?"

Sam nodded. "You know I love science fiction and science almost as much as I love heavy metal rock bands."

Quickly John explained his predicament. "But it doesn't make sense. If the magic ring disappeared because Muriel isn't my girlfriend, then why did the first wish come true?"

"I'll say this, John. You may be a little crazy, but you do have some great SF ideas."

"I'm serious, Sam."

Sam tilted his head. "Look, John. You said that Muriel mentioned the genie of the ring isn't as powerful as the genie of the lamp, right?"

John nodded.

"It doesn't seem that a less powerful genie could completely remake the world. What if the genie simply took advantage of the world's existing reality?"

John blinked. "What?"

"Physicists believe that there are many dimensions. There are many alternate realities that exist in essentially the same space as we do, but they are separated from us mostly by our own perceptual limitations." Sam leaned forward. "You've heard of Schrodinger's cat, right?"

"Yes," John said, remembering his high school physics class. "The cat that was sealed in a box with something like a radioactive atom that could kill it. It could not be examined, so its state was unknown, neither alive nor dead."

"Right," Sam said. "And we have many possible outcomes and realities around us all the time, but we have no way to perceive them. What if the genie found a way to transfer your consciousness to one of those realities? The world where you and me are roommates and where Muriel ended up with Blaine."

"You and I," John said absently. He frowned. "How do I get back?"

Sam shrugged. "You say you didn't have the magic ring when you woke up here. Presumably it remained in the alternate reality you left." A thoughtful expression crossed Sam's face. "Hmm... Did Muriel tell you where she got the ring?"

John nodded. Then he jumped to his feet. "The ring could still be at that store!" He glanced at his cheap wristwatch. "They'll probably close in half an hour!" He turned back to Sam. "I haven't known you long, Sam, but thanks!"

Sam stood up and grabbed his jacket. "Just shut up and let's get going!"

"Why do you want to come with me?"

"Obviously, once you've used up your three wishes, I will want to have the ring you leave in this world."

The little antique shop was still next door to the sandwich shop, but Ye Olde Sandwich Shoppe was now a Happy Belly Burger. John tried to remember everything Muriel told him about buying the ring. He peered around the cluttered antique shop, which was overstuffed with random bits of furniture and odds and ends, a veritable tight maze of stacks of dusty, old objects.

Muriel had mentioned finding the ring on a table.

"May I help you, gentlemen?" A short, plump woman asked them. "We'll be closing in fifteen minutes. Are you looking for anything in particular?"

"Do you have any small, dark rings?" Sam asked.

"We have many rings," the woman said. "But there isn't a central collection of them."

John pressed on deeper into the store. He heard Sam and the woman follow him.

There! A small dark circle upon a tiny, worn wooden table. With trembling fingers, he picked it up.

"Did you find what you were looking for, sir?"

"Yes," John said. "Is it alright if I try it on?"

"How much are you asking for the ring?" Sam asked.

"Let me see it," the woman said.

Reluctantly, John passed it to her.

The woman pursed her lips, taking in John's worn jeans and t-shirt. "$135."

John reached into his pocket and brought out his wallet. He had $35.

"Sam, how much do you have?"

"Do you take credit cards, ma'am?" Sam asked.

"Sorry, our machine is on the fritz. It will need to be cash."

"I have $85," Sam said. "Together we have $120. Will that be enough?"

The woman considered. "A joint gift, eh?"

"Something like that," John muttered.

She looked at each of them, then nodded, taking their cash. "Would you like this wrapped?"

"That won't be necessary," John said. He clutched the ring and exited the store, followed closely by Sam.

"There's an alley around the corner," Sam said. Then, "I sure hope this ring works. I can't believe I blew $85 to help you out."

John flashed him a quick, nervous grin. "Just remember to be careful what you wish for."

They squatted behind a dumpster that blocked the view of the street. John took the ring out of his pocket and spun it around his finger.

The diminutive genie appeared in a flash of darkness.

"Good lord!" Sam said. "I can't believe this is really happening."

The genie looked amused. "You have one wish remaining, John."

"Here's my wish: I want you to return me back to my original life, where I'm together with Muriel," John said.

"Wait!" Sam said. "You have to be really careful with your wish."

"Your wish is my command," the genie said with a smile and a bow, vanishing.

The world blurred again. Everything went dark.

Someone held John's hand and wrapped it around a small, cold, hard object.

Deja vu–the ring!

"I was too excited to bother wrapping up this gift," Muriel said. "Open your eyes."

John's heart thrilled to hear her voice. He opened his eyes.

Inspiration

As an author, I enjoy stories that deal with parallel universes and interdimensional travel. In such tales, it is interesting to see what differs between two worlds that might otherwise be identical save for one act. What if the son from a wealthy family got a woman pregnant and abandoned her? What if he didn't? Many lives would be impacted. Traveling between them would be a shock.

The other inspiration comes from my long appreciation of stories from 1001 Arabian Nights. Everyone now remembers the story of Aladdin and the magic lamp that housed a very powerful genie. Few, however, may remember that there was a second genie in the tale, the less powerful genie of the ring. I enjoyed bringing that ring and genie into my story.

Date of Death

ELIZABETH SANFILIPPO HALL

9:00 p.m.

The kitchen timer beeped and Mandy jumped.

Her fingers shook as Mandy reached to turn the timer off. She nearly hit the wrong button but it beeped one last time and fell silent, so she must have hit the right one. As she opened the oven to grab the filet mignon, she wondered: *Is this the moment of death? Is this when it happens?*

Her gloved hands firmly held the heavy cast iron pan. She set down the pan onto the metal stovetop. It clunked, sending up a small spark. She jumped again.

Mandy stared at the steak. Red oozed out the charred sides. She poked the top with one finger. Without intending to, she stepped backward, moving from a black tile to a white one on the checkered kitchen floor. But the meat was done, just the way she liked it. The steak didn't explode. Even when she stabbed it with her last fork and put it onto her last plate, her favorite piece of china.

Mandy shook her head. A piece of meat wouldn't explode. But she was running out of ideas of how it might happen. She was home now, standing in her kitchen with its empty shelves and cabinets, after using all of New Year's Eve to spend the last of her money.

The steak continued to bleed onto the plate's flower designs. Distracted by the thought that the steak looked like it was hemorrhaging, her right foot stepped onto Roger's dog ball and the world spun for a moment as Mandy stumbled. When she regained her balance, her plate held high and the ball still rolling away across where the oriental rug used to be, she stood in place to catch her breath. Her heart pounded as she looked around the barren dining room, her table free of the knick-knacks that used to always be there. The only sound came from the kitchen: the clock ticking.

If she had fallen... she could have hit her head on the chair or table. Or maybe she would have fallen onto the plate and it would have broken into shards, slicing her hands, or worse, her head.

Stop, she told herself. *It's pointless to consider all the what ifs. That's not how I want to spend my last night.* She'd heard of plenty of people who decided to stay home all day when their computer-generated date of death came up, thinking they'd somehow cheat and survive the day. But the government's computer system was always right. Something always happened. A heart attack. A fire on the stovetop. She once read a news story about a tree falling right into someone's living room and, of course, the person sat right in its path.

Her fingers shook again as she sliced into the meat with the only knife she hadn't yet donated or given away. She brought a slice to her lips and chewed slowly. Choking, all alone, would be a terrible way to die.

9:30 p.m.

The plate sat empty, just a small pool of blood left. She crumpled up the paper napkin, put it on the dish where it soaked up the blood and looked around. Her china cabinet stood empty. All her family china... gone, given to cousins and twice removed family members. She had no children to give the things to. No husband.

She walked into her living room and stared at the bare shelves that lined the walls. Only a couple of paperback books remained. She had already told

Ellie, her coworker, that she could take them if she wanted. Or Ellie could donate them along with the handful of things left around the apartment: a blanket, the pillows. Mandy had saved only the necessities for the last few days of her life.

She plopped down on the couch. Roger ran over from under the kitchen table and hopped up onto the couch next to her. She never used to let him up on the couch, not wanting to get his shaggy Golden Retriever hair all over; but if not now, then when?

He laid his head in her lap and stared at her with big, brown eyes. As she rubbed his head, she hoped he'd be okay. Ellie said she'd get him first thing tomorrow. Thank goodness for Ellie and the fact that her date of death wasn't for a few more decades. There were so few people in her life, but at least she could count on Ellie.

10:00 p.m.

Mandy flipped open a book and for a split second, she wondered if she should go out since it was New Year's Eve. That's what most people did on New Year's after all, right?

She stared at the opening page of a contemporary book she'd read at least twice before. Even though it was her last day on earth, her last night, going out–spending time with strangers and drinking at bars–it wasn't her. Staying at home and spending time with Roger: that was how she wanted her final moments to be.

Yet as the pages fluttered by–she wasn't even really paying attention to the storyline–she trembled again. The clock kept ticking. How was she going to die? With all their technology that told them when someone's life was up, why couldn't they figure out
the *how*?

She strummed her fingers against the couch. Would someone burst in and start shooting? Her eyes popped open. How ridiculous. She had nothing left to steal. But how would the robbers know that? Sometimes people whose expirations were approaching were targeted like that.

Every last cent of Mandy's bank account was gone. She had taken a big vacation to Europe a couple of weeks ago; she lounged on Greek beaches, strolled through Roman ruins, and dined and drank her way through France. She finished her job, where she edited manuscripts, just yesterday, a job she mostly enjoyed. Plus she wanted to make sure Ellie would take Roger when all was said and done. Lastly, today, she gave the rest of her money to the local animal shelter.

"Today's the day for you, huh?" the man at the shelter said as he gave her a sad smile.

Mandy nodded. They were used to things like this. After all, no one can take their money with them when they died.

Now Mandy just wanted it to be done with. All this waiting…it was tiring.

∿ ☆ ∿

A noise startled Mandy awake.

Roger had jumped off the couch and landed with a thud. Now he stood at the door, tail wagging, whining to go out. Through the thick-paned windows, she heard a cheer erupt from the bar at the corner.

Mandy stood and, after regaining her bearings, walked over to the door and slid on her shoes. She hooked Roger onto his leash and out they went. A light snow fell and Mandy took in a deep breath of icy air, wondering if this quiet, this peace was what death felt like.

Someone stumbled into her and she caught them before they hit the ground. They stood and slurred, "Happy New Year!" and off they went again.

More people streamed out of the bar down the road. It looked as if they were leaving and going home…but why before midnight?

Back inside, Roger shook his fur, spraying a fine mist of snow. As Mandy took off her coat she glanced at the clock and did a double-take.

12:15 a.m.

A new day. A new year. But that couldn't be.

Mandy rushed over to her computer and clicked into the website that housed everyone's info.

The list of people flashed before her. The system updated at midnight, as it did every night, with all the causes of death. A car accident here. A heart attack there. Someone who died of cancer. Next, an array of home accidents: a slip, a fall. Food that exploded–well, that did happen.

Then her own name: Mandy Robinson.

Age: 42.

Date: December 31, 2032.

Cause of death…

The website blinked for a second as if reloading.

Cause of death: blunt force trauma to the head.

Mandy gently touched her hair. But she was fine. She was alive. Wasn't she?

Roger ambled over, shoving his wet snout into her leg. It left an imprint on her khaki pants. Mandy felt very much alive, even though she wasn't supposed to be.

She sat still, staring at the computer, at her supposed death. The only sounds in her apartment were Roger's sighs and the clock ticking.

1:00 a.m.

Mandy waited. But she no longer knew what she waited for.

Inspiration

The idea for this story started with a "simple" question I wondered about: would we live life differently if we knew when we were going to die? My short answer to that question was "yes," that for me personally, I'd live life more fully, somewhat like the main character in "Date of Death" does by going on vacation and spending all of her money. But the answer to that question isn't really all that simple, because it's about more than knowing just "when," as I hope I portrayed in this story.

Stranded in Time

SAVANNAH REYNARD

Italy, 1348

Angeletta De Acutis lay in the small candlelit room and waited for death. Her entire body paralyzed and consumed by the fire of fever. Painful bulbous tumors left no amount of skin untouched and the ability to breathe lessened with every gulp of air. There was no time, no counting of hours, just the unending vacillation between awareness and nothingness.

Amidst the haze of death, there was one person who never let her suffer alone, her Marcuccio. A warm glow traveled through her, momentarily blocking out the pain.

She wished she could see him one last time. The world around her was nothing but light and shadows. And yet she knew it was her Marcuccio who knelt at her bedside, his large hand enveloping hers, one of the only places agony hadn't besieged. With everything she had, she willed her fingers to twitch. Her attempt at a goodbye, at 'I love you.' He squeezed her slender fingers in response. Sweet relief. The last exchange of their love.

She felt the weight of his head on her hand. "My Angeletta. My Angel," he whispered. "I have done something unforgivable." His whispers turned into sobs.

She lay there. A witness to his confession but unable to comfort him.

"The witch." He choked out. "I have sent for Strega Ezzo."

No, Marcuccio. No.

Fear's icy fingers wrapped around Angeletta's heart. She yelled, but no words formed. She screamed, but no sounds left her lips. She willed herself to sit up, to stop him, but she was stuck in her body, isolated from the world by the cocoon of death.

The sound of the old door creaking filled the room.

"You sent for me," croaked a scratchy voice from the direction of the doorway.

"*Dio mi perdoni,*" he said softly.

Angeletta coughed, blood warm and metallic filled her mouth and pooled in her throat, choking her. She struggled to swallow, to breathe. Marcuccio scooped her up and cradled her head upward. The liquid flowed back down her throat. He stayed there, ensconcing her in his protective arms.

Uneven footsteps and the thump of a cane signaled the old woman drew near. The scent of damp leaves filled Angeletta's nose. The thump circled around her like a death march as the witch chanted something unintelligible, stopping at her head. "There is nothing I can do. Death will come for her within the hour."

"You must do something…please…" Marcuccio's words trailed off. "Please help me."

The pain in his voice hurt more than all the pain in her body combined.

"I can do *something*. I can promise you will meet in the next life."

Angeletta desperately wanted to believe the witch, but she knew there was something more to that promise. Something that waited for her on the other side because of what she had done to the old woman.

There was a long stretch of silence, or maybe it was unconsciousness, before Angeletta heard anything else.

"Put a lock of hair from both of you in this pouch," the witch ordered sharply. "*Capelli per ogni anima.*"

Hair for every soul. Angeletta repeated the witch's words in her head.

"Now, blood. Use this blade."

She felt the sensation of Marcuccio gingerly lifting her hand, but it no longer felt like hers. The veil to the next world thinned as the end drew closer.

He brushed a kiss onto her palm, easing the sting that followed.

"*Il sangue ti lega,*" scratched the Strega.

Blood binds you.

The scent of fire surrounded Angeletta, suffocating her.

"*Per sempre,*" the witch shouted. "*Per sempre.*" She repeated the words until they melded into a whirlwind circling Angeletta's body. *Was this magic or death?* A black hole empty and hollow swallowed her, spreading its despair throughout her being.

"One last thing. Your rings."

Marcuccio said nothing, but she could feel the slight lift of her finger and the smooth gold of their promises slide off.

"Drop them both into the candle wax and press them together," the old woman paused. "Now, into the bag…*la cera ti copre.*"

Wax covers you.

"It is done," the witch said finally.

And with that, it felt as though someone had let all the air out of the room. Angeletta gasped and attempted to fill her lungs with the emptiness around her. Marcuccio clutched her hand and squeezed. His tears fell upon her cheek. "Wait for me, Cara mia. I will find you." His whisper sounded farther and farther away. "Wherever you are. I will find you."

The last words she heard from the lips of her love echoed inside her head, slowly dissolving into the void.

Italy, present day

Angela sat in a café in Valerio Catullo Airport just outside Verona, doodling a picture of her cat Sofie from her previous life on a square napkin, as she waited for her taxi. She had owned Kitty Kat the life before that and Max the one before that, but Sofie had been one of her favorites, all white and fluffy and a complete diva.

Remembering all her past lives wasn't as great as it sounded. That meant she remembered every scar, every humiliation, every painful detail of them all. That wasn't normal, of course. Not for one life, let alone multiple. But it was her punishment. Strega Ezzo had fully intended for her to be able to recall the harshness of life. Vividly. She let out a deep sigh. Her most painful memory being the cause of the sigh. Her Marcuccio.

Wait for me, cara mia. I will find you. Wherever you are. I will find you.

Those words never stopped repeating. In all this time, in all her lives, she had never found him. She figured that too was part of her punishment, always searching but never finding. Each time she was reborn, she desired only him, only Marcuccio. She dated, of course, but real love was elusive. It was as if their souls were somehow attached through time, but something kept them apart. The something being the curse Angela was sure Strega Ezzo had put on them. So, Angela was forced to walk the world alone, looking for her true love, stranded in time, maybe forever.

Angela sipped her drink, the liquid coating her throat, warm and soothing, contrary to her last memory in Italy. The burning. The pain. The lingering iron-like taste of blood.

Crumpling the napkin, she stuffed it into her now empty saucer. She hadn't been back to Italy for lifetimes. There was always something heavy about returning. Beautiful yet terrible. She remembered their country manor so clearly and how her Marcuccio's dark eyes devoured her. How his touch made her tingle in all the right places. How deeply she missed him.

Slinging her carry-on over her shoulder, she left cash on the table and proceeded over to her awaiting ride. She was headed to meet her best friend Sandra's Nonna. Her bestie offered to come with, but Angela knew she had to do this alone. She had been to psychics, mediums, a few Wiccan witches, anyone she thought might be able to help, and some actually had. That's how she put the pieces of the curse together. But from what Sandra said, Nonna could be the one to help her break it.

An hour Southeast of the airport, hidden in the Euganean Hills, was a small village tucked inside the vast woodlands. Oak and Chestnut trees lined the slopes with their deep russet colors and olive crops ripe for harvesting.

A rustic stone cottage welcomed Angela as Nonna burst out the front door, arms open wide like they were old friends. *"Benvenuto Bella!"*

Angela couldn't help but laugh as Nonna gave her a big squeeze. She liked Nonna already. Ushering her inside, the jovial woman sent her straight to an awaiting feast. For the rest of the evening, Angela's wine glass remained ever full and her plate bottomless. She met Sandra's fourth and fifth cousins, her great-great uncle Bruno, and neighbors from either side. Angela had thought she'd be having a quiet, personal visit. Nonna didn't work that way.

Later, after all the guests left, Angela helped Nonna clean up, taking her back to the days of her small country estate, helping her kitchen servant and confidant Maria...and her Marcuccio.

As she washed the dishes, Marcuccio's strong jawline and hearty laugh invaded her mind.

Nonna sidled up next to her. "I think it's clean by now," she laughed.

"Hmm...what?"

"The dish. You've been washing it for the last ten minutes."

Angela's cheeks heated. "Oh. Right." She put it to the side and grabbed another.

"Enough dishes. We sit and have some wine and talk about your problem. You know I'm a *Chiromante*, yes?"

"Yes, and from what Sandra says, you're the best fortune teller that's ever lived."

"My biggest fan."

Angela chuckled and nodded.

"More wine?"

"Nonna, are you trying to get me plastered?" Angela teased.

"Bah," Nonna waved off the question. "It's only wine, Mimma."

Before Angela could say yes, her glass was full. Again. "If Nonna says I must, then I must."

Nonna smiled, warm and comforting. "Mimma, you've got a darkness all around you." Her sweet smile faded. "So much so, it's hard to even see you."

Angela took a sip of wine. "I do?"

"It almost hides you completely from my third eye." She tapped a chubby finger in the middle of her forehead. "You have walked this earth many times, but you know that."

Gulping the rest of her wine, Angela nodded.

Nonna filled Angela's glass again and then her own. Taking Angela's hand, she held it between hers. "And…Mmmm…hmmm." She closed her eyes and shook her head.

"And, what?" Angela's heart raced.

"And you are bound to someone."

Angela had known it all along. She let out a slow shaky breath. *Marcuccio*. "You can see that?" Her legs felt jelly-like. They *were* bound, they just hadn't found each other yet.

"Yes, but…" she rubbed Angela's hands between hers. "I've never seen anything quite like this shrouding before." Staring straight ahead, Nonna bit her lip, warming Angela's hands with the friction of hers. "It's dark magic or low magic some would call it."

Strega Ezzo came to mind as clear as day. Deep lines etched her expressionless face.

Nonna furrowed her brows. "What did you do to bring on this curse?"

Angela lowered her gaze. She couldn't look Nonna in the eye. "Ran her out of town. Called her false. Blamed her for bringing the black death to us."

"Mamma Mia, child. A false witch she wasn't."

Angela remembered the panic, the stench of death. "We didn't know what was happening..." She choked on her words. "Can we fix it?"

"Tomorrow, we find this Strega. We see what she wanted."

"She's dead."

"The dead speak too, you know."

It didn't take long for Angela to get her bearings and find the road that led to her once beloved estate. Nonna's ancient VW Beetle vibrated along the old gravel road. Where memory failed, a pull guided her. She tightened her grip on the handle of the door, the urge to bolt out of the moving car and run the rest of the way overwhelmed her.

They pulled up to the dilapidated mansion, long abandoned, the stone worn by time.

Angela clutched the fabric of her shirt and whispered, "This is it." She drew in a breath to steady herself. "Home."

"Be careful, child. The building's not safe," Nonna called out.

Angela nodded as she ran through the grand archway, remembering the summer strolls she and Marcuccio used to take along the walkway. Shards of wood, jagged and dangerous, protruded where the large front door had been, and the ornate wolf knocker that used to signal visitors was long gone. The stairway to the second floor, once splendid, had rotted away, but its absence could never erase the memory of that night when Marcuccio carried her up to their wedding bed.

Standing in the middle of the foyer, the house came alive. She was surrounded by tapestries, furniture, the aroma of Maria's cooking emanating from the kitchen. Why had she waited so long to return? So many lovely memories.

The gardens beyond the house beckoned her. The place where she and Marcuccio had spent many an evening dancing among the spring blooms. The scent of violet and jasmine filled her nose as she spun in circles, happy and comforted, until…she spied what lay at the edge of the property. Reality, harsh and foreboding.

With purpose, she followed the stone path that led to the family cemetery. Overgrown shrubs and weeds hid the many headstones of her ancestors. Two large ones jutted out from the dense greenery off to the right. Clawing and tearing at the overgrowth, she yanked off the weeds, revealing the faded names Angeletta and Marcuccio De Acutis. She fell to her knees and brushed her fingers along her husband's name. *Marcuccio.* She lay down on her side along the cool grass as tears streamed down her cheeks, the ache palpable.

After some time, she realized Nonna was standing behind her and turned to meet her gaze. "It's me…us."

Nonna smiled, a knowing look on her face.

Angela sat upright on the backs of her heels. "Now what?"

Nonna rubbed Angela's back in small circles. "Now we find your Strega."

A small village shrouded in the middle ages lay just down the hill. Stone houses clustered together, untouched by time. Angela stopped at the edge of the town. What was she thinking? Was she going to walk up to a stranger on the street and ask them if they knew a witch who had lived there in the thirteenth century? That sounded completely ridiculous.

"It's not though," said Nonna.

"Not what?"

"Ridiculous."

"Oh, and a mind reader too. That's kind of creepy."

Nonna let out a full belly laugh. "I amuse myself."

In the distance, the town square was alive with music and dancing and Angela was drawn to the sound of celebration. Before she could take another step, the hairs on the back of her neck stood on end and a gust of wind whipped through her, chilling her. "Nonna? Are we—"

"Being watched? Yes."

Compelled, Angela slowly turned her head, coming eye-to-eye with a young dark-haired woman standing in front of one of the larger houses on the street. She was beautiful, with large dark eyes and a cascade of raven curls. The woman studied the two of them as they moved along the road, causing a shiver to snake along Angela's spine. "I think I'm supposed to go to her."

"Then you should."

Angela walked tentatively toward the woman. "Hello," she said, unsure of what to say next.

"*Ciao.*"

Clearing her throat, she continued. "We're here—I'm here." She stopped in front of the woman and scratched her head. *Just say it already.* "I'm here about a witch."

"We've been expecting you...Angeletta."

Angela's mouth fell open.

"Well, that was easy enough," said Nonna matter-of-factly.

"Follow me." The woman headed toward the back of the house.

Angela turned to Nonna for guidance, but her companion just stood there, one eyebrow raised as she watched the woman walk off.

Straightening her sweater, Angela took a deep breath and set on the path the mysterious woman took. When she reached the back of the house, the young beauty was gone. Nonna caught up as Angela stood dumbfounded, scanning the area.

"She's gone," said Angela, irritation lacing her voice.

Nonna nodded. "So she is." Then headed toward a cluster of trees.

Angela could see a single headstone near the thick trunk of the largest tree, but she was still stuck on the dark-haired woman who had vanished. "How did she know I was Angeletta?"

Nonna shrugged her shoulders. "A false witch she wasn't."

"I guess not," said Angela.

They stopped in front of the single grave as a gust of wind whooshed past, the branches of the old tree swaying vigorously. Peering up at the tree, Angela noted how the poor old thing's limbs drooped as if they were weighted down.

"This is the husband." Nonna gave the top of the tombstone a friendly pat. "And that patch of grass must be Strega Ezzo." She fixed her gaze on Angela. "She was never allowed to come back, you know. Never had a proper burial. Never even had a stone to mark her grave."

Angela felt her cheeks heat with shame. "Why didn't anyone get her a headstone in all this time?"

"It must be undone…not ignored or her soul will never be at peace. And only she who made it so, can make it right."

Clearing her throat, Angela knelt at the edge of the trimmed patch of grass. "Wait…how do you know all this—" She held up her hand. "Never mind." Sitting back on her heels, she blew out a breath. "Now what?"

"It is up to you."

Angela sat there for a moment, facing the grave of the woman she had wronged so long ago. When forced to flee her home by the angry villagers, Strega Ezzo made no fuss, put up no fight. Just grabbed a few things and set out on foot in the middle of the night. The picture of the frail old woman walking into the darkness and her husband's wails burned in Angela's brain.

Brushing her hand back and forth along the wispy blades of grass, she considered what might make things right. "I'm so sorry Stre—Signora Ezzo." Her shoulders slumped. "I'm so sorry I blamed you for all of those deaths." She wiped a tear away with the back of her hand. "In truth, I think you saved more than one person with your skill in herbs."

Not even a rock to mark her grave.

Angela decided that's where she would start, marking Signora Ezzo's grave, the least she could do. With care, she gathered stones of all shapes and sizes from the surrounding area and made a temporary basket with her outstretched sweater. Dark ones. Light ones. Smooth ones. Textured ones. All the while, Nonna just sat under the tree, watching. Every now and then, she'd catch her chuckling and nodding her head.

After multiple trips in all directions, Angela finally had enough to make a proper marker. The sun began to set casting rich hues of orange and gold across the sky. Carefully, she outlined the perimeter of the grave with the larger stones, reciting every prayer she could think of. Inside of the rock outline, she spelled out Signora Ezzo's name with the smaller rocks. Then, she handpicked a bouquet of wildflowers from an adjacent field, setting them in the center. As she sat back, admiring her handy work, a quiet stillness settled in the area. Not even the gentle whir of an autumn breeze stirred the night air.

Sighing, Angela scratched the back of her neck. Somehow, this didn't seem enough. She glanced at Nonna who had fallen asleep against the tree. The hazy curse ritual invaded her mind. The hair, the blood, the rings, the wax were all collected into some kind of holder. Thinking back, Signora Ezzo often wore multiple leather pouches around her neck. Angela stared at the ground beneath. No. She couldn't. She wouldn't. She drew her legs in tight and wrapped herself in a hug, burying her head in her knees, sure that digging the poor woman up and looking for an old pouch around her skeleton-neck wasn't what she would have wanted.

The sun had completely set, and the sky was velvety black with a sliver of moon highlighted by the glitter of thousands of stars. Staring upward, she pleaded. "Signora Ezzo, please help me help you."

Another whipping wind surged through the branches of the tree, rustling and rattling every branch. Angela saw something she hadn't in the light of day. She bolted to her feet and ran all the way around the tree. *God in heaven.* There, along every branch, dangled hundreds of pouches. Some red, some black, some small, some large. *Holy hell.* They must have been there all along, invisible.

Clasping her hands together, she held them up toward the sky. *Bless you, Signora Ezzo.* She needed to find her own pouch. But how? Hundreds of pouches swayed in the moonlight. How was she to find her own? She jumped and grabbed at one. An electric current sizzled her fingers. *Ouch.* She swatted another and the same thing happened, and another and still the same. She pressed her singed fingers to her lips to cool them. This was going to be a very long night.

Looking for guidance, she glanced at Nonna, but her eyes were still closed. She didn't really have to ask; she knew she had to climb the tree. *God, I hate heights.* Ever since little Jimmy Wilkes fell off her roof and took her with him in Atlanta, before the Civil War, she couldn't stomach them.

She held her breath and jumped, grabbing a sturdy limb and hoisting herself up high enough to be able to step onto a knot. Her foot slipped, and she fell flat on her butt. Why did she have a feeling Signora Ezzo got a good chuckle out of that? Two more failed attempts, plus a few scrapes, and she was able to make it to the lowest branch. Her heart raced as she scooted along the limb to get close to the trunk. Flattening her body along the rough bark, eyes closed, she slowly stood up.

She stretched out her arm and waved it under a cluster of pouches, trying to touch as many as she could at once. Orange and red sparks attacked her skin and she yanked her arm back. A cloud of sulfur surrounded her. "Why are there so many?" she shouted. "Why so many curses?"

"They're not all curses, Mimma." Nonna looked up at her, one eye open. "Some are love spells, fortune spells, fertility spells."

Angela wiped the sweat off her brow.

"She wasn't evil. Misunderstood, maybe."

"You remember she cursed me for lifetimes, right?"

"You remember you ruined her life, *corretta*?"

"Good point." Angela couldn't argue that one.

"You might try to go higher. If you touch every single one, it's going to be painful."

"Yah think?" A knot the size of Italy, no Texas, balled in her gut. Trying not to look down, she climbed a few more branches and then a few more. She spied a pouch at the very top of the highest branch. If she was pissed at someone, that's where she'd put their salvation. By this time, her arms and legs were sore, and any skin not covered was either singed or scratched.

Sucking it up, she brushed herself off. She would get that damn pouch or die trying. Finally, she got high enough where she could bat at it with the tip of her fingers. Reaching up as far as she could, she tipped it. Nothing. She tested it again. No zap or fiery pain at all. She closed her eyes as a rush of relief surged through her. Tears pooled behind her eyelids. She almost had it. Reaching up a little higher, she gave it a good whack and sent it hurtling to the ground. She couldn't believe it. Now, if only she didn't have to climb down.

It took a few moments of crawling around the grass before she found where the pouch had landed. Grabbing it, she kissed it and raised the small leather sack to the sky. "Thank you, Signora."

"*Pace a te Signora Ezzo,*" said Nonna.

"Aren't you awake at all of the convenient times?"

"Asleep? You think I could sleep with that witch talking my ear off the whole time?"

"*She* was here?"

"Of course."

"Of course," Angela said mimicking Nonna's nonchalant attitude.

The celebration in the town square was still going strong and the laughter bounced off the stone houses, surrounding them with joy. On the trek back to the car, Angela peered over her shoulder for one last look. An old woman stood there with a cane in one hand and the hand of an elderly gentleman in the other. Angela squinted. Signora Ezzo? Signore Ezzo?

The woman let go of her companion and waved, a slight smile on her face. Angela turned completely around to face them and slowly waved back. Walking backward, she continued to wave at the couple. Peace, Signore Ezzo *had* found peace.

As the distance grew, they became harder to see, translucent almost. Then, one minute it was the old woman waving, the next it was the young raven-haired beauty they had met when they first arrived. Her husband changed too, becoming young and muscular, a brown cap askew on his head. Angela stopped at the very edge of the town. "Goodbye," she mouthed.

The couple turned and headed toward the celebration hand-in-hand. He gave her a twirl and pulled her in for a sweet kiss in one fluid motion.

"*Addio,*" whispered Nonna.

Back at Nonna's, they dumped the perfectly preserved contents of Ezzo's pouch on the table. Two wax-coated rings fell out with a thud.

"My heart," said Angela and scooped them up. She turned them over in the palm of her hand, a warm feeling settling in her chest. "Are we going to burn it all or something?"

"No Mimma. We only want to break the bad part. The part that keeps you veiled." Nonna peeled off the thin layer of wax that covered both rings, tossed them into hot soapy water, and gave them a gentle scrub under the sink. After they were wax free, she slipped them back into the pouch. "*Finito.*"

"That's it? Scrape some wax off and it's done?"

"It's magic my dear, not rocket science," said Nonna with a wink.

Angela didn't know if it was happiness or the fact that the curse was lifted but she felt lighter, no longer weighed down.

The next morning went quickly. Angela thanked Nonna and tried to pay for her help and hospitality, but she wouldn't have it. A car honked outside signaling it was time to go. Angela gave Nonna the biggest hug ever. "Thank you."

"*Prego*, my child. You must let me know if you find your Marcuccio, *si?*"

Angela nodded and choked back tears. That might be possible after all. She had renewed hope. Someday, she'd find her Marcuccio.

She boarded the plane and found her row empty. So, she helped herself to the window seat. The terminal didn't look too crowded, so she had hope that she'd get a whole row to herself. Getting comfy, she pulled a book up on her kindle and began to read.

A slight bump to her arm jostled her out of the world of dragons and unicorns. No row to herself, apparently. Another bump, only this time Angela felt a spark that sent a tingle up her arm and through that entire side of her body. She was afraid to turn her head, but she did. Staring back at her just as intently were a pair of dark eyes with the longest blackest lashes. A flicker of recognition whooshed through her and her heart caught in her throat. A strand of hair fell into his eyes and he ran a hand through his tousled jet-black waves. He smiled, highlighting the jawline that she had never forgotten. *Marcuccio.*

She had no words for this moment, but she didn't need them. Tears blurred his sweet face as they reached out for each other's hand.

He ran his thumb along the outside of her hand. "Hi…I'm Marc," his voice was low and velvety.

Tears burst through like a river un-dammed and she threw her arms around his neck. "Is it really you?"

Wrapping her up in his arms, he whispered, "Yes, my Angeletta. My angel. It's me."

Now, they'd have all the time they'd ever need to get to know each other again. Now, they had forever.

La fine.

Inspiration

The inspiration for Stranded in Time came about several ways. I like to write stories about past lives and second chances at love. Since our theme was stranded, I wondered how someone might get stranded in time. I'm sure there are lots of interesting ways, but the one that came to mind first was a curse and who better to put a curse on someone than a witch? Death often goes hand-in-hand with stories about previous lives whether it's described in detail, conveyed in a vision or memory, or relayed in some other way. I wanted to capture the isolation, the feeling of being trapped, and the desperation it can often bring to both sides. And then, of course, being a lover of romance, there had *to be a happily ever after for all.*

Happy Travels!

Barbara Lipkin

"A wonderful good morning, ladies and gentlemen. This is your cruise director. We will be boarding the buses for our tour of Wertheim in one hour. Please remember your boarding cards and whisperers."

Tim Prentice wearily opened his eyes. He looked around the tiny cabin without raising his head from the pillow. The hard bench on the opposite wall, only eight feet away, upholstered in dull yellow. The wooden panel above it that hid the fold-out bed within. Next to the identical bed on which he lay, a tiny round table. A barricade of miniature chocolate bars standing guard on it. He never ate the little piece that appeared on his pillow every night anymore. There were more than thirty of them. It just made him feel worse.

Everything was just the same as before. He couldn't help himself. The tears overflowed onto his cheeks.

"The Green Group will be boarding the bus with Lara," the voice elaborated.

Tim didn't recognize the voice coming over the loudspeaker. It must be a new cruise director this morning. None of them lasted very long. Only the length of one trip upriver, and then they were gone.

"We'll be exploring this fascinating German town, at the confluence of the Main and Tauber Rivers, which dates from the 8th century. We'll drive up to the Castle, but later we'll be touring on foot, so be sure to put on your walking shoes."

How many times had Tim heard these very words? He couldn't remember. The whole Rhine-Main river system blurred. The only image he retained was that of green water flowing past endless river banks, each town looking just like the one before and the one after. Often, the riverboat floated into a lock and the view became one of cement walls rising high above. Slowly, the water-filled the lock. Then the gates opened and the ship continued on its way at a higher elevation than before. Tim could see the entire operation from his narrow balcony. He had seen it many, many times. He no longer bothered to look.

He'd never wanted to come on this cruise in the first place. Natalie had chosen it from a brochure that had come in the mail. She thought it would be a wonderful romantic getaway, just the two of them. A sort of pre-honeymoon. Tim wanted to go fishing up in Wisconsin.

They'd quarreled about it all the way to Amsterdam. Neither of them got any sleep on the flight. By the time they landed, the relationship was over. He should have turned around and taken the next plane back home. He gave Natalie well-deserved credit for having had enough sense to do exactly that, even though the trip was already paid for. But Tim stubbornly boarded the ship. He'd be damned if he'd let the money go to waste.

His stomach growled. At least, something was still normal. Wearily, he rose from the bed, unrested, his back aching. He stooped on the floor to open one of the two drawers stacked under the bed. He pulled out some underwear and a clean shirt and laid them ready on the shelf sticking out from the wall over the bed.

He washed out his underwear and shirt every night but the jeans were too heavy to manage in the little bathroom sink. He'd lost count of how many times he'd already worn the pair he'd draped over the bench the night before. He'd been alternating the three pairs he'd brought on the trip. They'd have to do. There wasn't a lot of choice. The last time he'd tried to send his clothes to the ship's laundry, he found them still in their plastic bag at the bottom of the little closet the next morning. Even the clothes couldn't break out. He put on the jeans.

With one baby step, he was inside the minuscule bathroom. Washed, teeth brushed, shaved, sandy hair slicked back with water. Ready for another day. *What would happen if I never left the cabin? What if I refuse to play?* Tim already knew the answer. That didn't seem to be an option. Still, he asked the same questions each morning.

Why is this happening to me? Why is it all going so wrong? Does Natalie even think about me anymore? I just want to go home.

He opened the cabin door and peeked out, reluctant to begin the day. He could just close the door and get back into bed. It was tempting. He stood at the door thinking about it.

No! I won't give in. I don't know what this is about, but I have to keep going no matter what. Today is the day something is going to change. I can feel it.

Tim straightened his shoulders and stepped out into the corridor, but then stopped again.

Oops! Almost forgot the whisperer. Even the name of the audio receiver was spooky. *Whisperer. Whisperer.* The sibilance made him shudder.

He grabbed the thing from the shelf and hung the lanyard around his neck. The earplugs were already attached, the cord dangling. He coiled it up, tucked it in a pocket and left the cabin. He knew he'd never get off the ship without it. The cruise director always insisted the passengers were properly equipped before they went out.

Sometimes he recognized people at breakfast, for a week or so. Then the cast changed and everyone was a complete stranger once again. It was uncanny though, how much the newcomers resembled the ones who'd come before.

He'd lost track of how many different times he'd introduced himself to strangers. He no longer bothered. He just grabbed some eggs and toast from the buffet and sat in the nearest vacant seat. The tables were set for six. If one of the others at the table offered to make conversation, he'd just look up and nod briefly, before addressing himself to his food once again. He didn't like being rude. He just didn't have any more energy. The waiter, a new one, poured coffee. Tim nodded his thanks.

Breakfast done, Tim walked down the hall to the lobby and joined a short line in front of the desk. When his turn came, he told the receptionist, "Four-sixteen, please." She handed him a plastic card that had his picture on it. They wouldn't let him get off the ship without it, or back on, either.

What if I don't get back on the ship? What then? Could I pull that off?

The sliding glass door leading to the ship's deck was standing open just to the right of the lobby. Beyond the deck, a narrow gangplank connected the ship with the pier. Beyond that lay Germany. Beyond that lay freedom. Tim made sure the cabin key was in his pocket, along with his passport, boarding card, phone, and wallet. He shifted his sunglasses from the top of his head to the front of his eyes. His heart was pounding. *Can I do this? I have to. I have to try.*

The couple walking along the pier just in front of Tim chatted excitedly to each other about what they were going to buy in Wertheim. Or rather, the woman was chatting. Her husband nodded now and then. Tim recognized them. They'd appeared at breakfast a while back. Was it a week? Was it longer?

The woman was chunky and short, with thick salt-and-pepper hair caught up in a bun at the back of her head. Her husband topped her by at least six inches. He was the designated carrier of his wife's plentiful purchases. Tim expected that he'd be laden with bags and boxes when they returned to the ship. *But I won't see them!*

He inserted himself between the two of them. He didn't understand why, but he knew he needed to remain inconspicuous. His freedom depended upon it.

Several buses lined up just past the dock, waiting for their daily load of travelers. Each bus had a different colored card posted in its front window. Tim belonged to the Green Group. *What would happen if I got on the red bus instead? What if I don't get on any bus? What if I don't follow the rules? What if I make my own rules?* The very thought started sweat dripping down from his forehead. *Stay calm, now. I can do this! I know it. Today is the day.*

He turned his head aside as he passed the ship's officer stationed on shore, avoiding eye contact. He followed close behind the Shopper, ignoring the fact that her husband was trying to scoot ahead of him. They belonged to the Green Group too. In a single file they walked quickly along the line of buses, looked for the green sign, found it. The wife got on first but Tim swerved aside at the last minute. He kept on going, past the Red Group, past the Blue Group, on toward the first bus, the Yellow Group. He hesitated a second, suddenly afraid. *Don't be a fool*, he told himself. *Go for it.*

He crossed in front of the Yellow Group bus. Just beyond, just there along the dock, was a set of stairs. Above them lay the town. Tim could barely breathe, but he kept going.

Look normal, he reminded himself. *Take it slow.*

He ascended the stairs at a moderate pace instead of racing up them as he wanted to do. At the top of the stairs, the Bavarian town of Wertheim, between the Main and Tauber Rivers, just as the cruise director had promised, spread out before him. High above the town rose the fairy-tale red sandstone towers of the Castle. Medieval-looking buildings lined the cobblestone streets, but those streets were filled with people, walking, shopping, eating ice cream – so ordinary, so right.

I'll just call a cab, and I'll get to the airport in no time. People do it every day. I've done it zillions of times. Nothing to it. I can be home in a matter of hours, he exulted. *There's a cab coming right now.* He waved it over to the curb, opened its door and slid into the back seat. "Take me to the airport," he told the driver.

He relaxed against the seat and closed his eyes. *I did it! I'm free!*

"A wonderful good morning, ladies and gentlemen. This is your cruise director. We will be boarding the bus for Wertheim in one hour. Please remember your boarding cards and whisperers."

Tim turned on to his stomach in the hard, narrow bed and his body shook with sobs.

Inspiration

There are 66 locks along the Rhine, Main, and Danube Rivers between Amsterdam and Greifenstein, Austria, a distance of around 450 miles. As the boat that my husband and I were cruising on traversed the 30th*? 40*th*? 50*th*? lock, I began to wonder if we were indeed progressing toward our destination or if we were trapped in an endless cycle, going through the same lock again and again. My mind wandered along those lines, and as soon as I got home, I sat down at my laptop and out came "Happy Travels." The story continues to morph in my head, and will soon be expanded into a full-length novel, with the working title* Time Warp. *So Reader, what do you think happened here?*

The Tapestry

KAREN STUMM LIMBRICK

Alyssandra Marchand sneezed into her arm, a great shuddering expulsion of the dust that had infiltrated the pile of textiles she'd been sorting through.

"*Gesundheit,*" a voice called from around a stack of the rugs and weavings.

Alys rolled her eyes, calling out, "We're in France, Maxine. Don't piss them off by speaking German." Alys smiled even though Maxine couldn't see her. "And your accent is lousy," she added in a singsong voice.

"Not that you're an expert," Maxine came around the corner holding a bright pink shag rug. Alys made a face at it and Maxine began to rummage in a pile near Alys. They fell into a companionable silence.

Flea marketing was one of Alys's favorite pastimes. You never knew what treasure lay hidden under the depths of old castoffs. It was the same reason she loved her archival work as a professional, collecting rare items for people. They all had a past, a story to tell. Today she put aside the more valuable and rare to relish the dust of discarded and well-worn furniture, books, and musty fabrics. She enjoyed the thrill of the hunt. It took patience and a good eye for the unusual to scavenge really good treasure amongst the debris and detritus of past lives.

Alys sneezed into her arm again. When she looked up she noticed a very shabby tapestry, shoved back behind the pile she was sorting through. She removed the stacks and reached out to grab it. The moment her hands came into contact with the woven piece, her vision darkened and a wooziness come upon her. She thought she was going to faint and reached out for something solid to block her fall.

"Alys? Alys?"

Alys heard her name being called from far away. As quickly as it hit her, the dizziness receded leaving her feeling weak and off-balance. She clutched the tapestry tightly to her chest, although she had no recollection of actually picking it up.

"Alys? Is something wrong?" Maxine looked confused and very upset. "I've been talking to you and you were just standing there looking blank, totally unresponsive. Why are you crying? And you're white as a sheet." Maxine held her hand to Alys forehead. It was cool against her feverish skin. A deep sense of fear had unexpectedly settled into the pit of Alys's stomach.

"I'm fine. It's nothing. Probably all the dust." She didn't want to worry Maxine, but this was the beginning of a mystery she knew she would have to solve. Based on past experiences, if she did not try to solve it, the episodes would get more and more intense until she was about to lose her mind.

Alys dropped the tapestry and put on her leather driving gloves as a shield. She recently learned she had a gift. Random objects of the past came alive to her when she laid her hands upon them. These objects carried a message from the past, a connection to the lives the objects had once been a part of and to a soul trapped somewhere in the hereafter. She had to discover the reason behind it to free herself from the connection, as well as the soul tethered to the object.

To be able to receive messages from another person lost in the afterlife or an alternate reality of some kind she considered a gift so far. But, the peril to her personally while trying to solve the cryptic messages she received any sane person would consider a curse.

Alys didn't know why she had this gift. She used to think it was because she had a personal connection to the objects and people in question. She soon realized this was not the case. Once a connection was made, her body remained in the present, but her mind became immersed in an alternate world. If she didn't solve the mystery she would eventually become stranded in another lifetime with no way back to reality or her own life. The soul of the person reaching out to her would be stranded in eternity, leaving the mystery of who and what the message is unresolved. She would buy the tapestry and take it home for further inspection.

Alys and Maxine paid for their purchases and left the *Boquelet Flea Market*. They walked the few, short blocks to the car park and climbed into Alys's sports car. After dropping Maxine off at her house, Alys sped off towards her own home, a chateau just outside the city limits of Senlis in the Picardy district of France.

Entering through the massive wooden doors of the front entrance, Alys was greeted by her dog, Edwulf, tail wagging and waiting for fur ruffling hugs. While she dug her fingers into Edwulf's dense fur, giving him a good scratching, squeals of laughter echoed across the hall from the outside. Alys glimpsed a child speeding across the back terrace. Her husband was nowhere to be seen. He was probably in his workshop in the east wing. As usual, the children had escaped the Au Pair. She smiled to herself, remembering her own childhood days of freedom in the great expanse of fields and forests that surrounded the estate.

Alys took her new acquisition into her study. She placed the tapestry on the floor and undid the wrappings, keeping her gloves on as she unrolled it. The sunlight enhanced the details so she could study it closely.

She surmised it to be about late thirteenth century by the detail of the workmanship and the style of clothing. It depicted a woman and a man seated in a garden sharing a goblet as they gazed into one another's eyes. Probably a wedding or engagement scenario. Perhaps it was given to the bride and groom as a gift for their new home, or it was commissioned by the groom for his bride or vice versa.

To Alys, nothing stood out as unusual, unique or special, at first glance. But it was. There was more to it than just a fantasy rendering of a damsel being courted.

Preparing for the inevitable, she sat on the floor and took off her gloves. Cautiously, palms down, she pressed fully on the surface of the woven piece. She felt the pattern of the weaving and the texture of the woolen threads used to create the now threadbare masterpiece, each fiber coming alive. Her surroundings faded, she felt like she was falling through a black hole. A cacophony of sounds surrounded her. A fierce shard of pain shot through her head, fear consumed her, and she trembled uncontrollably. It was all so intense. She couldn't take the onslaught and lifted her hands off of the piece. The feelings vanished, except the residual sense of fear.

She knew intrinsically this fear she was experiencing was at the root of whatever message she was supposed to understand. She suspected the creator of the tapestry was somehow linked to the message and the fear came from them. Male or female she couldn't tell, but there was a soul here waiting for someone to set it free. She would need to hold on longer to allow the story to reveal itself.

She heard her children call her. The spell was broken for now. It was time to go to them and see to their needs.

"I need a bit of normal in a day of definitely not normal," she mumbled, rising from the floor. Tonight she would make dinner for her family, hug them, read them bedtime stories and pretend all was normal. Tomorrow she would try to breach the boundaries between this world and the other, and pray she came back to her own in sound mind and spirit.

Alys woke the next morning to the sound of birds chirping. She blinked, adjusting to the brilliant stream of sunlight creeping in across the room, dissolving the shadows of the night. Lying on her side in bed, she faced the window. The yellow orb peeked its head up, surrounded with a glorious array of red and orange. She smiled at the gentle rumble of snores coming from under the covers behind her. Normally, her husband woke before the sun.

She crept out of bed so as not to wake him. Putting on her slippers and a heavy sweater over her pajamas, she went down to the kitchen to make herself a cup of coffee. The aroma of rich coffee always evoked a sense of calm comfort. While it percolated, she thought about the task ahead of her.

Alys took her coffee into the library and sat on the sofa next to the tapestry contemplating the pattern once again. Sunlight picked up the shimmer of a golden thread woven throughout the piece, appearing to be random. She hardly noticed it the day before. Probably because of the different angle of the sun. She was curious about that thread. It seemed out of place. She ran her fingers across it. A tingle raced up her arm. She pulled it away as if it burned.

Alys studied the people in the weaving. The lady's expression appeared happy. Alys focused on a third figure in shadow, woven into the pattern. She could barely make out her face, but Alys thought maybe it was fear on the face of the younger woman as she gazed upon the couple. She thought about her own feelings of fear she felt when she'd held the weaving. What could this mean?

While she was contemplating this, she hardly noticed she had placed her coffee mug on the side table and was being drawn toward the tapestry, not of her will. She knelt on the floor next to it, and in a transfixed state she placed her hands palm down upon the face of the fearful girl in the shadows.

The room spun, she felt herself falling through a vortex, darkness swirled around her. Voices and images appeared, blurred and jumbled. She closed her eyes and focused on separating one of the voices from the others in the hope to control what was happening. She heard music, like a string instrument, and laughter. The sweet fragrance of flowers assailed her senses. When she opened her eyes, she stood in a garden. She was surrounded by seated women dressed in elaborate costumes with wide skirts and high hairdos while men dressed in knickers and white curly wigs fawned over the women. In the center of the lush garden was a canopy decorated with flowers, under which sat two people. Lovers by the way they were entwined, or a bride and groom, sharing a silver goblet while gazing into each other's eyes.

Alys spun in a circle, taking it all in. She noticed someone peering out from a stand of trees. Closer inspection revealed a young girl, her hands clutched together, an anxious look upon her face. Alys recognized her by her silhouette as possibly the shadow figure she'd been drawn to in the tapestry. Alys started to approach her. The girl turned to speak to her but Alys couldn't hear her. She watched the pleading look in the girl's eyes. It wasn't until she got very close that she heard what the girl was saying. "I wanted to stop it. But it didn't work."

"What didn't work?" Alys asked her.

The young girl grabbed Alys' hands in desperation.

"The charm. The witch said if I wove a tapestry with the golden thread, my mother would be free of the Duke's attention and he wouldn't marry her. But, you see? It didn't work. They are married. He only wants her for her dowry and now I fear for her life." The girl started to wring her hands while peering around the tree watching her mother and the Duke.

"So, why would you fear for her life?" Alys felt like she was parroting the girl, who told Alys her name was Meridian. Meridian who looked to be about 14 years of age, was the daughter of the supposedly ill-fated bride, Lady Beatrix.

Meridian looked at Alys as if she was slow-witted. "Because once he has her dowry, he has no reason to keep her alive. He's buried three wives already." Suddenly, Meridian stopped shaking her hands, stood straight, and looked squarely at Alys, as if she just realized she was speaking to a stranger. "Who did you say you were?"

"My name is Alys. I think I was sent here to help you." She hoped that was a good enough answer. How to explain that one fell through a weaving from the future? It isn't something you wanted to just say out loud. Especially not in the 13th century. In fact, it's kind of amazing that the girl spoke openly about seeking out the witch in the first place.

"Help me how?"

"Well," Alys hesitated briefly while she tried to think how she could help. "Why don't you tell me about the witch. Let's start at the beginning." Meridian told Alys all about the courtship and her warnings to her mother who seemed to fall under a love spell of some sort. Meridian said she never trusted the old man and was confirmed when one day she overheard him speaking to someone in the garden about the riches her mother would bring to the marriage. Lady Beatrix refused to listen to her daughter's warnings so, in desperation, Meridian sought out the witch and asked her for help.

"The witch gave me a charm after she whispered an incantation over it. I was to hang the charm around my mother's neck. Then she gave me a golden thread and told me to take 3 strands of my hair and wrap them together. Then I was to weave them into a tapestry of a wedding feast. My mother's wedding feast. Supposedly it would reveal the true nature of the groom and my mother would no longer be under his spell."

"And then what happened¿' Alys asked.

"And, then I stood by while they were married," Meridian stated, shrugging her shoulders.

Alys and Meridian were each lost in their own thoughts, contemplating the situation. Neither one took notice as the bride and groom sipped from the loving cup. Suddenly a piercing scream shattered the silence in the idyllic garden. Alys and Meridian turned to find that Lady Beatrix lay crumpled in a heap in the grass at the feet of her new husband.

Alys became unaware of anything else as a sudden darkness descended upon her.

Silence permeated Alys' consciousness. A telephone rang somewhere. She opened her eyes to discover she was lying on the floor in the fetal position, her hands clasped together at her heart, tears streaming down her face soaking the rug beneath her. Alys looked up to see her husband standing over her.

"Are you alright?" Her husband looked frantic and disheveled. She stood up slowly, feeling a little off-balance and almost knocked him over as she wrapped herself around him.

Nicholas took her trembling hands in his and led her to the sofa, making her sit down next to him. She told him about the tapestry and what happened when she found it in the antique shop and continued with events up to this morning. "I found myself smack in the middle of this medieval wedding."

"It sounds like something out of a gothic fairytale," her husband said. Alys ignored him.

She paused a moment, her brow furrowed in thought. "I don't recall what happened next. Just suddenly here I was, curled up on the floor."

"Maybe we should call the Doctor?" Her husband asked.

"No, I'm fine," Alys answered, distracted. "There is dark magic here. That golden thread is not just any thread. And that's no simple witch charm or spell. It's a curse. I suspect the girl, Meridian, got herself mixed up with the wrong end of things. That's also why she shows up in the shadows, it's part of the curse."

"What do you mean?"

"I suspect that thread holds a piece of her soul. When she wove the tapestry with it, she bound herself forever into it."

Alys continued solemnly, looking directly into Nicholas's eyes. "I don't know if you can do anything. I don't have the knowledge to help free her from this earthly prison." Alys stood perfectly still as the horror washed over her. "I can't leave her trapped in eternity forever," Alys's head was pounding. She felt the pull once again to be in the other world. It was like an addiction. Her husband held her and whispered in her ear, calming words that fought against the urges.

After a few moments Alys said, "I could pull the thread from the tapestry, maybe that will untether her?"

They tried to unpick the threads together. But, hard as they tried, it wouldn't come undone.

Alys sat back on her haunches. "I will have to go back. I have no choice."

"No, it's too dangerous for you to crossover again," Nicholas said, urgency filling his words. "There must be another way."

They both sat quietly struggling for a solution. Alys thought of something Meridian had said earlier about the soul and the thread. It was only a hunch, but she had to try. Before her husband knew what she was doing, she launched herself upon the tapestry. Instantly she found herself hurtled through the vortex of time and space. She found herself back in the garden, holding a weeping Meridian, this time evidence of the wedding feast just beginning.

"I know what you are going to do," she said stroking the girl's long hair. "I know how we can save your mother. You don't need to go to the witch."

The girl looked at her bewildered. "How did you know? Who are you?"

"Never mind that. I just know. I also know the witch will trick you. Your mother's new husband isn't the one trying to kill her, and it won't be your mother the witch saves, but herself. My guess is, somehow that golden thread entwines your soul with hers and by telling you to weave a tapestry with a golden thread, traps your soul forever and this gives her eternal life."

Meridian held up a single strand of thread that glimmered in the sunlight. "You mean this golden thread?"

"Yes, that golden thread." For a moment Alys felt again the disappointment of failure. She was too late. But, just as quickly she had another thought.

"Instead of weaving a tapestry, you must weave it into your own hair and you must never take it out. That way it will always be a part of you and the witch will have no power over you or your mother."

The girl hugged Alys and instantly started weaving the thread into a fine braid at the nape of her neck where it couldn't be seen. As Alys watched, she noticed the images around her were fading until a black void surrounded her. She heard the distant murmur of Nick's voice calling her name over and over. She closed her eyes as she prepared to return to her world, fully and completely relieved of this connection.

When she opened her eyes, her husband wasn't there next to her and she wasn't in her library. The voices faded to silence.

"It's alright," she said to herself feebly. "It's over. I saved the girl." Alys took a deep, slow breath and blew it out through pursed lips against the terror of what she now faced. The decision to return that last time was her undoing. Alys had to accept the outcome.

Meridian is no longer stranded in an eternal loop waiting for help. The words echoed in her mind. *But I am.*

Inspiration

I am a writer of historical fiction and a fan of dual timelines. A few of my favorite authors are Susannah Kearsley and Diana Gabaldon. The ideas of having ancestral memory or alternate realities and of being capable of traveling to those other worlds have always fascinated me.

I started writing Alys's story twenty years ago. Alys comes into contact with a family heirloom and is transported back to the time of an ancestor in the tenth century. She becomes involved in a mystery that she must solve through her own wits and research as well as living in the world of the past even though it threatens her life and her sanity. So for this piece it was easy for me to consider the idea that she actually is stranded in one of her adventures into the past.

I picked the thirteenth century for Alys to travel to a time when wise women or healers were called witches. I grew up on fairy tales and it seemed natural that this story evolved as it did into a semi-fairytale with a twisted ending. I hope you enjoyed it.

Waiting For My Family

GREG WRIGHT

I like the new family. There are two little boys just like me. One of them is really small, he can just barely crawl, and the other is just a little older, taller, constantly running. He ignores me, but I like him just the same. I watch them as they play with the plastic blocks in my room - or with the army men. A lot has changed in my room since I last slept here. There are new beds, and the shelves are different and there are a lot of toys here, some I've never seen before.

I want to play with them, but I am afraid the boys will get mad at me and won't want to be here, so I just watch them. The little one looks at me and giggles as he tries to touch me, but I stay just out of reach. Sometimes the children get sick and I watch over them until they get better. I remember when I was sick, although I don't recall when. I do remember the smell of the horses from the street and the streetlights being lit by the man with the ladder. I lay in bed and I kept trying to breathe, but it became harder. I watched my mom cry and my dad looked so worried. It was as if a ton of stones were on my chest and I could feel my lungs pop and crackle whenever I breathed. There was water in my throat and it was rising and rising and it was harder and harder to breathe.

Then everything stopped.

I could breathe again, but I couldn't get up. Memories were in pieces. I remember them changing my clothes followed by taking my picture with my parents and with my sister, who was looking at me with a horrific look on her face. She couldn't stop crying. Afterward, I was here alone.

Well, not really alone. There have been so many children that have come through my room. I love to be with them, but as they get older they grew distant, like they didn't see me anymore. When they started to ignore me, I stayed closer to the fireplace. The warmth is long gone, in fact, it is rarely lit, but I feel safe there. When I felt scared I used to sneak out of bed and lie by the fire to watch the flames until I fall asleep.

When the children are playing somewhere else in the house, I like staying here, in my room. At times when they are gone from the house, I stroll over to the window and watch for them to come back. I don't mind waiting. There is so much to look at. When I see them walking up the front sidewalk, the young ones always glance up and see me at the window and they wave to me. I wave back and they smile. The parents look up to, but they seem to be confused. I wave at them anyway, even though they don't wave back.

What I also look forward to is the little dog that visits my room when the two boys are gone. He comes over to the fireplace where I sit and he looks at me. He is very quiet and he sits there and watches me. When I reach out to him, he growls and sometimes barks, but he never tries to bite me. When I pull back, he continues to watch me until the other people call him away. He is a good dog, he loves the children and is always on guard. Occasionally when I am sitting alone in the room by the fireplace, he comes over with a ball and drops it in front of me. He does it lots of times and it makes me laugh because he has forgotten that I can't pick it up.

I really miss my mom and dad. I remember my mom reading to me and the smell of my father's pipe. I want to hug them and talk to them, and I can feel them wanting that too. Before, I could only feel that they were looking for me and couldn't find me. Now I feel they are much closer. My sister is closer also. They are very close. As I wait quietly by the fireplace, I'm very certain that they will be here to get me soon. Then we will be a family again.

Inspiration

I have never written a ghost story before and with the topic selected I thought now would be a perfect opportunity. I think flash fiction is perfect for horror pieces, and unless there is an element of romance or comedy where more of a story needs to develop, I think it leaves a lot for the imagination to think about. I wove in some of the thoughts about ghosts. Only young children and dogs can see them, they always appear in specific areas where they are safe, and they also appear in windows when no one is home. Also, by making the subject a child, I thought it would be easier to empathize. Although a little sad, it was fun to write.

Haunted

ELAINE FISHER

Peeking from a veil of thin clouds, a pale moon illuminated the grounds, casting an unnatural light on Vixie. Slowly, she made her way around the exterior of the old nursing home, her delicate fingers gripping a suitcase, her nervous eyes scanning the windows.

In one of the opened windows, an elderly woman outlined in a yellowish glow began to rant, and a surge of energy filled the air. Vixie kicked and trampled through the blood-red leaves on the ground. Stop! I don't want to do this. Her feet were not listening.

Vixie looked upward toward the window. Why can't you leave me alone? Her jumbled memories swirled around her as the rustling wind pushed her toward the building's arched entrance.

Something was wrong. The glass doors should have been overlaid with intertwining shiny brass branches and exotic birds, instead of this dull metal lattice covering.

Where was the doorman? In her mind, she could hear his familiar greeting —Welcome to Hotel Ballyhoo! Instead, there stood a quiet man in a dark jacket. After a while, his name appeared in her mind—Emanuel. He worked in the building. Now he stood near the doorway and looked at her, a glowing cigarette dangling from the corner of his mouth.

Vixie longed for a smoke. Memories of her diamond-embedded cigarette holder—an expensive gift from Joey 'Bulldog' Morelli—flashed in her mind.

A woman, dressed in pink nurse scrubs with a playful puppy design, approached Emanuel.

"Manny, did you hear those cries? I think it's Gabriella. I know I shouldn't be telling you this for confidentiality reasons, but her Sundowner's Syndrome is becoming worse."

Emanuel interrupted, "Lena, I'm aware of this. I work around our residents, day in and day out, and have noticed the changes in Gabriella. Usually, she's a sweet old woman always pulling me aside to say, 'Hello dear, so nice to see you again.' I can tell she's lonely and wants to talk. But there are times she makes no sense and later becomes agitated, especially toward the end of my shift."

"I worry about her, Manny. Especially when she wanders off at night. I hope tonight will be quiet for a change, but I have a feeling it won't."

"It's that time of year. Halloween. Haunted spirits. Full moon. Ahwoo!" He howled.

Vixie lingered nearby and listened to their conversation.

"You and your ghost stories. You're probably riling up the residents," Lena said.

"My ghost stories are only for you."

"Me—the non-believer?" She gave him a crooked grin and rolled her eyes. "Lately, the residents have been restless. More so than usual. These ghosts of yours must be out in full force."

"Only one. I don't know her entire story. I do know she's been haunting this place for over 90 years. My grandfather was a gifted psychic and ghost hunter. I've inherited some of his abilities. Throughout my childhood, I was told about this place and the ghosts that inhabited it. She's the only one from that time that still remains."

"Is she here now?"

"Yes," Emanuel said.

Vixie smiled at the acknowledgment.

Lena shook her head and watched the smoke from his cigarette float away like a thin apparition.

He lowered his head and muttered, "I know, I know, I'm trying to quit."

"Hope you do. But then—maybe you want to be with that old ghost." Lena snickered.

Vixie moaned under her breath, I'm not old. Only eighteen.

Emanuel looked at his watch. "I guess it's time for you to face the inmates."

He crushed his spent cigarette into the ground and opened the door for her.

Before the door closed, Vixie slipped in behind the nurse and gave Emanuel a nod. He nodded back and left. Once inside, she turned and looked back out. Through the metal lattice, the night sky broke up into tiny segments like a kaleidoscope. Vixie turned to view the lobby ahead of her, looked at her suitcase with all of her valuables. Where was the bellhop?

She followed Lena through the lobby, passing handkerchief ghosts floating from the ceiling, smiling jack-o-lanterns on the end tables, and plastic spider webs in the corners. What would the hotel's concierge think about these ridiculous decorations?

Her head was spinning by the time she reached a wide hallway. At the end were two elevators. Vixie felt a pull toward them that made her flinch. She got there in time to see a slit of Lena's pink uniform disappear behind the thickly shellacked, creaking, wooden doors. Where were the beautiful brass gates? This place was so confusing. She needed to go up to the top floor, but couldn't remember why. But it didn't matter since she could no longer push the buttons.

Vixie paced back and forth waiting for the elevator doors to open. A sudden urge to flee raged through her head, but the reason was beyond her grasp.

Then the elevator opened. Before she could enter it, an old woman inside shouted at her, "Get out of my way!" Vixie stared at her. Something nagged at her mind, but before she could remember, the woman plowed through her.

It was only human energy, but it hit Vixie hard and deep. The momentum created by this force zoomed through her, knocking her backward toward the lobby. She skidded into walls and furniture, whirling around like a tornado, knocking things over. Her suitcase went flying. There was a time when she was able to do the same thing to the living. This time she saw it reversed—a human manifesting the chaos. In the middle of the disarray was the old woman.

Again, the elevator opened and Lena dashed toward the lobby. She watched the old woman moving furniture, looking under chairs. Searching.

"Gabriella, when you wander off, I worry about you," Lena gently said, approaching her slowly, not to startle her. "What's wrong?"

The old woman ignored her, continuing her search, her face streaming with tears.

"Nappy! Nappy! Where are you, boy?" Gabriella bawled in the most mournful tone. She then slowly walked to the entrance doors, Lena alongside her.

Vixie picked up her suitcase and nervously followed them from a distance.

At the entrance doors, Gabriella moaned, "I've lost him, I've lost him. He must be out there… somewhere… somewhere… somewhere." Her body quivered for a moment, then stiffened with rebuke. "Napoleon. Bad boy! You'll just have to spend the night outside." Then she looked at Lena. "I'm tired. Can we go back up to my room?"

"Yes, we'll do that, but first let me straighten up this room." She picked up a jack-o-lantern from the floor, placed it back on a table, looked with troubled eyes toward Gabriella, and then continued her task.

Vixie followed them back to the wide hall with the elevators. They waited and waited. It seemed to take forever. Gabriella burrowed her head into Lena's shoulder and started to cry again.

Then the doors squeaked opened and Vixie rushed in. Gabriella shoved past her, giving her the creepiest grin. She had to get away from this crazy old woman.

Hurry, elevator! The top floor's Penthouse was waiting for her return. Vixie looked at the suitcase in her hand. Soon, she would be able to put her belongings away.

The morning sun streamed into the large room lighting up the wild collection of houseplants that grew toward the ceiling. These plants were different. Who replaced them? On the window seat sat Vixie's opened suitcase with her belongings spread out from the night before. She faced away from the window, the light bedeviling her eyes. With a delicate touch, she caressed the objects from her past, the only things her fingers could hold, could manipulate. Vixie was finally home.

Wonderful aromas wafted toward her—roasted coffee and cinnamon rolls. She called out, Joey, I think room service is here!

She yawned, stretched, and waited for him to come out from his office. He was always up at the crack-of-dawn doing business. She strained to hear his voice on the phone as it penetrated through the thick layers of time, gradually getting louder.

Yeah, it doesn't look good. It's a dog-eat-dog world. And I've just been eaten. Heard word that Gambino's sending out his chopper squad, tonight... yeah, it's Halloween night. You should stay away, too.

Vixie never paid much attention to Joey 'Bulldog' Morelli's conversations. As he often told her, don't worry that pretty little head of yours about my business. Your main business is pleasing the hotel's guests and me. Vixie remembered when she first met Joey. Her name was Vivian then. Boring, he told her and renamed her Vixie because he thought she was a little vixen. He got her a job as the head elevator operator during the day and a flapper on the speakeasy stage at night. It wasn't too much longer until she moved into the Penthouse. How did she get to be so lucky?

She continued to touch her belongings from her suitcase, the only things she had left in the whole world, most of them she received from Joey. Everyone called him Bulldog but her. Joey named her Vixie, but he never called her anything but 'hey babe' or 'doll-face.' She minded at first. But the expensive gifts, the last one being a long fur coat, made up for it.

Loud hammering and drilling interrupted Vixie's memories.

She glided down the hall, following the sound, stopping in front of one of the rooms to peer inside. It took her awhile to connect the names to the faces. The old woman. Gabriella. Now standing by the bed watching a young man work. The man who'd been smoking by the entrance. Emanuel. Vixie listened to their conversation, relieved that the old woman never looked her way.

"Hello dear, what are you doing? It's very loud." Gabriella spoke to Emanuel while covering her ears.

"These motion-detecting alarms will alert Nurse Lena if you need help through the night, Gabriella," Emanuel said looking up from his work. "She told me that you might have been looking for a dog last night."

After attaching an alarm to the door, Emanuel nodded to Vixie. He then went to the bed and attached another alarm to the mattress.

"Do I have a dog?"

"Maybe when you were young. But you don't have a dog now. Lena thinks the therapy dogs that came here yesterday might have triggered a memory from your past."

Emanuel bent down and put his tools into his toolbox. He straightened up and held Gabriella's hands gently in his own.

Her face lit up, then crinkled with confusion. "What about my dog?"

"Don't you worry about your dog, Gabriella, it's breakfast time. Why don't I walk you to the dining room." He laughed and said, "Then on to my next job—a plugged toilet, yuck."

Gabriella laughed. She turned and finally saw Vixie scowling at her.

Emanuel looked at the ghost and then the old woman. The tension in the air was thick. He said to both of them, "OK, girls, you need to be friends."

Gabriella's eyes darted back and forth between Emanuel and Vixie. Without waiting for him, the old woman rushed off toward the dining room.

Nervous energy slid through Vixie as she veered off down another hallway, the sound of his footsteps following her.

Along a wall, an old man, wrapped in a wool blanket in a geriatric recliner reached out with trembling fingers, the other arm hung limply by his side. Vixie looked down into his sunken haunted eyes, his face grooved with wrinkles. Hoarsely he whispered, "Help me, help me!"

She watched nurses and assistants walk by him as if he wasn't there. Vixie's eyes could no longer produce physical tears but she could swear her face felt wet.

Behind her, Emanuel whispered, "Poor Leonard, it's just something he does all the time and doesn't even remember doing it. He's fine. See, he's resting, now."

Emanuel's warm breath floated down on Vixie who shivered from the coldness that suddenly moved into the hallway. As she transfixed on Leonard, her hovering feet felt as if they were embedded in the ground. Fear had a firm, heavy grip on her and wouldn't let go. The words, 'help me, help me,' vibrated violently through her, racking her with pain, and she remembered calling out just like the old man did. And no one came to help her, either—the night that she died.

～ ☆ ～

Loud music broke through Vixie's unsettling memories. Her feet rose up from the ground and she was back among the living. She absentmindedly meandered her way toward the dining room. From the wall speakers, a deep, mellow female voice sang an old tune. A few residents joined in, but most slept in their wheelchairs, their contribution a snoring accompaniment. Brass instruments played in the background and Vixie was transported back to Hotel Ballyhoo's underground speakeasy. She smiled at 'Slidebone' Washington and his jazz band and their singer, Ruby.

Then the music changed and the Ballyhoo Flappers danced the Charleston on the speakeasy stage. The spotlight shined on Vixie.

A voice drifted toward her ear. "Hello dear, do you want to be my friend?"

Vixie ignored the strange request. Her attention was on all of *her* friends—the young, the rich, and the beautiful—who came to see her dance. She wildly twirled her long beads, flapped her elbows, and did tricky kick steps.

"Watch where you're dancing!" The voice was back.

Vixie felt the energy before noticing the old woman. With fearful eyes, she glanced around the room—the speakeasy had disappeared. The music had stopped.

Vixie watched the nursing home residents leave the dining room. One woman with a cane stopped in front of Gabriella.

"Gabriella, you were talking to yourself again."

"I was? Sorry about that, dear." Gabriella mumbled.

"Are you going to the Halloween Party after dinner tonight?

"Maybe…can I bring my dog?"

"Does he have a good costume to wear?" The woman with the cane laughed and laughed.

"I don't know." Gabriella said.

"Don't think dogs are invited anyway." She laughed again, more gently this time, and patted Gabriella's shoulder in a reassuring way.

Vixie listened to their conversation and another Halloween popped into her memory. Hotel Ballyhoo's Masquerade Ball—everyone was going to be there! Partying, dancing, and drinking! All that illegal glorious booze down in the speakeasy. All night long! Her costume was a fancy, sexy version of her elevator operator uniform. Joey's idea. She wanted him to wear a diamond-studded dog collar and she could lead him around on a leash. Vixie had to cover up her bruises with make-up after that suggestion. She thought she was being cute. But she forgave him. After the party, he was going to take her on a trip to Vegas. She was all packed and ready to go. Vixie remembered that she left her suitcase back on the window seat in the Penthouse.

As she made her way back, she took a wrong turn leading her down the hallway where Leonard slept in his chair, his uneven breathing rattling deep within his chest. She paused for a final look at him, a soft titter escaping from her lips. How silly to be afraid of this frail old man. As if he could hear her thoughts, his eyes blinked wide open.

Again he called out, "Help me!"

In a panic, Vixie flew down one hall and then another. I'm trapped in this maze. I'm lost! Finally, the Penthouse appeared in front of her. She grabbed her suitcase, made her way toward the elevators, and waited for one of them to open. When the doors opened, a family walked past her. The mother held back tears while reprimanding her teenage daughter. "We're not going to stay long. Stop chatting on your cell phone. Have some respect. Grandpa's dying." Vixie entered the elevator and waited and waited. Finally, it started downward and opened on the second floor. Vixie ignored the two nurses entering. With panicky eyes, Vixie all of a sudden remembered another time. Another elevator.

TAT-TAT-TAT. Rapid, piercing, staccato sounds startled her. She shrieked, grasping her chest, slowly sinking to the ground. As she pressed the gaping wound, the color red filled her thoughts. Then the door closed and the memory was lost. Until the doors opened and the shots rang out again. In shock, Vixie remained in the elevator, huddled in the corner, shivering, as passengers entered and departed. She rode up and down, as the doors closed and opened. It seemed endless. Until Emanuel entered the elevator and pressed the button for the first floor. He looked down at her and gave her a nod. When the door opened, Vixie looked up at him with frenzied eyes, her breath floated out, a frosty mist hanging in the air. The elevator was icy cold. She desperately wanted to leave but her feet were stuck in the past. Please, don't leave me, she begged to no one in particular.

But as with all of her memories, her violent death quickly dissolved. She rose in one smooth flowing movement and followed Emanuel, past the lobby with the plastic spider webs in the corners, and out the entrance doors. He lit a cigarette and waited for Lena to show up for her night shift. Vixie hovered nearby.

"Well, is your ghost out tonight?" Lena asked, taking the cigarette from his mouth, and crushing it out with her shoe.

"She is and I think she's figured out how she died. Now I know, too. She was killed in an elevator trying to escape during the infamous Halloween massacre. Her suitcase in her hand. The story goes: she was mobster Bulldog Morelli's moll and was going to Vegas with him after the Masquerade Ball. But he knew something was up and stranded poor Vixie. Everyone in the hotel died that night."

Vixie listened to the story, trying to understand it. Then his words disappeared from her mind. She looked down at the suitcase in her hand, trying to remember why she had it. The sounds of moaning and shrieking filled the night sky.

Through the opened window on the third floor, Gabriella bellowed, "Napoleon, you bad boy, come back here now!"

Vixie felt the wind charge through her as she looked at the old woman. The blood-red leaves swirled around her feet as she drifted back to the entrance. Again, she wondered, where is the doorman? With haunted eyes, Vixie followed the nurse through the doors, past the lobby to the wide hallway with the waiting elevators.

Inspiration

I wanted to tell a 'ghost story' from the perspective of the ghost. I felt the Roaring Twenties was a fascinating time for my main character to have lived and died in. It was interesting showing her confusion and fear as the place and time she found herself in kept changing while she endlessly relived her untimely death. The present-day nursing home setting had special relevance since my mother spent her last two years in one. It was hard watching my independent and competent mother slowly change to become more 'stranded' in her own world of sadness and dementia. I'll forever be 'haunted' by my memories of her, the nursing home, and its residents who all played a part in my story.

It's About Time

JENNIFER STASINOPOULOS

"C'mon! Live a little!" said Patrick as he prodded me out of my chair.

"Stop poking me!" I said, standing. "Go on without me. I'm fine here."

"You're fine here? When is the last time you went out?" he asked.

"Recently." I avoided his gaze.

"How recently?"

"I went to the grad Christmas party," I said, trying to sit back down at my desk.

"Tabitha," Shelby shook her head in exasperation. Even in the fluorescent aisle lights of the library, her curls reflected honey gold like a summer's day. "It's October."

"So?" I backed against the wall and glanced out my little window at the shimmering lake 13 stories below.

"That was ten months ago!" They both said in unison.

"I like it here," I said, trying to ignore Patrick's earthy scent, like leaves and spice. "I smuggled up Fred," I pointed to my little cactus, "I have a throw for when I get cold, and they even turn a blind eye to my tea and cookies."

What I didn't say out loud was that I didn't have to deal with people here. No one asked me for favors, no one judged me, and no one made cutting remarks. "Besides, I have a lot of work to do."

"You always have a lot of work," said Shelby, playing with the bangles on her arm. "You need to go out." As I had discovered in the month since I met her and Patrick, my new suitemates at Hollingsworth Graduate Dorm, Shelby wasn't one to take no for an answer.

Five minutes later, I found myself marching away from the library, its marble facade a muted white beacon calling me back to safety. I glanced up at Patrick and felt something in me thaw, loosening a cool joy that flowed like the first trickle of fresh water in a spring creek. It wasn't his handsome face that did this to me, not his velvet blue eyes or smooth olive skin. It was something else. He seemed a centuries-old man living in the body of a 25-year-old. In the one month I'd known him, we had developed a comfortable rhythm, spending countless hours chatting over late-night sandwiches after the main library closed. His tales of traveling the globe fascinated me, cracking open a door to possibilities I had never contemplated before. Sometimes I would catch him gazing at me lazily, a sweet curl playing at the edge of his lips, but beneath his laid-back exterior, I sensed a wild intensity that both drew me and set alarm bells ringing.

He gave me a lopsided grin. "There's no turning back now!"

"And what's a little time out of your schedule?" added Shelby with a small laugh.

Patrick's arm tensed on my shoulder. "What do you mean, Shel?"

She waved his concern away. "Just an expression! Take a chill pill!

"Don't worry, Patrick," I said. Their bickering made me nervous. "I don't mind losing a little time. You're right, I need to get out." His arm relaxed, and we walked on.

The crisp evening air and frost-glazed surroundings, sparkling in the moonlight began to work their magic on me. The warm weight of Patrick's arm slung around my shoulders and the music of Shelby's constant chatter melted some of my pent-up tension. Robed in glistening reds and yellows, the 100-year-old oaks standing guard over the quad seemed to whisper ancient secrets and warnings in the gentle October breezes.

At Fifth Street, Shelby started to go north, but Patrick stepped off the curb and headed west.

"Where are you going?" Shelby crossed her arms.

"To The Sunrise," said Patrick.

"You are kidding, right?" said Shelby in disbelief.

Patrick's jaw clenched. "I thought for the first time out, a little quiet place like that would suit."

"We've been through this already." Her eyes flashed with anger that didn't match the situation. "She needs to be among people."

"Yeah, well. That can wait," said Patrick evenly.

"No. It really can't. It's about time," she spat. "And I, for one, am very hungry."

"Hey guys," I waved. "I'm right here!" This was why I didn't like to be with people. They were too complicated..

Shelby's voice turned sugary. "I know this great place called The Library. You'll love it!"

Patrick sighed heavily. "The Sunrise would be ..."

"Hey!" sounded a voice from up the block. "What are you doing out here?" A figure in a black biker jacket and a red cashmere scarf stepped into the lamplight.

Our other suitemate, Clara, strode up to me without a glance at the others. She and I had been in the same dorm suite for two years, but I couldn't say I knew her any better than I did Patrick and Shelby. She had her friends, and I had... well, I had my work.

"We are going to The Library," I said as Patrick withdrew his arm and walked ahead a few paces with Shelby.

Clara glanced behind me towards the main campus library, my usual haunt.

"Not that one," I ignored Shelby's victorious expression. "The one on

Main Street."

"What? You? Having fun?"

"I go out sometimes," I said flatly.

"Yeah," she said with a knowing smile. "I bet the last time you went out was to the grad party at Christmas, and even then you only lasted to 8:30."

"Well, we are going out now," I said.

"We? What do you mean we?" Confused, she scanned the space behind her. I couldn't understand her coldness to our new suitemates. If they ignored her, they did so only because she pretended they didn't exist.

"Why don't you come?" I asked, regretting the words the moment I saw Shelby's frown.

Patrick, on the other hand, smiled at the invitation. "That's a great idea!"

Clara paused. "The Library, eh? Pretty swanky, but at least the prices keep out the riff-raff. Yeah, sure. I'll come."

She took my arm and walked to the front of the group. "I was supposed to meet Jessica, but she canceled last minute. What timing, eh?"

Patrick and Shelby silently fell in step behind us.

When we got there at 7:00, posing grad students and glassy-eyed undergrads filled the entry. Puddles of grey-haired administrators and professors dotted the great hall.

On our way to the bar, I picked up a brochure detailing the history of the restaurant. The ornate Georgian mansion, built during the infancy of the republic, had been renovated into an eclectic pub and eatery, where each room was decorated in the style of a different era. The bar, imported from Ireland, was made just over a half-century ago, before WWII. Each room had at least one bookcase stuffed with books, though some rooms had an entire wall of bookcases. Customers took and left books at their whim, so there was a constant renewal of reading material.

I got my drink, a Cider Sidecar Named Desire, and we followed Clara to a cozy room with a crackling fire. Patrick settled into one of the brocade chairs encircling a marble-topped coffee table, while Shelby leaned against the doorframe surveying the room. I set my drink on the coffee table, hung my coat on a lion paw hook by the door, and stepped over to the bookshelf.

Clara draped herself over a velvet button-backed armchair near the door and watched me, continuing the story she'd started outside, her lilting Tennessee accent growing stronger as the whiskey disappeared from her tumbler.

"...And when the professor found out I meant Paris, Tennessee, she was madder than a wet hen!" she ended, clinking the ice in her now empty tumbler.

Shelby, leaving the door to join Patrick, guffawed at the story. "Who'd have thought you could be the life of the party?" she said, slapping the top of Clara's chair as she passed, making Clara jump in surprise.

"Great story," I chimed in, hoping to cover the sarcasm in Shelby's voice.

"Huh? Oh, yeah. Thanks." She twisted and scanned the space behind her.

"I could have sworn someone tapped my chair."

"It was just Shelby," I said.

"Shelby?" Her brows knitted.

"Yeah, she walked away before you could turn around."

"Shelby... Right. That's funny," she said, but her voice held no humor. "Things seem a bit off tonight."

"Maybe it's the whiskey?"

"Naw, this is what I usually start the night with. In fact, I'm gonna get another drink." She stood up.

"Why don't you try something tamer?" I called after her. "That one seems to be playing with your head,"

Her eyes crinkled with laughter. "Ha! You're one to talk!"

The night could be better, but at least Clara was hanging out with us, even if she was a bit cold, and the rest of the group was actually talking to her.

Clara had picked the perfect room. Books filled the wall opposite the fireplace. I scanned the titles, hoping to find a book that would help ease the strange tension between Shelby and Patrick, who now sat brooding in his chair.

"Tabitha! Are you for real?" Shelby cried in exasperation as I pulled book after book from the shelf. "Haven't you read enough for one day? Come on! Sit down and drink your drink!" She waved a hand to the chair opposite her.

"Just a minute," I answered. *Vatican Treasures, Death at the Hermitage,* and *Love on an Iron Shelf.* I spotted a lighter title that suited my purpose: *Alaskan Outhouses.* I pulled it off the shelf, and held it up triumphantly.

"Hey Patrick, here's one that might catch your fancy," I teased.

I handed it to Shelby to pass to Patrick. When she took it, our hands touched. As if I had touched an open wire with a wet finger, a jolt ran through me. For a moment, Shelby's green eyes blackened into gleaming onyx orbs. A scream climbed my throat.

Everything skipped like a needle of a record player on scratched vinyl. My vision cleared and I found myself gazing at Patrick as he leafed through the book. "Hilarious!" he hooted. Shelby, leaning over the arm of her chair to better see the book, smiled sweetly. Her chin was lowered, but I didn't think she was looking at the pictures. Through the veils of her long lashes, she was watching me.

"Get you another drink?" she asked as if she were offering me the prize at a county fair.

I looked down at the empty glass in my hand. "I don't even remember drinking this!" I blurted. A wave of dizziness hit me. Sweet cider and cognac still clung to my lips and a delicious warmth spread through me. Had I blacked out?

"You know what they say about how time flies with fun," Shelby said. "Right, Patrick?"

But time hadn't merely flown by. It had disappeared. "I-I think I should go home." I tried to scoot forward in my seat, but I couldn't move.

"You're just not used to relaxing," Patrick answered in a soft growl. He glared at Shelby. "That's all this is, right? A night to relax? To live a little?"

A student in a red t-shirt that read, "Geology Rocks!" stopped at the entryway, swaying on unsteady feet. From the baby-smooth skin peeking through his scraggly blond beard, I pegged him as close to 21. "Here's an empty room!" He slurred over his shoulder. He turned back to face the room and his eyes caught mine.

"Oh! I didn't see you sitting there! What's your…" he started to say, but stopped abruptly and gasped. His eyes did this strange thing like they were going in and out of focus, and then his face blanched. He scanned wildly about the room, shook his head, rubbed his eyes, and looked back towards me, not exactly at me but at the chair I sat in. He backed out of the room, tripping over his own feet and falling to the ground. His friends started to step over him to come in, but he threw up a shaking hand to stop them.

"Don't go in there!" He gulped. "It's haunted!" Using the door frame, he pulled himself up and careened down the hall. His friends stuck their heads in to look for the supposed ghost and left without a word to us, except for the last guy, a short freckled student in large aviator glasses carrying a lemon-lime soda.

"Sorry about them," he winced. "It's his 21st birthday, and they've been celebrating for a while." He started to go but turned back. "Why don't you join us instead of drinking by yourself?"

"Uh, no, that's OK. I'm here with my friends." I tipped my head towards Patrick and Shelby.

"Whatever," he backed out again. "We'll be down the hall if you change your mind." His right hand twitched in a shy wave as he left.

"That was weird!" I forced a laugh. "I may be thin, but you can still see me when I turn sideways."

Patrick frowned. "Shel, you didn't–it's too soon!"

Shelby grabbed my empty glass headed towards the bar. "Be back in a minute."

"People don't always know what they want!" Patrick said to her retreating back.

Shelby returned with a pink chilled drink. She handed it to me with one hand, and with the other, she stroked my cheek.

"Are you OK? You look a bit pale."

An electric current coursed through me. The world stretched like taffy being pulled and then snapped back into place. I squeezed my eyes shut, trying to block the sensation. A low moan seemed to come from Shelby, but when I opened my eyes, she was silent, looking at me with concern.

"Ok, now?" She sat down next to Patrick again and picked up *Alaskan Outhouses* again.

"Sure," I lied, my heart pounding. A bead of sweat ran down my chest. Trembling, I tried to stand, but a strange numbness tied me down. I needed out. Run! I commanded my legs, but they didn't obey. Something was wrong, terribly wrong.

The glass Shelby had given me sweated in the heat of my hand. I jerked it to my lips, sloshing sticky strawberry and rum on my shirt, and drank deeply. My heart rate slowed. I was going to be OK I told myself. Everything was going to be OK.

Clara popped her head in the room. "Hey, Tab! I am soooooo sorry to leave you here alone." She looked around the room. "I can't believe no one else has joined you by now–it's getting pretty crowded out here!" She shrugged. "Anyway, I ran into my advisor. She asked me to join her and a couple of other grad students for a drink. Come with me. You'll like her." She said, urging me out of the room with a wave.

"No, you go. I'll just hang out with them." I said, throwing a glance at Shelby and Patrick.

Clara slumped against the doorframe, her face creased with worry. "I've really got to go. This conversation could make or break my opportunity to get the Fountly internship."

"Then go!" I forced a smile. "We are fine!"

"Go, Clara," whispered Shelby, "We've got things covered."

Clara hesitated, then came to a decision. "I'll get away as fast as I can, and we'll hang out the rest of the night. Promise." She caught sight of my second drink. "Take care–the ones with the umbrellas can be deceivingly strong."

She must have been right. The second drink relaxed me. From panic to calm in record time.

"Look!" Shelby pointed at a small photo in the book. "Isn't this the outhouse we saw back in 37?"

"Shelby!" Patrick's sudden anger made me jump.

"No worries anymore, Sweetie." She bent close to him and kissed his cheek. "It doesn't matter what we say. It's happening."

Patrick clenched his teeth, hissing, "We never agreed."

She shook her head. "I am not waiting any longer." She faced me and as I watched, the black of her pupils spilled across her irises into the whites of her eyes. "I need her potential."

Panic percolated in my chest.

A woman started in the room, grabbed the doorframe, and twirled back out, her flowing blue skirt swirling around her legs.

"Why aren't you going in that room–it's empty?" A man's voice boomed behind her. "All the others are full."

"It's got a weird vibe. Let's go upstairs. It's not as claustrophobic up there."

She was right about the vibe. This room–these drinks–I was imagining things. I needed out.

"I know you all are going to think this is strange," Straining, I pushed off the arms of the chair until I stood panting, my legs as heavy as statue plinths, "but I've never been dancing at any of the discos around here. I would love to go!" I said, hoping my toothy smile would make my panic pass for excitement.

"Great idea," said Patrick, rising to face me. "Let's go dancing." But he didn't take a step towards me or to the door. He stood unmoving, a white flag planted in the ground. Whatever battle they were fighting, he had lost.

Shelby rose and taking his face in gentle hands, she turned his head. Their gazes met. With rare tenderness, she whispered in a voice I could barely hear, "She is ready now. We take 40, but she only loses 10."

For a moment we stood as still as statues. I held my breath, but their chests rose and fell in unison. A silent minute passed until, as if punctured, he deflated. "Only 40." Defeat edged his voice. "No Rip Van Winkles."

"No Van Winkles," echoed Shelby, stepping back to create a clear path to me.

As he faced me, the creases of concern that lined his forehead smoothed and his expression hardened into one of lusty yearning. His blue eyes flickered into black onyx orbs, and on silent feet, he stepped behind my chair.

"What's–what's happening?" I could barely get the words out. Patrick put his hand on my shoulder, his fingers feather light. His voice tight with emotion, he leaned close to my ear and whispered: "Please forgive me." I tried to turn my head to see his face.

"Forgive you? For wha–"

He interrupted me and uttered the four last words spoken directly to me: "It won't be forever." Then there was nothing.

Hours later, in the grey of dawn, I woke up. It all felt so…off. I shook my head, feeling like I was coming out of anesthesia.

I stood up on shaky legs and called out for my friends, my voice small in the expansive mansion. Except for the creaks an old house makes as the sun overcomes the chill of night, all was eerily silent. In the fireplace, the ceramic logs lay cold, mocking the cheery glow of the night's fire.

I stumbled from room to room, calling out my friends' names and then for anyone at all, but there was no answer.

Had they really just left me while I slept? I made my way back to the room with the brocade chairs to grab my coat, but the lion paw hook was empty. After searching a number of rooms, I found my coat under the bar in a box marked Lost and Found. How could the staff be so utterly incompetent as to find my coat but miss the person sleeping in a chair not 10 feet away?

I groped for some sense in the situation, settling on the most obvious answer. It was a joke. My so-called friends had paid someone to pull this prank. Ply reticent little Tabitha with alcohol and catch her reaction on Candid Camera when she finds herself alone in The Library. An angry flush crept up my neck.

Righteous anger burned through the black numbness I had worn for so long. I was used to being ignored and going through the world unseen. Growing up, I had been no more than a ball and chain to my mother and had learned young the value of silence. The more I could become a mere furnishing in the room, the safer I was. But at this instant, I wanted to be anything but silent.

"You idiots!" I screamed, shaking with rage. "How could you leave me?" My voice reverberated down the hall, swirling dust motes in streams of morning light. There was no response.

The burning anger subsided as quickly as it had surfaced. "Friends just don't do that," I whimpered.

I caught my reflection in the mirror above the Irish bar. "Why would they do this to you?" I whispered. The forlorn image gazed at me with an expression that spoke of a horror I wasn't ready to accept.

"No!" I shouted back at her.

I was leaving–not just The Library, but I was leaving the dorm. I would demand a new room on the other side of campus. They couldn't make me stay with the kind of people who would do such a thing to a fellow student. I strode to the door only to find it locked tight with the kind of double deadbolt that needed a key to open. I ran to the back door and then the side door and found the same locks. Fine. I could wait for the morning staff. It wouldn't be long.

I lay my coat over the end of the bar and waited.

Within minutes, the sound of people approaching broke through my thoughts.

"Thank you so much for letting me in," came a ragged voice.

"No problem, but I can assure you that she is not here. The staff check and double check all the rooms," answered a man. Keys jangled and a second later the deadbolt slid open. In walked the manager followed by Clara.

"Oh my God! Clara!" I cried, awash with relief. I ran over to her. "I am so glad you are here! I can't believe–"

"What did the police say when you called them?" Interrupted the man, closing the door behind him.

"I didn't–I thought I had to wait 24 hours to report a missing person," she answered.

"Who's missing?" I asked, but she ignored me.

"That's a myth," he answered with a frown. "If you're worried about her safety, then call right away. Use the phone on the bar while I go check the rooms for–what is her name? Tyra?"

"Tabitha–her name is Tabitha." Clara picked up the phone with a shaking hand.

"Clara! Hey! Clara!" I followed her and tried to grab her shoulder, but my fingers couldn't touch her. Like the force between two magnets, the closer my fingers got to her, the stronger they were pushed away.

"What the hell!" I shouted. "Clara!" I got right up into her face, but she dialed the phone, oblivious to me.

"This isn't funny!" I pleaded.

"Hello?" she said into the telephone. "I want to report a missing person."

"Clara! Please–"

"Tabitha Eremitia." Pause "E-R-E-M-I-T-I-A, Eremitia." "Yes, I do believe she could be in trouble. She…" She leaned down on the bar, resting her forehead on her left hand. "she has been talking to herself."

She took a deep breath and listened to the speaker on the other end of the line.

"Yes, she mentioned new roommates a few times, but I am the only other grad student living in our suite - just us two."

She grabbed the phone tighter.

"Because I thought it was a quirk, you know. Like a tic or something. I - we hardly talked. She kept to herself. I thought last night… I thought that it might help. O God! I shouldn't have left her alone!" A quiet sob rose from her. I saw a tear splash on the burnished wood of the bar.

I backed away. "No, Clara… That isn't true. You know it isn't. Shelby, she is so sweet like sunshine in the spring, and Patrick, he is… he is … we share sandwiches," I stammered, but Clara didn't hear a word.

As she talked on the phone, her eyes flitted about the room, alighting on my coat.

She gasped. "Her coat! It is still here in The Library!"

She gripped the phone, listening impatiently.

"No, not a campus library - the restaurant! Hold on!" She set the phone down and grabbed my coat from the far side of the bar.

"Oh my God! It's her coat. Her keys are still in the pocket!"

The manager came back in. "I'm sorry, Clara. There is absolutely no one here."

"Her coat!" Clara held it up. "She left without her coat!" A small sob caught in her throat. "Or she was taken. Oh my God!"

I stumbled to the door. It was open now. I could leave. I could go home. I would find Patrick. What had he said? "It wouldn't last forever"? He knew something. He would tell me.

I grabbed the doorframe and pulled myself through, but at the edge of the first step of the landing, I hit an invisible wall. Tentatively, I reached my hands out and pushed, but whatever it was, it wouldn't budge.

There was a noise from behind me, and Clara burst out of the door.

"Clara!" I yelled, grasping at her red scarf. She breezed down the steps, tears glistening on her face. It was then the horror hit me full force. I was finally getting what I wanted: a chance to live unnoticed. I was stranded in The Library, my sanctuary turned prison. I wasn't going to leave this place, not for a long, long time.

Inspiration

The inspiration for "It's about Time" is an episode of the new Doctor Who, "Blink," in which creatures that appear like weeping stone angels feed off the potential of other creatures. The angels, when stilled with a stare just as they are about to attack their victims, sport stone teeth like those of a vampire. As moments of that episode drifted through my mind, I got to thinking about a kind of time vampire, one that had started human. I wondered what its moral compass would be, what would be the effects of his not eating for a time, and what would the effects would be on his prey. Time doesn't behave like the little pointy line gracing the pages of every elementary math book. And when it is consumed in "It's about Time," it isn't eaten like regular food. If you eat half a hamburger, then half is left on the plate. But if a time vampire eats 40 years, only 10 physical years are taken from the victim. However, the victim loses 40 years of potential. The repercussions of this is that the victim lives a ghost-like existence until she catches up to the amount of time eaten–she is a "ghost" for 40 years. In "It's about Time," a slice of interaction between vampire and prey is recorded from the viewpoint of the victim.

Ghost Diner

Julie Rule

There had only been a few clouds ten minutes ago, but now lightning was streaking across the sky and the rain poured down. The windshield wipers on the car were going full blast and Charlie could barely see the road in front of him. Few lights illuminated the winding two-lane highway.

It was almost as if someone was trying to tell him something.

His phone rang. It was his brother, the last person he wanted to talk to right now.

He let it go to voicemail. Charlie had completely abandoned the restaurant, and his brother was probably getting a little concerned. Of course, it was usually Charlie who did the worrying. There was no way they could keep that restaurant open more than a few more months. Another one of his brother's terrible ideas, and Charlie had given up his good accounting job for it.

A few minutes later, the phone rang again. This time it was his wife. Maybe she was worried about him. He couldn't talk to her, though. She had been right that it was a bad idea to open a restaurant with his brother, but Charlie hadn't listened to her. He cringed as he remembered some of their recent fights. He couldn't stand to tell her just how bad their finances were now. She would be better off without him.

A lightning bolt hit the ground uncomfortably close to his car. The storm was getting worse. He needed to find someplace to pull off, but he was in the middle of nowhere.

A light appeared up ahead. Charlie squinted through the windshield. He could just barely make out the red "Diner" sign. He didn't remember a diner being there before. Maybe it was new. He hadn't been out this way for years.

Charlie slowed down, searching for the turn to the diner. He nearly missed it and had to slam on the brakes. Thankfully, nobody rear-ended him. Of course, who else would be out on a night like this? He shouldn't be either, but here he was.

Pulling into the parking lot, Charlie was surprised at all the old cars. Was there some kind of car show going on? A few newer cars mixed in with the old Chevys and Fords but not many. Even an old Model T sat in the lot. When was the last time he had seen a model T? There had to be a car show, he thought. Why would so many people be at this diner all the way out here, a good 50 miles from the nearest city? They also must have decided to stop because of the rain.

He looked at his phone. No signal. Well, there were probably no cell towers anywhere near here either. And who would he call? This was supposed to be a fresh start.

He looked around in the car for an umbrella, but that was one thing he forgot to bring. For the first time in his life he wasn't planning what he would do next, and he was already paying for it.

Charlie sat in the car for a few moments, waiting for the rain to subside, but it wasn't letting up. He sighed and opened the car door. He was soaked before he even started running toward the door.

All conversation stopped as he walked into the diner. The waitress and customers turned to stare at him.

Charlie stared back at them and noticed something odd. Was there some sort of costume contest along with the car show? Charlie was no expert on fashion, but some of the people there looked like they had come straight out of the '70s or '60s or even the '20s. One man in a booth looked like a hippie with long hair and a tie-dyed shirt. There was a woman in the booth behind him in a bright yellow dress and a beehive hairstyle. A woman sitting on a stool was undeniably dressed as a flapper.

"Um ... hello," Charlie said, looking around as everyone stared at him. What were they looking at? Yes, he was soaked from head to foot, but it was pouring out; of course he would be soaked. That didn't change the fact that he was the only one dressed normally here.

The waitress walked up to him, looking him up and down. "We've been waiting for you. We have a seat all ready right over there."

The waitress pointed to an empty booth between a man who looked like he just came from a '50s private eye movie and a woman in bell bottoms. That was when he noticed something else. Everybody was sitting alone.

Charlie turned back to the waitress. "What do you mean you've been waiting for me? How could you have been waiting for me? I had no idea I was coming here. I didn't even know this place existed."

The waitress didn't answer. "Take a seat," she said, gesturing again toward the booth.

Charlie looked at the booth and then back toward the door. He shivered. He told himself it was just because he was soaked. Still, he could warm up back in the car. There had to be someplace else he could stop.

"You know, I'm not really that hungry." Charlie slowly moved toward the door. "I think I'll just keep driving."

"Don't be silly." The waitress set a coffee cup and napkin down on the table. "This storm isn't ending anytime soon. Take a seat. Have some coffee."

He looked back out at the storm again. The waitress was right. No matter how strange this place was, it probably wouldn't hurt to just have some coffee while he waited for the rain to let up a bit.

"Alright," he said, taking off his wet jacket and sitting in the booth. "Just one cup of coffee."

The waitress walked back up to the counter and came back with the pot of coffee. "Just let me know when you want a refill, sweetie. My name is Marge, by the way."

"I'm sure one cup of coffee will be enough," Charlie said. "The storm has to let up at some point."

"The storm never lets up." Charlie turned around. The man who spoke was wearing a trench coat and a hat. He was sipping coffee, too. Charlie looked around and realized that everyone there was just drinking coffee. Nobody had any food.

"What do you mean, the storm never lets up?" Charlie asked, frowning. "It has to end at some point."

The man shook his head. "You'll see."

What strange people this diner attracted, Charlie thought. Still, as the minutes ticked by, it started to seem like the man in the trench coat might have a point. The rain hadn't let up at all.

Well, he would just have to find his way through the rain. He didn't want to stay in this place a moment longer. Charlie threw a few dollars on the table and headed toward the door. Everyone was staring at him again.

"Where are you going, sweetie?" Marge asked. "It's still pouring out there."

"I'll be fine," Charlie said, opening the door. "Thank you for the coffee."

He had only started drying off in the diner, and he got soaked again on the short walk to his car. He was relieved as he sat down in his car. That diner was the strangest place he had ever been. Surely he could find a motel to stop at somewhere along this highway.

He put the key in the ignition and tried to start the car. Nothing happened. He tried again. Still no sign of life from the engine.

"But I just had this serviced," Charlie grumbled. He tried to start the car again and again, but nothing happened.

He sighed and trudged through the rain back into the diner. Everyone stared at him again, but Charlie ignored them and walked up to the waitress.

"My car won't start and I can't get a signal on my phone," Charlie said. "Do you have a phone I could borrow?"

The waitress shook her head. "No, we don't have a phone here."

Charlie stared at her. "What do you mean, you don't have a phone here?"

"Who are you going to call anyway?" Marge asked, leaning against the counter. "I thought you were leaving everything behind."

Charlie's heart began to pound. "How do you know that? And why did you say you were expecting me? Why don't you have a phone?" He was shouting now and gesturing around wildly. "Why is everyone here dressed like they're going to some crazy costume party? With cars to match. What the hell is this place?"

"Do you really want the answer to that question?" Marge asked. "Maybe you should just sit down and have another cup of coffee."

Wait, he thought. This must be a nightmare. He was at home in his bed, just having a crazy dream. He just needed to wake up. He pinched himself. Nothing happened. He pinched himself again. Why wasn't this working?

"This isn't a dream." It was the man in the trench coat again. "I can't tell you how many times I've pinched myself over the years. I never wake up."

"Years?" Charlie gaped at him.

"Yeah, I have no idea how long I've been here. No one does. My name is Ernie, by the way. You might as well get to know all of us. As far as we can tell, we're stuck in this place forever. The storm never ends."

Ernie went back to sipping his coffee and staring out the window. Charlie turned back to Marge again.

"What does he mean, we're stuck in this place forever?"

"Well, that's what you wanted, isn't it?" Marge said with a smile. "You wanted to get away from everything. Now you'll never have to go back. Why don't you sit back down? I'll get you another cup of coffee."

Charlie dragged himself back to his seat. He stared out the window again. The storm wasn't letting up. It was raining just as hard as it had been when he arrived.

Marge came back over and filled up his cup with coffee. Charlie looked around again. No one else worked here. He sat there, drinking his coffee and tried to figure out what to do. Maybe he could just walk. Surely he would get somewhere eventually. He could even hitchhike if he needed to. Charlie turned around to look at Ernie.

"Have you ever tried walking? Finding a car to pick you up?"

"Of course," Ernie said. "There's no way out of here. Feel free to try it, though."

Charlie got up and walked out the door. This time, nobody stared at him. They just kept drinking their coffee.

Charlie trudged toward the highway. He was oblivious to the rain at this point. Even the lightning hitting the ground didn't scare him. He could swear that it just kept hitting in exactly the same location every time.

He walked and walked. Where was the highway? He felt like he had been walking for hours.

Then he saw it. Lights ahead of him. His stomach dropped as he realized it was the same diner. How was this possible?

As he walked back in, only Ernie looked up at him. "Told you so."

Charlie slogged back to the booth and collapsed into it. He took his phone out again and tried to check his voicemail, but there was nothing there. He might never know what his wife or his brother wanted to say to him. Right now, he would give anything to talk to them.

Marge walked back over with the pot of coffee.

"I just want to go home now," Charlie pleaded. "Isn't there any way I can go back? Isn't there any way out of here? I should never have left home."

Marge sighed and shook her head. "Everyone here regrets leaving in the end. When they realize they had something to go back to after all. More coffee?"

Inspiration

I was inspired by The Twilight Zone and the spooky stories I've enjoyed since I was a kid.

At the Other End

Tauna Sonne leMare

I was born in the fifty-fifth century since mankind acknowledged their existence. As I sit here, in fifth dynasty China, I am Pan Yu'er. I am the Chief Dancer in the Imperial Court of Emperor Xiao Baojuan. In the future that existed I was Ying Mae. I studied ballet for seventeen years and waited for my chance to become a renowned dancer. You might note the time discrepancy.

I am writing this letter, hoping it will be discovered in the future. If our journey to the past was successful no record will have survived in your time. Tests will prove my writing style didn't exist yet and language differences could not have existed in the past or your time either. Carbon dating of the pigments, and parchment I write upon, will prove ancient origin 25 centuries earlier. This should serve to authenticate the history I am about to relate.

We can only hope that your circumstances now are better than ours were when we took the extreme measures of traveling back in time. I am a member of one of several teams of time travelers sent back to our past in order to change your future world for the better.

We had peace and prosperity. We even attempted to treat all people equally. I am no expert, so I do not claim to understand what went wrong.

But, it did, and the outcome was so dire, we realized we were facing the end of days.

Our world became overcrowded. Eating animals was outlawed, since they required more sustenance than they provided. Food animals were eliminated completely. Then those requiring space in the wild, and lastly pets. By the time I was born, no animals except man existed for one hundred years. No, that is not quite correct. No animals except women existed.

Men were genetically altered at first to remove traits of violence. Then for less altruistic reasons and more aesthetic ones. Lastly, their numbers were reduced. With multiple wife situations, fewer were needed for reproduction, especially with an already overburdened population.

Decline in vegetation followed due to climate and lack of necessary animal and insect interaction that contributed to their existence. In spite of good intentions, everyone was not equal. People are all different and trying to pretend otherwise, diminished our value as individuals. I know that is how I felt. No matter what people said, their behavior proved that they believed as I did, but were afraid to say so.

Our world was bleak, except art in all forms was raised to a level reaching adulation and worship of aesthetics. It became a way to control people, give them something beautiful to focus on, where beauty no longer existed in nature.

Those who excelled in any of these art forms became national treasures, ensuring special treatment for themselves and their families. I studied ballet to the exclusion of all else. My goal was to be one of the acclaimed. If benefits for my family resulted, that would be alright with me.

I hope our interference created a better world than the one we left behind. I am only including my history, to explain how I was recruited for the project and perhaps, as a cautionary tale. Do not be blind to your surroundings, ignoring truth. This is how my involvement began.

With hope, Pan Yu'er

My elder sister Ahn married Mr. Gao, becoming one of four sister wives, who each had predetermined duties. When our parents died, sister and her family, with their four children, took me in. Ahn and her husband paid for my training and were the sole support of our combined family.

When Ahn's husband died, it left her to provide for the entire family. Still, she encouraged my dreams, for it gave the whole family hope of a better future. When Ahn became ill, the doctors said she needed a transplant. Money had never been plentiful. With funds no longer coming in, the outgoing trickle became a flood.

I never considered giving up my dream. I didn't think it fair. The burden of a family was not mine. I might have wallowed in self pity until Ahn was dead, but any decision was unnecessary. Unbidden by me, I received several applications from the Benevolence Institutes.

These were groups established under the Law of Due Process, to help people who had fallen below what was considered the average acceptable level of achievement. I was insulted, but it could provide a way out from under a burden I was expected to carry.

Everyone agreed I was talented, but I had never been lucky enough to dance for the right people. I always wondered if there was something hidden behind the eyes of those officials who never committed to giving me a contract.

I have small feet. Their size didn't stop me from dancing, but in a world of big feet, perhaps people found mine distracting. They didn't say so, but lack of a contract, or eye contact did make me doubt myself.

Applications received without request seemed confirmation that some-one thought my small feet were odd enough to qualify me for intervention.

If I were chosen, the institute would fulfill a wish in exchange for a personal sacrifice to show their benevolence.

All I had to do was humiliate myself by agreeing with my silent critics. If chosen, at least Gao Ahn could take care of the family once more, and I could still dance.

∽ ☆ ∽

Each edifice I entered made me cringe. I was used to places where you bumped into someone anytime you moved. These places were obscene in their grandeur, and each more disturbing by its waste of space.

I turned in the applications and took the exams of Worthy Purpose. On four separate occasions I was turned away. Then twice I made it through the lines of endless petitioners. It was the final line. My last chance with only one other woman left.

She won her plea because her ears stuck out. How could that compare with Mae's life and death problem?

I would have laughed, if I weren't so close to crying. All pretense that this had been about Ahn's life aside, I admit I felt sorry for myself. I sat in my chair, two hundred empty ones for company. No one remained, but I couldn't stand I was shaking so. I came here to be humiliated. My mood was darker than the approaching night.

"Excuse me Miss, are you Ying Mae?" asked a person so nondescript that I barely noticed him. Interviewers were women of stature. Any man present had only been an assistant, and pleasant to look at. This man had no more bearing than a fishmonger on a street corner.

"Yes," I answered. "Why do you ask?"

"I belong to an institute. Not one that you applied to of course. One less known. The Prioress of the Great Council shared your application with us. She knew what we were looking for and thought perhaps you would fit our project."

"I am not looking for work. I need permission for my sister to cheat death, the organs needed to do so, and a great deal of money for her care and our family."

"We read all that in your application. All your needs will be met, if you take on an assignment for us. You only need dance on your toes. Your paper work indicates you can."

"Is this a joke? Yes, I can dance, very well thank you. Everyone agrees, but they look at my feet and that's the end of it. So what if I wear a child's shoe size. Now, you say I can dance for others as I have always wished? Why should I believe you are willing to fill my needs, by fulfilling my wish as well? Do I look stupid?"

"Oh, I'm not pulling your leg, Miss Ying, I assure you," said this creature, who had the audacity to chuckle at his rude comment. *I had half a mind to hit him over the head with my chair.*

My displeasure must have shone on my face, because he bowed incessantly to placate my temper.

"You do not understand. We need someone with your skill, and extremely small feet. The person you will dance for is royalty, Miss Ying, and he likes tiny feet. Please do not disappoint us. Just a few formalities and every thing can proceed."

"I will be paid in advance, and you can arrange for the medical care my sister needs? Whatever the cost? It sounds too good to be true."

"Everything you request is in the contract. Only first, may we inspect your feet, please?" the little man bowed again, several times.

I don't think he ever said his name, he was just beige. *He was offering a contract, so I would think of him neutrally, as Mr. Beige. No need to know his name.*

I put my feet forward warily. I bit my lip, removed my shoes, and made a vow. I had no intention of baring my feet and then be turned down because of their tiny size. If that happened this time, I was going to crush this insect's skull.

"They are very small." A man I had not noticed spoke from a shadow. I jumped. It was one thing to show my shame to the beige toady, but to this stranger? I suddenly felt naked. I tried not to look at my shoes sitting there, one size bigger than I needed.

"I know, I am sorry, but I really am a good dancer." Why *must I always apologize?*

"Do you mind showing us your style? Mr. Wong and I have heard of your exquisite form," said Mr. Beige.

"I have no ballet pointes with me." I couldn't look up. I knew Mr. Wong must be a dance expert. I could feel my face color in blotches. He was there to judge me unworthy.

"Here is some lamb's wool for cushion, and silk you can wrap around your feet. A full pointe is not required. When you perform, these are the same items you will be expected to use." Mr. Wong spoke as he placed the fabric in my hands gently.

I looked up for the first time, speechless and bug eyed. I cast my eyes down immediately.

Mr. Wong wore a silk suit and spoke with a French accent. I would have to be blind and deaf not to recognize the tall, elegant Wong Sai. He was the most illustrious dance entrepresario of all time and a poster of him hung above my cot at home.

I wrapped my feet as instructed and took a breath. I emptied the room in my mind and danced in a way quite singular, I was perfection. This was my dream come true whatever happened.

"Bravo! You are magnificent. Arrangements for your sister's care will begin as soon as you sign the contract." Mr. Beige had spoken.

Far more important was the nod of Mr Wong's head and bow he made before me.

"Is the performance soon?" I asked my voice trembling.

"No, actually it will take place a little over a month from now. We thought you would like to see your sister come out of surgery and in recovery before you leave."

"Leave?"

"I didn't say, did I? The venue is in another country. As mentioned, you will be dancing for royalty. You might encounter some troublesome behavior, royalty expect things. Certain dangers are associated with the location as well."

"You mentioned none of that. But, I expected there would be a catch."

If I had been thinking at the time, I would have caught the mention of another country. We didn't have separate countries. We were one large united world. I might also have wondered if my sister really was sick and how I came to be approached, but I didn't– then.

"We are confident all will work out to everyone's benefit. Foreign relations can be tricky. You do understand, I'm sure."

"Yes, I suppose." I answered but I wasn't thinking. I could die on the spot and be happy. I danced for The Mr. Wong Sai. To have him acknowledge my talent, was everything. The fact I was to perform before royalty was immaterial.

I couldn't wait to comfort Ahn, and tell her about her own good fortune.

To think, if Ahn hadn't gotten so sick, I would never have been given this opportunity. How strange fate can be. *At least that is what I thought at the time.*

"Deciding incident established at all six historic time frames.

Check.

Ten global locations, verified.

Check.

Confidence is high gentlemen. We have calculated every aspect and possibility. You can all be proud of your efforts. Our future rides with them," said a small man.

Two hundred technicians never took eyes off The Director, as they stood and applauded. He was inconsequential in the eyes of most women. Outsiders might pass him by as if he didn't exist. But, He was a great scientist, and the person on whom mankind's survival rested.

The women of the Great Council tolerated him only because their genetically modified males didn't have a brain between them. They needed him, which gave him certain license in exchange for his facility with their problems. Otherwise, he was ignored, leaving him to blend into the background.

Luckily, some women realized that the world needed change, and believed his solution might be the only hope for human survival. If he succeeded, he wouldn't be thanked or remembered. He might not even have been born. A fact he secretly prayed would be the case if his project worked.

The mission's second in command asked,"Don't you find it ironic the future of mankind relies on women?They led us to the brink of disaster, yet we rely on the outcasts among them for our salvation."

"It is these women in particular, that give me hope for success.. While each takes something with them to beguile their sisters, it is their personal need to be best and survive that will win our cause. Each one of them has refused to fit into the neat box our society has put them in. That trait has not been bred out of them, otherwise there would be no hope for us at all." He nodded to the man at the controls.

The mission coordinator nodded back.

"Gentlemen, monitors indicate our teams are in position. Countdown for the first launch on my mark. Subsequent launches to follow at designated intervals. If you believe in any god, pray to him now."

The countdown began at ten and descended to one.

The mission coordinator pressed the button. There was no turning back, no rethinking the final solution. The time bombs were on their way.

 ∽ ☆ ∾

"None of you felt the flash of nausea?" the girl asked.

Once the cold black moment passed, Ying Mae addressed herself to the two men present. She ignored the girl who spoke, "I'm not the only one? Is she my competition?"

"I'm not your competition, I'm a fellow conspirator. Dance is not my area of expertise. My name is Mumu by the way."

Mumu glanced at the two men, who were looking green at present. They needed to display some gumption when the doors of the time capsule finally opened. If the doors opened.

"So, I am the only one chosen?" asked Ying Mae

"You are," said the oldest of the two men.

"He means on this team you are the only dancer," said Mumu.

"This team?"

"Why do you have to complicate matters?" asked the massive hulk. His voice high pitched like a woman, startled Mae. It was quite contrary to his form and manly features.

"She has a right to know. Forewarned prevents needless mistakes," said Mumu.

"Know what?" asked Ying Mae.

"The basic plan. This old man, Pan Baoqing is your uncle now. He gets us where we need to be. Then Court Eunuch Woo, the heavy set dude with the voice of a diva gets us positioned in Xiao Baojuan's court among the Imperial Concubines. No small sacrifice on his part," Mumu said with a giggle.

"Sacrifice?"

"Yours is dancing for that lecherous emperor and all that might entail. Ours is setting the stage for your success." said Mumu.

"Where is this place?" asked Ying Mae.

"A better question would be when. China, in Qi, about the year 350. You will take the place of a minor historical figure here. Our information is vague. Then dance. Hopefully with the desired effect. Four centuries later in Southern Tang, Yao Niang will be replaced. But, you have to make the first step count."

Mae's new uncle stepped forward, "You are crucial to the plan. Become your new name. You are Pan Yunu or Pan Yu'er. History gives both versions, who knows which is right, so pick the name you like best and be her. Leave it to historians to spell it wrong. Remember that, and we might survive."

The Eunuch Woo added, "If you do your job to perfection, you give the next team a better chance to help change society as we knew it."

"I'm Mumu, as I said. I was trained to be a spy, infiltrator, and manipulator of thought. I will wish out loud, that I had your delicate crescent moon feet."

"I wasn't told why my foot size and ballet is important now. What else haven't I been told?" Mae asked. Mid-question she remembered she was now Pan Yu'er and stood straighter.

"The Emperor has a foot fetish, something about the Buddhist legend of Padmavati, under whose feet lotus springs forth. You need to dance seductively, appear to be floating on air, so that he desires you and moves you up the concubine chain. Simple as that."

"Once I have him besotted with me and my dance, how do you fit in?"

"I am the thought that whispers in the ears of the other concubines. Make them envy the gifts the Emperor will bestow on you, and fear your rise in status. Make them want to dance like you, better if they can. Which of course they can't, because of their big feet. They also lack the intense training that has altered your musculature and skeletal structure. It is why you dance as you do, and will prevent them from doing the same. They will try anyway, especially when I tell them the real benefits of small feet and dance," said Mumu

"Like what?"

"I'll make something up if I need to, depending on what will manipulate my audience best," said Mumu.

"To what end?"

"Women control our world. Multiple wife situations gave them the platform to achieve power. Men, happy with the sexual benefits, did not anticipate the strength a group of women bonded for a single purpose possess. Men reduced their own numbers for sexual greed. We hope to sow seeds of mistrust in other women. We must set them on a course of self survival and jealous competition. Win at all costs."

"You expect women to be that stupid?"

"Yes, to change the world. Change isn't all balanced on your toes. More will come as I said. Some prepared to squeeze their guts in like sausages so that debilitating style makes them catch their breath, and other women mimic them. Some will take over high heels reserved for men and raise them to a new height in torture. Anything to handicap women to the point they forget about control and focus on attracting one man all their own. The endeavor is immense and hopefully will unbalance the current state of affairs in our time," said Mumu.

"We are attempting to change the past, you mean?"

"Got it in one. Doe-eyed you might be, but not dumb as the Dodo," said Mumu.

"What does an extinct bird have to do with anything?" asked Mae.

"Why everything! If this doesn't work, then we will be extinct in short order," said Mumu.

Eunuch Woo moved into Pan Yu'er's path as he spoke, "I believe in our task so completely I gave up my manhood, my balls, for this. The girl you are replacing was not up to the task. You must be. Oh, she was a good dancer for her time, or history wouldn't have mentioned her at all. You were born with elegant feet and have been trained for this. It is fate."

Mae's new uncle pushed Eunuch Woo aside, "Women banned war! Stole our manhood. Everyone shares the bounty, even if they sit on their arses. Peace at all costs and equality for all was a horror story not a fairy tale."

"But, aren't those good things?" Mae strained to keep up, she never thought much about what others did.

"You can't be that naive," Mumu said looking dazed. "What do you think led to our world. We ingest chemically constructed food and recycled water. They keep the worst hidden from people so there won't be riots. You aren't stupid, you had to realize."

"I only recently noticed that the Institutes had an excess of land," said Mae, her eyebrows squeezed together in thought about something beyond dance for once.

Eunuch Woo stood with his arms crossed and chin cocked judging her, "You didn't volunteer out of a sense of duty. What did they promise, to coax you into this?"

"Duty to family. My sister's surgery, and money for her and our family," answered Mae annoyed at her motives being questioned. She didn't add that she did it in order to dance.

"You don't have a clue," Mumu said, a tear in the corner of her eye.

"They didn't lie. Ahn had surgery and they gave the family a nice new home, before I left."

"It might have all been play acting for your benefit. Or if it was true, they displaced twenty or thirty people to give your family space. Killed somebody, perhaps a volunteer, to give your sister that transplant. Everything necessary to give hope."

"Hope?"

"Hope that you would be part of this. They might have faked your sister's illness just to rope you in to their plan. They needed you. All so men can rule and play at war," Mumu sighed.

"Why should men rule? How can it be better with wars?"

"There will be wars and plagues to cull off the undesirables, the weak, the lame, and the old," said Uncle.

"You are old," said Mae looking down her nose at him.

"Yes, and I'm here aren't I?"

"Why would anyone want chaos?" asked Mae..

"Order without chaos is extinction, oblivion, nothingness," said Mumu.

"Then they will send for us, we will go back?" asked Mae

Her new uncle laughed, "There were no plans to go back, that would not be possible in either case. Win or lose. Look around you. Things grow, animals live, look out the porthole, not a person in sight. Vast empty space. Why would we want to go back. It is like heaven here, compared to where we came from. Here we are back in the garden."

"Pan Yu'er," Mumu bowed. "If nothing changes back in the future, then by now humans are extinct. If we change the future enough, where we left doesn't exist any longer. Your sister or any of us might not even have been born. Who knows how many generations would be wiped out along the way back."

"We are stranded here? That was always part of the plan?"

"Yes."

"How are my feet supposed to change anything?"

"I was wondering when you'd ask. If women don't have small feet and they want small feet, they probably won't stop at anything in order to get small feet. Remember the fairy tales where the wicked stepsisters cut off their own toes to fit into the special shoe? Even fairy tales contain a kernel of truth."

The doors to the Time Capsule opened.

"Break a leg," said Uncle.

"Not something to say to a dancer, that's for actors," said Mumu.

"I know. This is the greatest part I have ever played," said Uncle.

Mae took a deep breath and exited as Pan Yu'er She took on an attitude of total disdain.

May sat cross legged on the floor painting a sign with the words *My body my decision* in blood red.

"You wouldn't believe the crap women put up with in the old days. I thought corsets, makeup and high heels were bad. At one time women in China broke their bones and bound their feet. They could barely walk, but they did it for over a thousand years. For what? Supposedly, great sex muscles and perverted men. Give me tee shirts and jeans."

"I know I'm not giving up my sneakers. You about done there, May? If we don't get moving we'll miss the bus to Chicago. Then we'll get stuck with another of those jerks in office."

"Not this time Ann, there are close to a million women joining us all around the country. We need more women in office for sure, 2020 should be our year. Over 65% of the men are with us on this one."

Inspiration for At the Other End

Catholic countries and the Protestant ones used different calendars. France and England from January till March were in different years, months and days for 200 years. Merely crossing the English Channel would put you in a different time. Actual dates of importance have been adjusted to try to agree, when in reality they did not. Some countries were still on a different calendar as late as 1920.

The year in the story says, "since the existence of man". In fact according to the old Chinese calendar 3761 BC. and according to tradition, the Hebrew calendar started at the time of Creation, placing 2018/2019 at the Hebrew year 5779. Of course 20,000 years would be somewhat more accurate, but I went with a date according to earth's oldest traditions.

Separate races, religions, etc. do not exist as entities in the story, as they have a society that in being "all equal" make no such distinctions. I have made 2020 at the end, because it is our world as it is, that they have created. Just after the year they left,

All the ancient people in China mentioned really existed, and did just what the story said they did. The dancer, the emperor, the uncle are all given their real names and can be googled.

Foot binding in China, corsets and high heels worn originally by men became female attire and became more and more restricting. All part of our actual history.

In addition the world's civilizations started out as matriarchal, including Japan, with Hamiko (170-248 CE) a shamaness-queen of Yamataikoku in Wa (Japan) Statues exist the world over, similar to the Venus of Willendorf, dated (c.25-20,000 BCE). All women, no male statues that ancient exist.

So the idea for the story started as questions. What if the world had stayed matriarchal? What if our past hadn't gone the way it did? Would we do as they did to create the world we have now? Would women have avoided wars and been so socialistic that they drove the world to a different type of extinction? The story ends with our world as it is now, for better or worse.

Lady Eve and Adam

Susan Wachowski

The parasol blocked the gear from turning and slicing through my trapped arm. I hadn't thought to bring a knife, even hidden in my skirts or corset. A simple tea party, the gentleman had promised. He was a viscount—*had been* a viscount. His twisted bloody legs stuck out from beneath the housing of the large steambox that powered these gears. It was a good piece of engineering that still attempted to run the airship now in burning pieces around me. I looked away from his smoldering trouser leg with a deep breath and blocked out the hints of other bodies, passengers and crew, scattered around me from the crash. There was no time to fall apart, I needed to get free from these meshed gears.

"You-birds look in need of assistance, my lady-birds."

Adam, the viscount's butler, rose from the wreckage and made his way toward me. Normally a reliable German automaton, he had an apparent 'birds' speech error, one empty shoulder socket with dangling wires, and an absent portion of his hair, well, his wig. Wigs on an automaton were impractical and silly nonsense. My father and I never used them on our prototypes. Wigs simply set the average man or woman at ease, seeing the familiar dashing head of hair and mustache on a butler, the lovely blonde bun on a maid. But obviously trouble to keep them tidy and attached, not dropped into your soup, or fallen into your bath.

Even damaged, my heart lifted to see him still mobile after the crash of the viscount's luxury airship, *Precosity*.

"My arm is tangled in this contraption, and the gear insists on turning, cutting off all circulation. Are you functional enough to help remove my arm from its grip?"

"Happy-birds to be of help-birds."

His operational hand reached through the hole of the large aggressive gear wheel, gripped the fabric around my arm and ripped the cuff and sleeve of both blouse and jacket from the metal teeth. I tumbled backward as he let go, once clear of the insistent gear. Adam removed the parasol with another hefty yank. The larger gear screeched and spun until steam whistled through growing cracks in the piping. Something clanked, pinged away above my head. In a final woosh of billowing white vapor and smoke, the steambox went silent. I was left with the wind, the waves, the crackle of small fires in the wreckage, and the whir and rattle of Adam.

"Your-birds parasol, my lady-birds." He extended the battered parasol to me, but I paused in taking it. He offered it to me exactly as he had the book I'd forgotten on deck mere hours ago. Like he'd handed me the teacup moments before the airship lurched in mid-flight. Before the sudden plummet to this blighted bit of land somewhere off the Mull coast of Scotland. The fault probably lay with a broken valve in the turbine coupling, or the *Precosity* would have exploded instead of crashed.

Adam politely waited with my parasol. He had issues with his speech circuits, but his civility to me in the midst of chaos made my breath catch. I could not cry yet. I took a moment to calm myself and focused on the work to be done.

Using the parasol and his arm to steady myself, I brushed at my ruined skirt, as if anything would help the burned and ragged hem. "Thank you, Adam. We must look for survivors and offer what help we may. Then we will need food and shelter."

"Certainly-birds, my lady-birds. Might-birds I suggest that you assess your own wounds, while I search the wreckage-birds?"

"My own wounds?" Checking my own situation as I'd been unable to do while trapped, there was nothing wrong with Adam's power of observation. Burns covered my calves above my boots, throbbing now that I stood, and my head ached badly enough to make me wince as I leaned over to look at my leg injuries. Blood ran along the side of my face, soaked through my once-pristine white blouse and trickled into my cleavage beneath the corset. Reaching up, my fingers touched a large painful cut over my ear. My arms were scraped, and the deep slice to my hand that had been caught in the gears still bled.

Adam anticipated my needs, popping back with a medical supplies chest. "Your-birds hand looks in need of stitches, my lady-birds. May-birds I assist-birds?"

He cleaned the wound, as I sniffled and did my best not to jerk my hand away from the sting and pain. I assured him I'd be fine through a clenched jaw, as we carefully stitched the gash closed.

He would have continued being my doctor if I'd not insisted I could see to the rest. "Please, continue to search for anyone else that may be in need of medical attention."

"If-birds I find supplies to assist your comfort, I shall endeavor to bring them to you, my lady-birds."

"Very good, Adam, I'll be fine for the moment."

His tilted gait as he walked away concerned me. Could be from the missing weight of the arm, or the dent in his head. He systematically coursed through the smoking wreckage of the engine, the bits of deck from the shattered airship, and the shredded balloon responsible for the *Precosity's* lift. He picked up and studied a twisted cart from the galley, then turned over one of the couches, the plush gold velvet now blackened tatters. The smoke made my eyes tear so much I had to look away and wipe them.

Inside the medical chest, I found a plentiful supply of everything needed for myself and other survivors. I used the cleansing solution on my leg burns as best I could, applied soothing lotion, then ripped my petticoats and used them as bandages. After seeing to my head wound as well, I tucked everything safely back into the chest and looked for Adam.

Grass and stone surrounded the crash, with a few gnarled trees that had escaped damage. The airship had left Glasgow and headed northwest, flying above the beautiful landscape of the Isle of Mull, out over the sparkling waves of the Atlantic dotted with myriad small islands off the coast. I whispered a prayer of thanks we'd not come down in the chill water.

"A simple tea excursion, dear Lady Digby, to brighten a dreary day," the viscount had airily enticed me, his invitation calculated to boost his suit of marriage so he could run my father's company, Digby & Associates, Automaton Engineering and Development. We'd set off for an afternoon of quiet entertainment on the *Precosity*, intending to return before going to the theater that evening. A play? Yes, but though I searched my memory I could find no detail of which one or any of my evening plans with… well, how embarrassing to forget the viscount's name. Certainly, he would have been my companion for the theater. I sat on a nearby rock and tried to remember, but nothing came to me beyond the horrific vision of his mangled legs beneath the steambox. I let out a slow breath, wincing at the sharp pain within my skull. Obviously, my own brain had some damage, as had Adam's.

I blinked at the sudden shade, startled to find Adam once again stood before me. Had he finished his search for survivors already? The sun glared much farther along the sky, but it had seemed such a short time since Adam left.

"My-birds lady, I have found none of the other crew or passengers in any condition to revive or assist-birds. There-birds is a more suitable seat for you, though, in a modicum of shade, if you will follow me-birds."

I searched his glass eyes and pale skintone, soot-stained, metal face for some form of familiar comfort. He waited expectantly for my answer, but my vision blurred and such bereavement engulfed me that I could not speak. He crouched before me and his remaining arm encircled my shoulders. I sank against the gray vest beneath his black morning coat, bedraggled as it all was, and wailed into his chest. No one to see me, no one to report what an absolute shameful mess I was at that moment. My human companion maid, Abigail, was gone. The hopeful viscount who'd invited me on this excursion was gone. The friendly crew that had greeted me upon arrival was gone. I was alone. Except for Adam.

"If-birds I may enquire, my lady, are you in need of sustenance-birds? Perhaps a nice cup of tea and a teacake?" He let go and produced a singed handkerchief for me.

I made myself presentable and slowly looked around with an eye to-wards my uncertain future. "Adam, where will you find a whole kettle, cup, and teacake? We will need to consolidate food, establish a drinkable water source, and create a shelter for the evening."

"Very-birds good, my lady-birds. I-birds am certain I can see to these requests, even in these trying circumstances-birds."

"Lead me to this spot of comfort you mentioned." I swayed as I stood and clutched at Adam for support. There, no more than two steps away behind another rock, lay the broken body of the captain, his neck severed almost completely, and his deep blue coat now a wet mess of deepest red. I could not stop staring at the body. I knew there'd be so many more.

"Adam, would you be willing to help bury these poor souls? Or at least cover them in orderly fashion for when help arrives and they can be returned to their families." I shuddered at the Captain's vacant eyes and wondered if I could remain standing if faced with sweet Abigail's remains, my young maid and companion no more.

Adam pulled a broken green velvet chaise from the wreckage and dragged it behind him as he led me away from the crash to a cleaner patch of scraggly grass and bushes. He twisted the remaining two legs off the chaise and set it neatly on the ground, assisting me to lie down. I tried to remain conscious, but exhaustion lulled me to sleep.

When I awoke, for a brief moment I lay in my own room in our country estate outside Glasgow, late to join Father in the lab where we worked on our latest prototype. The smell of smoke soon made me realize a fire blazed outside the doorway of whatever dark room I'd slept in. Memory of my circumstances returned.

I stepped out to find a passable hut built around my chaise with metal sheets salvaged from the wreckage. I sat on a newly bolted bench to warm my hands at the crackling fire. Sorted piles of parts lay scattered on the blackened grass of the crash site. On the far side, I saw the fabric of the *Precosity's* balloon, trimmed and laid out neatly over rows of lumps, held down by pieces of metal and rocks. I could only whisper prayers and turn away as the sun slowly set.

"My-birds lady, if you please, allow me to present a small supper and water for your thirst and for bathing-birds." Adam appeared with a covered tray of sandwiches, of all things, and a pitcher of water inside a large bowl.

I devoured the first sandwich and eased my dry throat with the water. "Amazing, Adam. How long have I slept?"

"A-birds day, my lady-birds."

I frowned at having slept so long with so much happening around me. My injuries must have been more severe than I thought. "Let me check your quadrary speech circuits. I think I can fix that 'birds' issue."

With standard tools retrieved from Adam's thigh compartment, I repaired some of his damage, including his arm that he'd discovered amidst the debris. A few wires replaced, a rotor and flexor cobbled together in the low light of the evening fire, and he was almost serviceable, even if the aesthetic was ruined. I removed the remaining hair, preferring the bald look on him. I also noticed that someone, probably the viscount, had installed additional upgrades to his programs, such as camping and first aid, accounting for his wide range of services displayed since we'd so abruptly arrived here. Upgrades were the rage among the rich and powerful, and I was grateful to the viscount, whoever he had been.

Adam flexed the fingers on the new arm, one of them not quite curling like the others. Clasping the errant digit, he bent it back into place and moved his fingers quickly in sequence with satisfaction. "Thank you, my lady, I feel more normal. I did not expect a lady to—"

I growled in frustration. "I long ago realized I am not a woman, Adam. I am an engineer." I'd heard the comments often in my life. *Women did not learn such mechanical things. A lady did not enjoy circuitry and steam engines.* "I partnered with my father to build prototype automatons and experimental circuits. I may be Lady Eve Digby, but I assure you that I am as educated and accomplished as my father." I snapped the lid of the toolkit closed and handed it to him.

Adam straightened his ragged vest and gave a small bow. "My apologies for angering you, Lade Eve. I am also sorry for the recent passing of your father. I overheard the viscount tell the captain when he planned yesterday's outing."

"I'm sorry, too, Adam. Father left me alone with a group of ancient men who think they can run the company without me, in spite of me, and surely handle finding new scientists who can take over my father's research. As if a mere woman could never deal with such matters."

Adam placed the toolkit back in his thigh compartment with care. "Digby Automatons are among the very best in the world, Lady Eve, far surpassing my own self."

"They are indeed, thank you. My father is not two weeks buried and the company board wants me married forthwith to a husband they can reason with. They'll make a shambles of our family's company."

I blew out a breath as I remembered my indignation when they'd suggested - *suggested* - that I choose from their list of acceptable bachelors. I had stormed out, but what could be done? I finally agreed to a meeting, and chose the viscount at random, but insisted that I would not marry for their convenience. I was more qualified than the board to run Digby & Associates; I simply needed to find a man who would agree.

"You seem reasonable to my programming, Lady Eve."

"I am well educated in physics, alchemy, and engineering, but those bloody men insist on shoving me aside. They've yet to realize they hold nothing but the factory without me. I have father's research secured, though they control the purse strings."

"You handled my repair very competently, if I may say so, Lady Eve."

"Thank you, Adam." I took in a huge breath and let it out slowly, calming myself. "You've seen nothing that indicates rescue or search parties? We should have been missed by now."

"Nothing, Lady Eve."

I stared at the blackened ground and then out towards the horizon, searching for the lights of a ship at sea or in the sky. I sipped the tea Adam handed me and wondered to what lengths the board would go to control Digby & Associates. As the sole remaining Digby, my mother and brother having passed from a fever before I turned sixteen, I had buried myself in my education and then joined Father in his research. Now, at twenty-four years of age, the board considered me an unreasonable woman and in their way. With me gone, the company would be turned over to the courts to award ownership to the board, as I'd not yet named an heir in the new will our family's lawyer had drawn up upon my father's death. Without me, the company was theirs. I reconsidered the reasons for the crash of *Precosity*.

The smells of the spilled and burnt oil, and the taste of ash and death in my mouth, were unbearable. I drank the rest of my tea in one go.

The following fortnight began and ended, each day, with Adam's cheerful 'good morning' and 'goodnight'. I switched his depleted battery with a fully-charged unit from our meager salvaged pile each evening before bed. I woke eager to discover what he'd constructed in the night——building a better hut, improved cooking fire, a pantry, and sheltered bathtub. Adam taught me to fish off the rocks along the shore. With his assistance, I arranged to boil the seawater and collect the steam, making certain I stayed hydrated. We kept our large bonfire burning and the smoke rising as high as we could with the planks from the wooden deck. I tinkered with Adam's cognitive core programming. And every chance I could, I searched the horizons for signs of rescue.

One evening I sat beside the fire, indulging in a bit of wine. A single bottle had survived intact. Mesmerized by the flames that licked along the wood, pieces of the Captain's desk, I looked up, alarmed, as Adam raced toward me. His glass eyes focused on me and his hand raised as if to strike. I screamed and cowered, I'm sorry to say. When all went still, Adam stood over me with a rather large snake held above my head.

"So sorry about the snake, my lady. Attracted by the warm fire, no doubt. A nice change from fish, don't you think, Lady Eve?"

He skinned the reptile and placed it over the fire to roast as I composed myself. My thoughts warred between thinking he'd malfunctioned and was about to kill me despite all programming, and the realization that I'd come to think of him as more human than that viscount I still could not name.

That's when I saw it.

A light glowed in the sky, out over the sea, heading toward us. It inched closer and grew larger. An airship! I couldn't speak and simply pointed.

Adam turned to see what had caught my attention. "You are rescued, Lady Eve!"

Yes, the airship would come and I'd be tucked away to recover while those heartless men rearranged Father's company and found another suitable marriage match to keep me under control. They'd lock me out of the lab, take away my own research. Force me to the altar and a marriage bed, so they'd not have to deal with a woman in charge.

I wiped away tears. "Adam, do you ever wish to be free?"

"I am a servitor, Lady Eve. That is my programmed purpose. I was owned by the viscount, and his family will have my disposition now."

"You've become more to me than a mere servitor. Is that all just your programming, your training? Merely the expectations instilled within you?"

"I do not have the freedoms a human would, Lady Eve."

"You mean the freedoms that any man would. My own freedom is very limited now that my father is gone. But I refuse to be used in any such manner." I stood and piled more wood on the fire, making sure the airship would see us. "I think I can take back and hold my father's company. If they will not allow me to head the company, I believe I could even start my own, if you would assist me."

"You will purchase me?"

I hesitated at the plan forming in my brain. "Yes. I will purchase your freedom." It wouldn't be easy, outrageous even, but if it worked…

"Adam, would you marry me?"

"Lady Eve, I don't believe humans marry automatons."

"There is no law against it."

"If this would help you, my lady, I would accept such a proposal."

"I'll marry you and we'll run my father's company together. You gain freedom and upgrades. The board will be apoplectic, but my father's lawyer will help us, I'm certain. He's a forward-thinking man who's always done his best by me."

I grabbed a long piece of burning wood and waved it back and forth as the airship came closer. Its foghorn sounded, signaling we'd been seen. I watched the future approach, already working out the cognitive programming updates for a Gentleman Automaton and Husband.

Inspiration

I chose a steampunk genre as I am currently working on a series. The news that day brought up a plane crash and I found my idea - a crashed airship and a stranded woman who must rely on a broken automaton. She's a strong woman up against the barrier of Victorian male-centric thinking, but she could overcome it. Stranded, but saving herself in more ways than one. I didn't even have names until I realized they were male and human female alone on an island, and they became Adam and Eve. I was also, at the same time, working on a historical figure bust of Lady Digby, a late 1800's woman who led a wild life. There was my inspiration for Eve Digby - who could Lady Digby have been in a steampunk altered universe?

The Ruin of Alder Lincoln

Yolanda Huslig

The camera hanging from the ceiling recorded every move Britta made. Creepy.

On Earth, she'd watched the Martian colonists doing ordinary things, like eating and working, on the reality television series *Life on Mars* and wished to be one of them. Now, after a week as a colonist in Discovery Settlement, the cameras spooked her. She shivered and peered inside the open drawer in Habitat-1's pantry. Empty. The third drawer she tried contained food, prepackaged single serving packets. Emergency rations.

"What are you doing in here?" Niels, the colony's leader, barked at her.

Britta jerked, trying not to look as guilty as his tone made her feel. How did he know she was here? She glanced at the camera. Why did he care? Skinny, like all the colonists, he towered over her. He'd arrived six years ago, one of the first colonists. They'd set up the colony, rolled out the long strips of solar panels, deployed the first greenhouse, and planted the first crops.

"Um. I'm on the cook team this week. They sent me for pasta and sauce." She squirmed under Niels' gaze.

"They sent a rookie in search of supplies?"

"I volunteered. Thought it would help me get oriented."

"Find it and get out. I don't want you loitering in the pantry."

She let out the breath she didn't realize she was holding and pulled out the next drawer. Empty again.

He glared at her.

Several drawers later, she found the pasta and sauce. She rummaged around but didn't find any protein to flavor the sauce. "When will the CMM get here?"

He squinted. "What?"

"The Clean Meat Machine, you know, the one that grows beef, for instance, without the benefit of a steer?"

"We're supposed to get one of those?"

She gave him a sidelong glance. How could he not know after the big deal Fred made of it? "Yes. In the spaceship we came in."

Four new colonists, including Britta, landed eight days ago. Shortly thereafter, the rovers picked them up and brought them to the settlement.

He shook his head. "No such machine was on the lander."

Britta straightened. "What? There had to be."

"I inventoried the supplies yesterday. Nothing like that was included."

A chill ran down her spine. Six months before Alder Lincoln sent them to Mars, Fred Huff, the company's CEO, had called her team of astronauts into his office. His eyes bored into each of them in turn when they shuffled into the conference room. Those eyes and his beak of a nose reminded Britta of a hawk about to strike. Her stomach quivered. She found a seat at the table.

"We have a tremendous opportunity with the Mars colony." Fred paused and leaned forward. "Britta, right? You're a nutritionist?"

"Yes." Her scalp tingled. Was he going to fire her? Unlike NASA and other government space programs, this one had chosen people with odd credentials to be astronauts: writer, software engineer, public relations expert as well as technical specialties like chemist and physicist. Her occupation shouldn't be out of line.

"What is your assessment of the situation on Mars?" He asked.

She blinked, took a deep breath. "From *Life on Mars*, I'd say they're doing well. I don't see any issues."

He nodded and pulled back. "We intend to train you on our Clean Meat Machine and send you there with one."

Her heart jumped. Wide smiles appeared on her teammates' faces. They'd waited years to hear that they were going to Mars on the next flight.

"Find what you were looking for?" Niels leaned toward her, his tone flat, quiet, intruding.

Britta jerked, nodded, gathered up the pasta and sauce, enough for all twelve colonists, and headed for the galley, Niels right behind her.

That evening, when Britta finally returned to her quarters, where there were no cameras at all, she logged onto her laptop. There, right at the top, an email from NASA blinked at her. From NASA? Intrigued, she clicked on it.

It said, "We're accepting applications for our next astronaut class. We have reviewed the application you have on file. Your credentials match our requirements. Please respond to this email to set up an interview."

What? She'd applied for that position two and a half years ago when Mars Ho!, the company she worked for at the time, announced they'd run out of money and would miss the next launch window. The hope that she would go to Mars had withered to a dull ache in her chest. She panicked and applied to NASA. They never replied. Good thing, too. Alder Lincoln purchased Mars Ho! and resumed the launches. She laughed. They were slow.

The next day, Britta found Niels unloading the compost from the toilet in Hab-2. The camera hanging in the corner of the ceiling pointed at him, red light blinking. She stood outside its range, watching.

He raised his head. "What?"

"What are you going to do with that?" she asked. The camera rotated to include her when she spoke.

"Greenhouses," he continued to shovel.

When the wheelbarrow was full, she said, "We need to find out what happened to the Clean Meat Machine."

He dropped the shovel blade to the ground and leaned on the handle. "Actually, I was hoping for solar panels this shipment, not people."

"It should be here. That was the whole purpose of sending us," she said.

"What do you want me to do?" He glared at her.

She sighed. "Find out what happened to the CMM."

"I have to deliver this first," he put the shovel on top of the compost and trundled the load to Greenhouse-2.

She followed him in. The air was drier than she expected for a greenhouse. Three tiers of plants on her left and two on her right, bean, potato, and squash, basked in the light from the fixtures running above each tier. No light penetrated from outside the dirt-covered tunnel.

Evania, the petite woman in charge of the greenhouses, sat on the floor, holding a water pump the size of her fist. Plastic tubing snaked between it and the cabinet below the bean plants. She stood up to let Niels and his wheelbarrow pass.

Britta touched a droopy leaf.

"We get that sometimes. A dust storm started this morning. Water supply is down." Evania punched her finger into the soil.

"Why aren't the plants larger?" Britta asked.

"Low power. Whenever something happens to the solar cells, they reduce the power to the greenhouses. It stunts the plants. Sometimes it's so bad I need to replant."

The lights dimmed.

Britta's heart raced. "What's happening?"

"Dust storm must be getting worse." Evania patted her arm. "Relax. Even during dust storms our array makes enough power to run all our critical systems."

Britta moseyed down the center aisle past Niels to the half-full, waist-high pool at the end. The water filtration system gurgled. Four living fish swam around in deep water. A dead fish floated upside down on the surface. She frowned and looked over her shoulder at Niels, half way between her and Evania.

"What's wrong with the tilapia?"

"Ask Evania," Niels scooped another shovelful into the finished compost bin.

"Not enough food," Evania called out. "I'm trying to maintain the population until I can find more food for them."

"One of them is dead."

Evania threw her head back. "Another dead fish?"

She pushed herself to her feet and rushed to the pool. Hands on hips, she blew a strand of hair out of her eyes. She raised her head toward the camera hanging from the ceiling and waved an index finger at it.

"We need more tilapia eggs and food for the tilapia! Do you hear me, Alder Lincoln?"

Britta wanted to stick her tongue out at the camera but feared corporate retribution for that act of defiance. After all, it was the income from the reality show that supported the colony.

"What should we do with the dead fish?"

"Compost pile." Evania returned to the water pump.

Niels handed the net to Britta and stood back while she netted the fish and dropped it in the pile to be composted. She watched the live fish swim in circles while he finished loading the bins.

She missed windows. On Earth, when something bothered her, it helped to stand by a window and watch the birds, or the dogs walking their humans, or whatever else was outside. Even a window onto Mars' stark landscape would help.

Niels set the shovel in the empty wheelbarrow and came to stand next to her.

"I'll send Fred a message asking him about the CMM." He took the wheelbarrow and left the greenhouse.

∽ ☆ ∼

All members of Discovery Settlement ate dinner together most nights. Fostered a sense of community.

On this night, the screen on the wall showed the next episode of *Life on Mars* and the red light on the camera in the corner of the ceiling flickered. She was beginning to realize the scenarios on the reality show were an idealized version of real life in the settlement, tailored to show viewers what Alder wanted them to see, success. No one sitting at the long table in the common room of Hab-1 paid much attention to it until the commercial touting Alder Lincoln and its products proclaimed, "Today the Mars colony received a 'Clean Meat Machine.' They now have all the meat they need."

Tired, hungry faces looked up. These colonists had left everything behind for a one-way trip to Mars. They'd all wanted to be part of something bigger than themselves, to extend the reach of humankind into the cosmos by colonizing a second planet.

"Alder Lincoln is going to take care of us after all," a tall, big-boned woman at the end of the table said.

A short man in a gray coverall waved his bean-filled tortilla at the camera. "Then why do we have to put up with low rations?"

"We were better off under Mars Ho!," a red-headed woman said.

"They had no money to support us," a blond, medium built woman said.

"They blamed us for that. Our videos weren't spicy enough." The man in the gray coverall glanced at the camera in the corner.

Someone laughed.

"Why did Alder Lincoln buy us, anyway?"

"Isn't it obvious? Publicity stunt."

A dark man tapped his handheld with slender fingers. "No ship landed here this week."

"Hey, Niels, where is this meat machine?"

He looked up with a fork half way to his mouth. "I sent Fred an email asking that very question this afternoon. He hasn't answered yet."

Silence.

"Maybe we should ask Mission Control," Britta said.

"Go ahead," Niels said. "It's your machine."

Britta pulled out her handheld and sent the message.

After the meal and the clean-up, Britta received an email with the CMM's Martian longitude and latitude.

"I have the coordinates," Britta danced up to Niels. Soon they would have all the meat they needed. She showed him the coordinates on her handheld.

Niels' head drooped.

"What's wrong?" Britta asked.

"Those coordinates are on the other side of the planet."

Sadness descended over Britta like a shroud.

Dreams about empty drawers in pantries, cameras spying on one's every movement, and disappearing Clean Meat Machines kept waking Britta up at night. She felt like the walls were squeezing in around her. Why did she want to come to Mars again? Why did she listen to the siren song of Mars Ho!, a company with the goal of putting humans on Mars. Forget about waiting for the hardware for the return trip to be built, the rockets that could lift the colonists off Mars or the spaceship that could bring them back to Earth. They were sending people now, on a one-way trip, using the hardware that had been developed to send probes.

In the middle of the third night, she sat up and pulled out her handheld. Twelve colonists, four habitats, each starting with food for four colonists for two years. But four colonists had been here for six years and four had been here for four. How much food was left? Hab-4's pantry should be full. It'd arrived along with Britta's team. What of the other three?

Only one way to find out. She pulled her robe on and tied it, slipped her handheld in the pocket and set out. She slipped past the cameras, their little red lights remained unlit, and started in Hab-1, going through the drawers, ruffling through their contents, and recording them on her handheld. An app broke down the data into calories, carbohydrates, fats, proteins, and fiber. It wasn't until Hab-3 that a camera revved up and turned toward her, the little red light blinking.

Halfway through Hab-3's drawers, someone grabbed her by the arm, covered her mouth and shoved her into a closet with mops, brooms, and buckets, and closed the door behind them. The light on a handheld went on. Niels leaned against the closed door in his robe, not a foot away from her. It gave her a queer feeling in her stomach.

"What are you doing?" He hissed. "Who are you?"

"Let me out," she tried to push him out of the way.

He shoved back. "You want this conversation to go on international television?"

She shook her head and crossed her arms.

"Good. Now, what were you doing in the pantry in the middle of the night?"

"Why do you care?"

"Are you Fred's spy?"

"What? No, of course not."

"I ask again, what are you doing in the pantry?"

"Inventorying our food stores."

"Why?"

"We don't have enough."

"Not enough to accommodate people's midnight snacks, that's for sure."

"You think curtailing midnight snacks will solve the problem?"

"It will help."

"Not enough."

"How do you know?"

"I calculated the number of calories available in the pantries versus what each colonist needs. At this rate, if we relied solely on the pantries, we'd run out of food in twelve months."

"You forgot the greenhouses."

"How much do they produce?"

His shoulders sagged. "The greenhouses never worked as well as the scientists on Earth said they would. The delivery Mars Ho! skipped was a gut punch for us. We've been in trouble since."

"How are you going to stretch what we have to last twenty-six months until the next supply ship arrives?"

"Are you sure you're not a spy?"

"I'm not. I live here."

"You're the nutritionist. Work out a plan and we'll review it."

"Why don't you have all the greenhouses deployed?" Britta asked.

He met her eyes. "Power. It's all a question of power. I asked Fred to send us more solar panels and/or an alternate power source. He sent us people and a phantom Clean Meat Machine instead."

Six months to the day after Britta received the first email from NASA a second one arrived. It said, "We have almost completed our assessment of candidates for our next class of astronauts and noticed you have not yet set up your interview. Please respond to this email to correct this discrepancy." She'd stared at the screen for a long time wondering why NASA didn't pass her over when she neglected to reply the first time.

Having accepted Niels' challenge to manage the food stores, she'd spent those six months worrying about calories and food production, calculating calorie requirements versus available calories. A two percent reduction in calorie intake across the board and a ten percent increase in output from the greenhouses would allow them to stretch their food resources until the next supply ship arrived. With the additional solar panels the ship would bring, they could deploy more greenhouses, increasing food production, and they would be well on their way to becoming food self-sufficient. All they had to do was make it through the next twenty months.

She replied to NASA. "I appreciate you're considering me for this position. However, I can't interview for it. I'm already on Mars."

They'd responded, "Thank you for your interest. We'll keep your application on file."

After focusing for so long on the food situation, she felt stale and cooped up inside Discovery Settlement. She volunteered to help harvest water.

Today, she walked beside Rover-1, a four wheeled multifunction vehicle about the size of a small pickup resembling a farm tractor, with a manipulator arm and a wing of solar panels. It pulled a trailer containing a load of Martian sand, dust, and rock. She followed Evania, Rover-2, and its trailer. Evania wore the body-cam.

Niels had tried several times to send a rover to bring back the CMM. On the last attempt, they'd almost lost Rover-1. Niels decided it wasn't worth the risk.

It felt good to see the horizon, to feel the sun, weak though it was. Britta imagined the wind blowing through her hair, although the spacesuit she wore protected her from it, as well as the carbon dioxide atmosphere, and the low temperature and pressure.

They approached the back of the settlement, eight structures resembling two story tuna cans, each large enough to house four people, lined up side by side. Walkways connected their second stories. Half were Habitats, half Life Support Units that provided the Habitats with electricity, air, and water. Two of the Habs sported tails trailing out their backsides, covered with dirt.

Britta had spent a great deal of time in those "tails" working with Evania to increase greenhouse output. And Evania had a thriving colony of thirty tilapia, enough that once in a great while they had fish for dinner.

The rovers skirted the end tuna can to reach the water processor chutes in the front of the Life Support Units.

Ten solar panels, each a football field long and about four feet wide, stretched out like the wings of a bird on the ground in front of the Habs, half the panels on one side and half on the other. Spacesuited figures with brooms swept the panels. In the last six months, the colony had eked out enough power from that solar array to produce two harvests from the greenhouses with a third on the way. Someone, Tomasz, the electrician, by the blue stripes on the arms of his spacesuit, bent over Solar Panel-1.

Rover-2 stopped at Life Support Unit-2. The water processor chute opened and the rover unloaded the sand, dust, and rock into it. Rover-1 made a sharp left turn, accelerated to its top speed of 25 mph, and headed for the solar panels. It bore down on Tomasz.

"Tomasz! Behind you!" Britta screamed, forgetting how loud it would be in his helmet over the intercom system.

"What?" Tomasz straightened and rotated. Face to face with the rover, he jumped to the side. The rover drove onto Solar Panel-1, missing him by a foot.

The air whooshed out of Britta's lungs. He was safe.

Evania jerked around. The spacesuited figures moved toward Tomasz. Niels, by the red bands on his arms and the body-cam, led the way.

The rover kept going.

"Hey!" Tomasz chased it.

Lot of good that will do. Britta rushed forward. "Use commands the rover understands."

"Stop!" Tomasz screamed.

"Ouch!" The broom wielders protested.

"Not so loud," Britta said.

The rover halted, on top of Panel-2.

"Go forward, slowly," Tomasz said.

The rover jerked forward across Panel-3.

"No! No! No!" Tomasz balled his fists.

The rover continued across Panel-4.

"Rover One, halt," Britta took care to enunciate clearly.

The rover ground to a halt.

Niels reached Tomasz when Britta and Evania did. The others clustered around them.

"Are you all right?" Britta asked.

"Yeah." Tomasz's voice shook.

"You sure?" Niels used a calming tone.

Evania touched the keypad on Tomasz's chest display. "His vitals seem okay for someone who's just had a scare."

He brushed her off and walked to Panel-4.

Niels spoke to the crowd. "Everything seems to be fine here. Go back to work." He followed Tomasz.

The broom wielders returned to sweeping. Evania moseyed back to Rover-2. Britta joined Tomasz and Niels. After visually inspecting the panel, Tomasz dropped to one knee and hooked up the multimeter hanging from the strap around his neck.

"How's it doing?" Niels asked.

"Function is compromised. Crushed where the rover ran over it," Tomasz said. "These panels are thin. They weren't built to hold the weight of a rover. Energy output will be decreased until we receive replacement solar panels."

"Decreased by how much?" Britta held her breath.

"Depends on how many of these solar cells I can fix."

Britta swallowed. She saw yellow leaves in her mind's eye. Granted, they were supposed to learn to live off the land but they couldn't very well eat Martian dirt. Or could they?

⌒ ☆ ⌒

The next morning, Britta found Evania in Greenhouse-1 touching an index finger to one tomato blossom after the other.

"Why hasn't the greenhouse for Hab-3 been deployed?" Britta's voice sounded sharper than she'd intended.

Evania jerked and missed a blossom. She licked her lips. "We had trouble getting Greenhouse-1 and -2 going and the solar array to work right. We didn't need another complication."

"We need to deploy it," Britta said. "To grow more food."

"Not enough compost," Evania said. "Or energy."

"There are twelve of us. We make plenty of compost," Britta said. "We'll find the energy."

"It'll take time to get the dirt on it."

"No dirt. We need the sun's rays."

"It's translucent."

"The sun's rays will get through, right?" Britta asked.

"Most of them," Evania said. "But the dirt protects us from cosmic rays. The thin atmosphere here wouldn't do that."

"I know."

"You want to eat radioactive produce?"

"It's better than starving."

Evania tilted her head to the side. She shrugged, "It's worth a try."

They spent the afternoon and the next day finding the long plastic tunnel, attaching it to Hab-3, and inflating it. Niels came by to check on them but didn't offer to help. They created a garden using dirt from the water processors fertilized with compost from the toilets. The processors heated Martian sand, dust, and rock to evaporate and collect the water. It removed toxins and left behind nutrient-rich dirt and clean water. Britta reprogrammed the rovers to keep them from covering the new greenhouse with sand and dust. No cameras were installed in this space. She didn't want them.

A week later, she planted bean, pea and lentil seeds, sunflower, and pepper seeds in Greenhouse-3. Working with her hands in the soil soothed her. The warmth of the sun seeping through the plastic cheered her. Her calculations said this garden would improve their chances of survival. Besides, doing something felt good. She didn't need NASA.

Britta spent the next six months worrying about the greenhouses and pantries. To relax, she read the monthly newsletter that had inexplicably started showing up in her inbox. It contained snippets of stories about exploring other worlds, looking for life there, and sterilizing spacecraft to avoid contaminating those worlds with life from Earth.

The third email from NASA arrived six months after the second. It said, "We're looking for a Resident Astronaut on Mars. Your credentials and your location make you a prime contender. Please respond to this email to set up an interview." Her stomach roiled. If she really wanted to get off this planet, that would be the way to go. NASA brought its astronauts home. However, that would mean abandoning Discovery Settlement. Who would manage the food assets? Who would understand their nutrition content?

For a week, she wandered around in a daze. What did NASA want? She didn't apply for the Resident Astronaut job. Why were they so persistent? She decided to set up the interview. It was the strangest interview she'd ever had. They sent her a list of questions. She sent them a video of her answers and her list of questions for them. After a 90-minute wait, she received their answers plus another list of questions. After three rounds of question and answer videos, they thanked her and told her they'd get back to her.

Two weeks later, when the third crop of beans in Greenhouse-3 was two feet tall with blossoms, Britta received the email from NASA. It said, "We're offering you a position as our Resident Astronaut on Mars." Hollow inside, Britta read it three times. It just didn't feel right. Now what?

Britta found Niels at the communications station in Hab-1.

Fred Huff's visage filled the computer screen. His voice pierced the air. "…drama into your daily videos. They'd put anyone to sleep." The video stopped.

Britta leaned on the console, tapping her foot, one fist on her hip.

Niels looked up. "What's wrong?"

"Turn the cameras off." Britta's tone was sharp and insistent.

Niels opened his mouth, then closed it, picked up the remote and pointed it at the cameras. They turned off.

"NASA wants to hire me." Britta showed him her handheld.

Niels' forehead creased. "What are you talking about?"

"When it looked like Mars Ho! would go out of business." Britta bit her lip. "I filled out the application for an astronaut position at NASA and submitted it."

"What?"

"I told them 'no' once but they didn't listen."

"They didn't even interview you?"

"Yes, they did. Long distance. It was the strangest interview."

"What do they want with you?"

"I don't know exactly. Eyes and ears on Mars. I'm a cheap way to get that because I'm already here. Maybe hotel services for their astronauts," Britta said. "NASA isn't going to help us. They think everything is fine here because that's what Alder told them."

"Alder won't release you to work for them."

"They said they'd buy out my contract."

"Maybe you should accept their offer."

Britta's eyebrows went up. "Why?"

Niels punched the start arrow on the screen.

Fred's eyes bored into Britta. She shivered.

"Niels, I received your request for more supplies. Unfortunately, the company is experiencing a decline in demand for our factory grown beef. We don't have the funds to launch a ship to Mars at this time. I'm sure, with the supplies we sent you last time you'll do just fine until the next cycle." Fred's eyelids fluttered. "Bear with us in this difficult time. Our analysts predict demand for our product will grow exponentially in the next few years." Fred rubbed the back of his neck. "For gosh sakes, put some drama into your daily videos. They'd put anyone to sleep." The video stopped, replaced by the start arrow.

The ventilation system whined.

Wilted leaves on bean plants and a fish floating upside down flashed through Britta's mind. Britta's legs seemed to have forgotten how to support her. She sat down, hard, in the chair next to Niels.

"They can't do that."

"They are doing that," Niels said, his tone flat.

"We've already reduced our calorie intake per person two percent." Britta poked at her handheld. "To have food until the next ship arrives in 419 days."

"Stretch the 419 day supply to last 1208 days," Niels said.

"1208 days?"

"That's the next opportunity they have to send supplies."

"What if they don't send them then, either?" Britta asked.

"Just do the calculation for 1208 days."

"1270 calories a day each." Britta raised her head. "It won't sustain us."

"The greenhouses?"

"That includes what we're growing in the greenhouses. Power output dropped due to the accident, remember?"

Niels set his jaw. "Reduce everyone's calories."

"I can't," she said. "We'll all starve. My fellow colonists would hate me."

"What are you complaining about?" he asked, "I have to decide who we're going to eat and in what order."

"What?" Her expression turned grim.

Niels sat with arms folded.

"We can't let Alder abandon us."

"Accept NASA's offer."

Pictures of the sterilization of NASA's spacecraft intended for Mars flashed through her mind. She stiffened. "NASA won't help us. They'd just as soon we all died. Less chance of us contaminating their precious Mars."

"What do you suggest?"

"Tell Fred our situation. Tell him they have to send us supplies."

The computer chimed. Niels leaned toward it. "It's from Fred." He touched the screen.

Fred's visage appeared. "I'm sorry, Niels, but we can't do that. We'd have to liquidate the company to send another load of supplies to Mars. I have the stockholders to think of."

Niels closed the video. "I can't ask him again."

"Let me try."

Britta sent Fred a video. "If we don't receive the supplies we need, we'll all die. Not sending them would make Alder Lincoln and the stockholders murderers. How would they feel about that?"

Three hours later she received Fred's response. "It can't be that bad. Surely you can find a way to survive."

Britta sent. "I suppose we could eat each other. You could show that on the reality show. We could roast one of us like for a Thanksgiving dinner, set out the fine china and white tablecloths. Hold a memorial service and then dig in. Give testimonials on how good our colleague tasted. Think of how many people would buy your manufactured meat after that."

They had to wait an hour and 20 minutes for Fred's response. "Niels, straighten that woman out. Tell her to stop joking."

Niels sent. "Actually, I've begun considering who to eat first."

It took 60 minutes to receive Fred's response. "Quit being facetious. You'd never do that."

Britta sent. "How do you know what we'd do if we're hungry enough?"

This time the wait was 40 minutes. Fred's face was ashen. "You know we'd never broadcast that."

Britta sent. "You think you could hide it? Stop it from going viral? It'd give Alder Lincoln a reputation. Wow, maybe their customers are really getting human flesh."

They waited for a response but none came that day. Or the next. It took a week for one of Fred's people to contact Niels to find out what supplies they needed.

Fourteen months later the supply ship fell out of the sky. All Discovery Settlement's residents, thin but still alive, came out to watch. First, the parachutes slowed the ship down. Then, when the parachutes released and flew off, the engines kicked in for a soft landing. Britta thought it one of the most beautiful sights she'd ever seen.

Alder Lincoln had put all their resources into sending Discovery Settlement the supplies they needed. They also included the Clean Meat Machine they'd promised earlier. When Britta turned down the job NASA offered her, they negotiated with Alder to perform tests on Mars for them. This shipment included test apparatus to look for Martian life. NASA had been emailing the colonists directions on how to use it and how to avoid contaminating the planet for a month now.

A shadow of what they once were, the financial prognosticators on the news predicted every week that Alder Lincoln would go out of business. But Alder kept hanging on, maybe because Discovery Settlement needed them, maybe because NASA contracted with Alder to obtain data from Mars, or maybe because they changed their editing policy for *Life on Mars* to show a truer picture of the hardships the colonists endured.

Once Discovery Settlement received the signal that the supply ship had landed, the rovers started rolling toward the landing site. The spacesuited colonists followed them on foot. Britta loved being outside. She loved how strolling through the red dust and gazing at the peaks and the horizon relaxed her mind, like a fresh breeze blowing through it. Mars had become home.

Inspiration

Humankind is curious. We've looked around the cosmos and wondered what was out there. We see Mars and wonder if we could live there. So far, we've developed the hardware to send robotic probes to its surface but we lack the hardware to return anything to Earth. Our space program continues to push back the date for landing humans on Mars. Parts of the private sector have become impatient. A few companies decided not to wait for the hardware to return people to Earth and plan to send humans to Mars on a one-way trip. I wondered what would happen to those humans, particularly if the company overreached its limits and ran into financial difficulties making it hard for them to support their colony.

Ready or Not

TIM YAO

Richie's voice echoed in the empty house above me. "1, 2, 3, …" Richie counted. "…40, 41, …" Then he skipped to the end, spitting out numbers so fast they tripped over each other. "98, 99, 100! Ready or not, here I come!"

What a cheater! Of course, I wasn't worried. I, Sam the smart one, had stumbled upon the best hiding place, a spot so clever they wouldn't find me in a million years. Maybe even two. I had discovered it and quietly crawled inside, repositioning the floorboards so Richie would never even think to look for me here.

I had to be quiet! Hearing Richie racing around the house, hunting us … it was so funny I had to laugh. Quickly, I dug out the sharp black rock from my pocket, squeezing it hard enough to draw blood from my palm.

"Hah! I found you!" Richie shrieked, his voice muffled enough that he had to be upstairs.

"Darn it!" That was Dougie, the brave one, the guy who had found the open window to let our group of nine kids into the abandoned house out of the sudden rainstorm. As we stood there in the dusty, darkened interior, it seemed the perfect activity for a lazy, wet, summer's day. Rumors at school had it that this house ate people and made them disappear. Of course, we knew better, but it made the house spooky enough to be irresistible.

"Now you have to help me find the others!"

I could just imagine Dougie rolling his eyes at that. Richie always was a stickler for the rules.

Over the course of the next twenty minutes or so, Richie and Dougie roamed around this dark, dusty house. They found Susan, then Alice, who had screamed when Richie found her; Jim, then Mark. The last person they found was Erica. They found her here in the living room. Had she seen me hide?

Creak, creak went the floorboards as my friends milled around above me. Their movements stirred up dust, but the sharp rock helped me focus.

"We've been all over the house, Richie," Alice said. "Maybe he snuck out when you weren't looking."

"I wouldn't put it past him," Richie muttered. "He is something of a sneak."

"Ow!"

I knew Dougie hit Richie's arm hard enough to sting. Dougie always stood up for me.

"Let's go over the house again," Dougie said. "Maybe he moved hiding places to one of the spots we already searched."

"See! He's sneaky!" Richie said.

I heard Richie scamper away before Dougie could approach him again.

The footsteps receded and I heard some faint shouting from other spots in the house. The thought of moving to another spot surfaced once or twice in my mind, but I just knew that this was *the* best place in the house to hide. Who would think of looking for loose floorboards?

A couple of times, I felt something creep over my arm or my leg. Cock-roaches. Their light touch made me shudder but I was no wimp like my sister Amy. She would have screamed and jumped around even at the suggestion that a cockroach was near. Me? I am made of tougher stuff.

"I'm bored." That was Susan.

I heard the footsteps of people gathering together above me. "Maybe you should call *olly olly oxen free*," Dougie suggested.

"I'm not giving up that easy," Richie grunted.

"I'm bored, too!" Alice said.

"Hey, I think it's stopped raining. We should head over to the park." Jim's voice rang out.

"I'll go," Mark said.

"Let's all go," Alice said. "I bet the little stinker is there already, laughing at us."

"Hey, if you're so sure that Sam is cheating, why not call him in?" Dougie again.

I could hear several footsteps move off in the direction of the front door.

"Guys!" Dougie again.

Then his footsteps trailed off too.

I waited. Maybe it was a trick. I had taught Dougie, Rich, and Jim how to use some sign language. I could imagine them feigning leaving the room, just waiting for me to pop out before tagging me.

Three cockroach trails later, I began to have my doubts. The house was utterly silent.

Well, not utterly. It was creaking, but not with footsteps. I imagined it empty, foreboding and dark, just the right atmosphere for ghosts and spirits to linger. Not that I believed in any of that garbage.

Okay. I'm patient and as sneaky as the next guy, but I was no man's chump. I brought my arms up and pushed up on the floorboards.

Nothing. Not even the hint of a movement.

What the heck?

I pushed harder and with as much force as I could muster in the limited space I slammed my hands up against the boards. Ouch!

The boards couldn't have been more solid than if they had been glued and nailed down, tongue in groove.

I felt sweat break out on my face. *Think, Sam, think.* I tried to slow my breathing.

A roach crawled up over my ear.

I couldn't help myself, clawing and slapping at my face. I heard the roaches skitter away around me.

"Hey! A little help here!" I shouted, slamming my hands upwards again and again against the wooden flooring.

I forced myself to be still and listened.

Nothing but the sighing and creaking of the old house. Even the cockroaches were quiet.

With my fingers cold and trembly, I felt the boards above me for the cracks. Maybe I was just hitting upwards in the wrong place. Ha, I might even have wedged the boards in a way that made them seem utterly sealed.

The wood felt entirely smooth as if I was beneath a solid piece of plywood.

Had I moved sideways somehow? Lost the loose floorboards?

The floor joists kept me from moving too much, but I repositioned myself and continued feeling the wooden surface above me. Smooth. Jointless.

My heart roared in my ears, as did my every dust-filled breath.

"Help!"

Inspiration

I have a lot of strong memories from playing hide and go seek as a child. I was a consummate hider, very adept at finding great and unusual places to hide. Invariably, though, I would find myself waiting. Waiting and wondering. Where were the searchers? Maybe they wouldn't find me. But what if they grew bored, gave up, and didn't find a way to let me know? I could be stuck hiding for a very long time.

Fever

SUSAN EKINS

Lying on a cot, John burned with fever. Why had he come on this safari?

After graduating from college, he and his friend Bill traveled through rugged terrain to view wildlife. Lions strutted, muscles rippling, in front of their jeep. Crocodiles and hippos basked in a muddy river. At night, the hippos grunted and wheezed, keeping them awake.

Recently they'd been staying in an inexpensive campground near the coast of Kenya. Disco music and the news in Swahili blasted over loudspeakers until 2:00 a.m., and at 5:00 a.m., the night watchman rode his motor scooter around the campground. Not a restful place, but John had thought it was fun.

The fun ended when Bill left him.

They'd met a man who offered to take them to get hashish. Bill said it would be an added adventure. John argued and refused to go.

But Bill snuck out during the night. When John realized Bill had deserted him, he slumped in his tent, head in his hands. He was alone, with no way to find Bill. He started feeling feverish.

He remembered nothing else until waking in a hut with a thatched ceiling. His body ached. How had he gotten here?

A scent of charred seafood, garlic, and cumin filled the air. A woman dressed in a traditional long black abaya was stirring a stew in a fireplace. She hastily pulled her niqāb over her wrinkled face when she saw that John had awakened, but he could see her piercing black eyes watching him.

He looked out the open door and saw sparse vegetation and red dirt. Maybe he was still near the campground.

Chills and shooting pains began again, and John tossed and turned. His head ached and darkness took over. He saw a bright light surrounding the silhouette of a man in the distance. Straining to see, John recognized the man as his deceased father. He shrugged. "I should go to him."

The old woman spoke with a heavy accent, "You will be alright. You will go home soon. Trust."

His father disappeared, and John glimpsed a slim young woman walking toward him with outstretched arms. She wore a long white dress. She spoke. "John."

He stopped thrashing and watched her come closer. She had red hair and green eyes. Calm settled on him, and the darkness lifted. But she was gone.

⌒ ☆ ⌒

Back in America, John grimaced as he completed another training session on the computer. Talk about boring. So far, working for a large software company wasn't as exciting as he'd hoped.

He sighed and walked down the corridor to get a drink of water, passing rows of white cubicles, gray file cabinets, and black carpeting. Out the window, the colors were the same. White snow, gray skies, and black tree trunks.

Up ahead at the water cooler, a slim young woman with red hair was sipping water from a paper cup.

Drawing near, he smiled, trying not to stare. "Hello. I'm John."

Her green eyes were watchful. "Yes?" But it sounded like "So?"

"I . . . I think I've met you before." His heart beat faster.

"Don't think so."

A few minutes of conversation didn't turn up a connection. John lived in Chicago, while Candice lived in the suburbs. He had gone to the University of Illinois, while she had gone to a small college. After a while, Candice threw out her cup. "Nice meeting you, but I have to get back to work."

The following week, John sat in a corner of the lobby, eyes closed. He'd been warned the fever could recur, and it had. He wiped sweat off his forehead with the back of his hand.

Candice walked into the lobby and did a double take. "John! Are you all right?"

"I'm fine."

She touched his forehead. "You're burning with fever." She went into the ladies' room and returned with wet paper towels. She patted his face and neck to cool him. "What else can I do?"

"Nothing, but thank you. I'm getting a ride home."

Candice hesitated. "OK then. I'll see you soon."

He nodded, and she left.

Back at work after a sick day, John found Candice's cubicle. A poster depicting palm trees by an ocean hung on the wall next to her desk. She looked up from her computer, and a gentle smile lit up her face.

He smiled also. "Thank you for helping me the other day. I didn't feel well."

"That was obvious. Was it the flu?" She sat back in her chair.

"No, it was a recurrence of malaria. I hope that was the end of it."

"Malaria? How did you get malaria?"

"Let's go out for lunch and I'll tell you about it."

"Sure." She stood. "How about seafood?"

They sat in the dining room at Candice's parents' house, eating dinner. Her mother frowned and set down her fork.

"But you've only known each other for a few months. You should date a while and have a long engagement before you get married."

Candice reached for John's hand. "That's the usual way. But we'll be OK."

Her white-haired, wrinkled grandmother spoke with a heavy accent. "Yes, yes. They will be alright." The old woman stared at John with black, penetrating eyes.

"Yes." John squeezed Candice's hand. "We will be alright. Trust."

Inspiration

People who find themselves drawn together sometimes see coincidences that seem like signs that their relationship is meant to be. For instance, my daughter's boyfriend bought his sports car from friends of my husband and me – who lived across the country. He and my daughter met online, but they lived only one mile apart. And our son once worked at the same company as him. So my protagonist having seen a woman in a dream could be a sign that their relationship is predestined.

It also interests me to think back on moments in my life and ask, "What if I'd made a different decision?" Long ago, I was invited to do something completely out of character: drive to another state, pick up drugs, and receive pay. No, I would never have done this, but what if I had? What would have been the impact on me and the people around me?

LOST IN LOVE

Stranded in Rewinds

SUSAN WACHOWSKI

space, you needed
and walked away
you left me
empty
my mind
a broken shore
stranded in rewinds
moments of need
memories tease
swirl through
my mind
again
you left me
you walked away
space, you needed
stranded in rewinds
my skin trembles
the touch of you
hands arms

legs lips

eyes

whirl dance

kiss laugh gasp

stranded in rewinds

trapped by the waves

moments crash boil

flood my shore

you left me

words

you used

done. never. mistake.

walked away and left me

stranded in rewinds

You left me.

Inspiration

Thinking on the anthology theme, I immediately thought of that feeling when a relationship ends. I didn't want to focus on a single moment, but on the recurring waves of memories and pain that hit you again and again at different times, day and night. Stranded in rewinds - trapped by memories that rewind and play again and again. It doesn't last forever, and you can make it through.

Static

Jessica Kosar

Every time I open my eyes in the navy blue darkness, I find that Grey has moved closer to my side of the bed, snoring and inching me toward the edge until I push myself up, grab my pack of cigarettes from the nightstand and head to the balcony. The summer breeze grazes my bare arms and shoulders. Sometimes a sharp gust envelops me, raising the fine hairs on my skin and reminding me that the season could end without warning.

Taking another drag, I scroll deeper into a repetitive newsfeed on Facebook. Everyone I graduated high school with is gloating about their new "real" jobs and how wonderful is life fresh out of college.

I'm so humbled to announce…

It's official!…

#Blessed…

Someone from my childhood Girl Scout troop is engaged. So is her best friend. They would combine their weddings, but then they couldn't be each other's maid of honor.

I erupt in a coughing fit and exhale the smoke in ragged bursts. My throat feels like leather. Deep in the consuming darkness of the bedroom behind me, I hear the creak of our worn headboard as he rolls over in the sheets and I freeze, wondering if he's woken up.

After a moment, the apartment is silent again and I force my shoulders to relax. Crossing the room and entering the bathroom softly, I draw a bath and let the water rush over my fingertips, fine tuning the temperature. Tossed against the wall as I step over the bath ledge, my day-old underwear falls to the cool tile floor. I'm warm now, hot even, but it won't be long before my muscles absorb all the heat in this porcelain tub, blindly grasping anything that feels momentarily good, leaving me shivering and dull.

I've started to doze off when I'm jolted awake by the squeaking of door hinges. There's a moment of complete stillness before the shower curtain is yanked aside so hard it nearly bursts from the rings that tether it weakly to the rod above me.

"Boo!" Grey laughs.

His dirty-blonde hair is pillow-pressed on one side and sticking in every direction on the other. The disturbed air around me is uncomfortably cold on my wet skin which has erupted in coarse goosebumps.

"Can I join you?" He asks, crouching beside the tub and dipping a hand into the lukewarm, murky water.

I have to prompt myself mentally before saying, "Well, I was actually just about to get out."

I steal a glance at him. The mischievous smile that was just there is now a firm line of lips and a clenched jaw.

The silence is frightening so I stand and water droplets fall from my body with faint plinks. I feel him continue to glower at me as I long for my towel hanging on the back of the door. Just then, I feel a familiar yet surprising sensation. Bright red blood trickles down my inner thigh in two diverging streams. It travels to the water where it disperses into thin wisps, losing vibrancy.

Grey's mouth twists with repulsion as he scoffs. The bathroom door slams shut behind him.

Days later and near the end of my period, I receive a phone call from an unknown number. It's early and I'm rushing to make it to work only two minutes late when my cell phone buzzes to life on the bathroom counter. I answer on the last ring.

"Hello?"

"Hi, is this Porter Jacobs?" It was a woman's voice. "My name is Jeanette and I'm the executor of Frida Nelson's will. I believe you were her niece, correct?"

I stare at my steamy reflection, absolutely dumbfounded. I barely would've remembered that Frida was related to me without someone mentioning her, and I certainly wasn't informed that she had passed away.

"Uh, yeah, she was my... yeah."

"I'm sorry for your loss, honey. She was a great lady. I was her next door neighbor. We used to play Double Solitaire together and host potlucks for the Camden Bird Watchers Society. She always made polenta."

"Oh, yeah, her polenta was really, uh, stellar." I pour myself a capful of mouthwash.

"It sure was," she sighs. "So anyway, I'm calling you because Frida left you her boat."

I pause for what feels like much longer than acceptable. "*A boat?*"

"Mhm, her little Hobo. She said she took you on weekend trips in it when you were a little girl."

Quietly and with composure, I realize that Jeanette is not speaking to the right person because Frida had not left her boat to the intended party. She had intended to leave the boat to my mother Portia, her niece, who visited her at her East Coast estate every few summers in grade school.

I pass the phone to the other side of my face. "Yeah, I remember that. Those were really fun trips."

"I bet they were," Jeanette says. "Poor Frida. She loved that boat but she couldn't drive it after her vision started to go. All she could do was sit at the dock."

The white noise of the bathroom fan surrounds me. I'm staring down the drain in my sink when Jeanette speaks again.

"So anyway, I just wanted to call to let you know about the boat. You'll want it out of the water no later than the start of September."

I scurry to dig for a pen in the kitchen junk drawer and write down the address Jeanette recited on the back of a crumpled receipt. It's in Camden, Maine, approximately a 14-hour drive from Mansfield, Ohio.

I could put the boat on the market from the comfort of my own sofa, but I already feel a relentless pang of guilt from accepting a gift that Frida obviously meant to give to my mother. She probably imagined Portia sailing around, reliving old memories of the two of them fishing and sunburning together. But I knew that Portia Jacobs-Steele would sell it herself and that she and her self-starting, Gucci-cologne-wearing CEO husband certainly don't need the extra cash.

I haven't received a dime from my mother ever since I left home when she screamed at me for not wanting to wear a purity ring at age 19. About $400 sits in my savings account as an emergency fund in case my paycheck-to-paycheck lifestyle suddenly becomes more demanding. Depending on the condition of the boat, I imagine I could get at least ten grand for it. What I can't imagine, is how it would feel to hold more money than I've ever seen.

I'll get a new phone, fix my car's A/C and replace all of my tired, old bras. The rest of it will be quietly put away. Grey frequently borrows money from others when he blows his paycheck on everything but our rent, and if he knew about this, he might just eat it away like an ash borer. So, as far as he's concerned, I'm visiting a friend in Nashville for a few days.

I pack light. Everything fits into my denim duffle bag except for an extra pair of shoes that I toss into the hatchback of my Honda Pilot.

Grey shifts his weight in the parking lot, wearing a hood up with hands deep in his pockets. He asks if I'd gotten my oil changed recently and if I have a full tank of gas. His attentiveness reminds me of the security I felt when we first started dating. Back when he was on his best behavior and we wanted to spend every minute together, he was the most comforting force in my upended life. When we met, I felt like everything would be okay as long as we were together.

"Be safe," he says as he hugs me.

I watch him shrink in the rearview mirror as I drive away and, for a moment, something seizes me and nearly brings me to tears.

The drive is long, my legs are restless just two hours in, and I constantly have to tune the radio between arid fields of static. I drink cans of iced coffee until I have to pee, buy snacks at the pit stops and continue on to Camden. I wonder about Frida and how her memory clearly failed her at the end yet she somehow remembered my name. I could recall seeing her at a Christmas gathering when I couldn't have been older than 8. Her tight grey curls bounced when she turned her head and her laugh was warm and wholesome. She gave me and all of my cousins a gift. They were wooden bookends that she made herself in her garage. Each pair was different. Mine were acorns.

My mother prompted me with her usual *what-do-you-say?* line.

"Thank you," I said. But I said it so softly and directed towards the floor that I'm not sure she heard me.

The further I drive into Maine, the fresher everything becomes. Lush evergreen boughs sway in the salty wind and the cool mist brings relief from the hot Midwestern summer I'm avoiding. Every restaurant claims to have the best lobster in town and they're all probably right.

The marina is closed when I arrive at 11 PM and I'm too exhausted to care. The hotel I check in to is old but homey. Its softly lit lobby is full of leather armchairs and lined wall to wall with full bookshelves. A mother and her young son tinker on the stand-up piano.

I turned off my phone halfway through the drive to preserve battery in case of emergency. Settling into my hotel room, I plug my phone in and turn it back on. My stomach drops ten stories when the device is bombarded with an influx of text messages. Its constant vibrations inch it toward the edge of the nightstand.

Hey babe. How's the drive going?

I hope you're doing okay. I love you.

Call me when you get there.

Is everything okay?

Porter.

I'm freaking out right now. You need to answer me.

PICK UP.

Are you leaving me? Is this really how it's all ending? Was that goodbye?

You can't do this to me. I'll die without you, you're all I have.

I took you in when you had no one and this is how you repay me? You never loved me, you're just a manipulative bitch.

Please come home baby. I love you more than anything in this world. I'll do anything for you.

My heart is beating me to death and my hands shake so terribly I have difficulty reading the messages. Taking a deep breath, I text back,

Hey, babe! I'm so sorry, my phone died and we've been having so much fun that I haven't been checking it. I didn't mean to worry you.

His speech bubble appears and disappears multiple times. I think he's about to send me a novel when my phone rings and his eyes in the contact photo burn through me. I answer.

"Hello?"

"What the hell are you doing in Maine?"

Thrown by his question I'm hit with the dark realization that I didn't turn off the "Share My Location" setting before I left. He knows exactly where I am and I had nothing to defend myself.

"Are you alone?" He asks quietly.

"Yes," I whisper back.

"Stop lying to me."

"I swear to God, I'm alone-"

"STOP LYING TO ME," he screams into the receiver. "Who the hell are you with? How long has this been going on?"

I tilt my phone upside down in hopes that he can't hear me cry.

"I'm so goddamn stupid," he continues. "This explains everything. You stopped sleeping with me when you started sleeping around. All I've done is love you and this is how you repay me, by being a slut."

I don't know which is worse: admitting to his delusion that I'm cheating on him and accepting the repercussions in order to still have a home in Mansfield, or telling him the truth which includes sharing the reasons I lied in the first place. I only have enough money to do this for a few days. There's no telling how long it'll take to sell the boat.

I choose neither and hang up. He calls back immediately and the vibration onslaught begins again. Between rejecting his calls, I reconfigure my settings so that my location can't be shared through any app. Then I turn off my phone, climb into bed and cry for hours.

Shortly after 3 AM I get up and fill a plastic cup with water in the bathroom sink. My face is puffy and red. I already know I'll look terrible throughout the day. I don't want to but I can't stop myself from checking my phone. I need to know what he's saying to me.

There are 14 missed calls and a stream of unread texts. He even tried messaging me through Facebook, Snapchat and Instagram.

I didn't mean what I said. Please talk to me, we can get through this. Please come home.

I love you more than anything. You're my whole world.

As I'm reading his confessions, a new text appears.

Are you up?

He seems subdued, so I reply.

Yes.

I accept the call but say nothing.

"I'm so sorry for the things I said to you. I didn't mean it, I swear. I just…" his voice is rough like he's been chain-smoking. "I just love you more than you could ever know. And the thought of you being with someone else made me lose it. But I don't care where you've been or what you've been doing. Nothing could be worse than losing you."

The phone rests on my face as I lie on my side. "You don't understand."

Then he says something I've heard so many times before: "I'm trying to be better for you."

My brain feels like it's ripping down the center and I might have to make myself throw up to expel the nausea lining my stomach.

"I need to sleep," I say.

"Can we talk tomorrow?"

"Yes, but you can't bombard me. You have to wait."

"Okay," he says quietly.

The sun shines directly onto my face and wakes me up. I feel hungover and I wish I was because I at least would've been drunk at some point last night. Eager to shake off the feeling that I've lost a layer of skin, I shower, dress and head downstairs to take advantage of the hotel's continental breakfast.

Having successfully kept down a muffin and coffee, I make my way toward Frida's marina. It's a 15-minute walk from the hotel and I've stepped into the most beautiful day. Passing through a slow-moving farmer's market, I admire displays of fresh vegetables, floral bouquets, and homemade preserves. Between passing clouds, sunshine pours through the vendors' canopy tents and for a moment the produce and crafts are illuminated with blues and reds. People smile at me.

Camden Marina appears to be empty aside from an elderly couple carrying fishing gear and life vests ahead of me. A tall, bearded man in faded overalls greets me at the office. Before he leads me to the boat, I peer over his desk at the four Red Heeler puppies asleep on a plaid blanket in the corner.

The weathered wooden piers bob beneath his heavy footfalls and my lighter steps. Freshly waxed rowboats and domineering sailboats adorned with coiled ropes sway gently from their tethered posts. I read each custom name painted on the long bodies as we pass: *Irish Goodbye, Star Boy, Sell 4 Bail.*

Frida's Hobo, *The Sunshine Daily*, is white with a mustard yellow trim. Surprisingly more spacious on the inside than it appears, it's complete with a stall-sized bathroom, a kitchenette and a pullout bed covered in an old afghan blanket. The hollow echo of my footsteps follows me as I explore cabinets of retro mugs, magazines, and sunscreen. I'm surprised to discover two things: a handgun under the kitchen sink and a photo taped to the inside of a cabinet door.

In the photo, I'm two years old wearing princess-themed onesie pajamas, delighted by the sock puppet Frida wears on her hand. I blink several times as I study the image, wondering why she kept it. The boat isn't haunted but I feel as though I'm with company.

I go outside for air and brush off a dingy plastic chair that sits at the corner of the boat's deck. Seagulls call to one another as they circle high above the pier. I squint against the bright clouds to watch them. From far away, the houses across the harbor look washed out in faded tones of blue. I pull at the strings on my hoodie. It's chilly in the best possible way.

Grey texts me, *Are you coming home?*

No, I think to myself, and suddenly whatever frayed thread my heart has hung from for the past three years snaps.

I'm surprised by the volume of my sobs as I hold my head in my hands. I'd rather leap over the edge of the Hobo and drown right here than return to Mansfield, and I know that if I do go back, I'll drown without dying. It'll just be expected misery interrupted by sporadic moments of pleasure. It'll be my life.

I start to hyperventilate. I feel like I'm four years old and separated from my mother in the grocery store. I feel like I'll never be safe again. Then, as quickly as I started crying, I stop. Everything stops. The past few years have been harder than they needed to be but I've been fine without my mother. Is there any real reason I couldn't be fine now?

I gaze back at the city's main strip and watch strangers carry about their days. As wind rushes over my cool tears, I imagine something so ridiculous I can't help but smile. I imagine myself cruising in the Hobo with one of the Red Heeler puppies from the office. It's my dog that'll grow up to be strong and protective and we're living on the little boat until I've saved up enough money for a deposit on a new apartment. I wonder how quickly I can sell this boat if I really want to. I wonder how much a waitress makes in Camden and which restaurants are hiring. I wonder if those dogs are for sale.

It'll be an abrasive, suffocating and crushing conversation, but I'll call Grey later today. Right now I can sit in this chair, watch the seagulls, and smoke a cigarette before I get up and ask for an application at the tavern beside the marina.

Inspiration

When I couldn't watch Netflix because two of my family members were already streaming on their devices, I found solace and entertainment in a British home renovation show on cable. The episode featured a young hipster couple working to maximize storage space and lighting in their tiny house boat, and I hoped that one day I could be lucky enough to take on a similar project.

The Cold Upon You

Stéphane Lafrance

One month before Christmas

"I didn't know that was how you felt," Tommy Oscar Jones said on his cell phone.

He got up from his brown soft touch recliner and rubbed a shaky hand through his dark shaggy hair.

"I mean," he pulled the phone away from his ear and cleared his throat, tight from where this conversation was taking him. Breathing deep, he let out a slow sigh.

"Leyna, are you sure?"

He listened. His next words came out as a half-whisper, "I missed us too." His eyes widened in surprise, and he lifted his hand as if Leyna could be stopped by it.

"No, I'm not just saying, I swear. I've been drowning here, Leyna. I never stopped loving you. Two years already this Christmas and I never moved on. But… what changed?"

Listening, he sat back down and reached for his Scotch, a cheap Cutty Sark. He lifted the glass in front of his eyes, looking through it. While his estranged wife explained, a photograph hanging on the opposite wall penetrated his mind. It was a three-year-old picture of him and Leyna at Christmas. She was holding his hand while they sat on a green and red love seat in front of a fake fir tree and a bold '1996' in the top right corner.

He slowly spun the glass and the picture took life like an old silent movie, worn out, missing most of its frames. The Scotch gave the images an old fashioned sepia tint. As he turned the snifter in his hand, a curved line from the sculpted glass slid below the chin of his younger and happier self, at an angle that gave the illusion of separating his head from his body. A cold chill like an icy blade pierced through his spine and neck, causing a momentary weakness. The drink slipped from his hand, the heavy lead crystal shattering on impact. Caught in his reverie, he thought he saw his head roll away from his body, as shards of glass scattered and the whiskey oozed away like blood.

The call had gone silent, hanging by a question that he could almost not recall. What was going on?

"It's ok. I dropped my Scotch. I'll pick it up later." He felt a pang of annoyance and anger at the waste, and that surprised him.

He had not felt anger since that last time as a child when it had nearly ruined his life. He had almost killed his drunken father who had passed out in bed after beating and raping his wife, Tommy's mother. He was eleven then, a bundle of twisting and raging emotions. Tommy had planned to bury a chef's knife in his father's heart. It would have been quick and his mother would have been saved. But she had seen him come into the bedroom and had noticed the blade. Silent, one eye swollen shut, she had just looked at him. She gave a slight shake of the head and laid back down, hugging her snoring husband. The next day, she had explained to him how it would have ruined his life to give in to his anger. Only hours after, Tommy found his mother on the floor bleeding, the one good eye glazing over. He ran to a neighbor's house and told them. The next morning, he started a new life in the world of foster care.

The events of that night flashed in and out in the span of a second, and he felt emotions that he thought were buried all these years. With an effort, he pushed them back, resurfacing to the present and to Leyna. He grabbed a towel he had left around this morning after his shower and threw it on the floor over the scotch. The conversation continued. But the incident, though minor, had cooled off Leyna's confessing mood.

After the call, Tommy reflected on how he had used the death of his mother as motivation to be different from his father. He refused to be violent and controlling. Yet, he wondered if perhaps, stranded on the desperate island of broken love, lost in a city that showed him no compassion, he had become part of what his father had been. Even his friends had slid into the shadows, leaving him to think dark thoughts in the Cutty Sark haze every night. A haze that was different yet the same as his father's, with the only purpose of escaping life's burdens, a shameful past or, in his case, painful memories. Leyna's attempt at reconciliation, he realized, shone a light of redemption upon him. She was coming back.

During the following weeks, she called him several more times, ultimately feeling comfortable enough to give him her private phone number. It got them closer, re-acquainted. With every conversation, Tommy's belief in love returned. His job at the local Ace Hardware was now tolerable. He renewed his friendship with his best friend Stephen Fuller. He stopped drinking.

When she gave him her phone number, Leyna suggested meeting for Christmas. She had rented a cabin in the mountains near Vail for the holidays and wanted to see him. The cabin seemed the ideal place for the reunion. When they hung up, he could not stop smiling.

He planned and dreamed of his Christmas with her. But occasionally when he least expected, whether it was in the running water of a warm bath or the cracking of an egg at breakfast, he saw in his mind the shattering glass, his head rolling away, blood spreading slowly.

December 24th, early afternoon

In his shiny 1982 royal blue Datsun 280zx, Tommy drove slowly on the small mountain roads near Vail. He had prepared for this trip, had made sure his car was in good shape, his brakes brand new, and he had bought chains for the tires. The weatherman had, the night before, forecasted snow flurries. But one could never really predict weather in the mountains. He had seen the dark low clouds from a distance and had known then that the flurries had turned into a raging storm. He stopped minutes before entering the storm, called Leyna to give her an update, and put the chains on. He was now in the middle of it, wipers at full speed, the odometer occasionally reaching 10 miles per hour. He knew at this speed, it would take him close to two hours to reach her. Prudence had always been one of his strongest traits. He felt great and confident in his driving skills. The Reaper was not going to deprive him of winning back his love today. He smiled.

The radio antenna was broken, but a good old cassette player was all he needed. *Kenny Rogers Greatest Hits* was his favorite album and the perfect song played: *Lady*. Tommy sang along with Kenny, his emotions a raging river ready to leave its banks. Concerned with looking his best, he looked at himself in the rearview mirror, perhaps for the tenth time, inspecting his appearance. A 5 o'clock shadow started to show, but he decided that the handsomely-rugged look suited him well. He smiled at his reflection and picked at a piece of food stuck in his teeth. In his mind's eye though, he saw Leyna stepping near, her hand caressing his cheek, her blue irises drowning his thoughts and closing in for a kiss. He did not see the avalanche coming at him from the high peaks on his left.

The white wave slammed into the car, pushing it over the cliff. Free falling among clouds of snow, the car spun. There was no up or down. The twisted roots of an Aspen tree crashed through the window, grabbing everything in its way. There was a loud crack and Tommy's head exploded. Everything faded to black. He did not have time to be afraid or to think of Leyna. His last thought was of an amber crystal sword severing his head.

Echos of a strumming guitar reverberated in and out, reaching him like the surf of a calm ocean. Tommy bathed in ether, aware of his surroundings but not feeling them. The words of a song finally made their way into his mind: *"If you're gonna play the game, boy you gotta learn to play it right"*. The engine had died, but his *Kenny Rogers Greatest Hits* tape still played. With an impossible effort, Tommy opened his eyes. It was dark, but he could see the lights from the radio and the Check Engine symbol glowing red in the console. He recognized the song as *The Gambler*, which preceded *Lady*. *I must have been out for a while... almost the whole tape has played. Or maybe it played several times.*

Leyna! The haze precipitated as the name brought clarity of mind and a flood of memories.

He was in his old house, standing in front of her. She sat at her desk, reading a letter, crying. Written words enunciated themselves to Tommy. "... What did I do to earn your ire? I was dedicated to you, did everything for you. How did I deserve this?"

Tommy recognized those words as he had written them to Leyna a month after their break up. This time though, he saw how they affected her. As she wrote a response, he heard the trembling words, pain permeating every whisper.

"Everything you did for me was kind and generous. This is what made me fall in love with you. But you were dedicated only to the way you saw me, the way I was when we met. But I changed, I matured. I wanted - needed - to give back to you, like a real relationship should work. But it seemed I never could. Love is not a one-way street..."

She sniffed and wiped the tears off with a tissue. "When was the last time you let me do something for you? When was the last time you told me what you wanted? You built a wall, like a double-sided mirror, where you could see me. But I, on the other hand, only saw myself. I'm sorry Tommy, but I got tired of only seeing myself."

"I don't know how to make this work Tommy. I'm sorry, but I just don't know!". Angry, she took the letter, ripped it, and threw it away. Straight through him.

Tommy came back to the present and heard Kenny Rogers slowed down to an almost unrecognizable noise. *Leyna, I wish you had sent me that letter. I'm sure I would have changed!* But Tommy felt he was in denial. He was reverting to his habit of centering everything around her. Guilt seeped in. He could not remember when was the last time he let her in. The music stopped, the weak lights flickered, the battery was dying. Consciousness evaporated, Tommy forgot who and what he was.

Leyna! The name was like an anchor and Tommy reminisced further.

"Do that for me Tommy, or better yet, do it for yourself," Leyna said, sitting in Tommy's blue Datsun, as they were coming back from the movies.

"It's ok Leyna, I don't need to do it. I forgave him many years ago."

"Ok, but does he know? Your father has been released from prison, on parole for more than three years. Yet you haven't spoken to him once. Why?"

Tommy, the ghost of present time, watched his younger self's reaction. All he saw was a blank face. His practiced voice betrayed nothing:

"He stripped me from my youth years ago when he killed my mother. But he was a drunk and he didn't know what he was doing. I've forgiven him." Tommy paused.

Leyna jumped in, interrupting Tommy's thoughts. "You should really go and see him. I'm sure he regrets what he did, I'm sure he missed you."

"I don't feel like I'm his son anymore." He snapped, clearly annoyed.

"The day I stopped hating him was the day I stopped calling him Father. He's only a stranger now."

He took a few breaths, calming down.

Tommy grabbed Leyna's hand and kissed it. "I would rather stay home, make us a nice dinner, and watch Svengoolie with you."

Leyna looked at him, seeing only his profile, searching for something. She decided to let go and smiled. "So many women would say you're the perfect man. Young, handsome, handy… And you're mine."

It was said with so much conviction that younger Tommy smiled and kept driving. But present Tommy saw Leyna's smile fade, replaced by such sadness as to break his heart. And he could hear her thoughts. *You're in denial Tommy, and you don't even know it. You lie to yourself and in the process, you lie to me. There's power in facing a person and forgiving them. There's redemption. But you won't listen to me. Will you ever open up?*

Tommy felt her words and her feelings deeply. Kenny Rogers' song came back to mind. *"If you're gonna play the game, boy you gotta learn to play it right"*. Tommy wondered what it meant. Was he really as closed-minded as she thought?

Oh, Leyna…

This time there was no fading, no passing out. The transition to the next memory was instantaneous, so abrupt it was almost violent.

The door to their house swung open too quickly and slammed into the coat hanger behind it. Tommy saw his best friend Stephen Fuller help him walk inside, followed by an upset Leyna and her friend, Lisa. Tommy knew that this was a year before they broke up, when two drunk guys in a nightclub had taken a liking to Leyna and Lisa. This quickly degenerated in the end, though not through Tommy's fault.

"He didn't even fight," said Leyna. "All he did was beg for them to go. Who does he think he is? Jesus of Nazareth? He should be thankful that Stephen went to his rescue!"

"Well, if you ask me," said Lisa, "Tommy does look and act like a saint. It's just sad he didn't call the wrath of God on them two jerks."

"He can be so stupid sometimes. And I was so scared when they ganged up on him." Leyna's voice broke but she regrouped quickly. Wiping a tear from her face, she said, "Which saint does he look like anyway?"

"Judas Iscariot as played by Ian McShane."

"What? Judas was never a saint," Layna replied.

They both looked at each other, then burst out laughing. But Tommy from the present only realized this had been the turning point for Leyna. She lost faith in her husband, lost respect as well. The change was subtle but insidious. The reference to Judas The Betrayer hit too close to home. Not that he would have betrayed her or cheated on her. But Judas was the bad guy, and Tommy did not want to be the bad guy. So much so, he realized, that he never let Leyna in, too afraid she would see the scars from his youth, the demons that still haunted his dreams.

Kenny Rogers had the right of it. *"If you're gonna play the game, boy you gotta learn to play it right."* He did not play the game right and by then he was only dealing himself losing hands. This was the root upon which discord grew and what brought his wife to slam the house door on him.

At the thought, he was transported one year later, to "The Day", seeing himself turn around and face the door closing in his face.

This time though, he was inside the house watching Leyna, her back to the door, crying silently, her beautiful face hiding a hurt so deep, he had to reach out with his soul to feel it. And then he sensed it, the pain, the anger, the frustration, … the love. Her emotions had become his. He cried, for her sorrows, for the pain he caused, for his stupidity.

Tommy slowly came back to the present. Still crying, he was determined to fix this and gain her back. He needed to show her he was a different man. He needed to play the game right. All this time, Tommy was blind to the truth of their relationship, dedicating his life to hers, slowly erasing himself and becoming her. The game of love is not a game, he thought. It is life. And life can only be lived if you let people in, if you make yourself vulnerable. If you don't, you lose.

He started yelling for help, determined not to lose consciousness again. He hit the roof with his fist, the only part of the car that felt hard enough. Some snow fell through the broken windshield. But he did not care and he hoped with all his might help would come. He quickly tired though and fell into a stupor again.

He heard the clang of metal hitting metal coming from the front of the car up above. The broken windshield had let in a lot of snow, and he was stuck in the back. He shouted and banged on the roof. Surely, whoever that was who made the noise must have heard him. Why was it so dark? Silence continued for some short moments and then he heard more metal on metal noise and grinding too. Rescuers must have seen something sticking out of the snow. They were going to pull the car out. He was saved! Thank God he was saved!

The Datsun jerked and he held himself in place. Quickly, he could see light shining through the snow above, through the windshield. And then the vehicle was out. The day was gorgeous, the sunlight invading everything.

"This must be the next morning," Tommy thought, "surely it can't be more than that."

A man in a bright orange vest, half standing, half rappelling, maybe 20 feet away, shouted commands into his radio. Tommy whistled and waved at him. He could hear the revving of a heavy engine some distance up, an industrial size tow truck he concluded, yellow strobe lights flashing.

The rescuer suddenly yelled, "Stop!" He peered hard into the car and took a step back. Tommy used that opportunity to get out through the broken passenger window. He reveled in the strong sunlight. Everything was white around him, covered in snow.

On the other side of the car, Tommy could see that the man had blanched and started to heave.

"Hey man, are you ok?" Tommy did not understand what was going on.

His rescuer bent over and emptied himself.

"Whoa, what's going on?"

The man finished retching, dry heaving several times. He ignored Tommy and started climbing up the cliff to where the tow truck was. He brushed past the roots of an Aspen tree and screamed, climbing faster and stumbling half of the time.

Tommy felt his anger rise and he did not know why.

"What the hell?! Hey! What's going on?"

Tommy started climbing the cliff too, not realizing that he did so without the help of a rope like the rescuer's. He stopped when he stood about 10 feet from the Aspen, staring at frozen mass stuck in the roots. The snow on it made it difficult to see what it was, but it looked like a head.

Tommy climbed closer. There was no doubt. A man's head, eyes open and smile frozen, gazed straight at him. The features seemed familiar. And then it hit him. It was his. Tommy's head was looking straight at him.

"No" he whispered, "Nooo!" An instant later, teleported, Tommy stood by his car.

In the driver's seat was himself, bloody shoulders and headless.

"It can't be... No, no, no, that can't be me!"

Rage and despair consumed Tommy as he realized he could never be with Leyna. He would never have his chance for life-long love! He looked up at the rescuers.

"It's a mistake!" He yelled, "I'm alive! I have to be! I'm here, am I not?" But no one could hear him.

He sat on the snow nearby, watching his Datsun being pulled up, crying. Life had played its game with him and Tommy had lost. His surroundings blurred, but this time he knew why. Fog settled in, a fog of ether or whatever made up the world of ghosts. Around him objects dimmed. But he didn't care. His anger made him blind but his despair was greater, and he could only think of Leyna. *I can't be dead, I can't.*

Time passed. On rare occasions, something would pull him away from Limbo, the world where lost, desperate or angry souls roam, perhaps eternally, and he would wake up and look around him. On one such day, warm and sunny, he saw something new beside him in the grass. A cross had been planted, beautiful flowers surrounded it and a small frame with his picture was attached and a note.

He recognized Leyna's handwriting: "In memory of Tommy Oscar Jones. I never stopped loving you."

Inspiration

I love sci-fi, fantasy and mystery books. Since I started writing, each of the three genres has had an impact, but more recently I've been influenced by Dean Koontz's work. I realize now that I love a little mystique in my stories. With The Cold Upon You, *I wanted to bring some of that dark supernatural feel. The idea of being stranded somewhere was not enough. I needed my main character to be stranded at multiple levels: thoughts of stuck cars, broken love and deep snow floated in my mind, but the ghostly element was what sealed the deal.*

The rest of the story was shaped by my own life experiences. The rocky love story was fictitious, but some elements like the unpredictable weather in the mountains, the Datsun 280zx and the Cutty Sark came from wonderful times in my life that have been stamped in my memory forever. And though I have never been around an actual abusive person, some dear friends from my past have been. Time has not erased some of the things they told me. Tommy's father in the story was my way of showing that sometimes abuse cannot be helped, that people find themselves in a vicious circle and are unable to get out of it by themselves unless an event of great magnitude happens. And in his own way, Tommy was as helpless as his father, even in death.

What Lies in the Cracks Between Us

DEBRA KOLLAR

My sister, Adele, was there when I arrived home from high school. Six sky-blue storage totes had been brought in and left on either side of the front door.

It reminded me of the blue forget-me-nots that bordered the aisle she had walked down six months prior to marry her husband. The person for whom she had left me behind.

She barely looked at me from the couch, a tissue in one hand and one of Mother's vintage highball glasses filled with whiskey and ice cubes in the other. I had never seen her drink what Mother dubbed her "refresher" cocktail, an evening aperitif she had claimed could always get one through the day.

I was sixteen, but I knew why she moved back. Adele and I both had lost our faith that someone could save us from Father; a husband for her, Adele for me.

We barely talked as the afternoon ticked away.

Father's first words to Adele after he arrived home from work at a punctual 5:30 PM: "Did he beat you?"

She said, "Of course not."

"Then go back to him." He walked into the dining room where Mother had his evening meal hot and ready.

It could have been because Father had complained he had spent $30,000 on her wedding. A sum which could be used as a down payment for a house.

It could have been because of Nick. Many dinner conversations the year before revolved around Father's belief that Adele marrying a used car salesman who sold lemons to innocent people, even to the elderly, would only bring her pain. "Movie star looks don't put food on the table."

It could have been because my parents had stuck it out. Father spent his free time at golf outings and Mother disappeared in her Red Hat Society functions—the most affection between them a pat on the back before they went off to work.

I imagine the true reason was rooted in the past, one Father would never share with us.

His words had always been paramount: statements without explanations and judgments without questioning. "A woman has her place in the home. A man is the sole provider. Kids should be seen and not heard. A wandering eye is an indication a wife isn't fulfilling her duties at home."

These commandments had been in our house well before my sister and I were born, as if they were the unwritten Bible of our family, decreed by Father long before he was married.

Mother had checked out long ago. I could pinpoint the exact time in the family albums: a slight decrease in her smile, then an anger in her eyes and finally an empty faraway look. She had married young, right out of high school, and she too had left a broken home behind—one with an absent father to one with a controlling husband.

My sister was different. She pressed, pushed, and wielded her way through life—at first. She believed in fairy tales and future dreams. She could do anything if she set her mind to it—that is, until Father got inside her head. By the time she turned eighteen, it did not matter who came around. Just like Mother, she was ready to leave one type of bad situation for another, hoping it would be better.

I did learn that night, once you left our home, you left it for good.

Adele went back to Nick. Father insisted she would have to pay them for the cost of the wedding if she did not and just to be sure, he had Mother turn my sister's bedroom into a TV room. He sat in there alone in the evenings, on a two-seater couch watching the golf channel, never looking up at the sky-blue picture frames of his oldest daughter growing up around him.

We rarely saw my sister after that. The cracks between us all turned to fissures too large to cross. I was angry she had left me; Father was angry because she had returned. Adele and Mother worked daily not to let the cracks of their own broken lives in. Strong spirits though were never made to survive broken lives for long.

A year later, after waiting up for a man who loved women too much, my sister ran her car into a tree and died on impact.

I begged for forgiveness at her grave because I learned I was more like my father than I realized. I had turned my back on her without hesitation.

Nick married a girl that graduated with Adele soon after, another wayward soul swayed by movie star looks and talk of ambitious dreams.

Father went back to sitting alone in his two-seater couch, watching golf games in Adele's room. The frames of my sister's life in photographs were taken down and stored in her closet in the few sky-blue storage totes she had left here.

Mother announced her desire to be the president of The Red Hat Society. I no longer recognized her faraway look in the group photograph; her expression had changed to a hollow shell.

Choosing to live fully for the sake of what my sister could not do, I left home for good when I graduated from high school five months later. I went into Adele's room and taped a sky-blue forget-me-not flower and a note to Father's television. The word "goodbye" —without any explanation.

Inspiration

When I was in college, my sister went into a shelter for abused women and filed for divorce. When she came back to her house, she brought a woman and her daughter who needed a place to stay for a while. The woman drove her car into a tree. I believe it was an accident, but the circumstances were strange, and it had a profound impact on me. Her two children went back to her husband.

Our country has always been a "can do" culture. We believe anyone can rise above the lot they were given. We wonder how kids grow up to be violent and others feel there isn't any way out except suicide. It's because people in this world need more empathy rather than judgement. Not everyone is born with the same coping mechanisms or the ability to get through life unscathed. This is when we need to forget the poor choices of our children, friends, neighbors and relatives and say: I will help you. Because you are hurting. Because you are a human being who doesn't see a way out.

Moonlight Sonata

Leslie Gail

The knuckles on the fingers of Andrea's right hand bent to create four peaks.

And cautiously straightened.

Peaked.

And straightened.

Andrea watched her knuckles arch along the stiff grey surface of the dashboard and recalled her childhood piano teacher. What was her name? Mrs. Owen. Mrs. Owen and her tight red lips.

"Curve your fingers dear, as if you are cupping them around an orange."

Andrea cupped her fingers at the memory, then continued bending until her right hand curled to a loose fist.

Andrea blinked sideways at the fading image of her fingers as they evaporated into radiant white warmth. A piano was playing. She recognized strains of Beethoven's *Moonlight Sonata* - mysterious, yet gentle. The quiet cadence of rolling triplets drew her into a memory of her last childhood piano recital...

Sitting in a pew awaiting her turn at the black grand piano, Andrea had reached the point where she must practice several hours a day or abandon lessons for other teenage pursuits. A slim, red and green plaid barrette secured the fair blonde hair that strayed in her eyes. Her insides trembled. Seated next to her father, she smelled the wool of his red sweater. After a smattering of polite applause, Andrea rose. Her father gave her cold hand an encouraging squeeze. Settled on the bench in her green pleated skirt, she prepared her left hand to ease into the octave. Her right began the opening triplets. The rhythmic lullaby of Moonlight Sonata filled the sanctuary...

A damp, burned rubber smell seeped into the rhythm as the Moonlight Sonata triplets in Andrea's head pressed on.

"Sweetheart?" Richard's faint, deep voice urged.

Bathed in incandescent softness, Andrea hovered on inaudible notes, unable to rise and adjust her head.

"Sweetheart?" Familiar and gentle, but with an unfamiliar edge. Richard stretched across the console and pressed his hand over Andrea's idle fingers, "Everything will be okay. No, no...don't try to move."

∽ ☆ ∾

The moment Carlos heard tires screeching at the intersection outside his pack and ship store, he reached into the front pocket of his navy chinos for his phone. After the exploding metal of the crash, a grave silence hung in the air.

"9-1-1, what is your emergency?"

Carlos responded, "I am reporting an accident."

Holding his light brown index finger toward a customer halted by the sound of the crash, Carlos mouthed, "One moment, please." The woman, in a smart beige overcoat, placed her kraft shipping box on the counter and rushed to the front window.

Carlos called to his assistant manager, yanked open the glass door, and sprinted across the cracked asphalt of the strip mall parking lot.

He continued with dispatch, "Corner of 4th and Main. Three cars, possibly a fourth."

A gas station attendant darted to the scene from the other side of the street. Carlos' eyes widened as he reacted to the condition of a silver sedan, "One driver's side took it hard."

…Adolescent Andrea's fingers froze. Her knuckles floated above the keys as she paused, unable to enter the piece again. Parents and fellow students waited in uncomfortable silence. She placed her hands and started over. Much to the relief of those in attendance, Moonlight Sonata triplets filled the sanctuary once again…

Abrupt sirens blared from every direction.

Carlos ran his fingers through the dark curls on his forehead. Observing. He turned from the accident scene to the gas station at the corner, then to the 24-hour pharmacy across the way. Impervious to the drizzly chill, he remained at the curb until the ambulance departed and the tow truck arrived.

Tubes connected Andrea's unconscious body to a percussive symphony of life-supporting beeps and whooshes. Helpless to the widespread swelling in her brain, she was neither awake nor aware.

Richard, sidelined after he answered questions and accepted a cool compress, sat on a taut, grey upholstered chair in the emergency department waiting room. The triage team had not allowed him to accompany Andrea to the ICU. Ignoring the ache seeping into his right shoulder, he counted ceiling tiles in their rigid rows as the evening sky darkened outside the tall, tinted windows.

A fair-skinned man with a navy jacket hanging open on his stocky frame rushed through the glass vestibule doors to the front desk.

"My wife!" the man, breathless and insistent, leaned in on the chestnut brown laminate counter with his palms. "They said Andrea is here!"

An attendant directed Andrea's husband forward into the clinical area.

Feeling exposed in the public waiting space, Richard trained his eyes on his grey canvas shoes. At the sound of the broad automatic door clicking shut, he rose to leave, then remembered his car was still at the pharmacy.

Richard sat in measured uncertainty. He attempted to suppress his internal hysteria by counting stiff grey chairs. His thoughts swerved to the time he encountered Andrea, a regular customer, in the back parking lot. She came to his pharmacy for refills of her husband's blood pressure medication; and he noticed when she stopped in for dental floss, nail polish remover, or a little red bag of milk chocolate caramel balls.

One day, Andrea brought in a new prescription for an antidepressant for herself and challenged Richard with questions. Uncharacteristically distracted, he found it easier to direct her attention to the instructions stapled to the white paper bag than hold eye contact while they were talking.

After his shift, Richard carried an unopened bottle of lemon tea to the back parking lot. Startled by the sound of sobs, he encountered Andrea's gentle face contorted with emotion in the driver's seat of her Acura. While he was privy to certain confidential conditions in his customers' personal lives, he was vigilant not to cross professional boundaries or to acknowledge them in public. Andrea looked up as he walked by and caught his gaze in a way he felt helpless to break. He stepped toward the opened window and extended the bottle of tea.

Andrea began waiting for Richard on Wednesday evenings when her husband had his standing racquetball commitment. They sat together in her car or drove a short distance to the arboretum to walk if there was still enough light on the horizon. Richard appreciated the simple routine and beamed as he drove home after their time together.

The pattern of the gentle hand-in-hand Wednesday evenings made Richard feel safe and appreciated. He understood that the medication would blunt the emotional impact of Andrea's discovery of her husband's infidelity, but it was not a solution for managing her abrupt change in reality. Nighttime was the worst, she confessed, especially when she received a last-minute text that her husband had "missed his train." Richard taught her to take comfort in the dark as he had, by seeking the light from the moon.

Richard paused his chair count to stand on his stiff limbs. He stepped across the tile floor of the lobby and triggered open the main doors.

Blazing light illuminated the Emergency Department driveway. Richard winced and tread out to the back of the empty parking lot. A closed dumpster lurked in the shadows to his right. He looked up at the dark sky, cool mist coating the lenses of his glasses. It was too cloudy for relief from the moon. Richard retraced the steps to his tweed seat to count chairs and ceiling tiles again.

Richard acknowledged to Andrea that he was married to his work. Back when he was called upon to open the new 24-hour pharmacy across from the strip mall, his wife at the time, a sixth-grade school teacher, tried to warn him, "It never closes. Your day will never end!" One predictably late night too many, he came home to an empty house. Having an affair with a colleague, she no longer attempted to hide it. Within a year, they divorced and she was gone.

Spending time with Andrea started to heal Richard in places he had long-forgotten were broken. The discrete rhythm of their clandestine meetings, however, began to seem insufficient. The more he experienced, the more he wanted to know her out loud - in the context of his family and a few close friends.

Once, when they stopped at the strip mall across the street from the pharmacy to ship homemade cookies to Andrea's son, the manager, a friendly, talkative man with thick dark curls, conversed when Andrea stepped back out to her car to retrieve the address. "Is it final's week?"

Richard nodded. "Junior year. One year left."

"My roommate's parents used to send him cookies too. Not homemade though. Chocolate Chips are the best!"

Richard smiled. Andrea's son didn't care for chocolate. "Yes. Can't go wrong there!" He recognized the young manager from visits to his consult window.

Surprised by how much he appreciated being mistaken for Andrea's husband during the casual exchange, Richard began to entertain hopes and dreams while simultaneously not wanting the cadence to change. He was content to live alone, but the thought of continued companionship with Andrea appealed to him. He wondered when she would confront her husband. It was not something they discussed.

An early sunbeam reflected off the Inpatient Unit through a floor-to-ceiling Emergency Department window, sending rays into Richard's face. Squinting, he reached into the deep pocket of his tan car coat for his phone. Heedless to where he spent the night, life had continued unaware. A message from Asha, the overnight pharmacy manager, *Why is your car here?* and two podcast episode notifications filled the lock screen.

A single tear slipped onto the glossy flat surface as he pressed open a ride-hailing service app. Smoothing the drop dry he ordered a ride to his car and wiped his nose. His shift at the pharmacy started in an hour and he had not eaten.

✎ ☆ ✎

Arriving at the pharmacy with two brown bags from Third Street Bagels, Richard unlocked the back door. He pulled out an old light brown cafeteria tray and paper plates and set them on the small, round café table. Ripping open the bags to better display the options, he arranged the plates, a cream cheese tub, black plastic knife, brown napkins, and two oranges he purchased on impulse from the check-out display on the tray, then turned to join Asha out on the floor.

Asha's voice filtered through the stillness, "Married? That surprises me." Richard's right hand came to rest on the white surface of the single swinging break room door. He looked through the slit of the door at the pain reliever display on the other side of the counter. The "Clinically Proven" portion of the red signage was at an awkward angle.

"Married?" Asha repeated. "…No, I know. It is just…well you know how he is."

Richard, ramrod straight as always, took two inaudible steps back and lowered his right hand into the side pocket of his lab coat, gripping a ballpoint pen. Frozen to the floor, his light brown eyes drooping under the weight of his moonless night, Richard raced to understand what he was hearing. Who was Asha talking to? He had not prepared himself for his staff to thrash about clickbait details of his circumstances so quickly.

"I mean," Asha's spirited voice maintained, "He does not seem like the kind of guy who would treat marriage so lightly."

Beyond the door, Richard paled. It all sounded so wrong when someone else said it.

The receiving area tone chimed and before Richard could respond, Asha swung into the break room.

"Oh, hi! I didn't know you were here!" She greeted him with an inclusive, pink smile.

"Seriously, Bahar, I have to go. The truck is here…Right, ok." She looked past Richard and his dark manicured beard, speckled white on the chin, to the round table, "You brought bagels!" Asha glanced at the screen and lowered her slim white phone into the side pocket of her lab coat. She approached the fresh breakfast display in high gear.

Richard released the grip on the pen in his pocket and opened the door for the delivery driver. He accepted the stylus and signed the screen to confirm the arrival of the shipment. The driver turned to begin unloading the red-lidded plastic bins.

"Sorry about that," Asha chattered, "This guy my parents wouldn't let me date in high school is getting married. I just don't get it." Her smooth dark ponytail shook at the nape of her neck for emphasis, "He just *met* her!"

For the second time in twenty-four hours, feelings overcame Richard that he could not show. Asha didn't know. Of course, she didn't know.

Richard forced his weary eyes to greet Asha's as she absently smoothed her hair and surveyed the table, "Oooh…Asiago cheese!" Richard swung into the pharmacy, then stepped out to straighten the "Clinically Proven" portion of the pain reliever sign.

⤳ ☆ ⤳

In Andrea's sterile room, audible beeps continued along the neutral walls. Incessant beeps. Long and low, short and staccato.

Andrea's husband watched her from the stiff aqua cushioned chair next to the metal rail of the hospital bed.

"Andrea?"

Beep.

"Andrea?"

Beep…Beep.

"ANDREA," with an edge. He reached for her fingers, "Squeeze my hand if you can hear me."

Andrea's knuckles, sidelined by the swollen moonlit triplets in her brain, did not oblige.

Inspiration

This story started in response to a writing prompt from an online workshop. The instructor, David Finch, author of the New York Times *bestseller,* The Journal of Best-Practices: A Memoir of Marriage, Asperger Syndrome, and

One Man's Quest to Become a Better Husband, *challenged participants to write in specific detail about the scene of a car accident.*

From Wikipedia, *I learned Beethoven left behind love letters to an unknown lady who became known as the "Immortal Beloved." I wondered, if Richard was never able to see Andrea again, if he would process his feelings to her in a journal as a way to hold on to how she made him feel.*

From one of Beethoven's letters, "You are suffering you my dearest … you are suffering. Oh, wherever I am, you are with me."

Quicksand

Elaine Fisher

My relentless companion follows me as I trudge
through the wetlands, the dripping leaves weep onto my face.

Leave me, I scream, my anguish finally surfacing.

He watches me with troubled eyes, double mirrors
reflecting the deceptive calm sea of sand.

You're lost, he tells me. His heartache forever deepening.
You're drowning in self-pity. Admit your blame. It'll set you free.

It's their fault.

That's not the truth.

Everyone hates me!

Deep down
you hate yourself more.

Why do you care? No one else does. I'm the muck beneath their feet!

I descend to my newest low, quickly engulfed
In the quicksand of denial, only to find that I've been deceived.
There's no relief in a bottomless void.

He extends an unwelcomed hand.
I bitterly laugh at the gesture while
we watch my mouth fill with vile grit.

You are stubborn to a fault. Never admitting when you've been wrong.

It's not fair, I argue.
Why should I be the one stranded in this torturous sand?

I gaze into his tired face. I see my own reflected back.
He looks at me and I sink into the mire of his eyes.

My answers never satisfy you. Your defiance is exhausting both of us.

My constant companion rests deep
in my mind. He knows I will continue
to slog through my guilt and self-loathing.

When he awakes,
We'll fight again. We'll never stop,
Even as his tears seep from my sand-filled eyes.

Inspiration

The narrator of my allegorical poem is a troubled and tormented person. He argues with his unrelenting, constant companion—his conscience. But gets no relief for he's stubborn in his ways. It's easier to blame others. He's unwilling to accept the guilt that he feels and the truth that he knows deep inside—he doesn't like the person he's become. So he's drowning in the 'quicksand' of his own making. I think we've all known people like this and hope they can pull themselves out of the sticky messes they've made of their lives, but many seem hopelessly stuck.

Heat

K.V. PECK

John leapt from the diving board with a hoot and cannonballed. Leigh scrambled up the ladder to outdo him. Her hair shimmered reddish gold in the sunshine and glare. The Midwest summer had baked John a lovely brown but to her irritation, Leigh freckled and turned a darker shade of pink.

Chlorine and the coconut scent of sunscreen imbued the air. Kids splashed under the watch of bored young lifeguards—the last throes of freedom before school reopened and they'd start high school.

Heatwaves refracted light and distorted images of kids wrapped in beach towels and mothers with novels on loungers. Teens shared earbuds. Triangles of color strung across the pool lanes hung straight down, the flags stirred only by the occasional, merciful breeze. An undercurrent of cicada song swelled and faded in waves.

Like the seeds in her mother's wildflower garden, the other girls had budded into young women. They swayed with sultry confidence, showing off their new breasts. In their wake, the scent of desire. Leigh's wet one-piece hung wrinkled on her slim body.

The whistle blew for adult swim. Leigh and John returned to their comic-book-making at the fenced-in tables in the snack area. Drooped and faded coneflowers pushed their heads through the diamonds of wire, watching. Beyond, new ornate houses had sprouted and overtook displaced farms. Dwarfed by development, an old barn's red walls flaked, the roof sagged and over the course of the summer, it disappeared altogether, leaving a builder's 'for sale' sign in its place.

Leigh took a swig from her chilled water bottle and John handed her one of the apples his mother had packed. A toddler's crayon, Infra-Red, had rolled off the metal table beside them. The hot pavement transformed the curves of the crayon into a rectangle. She thought, *that looks like my body.*

John toed the paper wrapper of the crayon. He signaled to Leigh to look a table over. Furtively, he swiped a handful of unguarded caramels. They scampered to the end of the pool deck, and each popped one into their mouths. John squatted at the edge of a shadow cast by the shade canopy. His dexterous fingers placed two caramels strategically—one in the sun, one in the shade.

When the lifeguards' whistles shrieked, Leigh and John jumped into the water. They dove for quarters, expelled trails of air bubbles out their noses and muted summer sounds with each descent.

"Let's check our experiment," John said and ripped his goggles off his face. The cube in the sun had flattened and continued to transform while they observed. The candy in the shade remained unchanged.

"What are you looking at, Johnny?"

Leigh rolled her eyes when Sherry (who stopped using Sheryl since her new boobs) stepped right in front of Leigh, blocking the sun. This girl between her and John left Leigh cool and empty, sitting on the cement in lanky angles. John traced his gaze up the girl's body before he flicked his eyes away with a small smile. A new and sour feeling hit Leigh full on. Leigh grabbed a caramel while Sherry chattered at *her* John. The candy gave as she squeezed it between her thumb and forefinger, warmed by her body heat. She unwrapped and slid the cube behind the girl's perfect little heel.

Leigh, legs pulled up, mouth hidden behind her knees, glared. Sherry transferred her weight from foot to foot while John talked about variables—time, shade, the angle of the sun. The girl arched her back and the curve of her torso accentuated her hips. Sherry's hands fluttered like hummingbirds when she didn't touch her hair or adjust her pink bikini bottom.

Step on it, step on it, step on it.

Sherry took a step backward, squashed the caramel, and kicked up her heel to peer at the mess. Leigh hadn't meant to laugh out loud.

"What the hell? Excuse me," Sherry said to John. She threw Leigh a contemptuous, then dismissive look and stepped away on the ball of her foot, which made her breasts bounce even more.

"Good riddance!" said Leigh.

"Not nice," John said but he laughed a little too. His sightline followed Sherry, and when he looked back at her, Leigh saw pink rise in his cheeks.

"I'll go see if she's okay," Leigh said to John in a pinched voice, but she didn't want that. She wanted to yell, to scream, to tell Sherry to just disappear.

Leigh had stumbled along through puberty, stick legs, thick belly, flat where she was supposed to be full. Now she attracted men who liked curves and creamy skin. Her lackluster relationships limped along despite an almost engagement. Emotion ticked forward as expected until the hands on the relationship clock stuck, refusing to push another moment further. Unfulfilled, she yearned for past desires.

At the market, she'd spotted his hands first, the way he gently selected the least bruised apple, then held it in his palm. John. In Los Angeles. Visions of cannonballs and caramels, the scent of youthful bodies slicked with oil, rushed back.

Girls had followed John since that poolside summer. Now, his broad back and muscled arms contoured his T-shirt. His dark hair fell in short lustrous waves. When he turned around and saw her, his smile reached his eyes. The vestige of interrupted blossoming hung in the air between them, the stuff of things undone.

She knew she'd sleep with him. And knew, the way he took in the fullness of her, the shape of her mouth, that he wanted her too. He called the next day and they met at Santa Monica's best cold brew coffee shop. She smiled at the stories of his boys, listened to his lament over the failure of his first business and his marriage. Leigh tensed as he spoke of his ex. 'The chemistry wore off fast. We were stuck,' he said. She exhaled the breath she hadn't realized she held. She reached out to touch his arm when he told her his mom had succumbed to cancer.

On the street, they fell silent and his hand brushed hers. They didn't discuss what they knew they'd do. They followed the trajectory of their impulses until they were in her small bungalow. He burned, and she cooled him when she ran the slick side of an icy glass along his chest. In her kitchen, she, wrapped around him, melting into him in a sultry dance, until they laughed out loud together in relief.

"I have to get home. I have Zack and Jason tonight," John said as he dressed. "I'll take every second I can get. Divorce sucks. Tomorrow?"

Even late in the day, it was still a scorcher. John shoveled mulch under Leigh's palm trees. She lounged on a recliner while he wiped his forehead. As he worked, she spied him through her shades, followed the movement of his arms, his hands. Sweat glistened on his exposed skin. His jeans hugged his thighs. Later they sat on her patio, sipped red wine, feet up, and reminisced. It's snowing today in Chicagoland, he said. But here the heat soothed her. They watched the sun dip below the horizon and the sky streak with gold.

"And remember old Mrs. Portico and her marigolds?" Leigh asked.

"Portillo, like the hot dogs, not Portico," John said and began a dissertation on architectural structures. John knew the stuff of houses, of angles and measurements; she knew the stuff of yearning and loss.

He trailed off and they gazed into the velvet purple sky.

"Do you ever think about Sherry?" John asked. Crickets punctuated the quiet evening. His thumb caressed the edge of the wineglass and dipped down around the curve.

"Too strong—I prefer wine," Leigh said.

"You know what I mean."

"No."

"I always wondered how she fell so violently. That it would *kill* her," John said.

It had been in the local paper—big news for suburbia. Headline news.

"Why think about that now, on such a nice night?"

John sat up straighter and caught her eye.

"You wouldn't talk about it. What happened in that shower room?"

Her eyes darted away, and she stared hard at her burgundy-polished toes. Without words she stood and crossed the short distance between them. Her lips moved close to his ear. Her hand circled his neck.

"What are you saying?" she hummed.

He moaned, an animal sound, and she lowered herself onto his lap, moved her mouth to his. He stirred beneath her and she relished his tongue's caress of her neck.

Mumbled words bled through. "I think maybe you—I thought I knew you." His fingers threaded through her hair, and he drew her head back to look at her. "I think you were jealous. I think you got over it pretty fast. You scared me."

He revealed want, not fear. His intensity made her desire him more. But she stood, turned her back to him, crossed her arms. Let him wait, she thought. Let him see how it feels to be cast away.

"I scared you? You dumped me." Tears welled. "We were best friends and you dumped me."

The lounger creaked with his movement.

"I wasn't sure how to be your friend anymore. It was easier not to be near you. I didn't want to think about if you…did or didn't…you know?" Apology bled through John's words.

"If I'm so scary, if you think I would *murder* a girl, why are you here?"

He stood behind her now. She thrilled at his breath on her neck and warm hands at her waist.

"You know why I'm here." His hands traveled. "Two reasons. This. And our past. Now, take me back. To then."

Leigh shook no. Maybe, she thought, he's stuck at that day too. His touch took on urgency. A seductive exploration.

"Yes," John said. "We both, we're both … stranded."

She faced him, forced herself to hold eye contact, took a deep breath and exhaled.

"I followed her into the locker room," Leigh said, barely above a whisper. He slipped a hand between her legs and made her breath quicken. He pulled off his shirt and dropped it to the ground. "She stood at the shower, prissy, nose in the air, while she waited for the water to get hot."

Renewed anger blended with arousal and made Leigh dizzy.

She let John maneuver her to the recliner. He paused over her.

"More," he said, barely audible. His hazel eyes pleaded. "Please."

Leigh's voice resonated from deep in her throat now, released.

"She pointed her caramel-covered foot toward the stream of water, like a prima ballerina. I hated her. I hated her tanned skin. I hated that you noticed her."

Leigh's temple pulsed and she kept her eyes on his. He moved closer and hooked a finger over the top of her blouse. The buttons slipped open. She trembled, welcomed him.

"Go on," he said, a low thunder.

"She'd picked up a bar of soap. Held it between her index finger and thumb like a dead thing."

His hands traveled, a fluid motion that urged her on.

"She rubbed it between her hands, and then bent over."

John's arms encircled her. Her heart thrummed and she rose to meet him, floating, Weightless and buoyed, she let him drown her in his fervor.

"What else?" he breathed into her ear.

"I heard the whistle, shrieks, splashes. I thought of you."

Leigh moved as quickly as she could (Don't Run on The Pool Deck) and peered into the Ladies Locker Room.

Sherry stood on her unsoiled foot, soap in hand, and waved her other hand under the water. Then Sherry stuck her foot into the shower stall.

This was *her* day with John. Sherry ruined everything.

"Hey." Leigh said. Heat rose in her cheeks.

She and John were friends. Best friends. For years.

"Hey! Are you deaf, *Sheryl*?"

"What do you want?" Sherry said with a yawn.

Leigh loved John, and Leigh knew he loved her too. They were supposed to be together. The way John looked at this girl—Leigh's sunburn pulsed with her anger. She looked down at herself, then back at Sherry, and tears blurred her vision.

"You need to scrub, you stupid bitch!"

Sherry turned to Leigh, red-faced, and gripped the soap so hard it popped out of her hand and skidded on the concrete. It left a slick trail behind. Sherry charged toward Leigh, ready to pounce like a lioness. Leigh smelled the bubblegum lip gloss, the shampoo scent of her perfectly wavy hair. Bared teeth and a scowl rushed toward her. Leigh pushed Sherry away with all that her slight weight could muster.

Leigh stood over Sherry's body, numb. How long had she stood there? Sounds from outside broke her stupor.

Panicked, Leigh checked the bathroom stalls, the other showers. No one there. No one heard them. No one saw them.

Leigh ran to him.

"Johnny!" she screamed. "Something bad happened!"

He rushed with her to the girls' locker room, and at the door, he hesitated, uncertain.

"Come *on.*"

Sherry lay in the shower room on the slippery floor. A metal-sweet smell emanated from a pool of dark liquid by her temple and mixed with the dank odor of wet concrete and chlorine. Leigh, wide-eyed, stared as the blood spread and formed one probing finger that lengthened toward the drain.

Disbelief distorted John's features. He peered at Sherry's face, reached to touch the puddle of viscous fluid, and reeled back, gagging. Sherry's bikini top had shifted, and a crescent of paler flesh peaked out the bottom of the pink fabric. Leigh wanted to tug the cup down, not for the girl's sake. John had seen it too. A chill ran through her body. John's skin goose-bumped.

"We've got to tell the lifeguards," he said. Leigh gawked at the girl's limp body until John took her hand and led her out.

⚬ ☆ ⚭

—oh—John," Leigh said, her breath hitching, "—she charged toward me. Her hands were fists, and her teeth were clenched."

He sent waves through her.

Silence hung between them. John stilled, waiting.

"I wanted her dead. I pushed her away and she lost her footing. Her head hit the concrete—I will never forget that awful thump and crunch."

Leigh's face crumpled. Tears ran. She clutched his back.

"I wanted her away from you ... and it happened. I ran for you," Leigh said into his chest, then looked up at him.

His scrutiny transfixed her. "So, did you—?"

Leigh shook her head. "I didn't mean for her to fall. Her skull against the cement—it was the most grotesque sound I've ever heard. It haunts me. And it drove you away."

John's expression softened, his brows knit in sorrow, and now he nodded a slow no. His uncertainty, his doubt seemed to lift, as if a submerged toy boat dislodged and floated up to breach the thin skin where water meets air. Relief bobbed on a shiny surface, like a pool on a Midwestern summer day. He planted a soft kiss on her cheek.

"Okay?" he asked, as he brought two fingers up to brush away a tear.

She nodded yes, her cheek now in the crook of his neck, his face buried in her hair, their coupling like underwater creatures swept forward by the current.

After, they lay, sweat beaded on their bodies, and let the words hang in the air. He exhaled years, rolled off her, and collapsed onto the second lounger.

"I never saw a dead body before then," he said. "It was terrible. Exciting," and he looked like both the boy she once knew and the man who left her tingling.

"It was my fault," Leigh said. "It seemed absurd—her caramel foot—her arrogant stride, and then she was gone before my anger cooled."

"We were just kids." John held his hands a foot apart, as though presenting her with this statement in a box. "She slipped. It was an accident."

He looked at her again, awaiting another confirmation.

Was it? She followed the flight of a bird until it disappeared behind a palm tree. Quietly, she answered, "Yes. It was."

He spoke now to the sky. "She was so *alive* when I saw her walk away. She set me on fire with it—this new sensation." His voice, full of longing, triggered a fresh pang of envy. "Life was never more real. Then I was embarrassed because you *knew* it."

Since that day, she'd been left forever poolside, shivering, and alone. The ugly girl in the saggy one-piece. He'd been stuck there too. And here they were. Together again.

In the silence, the past uncoiled, released stagnation and left space for newness, growth. When she met his gaze, he burned through her, scorched her body. The air between them seemed brighter. The connection between them, lighter. *Now he knows what I did. And now he can love. Love me.*

∽ ☆ ∾

The next evening, he arrived with a single plump apple covered in caramel and wrapped in cellophane held shut with a bikini-pink bow. He kneeled on one knee and held it in his open palm—an offering. When she accepted, they each tugged at an end of the bow. It slipped open easily.

Inspiration

Heat *was inspired by the smell of caramel and hot Midwestern summers poolside with my kids, watching the interaction of adolescents when play transformed into attraction and flirtation. The cement-floored locker rooms were often slippery, and I was always careful not to slip. I wanted to explore the effect of trauma at a time of sexual maturation and how one instance can leave people stranded psychologically and sexually. To go back to the "scene of the crime" so to speak, allowed these characters to abandon their stranded lives and find resolution and growth.*

AUTHOR BIOS

Author Bios

Barbara Bartilson

Barbara is a member of The Writing Journey and is published through two of their previous anthologies - *Reasons For Hope and The Love Anthology.* Her flash fiction story in this *Stranded Anthology* is titled *Beached on the Jersey Shore.* It is some romance, some historical fiction and all fun. She appreciates the assistance from the critiquing community who lead her to find positive stories to share and give encouragement to always dig deeper.

Her previous writing experience is in business where she consults and leads large-scale strategic corporate change. She uses evaluative and creative writing skills to produce business cases, organizational change recommendations, position papers, negotiations, and executive assessments.

Susan Ekins

Susan Ekins writes poems, flash fiction, and feature articles. Her work has been published in *Splickety, Prairie Light Review, Canticle,* and *Together in Christ* magazines. She has also contributed to the book *#Sisterhood Connection: A Year of Empowerment* and is currently working on a mystery novel. Susan's blog is *Women Making Strides*, which encourages women to be proactive in caring for themselves and living their lives. You can find her blog at *womenmakingstrides.com*. Susan also serves as a parish librarian in a Chicago suburb and enjoys walking and running.

Elaine Fisher

Since 2013, Elaine Fisher has been a member of the writing group, The Writing Journey. Several of her stories and poems have been published in the following Journey anthologies: *Voices from the Dark, Human: An Explanation of What it Means, Near Myths, Reasons for Hope, and The Love Anthology*. She is currently editing her first novel, *The Dream Traveler's Memoir*—A YA historical fantasy.

Besides her interest in writing, she's also an award-winning member of the camera club, PhotoGenesis. To find out more about Elaine, visit the website she shares with her husband, also a photographer, at *aephotoandprose.com* A collection of her short stories, poems, and photography are featured on the site, which is constantly updated as newer work is posted.

Leslie Gail

New to the Journey, Leslie Gail, M.Ed., is grateful for the accountability, feedback, and camaraderie from fellow travelers of the Journey Paths.

Leslie's research for a YA novel about a child making friends with the piles in her hoarded home resulted in a career as a professional organizer! She uses sensitivity, patience, and a dose of wit and whimsy to help clients reduce stress in their lives.

Leslie focuses the bulk of her forward-facing writing on social media platforms and blog posts for her business, Declare Order Professional Organizing via *declareorder.com*. Her expert advice has been featured on websites such as *MarketWatch.com, cleanplates.com, sparefoot.com, WomensHealth.com,* and *SupportForSpecialNeeds.com.* She is currently procrastinating a nonfiction book proposal about her experiences, *Life in the Middle of the Mess.*

Margie Gustafson

Margie Gustafson is an award-winning poet whose book, "Haiku Very Much", is available on Amazon.com.

Liz SanFilippo Hall

Liz SanFilippo Hall is a freelance writer, social media strategist, and beauty consultant who runs on caffeine and Reese's peanut butter cups. Her publication credits include stories in *Chicken Soup for the Soul: The Dog Did What?* and the *Hot Doug's The Book: Chicago's Ultimate Icon of Encased Meats.* Her work can also be found on SelfSufficientKids.com and CBS.com. She also writes a blog on a range of her favorite topics – including parenting, mindset, and working from home – at *www.oopsanddaisies.com.*

She has a Master's in Humanities/Creative Writing from The University of Chicago, where she earned an Honorable Mention in the 2007 Emerging Writers Series for Fiction. She's currently a member of SCBWI as well as the Writing Journey. Her current projects include editing a YA contemporary novel tentatively entitled *She Said, She Said* and querying agents with her picture book stories. When she's not busy writing or reading, she's chasing around her two young children and a bulldog named Kafka in the western suburbs of Chicago.

Todd Hogan

Todd Hogan, a Chicago writer, reads voraciously and enjoys learning from classical literary fiction while marveling at the excitement of modern literary fiction. He has traveled throughout the United States for business negotiations and appreciates the complexities and varieties of American cities, communities, and their citizens.

Yolanda Huslig

Yolanda Huslig escaped the corporate world by retiring. To pursue a lifelong dream, one that had been put on hold in the hustle and bustle of life, she enrolled in a creative writing course. Eight semesters later, she'd learned how to write a story. She continues to hone her craft, writing science fiction stories, the kind that could actually happen.

Her short stories appear in the Journey anthologies, *Near Myths* and *Reasons for Hope*.

Debra Kollar

Debra Kollar started writing at a young age and then later changed to public speaking in high school. She graduated from Purdue University with majors in speech education and public relations. After various jobs in communications, her love for the written word returned. She was a columnist for Catholic Charities and her memoirs and short stories have been published in six anthologies. Her seven-part series "The Marvelous Mary Alice" was featured in 2019 in Bravo Magazine, and she hopes to make it into a novel afterwards. Her writing is often a parallel of two opposites: inspirational, dry witty humor or dirty realism, a term coined to depict the seamier aspects and belly-side of contemporary life. She lives with her husband, two children, and an accumulated bunch of shelter pets; one of which is a cat who lies next to her laptop while she writes, whom she affectionately calls: The Boss.

Jessica Kosar

Jessica Kosar joined The Writing Journey in 2019 when, after graduating college, she longed for the familiar structure and accountability of creative writing courses. Since the first snowy meeting, she has undertaken multiple creative projects, including writing her short story *Static* which is featured in this anthology. She is grateful to have had the chance to learn with a group of such talented individuals and looks forward to reading their future published works.

Jessica's essays and poetry have been featured in *The Rum Bucket* and *Mosaic 57.*

Stéphane Lafrance

Stéphane Lafrance is a French-Canadian living in the US as a father of two and husband to Debra Kollar, co-author in the *Stranded* Anthology. He loves books and reading them naturally transitioned to writing them. This is his first published story.

Barbara Lipkin

Barbara Lipkin has been writing all her life but has only recently begun to publish her work. Her Bella Sarver Mystery novels: *Painting Lessons, Brush With Death,* and *Paint a Murder* are available on Amazon in both trade and ebook editions. Her latest, *Death on the Danube,* is due out in the Autumn, 2019. Her protagonist, Bella Sarver, is an artist and teacher who keeps finding herself at the heart of nefarious and often lethal situations in the art world, whether she stays close to home in a Chicago suburb or ventures out on European travels.

Lipkin is, coincidentally, also an artist and teacher, whose paintings hang in many private and public collections in the Chicago area. One of her short stories, *The Luckiest Block*, was published in the November, 2018 edition of Foliate Oak Literary Magazine.

Visit her website: www.LipkinGallery.com and sign up for her blog, where she regularly shares insights into writing and painting- related issues.

Edward Martin

Edward Martin is a recent graduate of Plainfield East Highschool who joined the writing group The Writing Journey in 2019. The Anthology *Stranded* is his debut, though he is currently working on a science fiction novel.

Sam McAdams

Born and raised in the Chicago suburbs, Sam McAdams has been a lifelong Cub fan and Monty Python enthusiast. In his spare time, he can be spotted in suburban cafes, pubs, and coffeehouses, typing on his laptop. Sam is a founding member of the Writing Journey and his short story, *When Bob's Dreams Come True*, appears in the Journey's *Drops of Midnight* anthology.

Mary O'Brien Glatz

Mary O'Brien Glatz began her writing journey with The Lighthouse, a writers' community in Denver, CO after retiring as an educational psychologist. Since she joined The Writing Journey, she has contributed to recent anthologies as both writer and editor. She has written a memoir, *Anywhere But Here: A First Generation Immigrant Life*. As a transplant from Boulder, CO to Naperville, IL, she follows her bliss in her most favorite role of grandmother.

K. V. Peck

K.V. Peck works as a freelance writer, editor, and marketer and has published in *The Matador Review, Prairie Light Review*, won Honorable Mention, Mainstream/Literary Short Story category in the *85th Annual Writer's Digest Writing Competition 2016. Spring* has been nominated for the *2018 Pushcart Prize*. Peck also contributed to the book, *Heart Guide, True Stories of Grief and Healing* by Diana J. Ensign, JD, (2018 *Independent Publisher Book Awards* Gold Medal Winner.) K.V. Peck holds an MA, Writing, Editing, and Publishing from North Central College and is looking for representation for *SHATTERED*, a novel about love across parallel realities.

Savannah Reynard

Savannah Reynard wanted to have a star on the Hollywood Walk of Fame and win an Oscar for best actress until she stumbled upon an abnormal psychology class and fell in love with the human psyche. She now combines her creative side with her experience working in the mental health field to write about characters who rise from their lowest points and achieve their undiscovered potential in her fantasy and paranormal romances. In these worlds, she makes sure everyone gets their happily ever after.

Her short stories *Echoes of Time* and *A Promise in Time*, about second chances at love, albeit lifetimes later, have appeared in two anthologies presented by Windy City RWA and can be found as stand-alone stories on Amazon.

Subscribe to her newsletter for all of the latest info on new releases, events, and extras or check out her website *Savannah Reynard* where true love knows no bounds.

Julie Rule

Julie Rule enjoys writing science fiction, fantasy, and mystery stories, and she is currently working on a series of young adult novels. This is her first anthology story. Her website is julierule.com.

Tauna Sonn-LeMare

My first published pieces were poetry, fiction, and non-fiction written for historical content on subjects of interest to fellow member of the Society for Creative Anachronisms.

I attended local SF&F conventions, and then five World Science Fiction Conventions. Back then meeting your favorite authors often involved sitting around and talking about writing until the wee hours of the morning.

I was fortunate to meet and have conversations with Heinlein, Rodenberry, Spielburg, King, Budrys, Harlan Ellison on no fewer than five occasions. I was lucky enough to take Algis Budrys' writing workshop at Barrington Library monthly for almost two years.

During this time I published six articles in three different Science Fiction magazines (now defunct).

I never stopped writing, but wrote every thing out by hand. Two years ago, I started typing out the manuscripts, editing as I went and adding new projects. I finished two NaNoWriMo with 100,000 words each. I have two stories and three poems due out in late 2020 and a novel near completion.

Jennifer Stasinopoulos

Jennifer Stasinopoulos was thrilled to join the Journey in January 2019 after discovering the group through NaNoWriMo. This is her first time being published, but she hopes that many more opportunities will follow. She is a nature-loving librarian and educator who is always on the lookout for unique coffee shops where she can find a nook to while away the hours writing. Her entry in *Stranded*, It's About Time, is an eerie fantasy, but she is currently working on an adult mystery novel as well as nature-focused works for children.

Karen Stumm Limbrick

Karen Stumm Limbrick loves researching & writing for genealogical purposes as well as writing historical novels, plays and the occasional children's story. She is also an avid reader, and likes to find free time to hike some new landscape or spontaneously discover some hidden corner of the world traveling solo or with her family. Karen is an active member of the Historical Novel Society and after searching for a writing family in the far west communities and cornfields of Illinois, Karen became a member of The Writing Journey and has been a member for several years.

Gwen Tolios

Gwen Tolios hails from Detroit but currently lives in Chicago with a cat who refuses to cuddle. She can be found on the weekends visiting one of the numerous coffee shops in the city. Her stories have appeared in previous Journey anthologies, as well as in *Today, Tomorrow, Always* and *The Overcast*. You can follow her on Twitter or Instagram as @GwenTolios.

Susan Wachowski

Susan Wachowski writes science fiction, fantasy, steampunk, cozy mysteries, and poetry. She manages the local writers group **Write Here! Write Now! Illinois**, found on FB, and volunteers for **National Novel Writing Month** (*nanowrimo.org*) as a Municipal Liaison for the *US Illinois McHenry and Lake Counties* region. She is also known as the award-winning mini-

painter artist PaintMinion (*Paintminion.com*), with numerous published articles in the hobby, most recently for the January 2019 **Fine Scale Modeler Magazine.**

Her current project is the series ***Sunset Lake Cottages Cozy Mysteries***, as well as co-author of the ***The Harrogate Chronicles***, a series of steampunk adventures involving a female duo – a British agent and a Fae shadow assassin – saving the world from evil magic and Bonaparte's schemes. Her latest short story, "Teacakes and Kraken Bait", set in ***The Harrogate Chronicles*** world, is on her website, *susanwachowski.com*.

Greg Wright

I have been writing on and off my whole life. Completed my first book at 25 which was a complete dumpster fire, yet I loved the process and over the years I have knocked off a few short stories here and there. When my son was born, I became a stay at home dad and really tried to improve my skills. Currently I am working as a manager at a west side university where I can close my door if I want to and knock out 500 words or so. Over the last five years or so, I have published short stories in previous anthologies, completed my first real novel ***Fortune's Mail***, and have completed another which I am shopping around to agents.

Tim Yao

Tim Yao is an author of science fiction and fantasy stories. He is a founding member of the Journey, the eclectic writing group that is publishing this short story anthology. Since 2005, he has been a volunteer National Novel Writing Month Municipal Liaison for the Naperville region that serves the cities and suburbs west of Chicago. In his day job, Tim is a Portfolio Manager for DevOps and Distinguished Member of the Technical Staff for a major telecommunications software company. You can visit his website at *naperwrimo.org/nmk.php*.

His short stories and poems appear in *the Journey anthologies*: *Infinite Monkeys, The Letter, Drops of Midnight, The Day Before The End of The World, Stories from Other Worlds, Voices from the Dark, Human: An Exploration of What It Means, Near Myths, Reasons for Hope, The Love Anthology*, and *Stranded*.